Beaumont Gregory had no use for virgins.

He drew away from Fortune, peering down into her face. Knowing that if he didn't do something soon, he *would* whisk Fortune away to his cabin and seduce her, Beau released his grip on her. He wouldn't—couldn't—do that. Cool air swirled between them to emphasize his loss, and he almost stepped back to her.

"I'm afraid that I need to . . . Patrick's waiting for me. I told him I'd be no more than a moment," Beau stammered, lying about the reason for breaking off the encounter. "Allow me to escort you to your cabin."

"No," Fortune whispered. "I'm not quite ready to go down. You go . . . you go on ahead."

Beau knew that this would be another long night, one among many. For, ever since he'd met her, she'd tormented his sleep . . . and his waking hours, as well.

Dear Reader,

Welcome to Harlequin Historicals, where the new year could be any year—from the turn of the twentieth century to one as far back as our talented authors can take us. From medieval castles to the wide-open prairies, come join our brave heroines and dashing heroes as they battle the odds and discover romance.

In Barbara Faith's first historical, *Gamblin' Man,* Carrie McClennon's simple life is turned upside down by a notorious saloon owner.

Jasmine and Silk, from Sandra Chastain, is set on a Georgian plantation soon after the American Revolution.

Louisa Rawlings's *Wicked Stranger* is the sequel to her *Stranger in My Arms,* and tells the story of the second Bouchard brother.

A luckless Southern belle finds herself stranded in Panama in Kristie Knight's *No Man's Fortune.*

Four new adventures from Harlequin Historicals. We hope you enjoy them all.

Sincerely,

Tracy Farrell
Senior Editor

No Man's Fortune

Kristie Knight

Harlequin Books

TORONTO • NEW YORK • LONDON
AMSTERDAM • PARIS • SYDNEY • HAMBURG
STOCKHOLM • ATHENS • TOKYO • MILAN
MADRID • WARSAW • BUDAPEST • AUCKLAND

Harlequin Historicals first edition January 1993

ISBN 0-373-28758-5

NO MAN'S FORTUNE

KRISTIE KNIGHT

is a native of South Carolina and believes that laughter makes the world go round. Though she resolved long ago never to take herself too seriously, the one exception to that philosophy is her writing—which she takes very seriously. Kristie, a former secretary and office manager, now makes her home in Decatur, Georgia, with her husband, Bob.

For Trey Knight,
a National Champion figure skater,
who will always be World Class in my heart

Chapter One

August, 1848

California!

Clutching the ship's railing in anticipation, Fortune Rosalynd Anthony peered across Charleston harbor as the California-bound ship cut through the shimmering water, beginning the longest journey of her life. The spire of St. Michael's broke the skyline, gleaming white in the parti-colored twilight as if to bid her goodbye. This trip would determine her entire future, a future she'd long speculated about, but had never allowed herself to dream could actually happen. Excitement surged through her, almost a physical presence, as she considered what this move really meant to her.

A journey to independence. Well, independence of a sort. Fortune was traveling with her parents to San Francisco to start a new life, so her freedom wasn't truly complete. She did have her mother to consider. Not to mention Nola Bell and Boaz, their servants, who treated Fortune as if she were still a child. Nevertheless, she was delighted. Filled with a passion for living each moment to the fullest, Fortune felt that this journey represented the ultimate adventure—and escape.

Escape. Fortune wondered if everyone equated independence with escape. Whether they really thought of it or not, she surmised that most people did place the two ideas together. She thought of the twenty-seven other passengers aboard this ship. Were they all escaping something? Running toward independence?

She, most probably, would never find out. Fortune decided that the prospect of her own freedom was sufficient for now. She had a lot of thinking to do on this trip. What would life be like in California? Were there other young people with whom she could share her dreams and aspirations? Or would San Francisco prove to be as stifling to her as Charleston had always been, with all its petty gossip, and the stringent rules of society that had long tormented her?

Though she had loved her hometown, she'd been terribly unhappy there for the past few months. Many events had shaped that dissatisfaction, but Fortune wasn't one to dwell on the past when the future lay so fresh and exhilarating ahead of her. The feeling of being unwanted at her grandfather's house was forever in the air, and now that her uncle had returned, the fate of Giles Anthony and his small family was the favorite topic of the elite's rumor mill.

Fortune knew she shouldn't concentrate so much on the adventure part of this journey, but she couldn't help herself. Few women—or men—had done what she was about to do. Instead of traveling to California by the overland trail, across vast plains, high mountains and sweltering deserts, or sailing around Cape Horn, an equally treacherous passage, they were going by a more untried route— across the Isthmus of Panama.

Because of her mother's frail health, Fortune's parents were in their cabins resting. Even though Letha Anthony had admonished her daughter to stay on deck for no more than a few minutes, Fortune couldn't bear to go inside yet; there was simply too much to see. Her excitement refused to be confined, and Fortune knew her fidgeting would disturb her mother.

Supper would be served in about an hour, so most of the other passengers had gone below to get ready. Eating didn't interest Fortune right now. Charleston's fading skyline did. She decided to walk around the deck to see what other brave individuals were flouting convention and risking the potential harm of the night air.

Hearing a sound, she stopped and looked up. The *Calhoun*, a packet making her maiden voyage, was a three-masted sailing ship. The brisk harbor winds billowed the sails into great white canopies, snapping smartly as the darkening sky, with its vibrant pinks and purples, quickly turned into night and softened the images that Fortune vowed never to forget.

The first day of my life, she mused. *The first real day of my life.* What lay out there for her, across that vast expanse of emerald water?

"Taking a turn in the brisk night air?" said a deep masculine voice from nearby. "It's a beautiful night for it."

Fortune spun around, her gaze scanning the deck for the speaker. A tall man stepped forward. She could hardly see his face in the dim light, but she could tell that he was several inches taller than her father. Imposing. For a few seconds, she didn't speak. Except for the few sailors working around the deck, she and this man were alone. When he stepped closer, she recognized him. She'd seen him board the ship soon after she had seen her own cabin. He'd been in the company of another man.

"I... Yes, I am." Fortune glanced around again, a bit nervously. "It seems that everyone else is below."

Beaumont Gregory didn't divert his eyes from her. In the last scarlet glimmer of sunlight, her hair appeared to be a golden-strawberry color, but he couldn't be sure. "I take it you aren't afraid of contracting some dread disease from the chill night air."

Fortune laughed. How many times had she heard her mother warn her against the chill night air? "I've never suffered from it thus far, sir." She tried to regain her composure. "And, of course, the air isn't that cool tonight. Charleston rarely experiences a cool August night."

Beau smiled as her laughter poured over him, sweet and innocent, like the clear, true tones of a pealing bell. The laughter was real, not the frivolous artificial laugh of a New Orleans society woman. "And you, I sense, are an authority on the vagaries of Charleston's weather."

"I've lived here all my life, sir," she said, watching him step closer to the ship's railing. He now stood beside her, his elbow nearly touching hers. "Well, all my life thus far."

Noticing the bitter note in her reply, he smiled, wondering what could have caused such a sudden change in her tone. "So wise for such a young age," he teased.

"I'm twenty-one years of age, if it's any of your business," she snapped, turning to face the rolling ocean once more.

"Please, excuse me. I never intended to cause insult to a...a spinst—" He stopped in midword. So far the conversation had been pleasant, a little banter that allowed two strangers to pass the time. He thought quickly, smiling at the reaction he knew his words would elicit. "To a maiden of your advanced years."

Spinster! He'd nearly called her a spinster! Well, in truth, she was. Fortune knew she was nearing the age when other women would whisper about her behind their fans, but she didn't care. They were already doing that. This move to San Francisco would make up for all the gossip she'd endured in the past—she hoped. "I am a spinster of Charleston, sir, and quite proud of that fact," she replied, lifting her chin defiantly.

Beau chuckled. Not the response he'd expected, but certainly a spirited one. "Well, Miss..."

He was obviously waiting for her to supply her name. Fortune smiled. In spite of his not having been introduced in the accepted way, she liked this man, who seemed to have a pleasant sense of humor lurking beneath a sophisticated, cool exterior. "Anthony," she answered, knowing her mother would rant and rave for the better part of an hour if she knew that Fortune had given her name to a strange man. "Fortune Anthony, sir."

"Fortune Anthony? What an unusual name," he remarked, studying her thoughtfully. "Very interesting. I'm Beaumont Gregory."

Tilting her head to one side, she gazed at him. *Beaumont Gregory,* she thought, smiling. She liked the name. It implied something...something, well, different, maybe exotic or exciting. She could see little in the way of details about him, but the strong planes of his face were appealing, as were the parted lips, poised as if he would speak again.

"Is your father a gambler, then?" he asked, resting his elbows on the railing. "Or perhaps your mother."

"Hardly," she answered, stifling a laugh. "My parents leave nothing to chance. Besides, my mother hates gamblers."

"That's a bit strong. Why does she hate gamblers?" Beau asked, turning to study her more closely. He liked what he could see—and he definitely liked what he heard. She seemed to be free of the constrictions of society, though her clothing and demeanor belied her words.

Fortune considered his question. Her mother had expounded long and hard upon the sin of gambling and the wicked ways of gamblers, but Fortune had always suspected that something *more* lay at the base of the towering contempt Letha Anthony frequently expressed. "You know, I'm not sure." Fortune's eyes narrowed, and she peered at the man. "But that never stopped her from warning me to avoid gamblers and gambling."

"And, do you?" he asked, trying desperately to hide his grin.

She looked up at him, a bit puzzled. "Do I what?"

"Avoid gamblers?" he asked, his interest suddenly piqued by this innocent with the lovely laugh. A wrinkle creased her forehead, and she inclined her head to one side. Damn, but he wished he could see the color of her eyes. In the darkness, all he could see was the glimmer of light reflecting the lantern behind him. He noticed the swell of her bosom, not overly large, but well-rounded enough to be pleasing. Then her scent caught him. He suddenly felt as if he were surrounded by lilacs, a garden full of them. The soft, feminine fragrance—along with everything else— caused a stirring in his groin, and he leaned against the railing to hide what might possibly be embarrassing to him.

"Why, I don't really know that I've ever met one." Fortune wondered why he was staring at her so blatantly, and decided that she should excuse herself. Her mother would be angry enough if she discovered that Fortune had been talking to a stranger. "If you'll excuse me, Mr. Gregory, I think supper should be almost ready. My parents will be waiting for me."

Beau grinned. This young woman was a challenge to him, and he loved a challenge. Young, beautiful, innocent, and with a mother that hated gamblers. "Well, Miss Anthony, I'll wager that *you* won't feel so adamant about gamblers. I . . . hear that they're a charming lot."

"Charming?" Fortune laughed, recalling some of her mother's accusations. "I doubt it."

"It sounds to me as if we're at an impasse here." He crossed his arms and tilted his head to one side thoughtfully. "I propose a wager. A real wager."

Fortune couldn't hide her interest. She'd never gambled on anything in her life. "What sort of wager?"

"I'll bet that you *would* like a gambler," he said, knowing that he could rely on his vast knowledge of women to bolster his end of the bet. To him, this was a mere dalliance, not a gamble.

"Well," she said pensively, "how would I know? I mean, we'd have to find a gambler to see if I like him, don't we?"

"We're bound for New Orleans. I'm sure we'll be able to find at least one gambler there." Beau leaned closer to her and caught the soft fragrance of lilacs. "Now, what shall we put up for this bet?"

"Oh," Fortune said flatly. "I hadn't thought of that."

"Suppose . . . I know!" he exclaimed, slapping his hand on the railing as if the thought had just occurred to him that moment. "A kiss."

"A kiss?" Fortune asked, wondering if she should turn and walk away. She considered it for a moment, but then she smiled broadly. What possible chance could she have of losing? As closely supervised as she was likely to be in New Orleans, she'd never get close to a gambler. She stuck out her hand to shake his, to seal the wager. "You have a bet, sir."

Beau bowed from the waist and caught her hand. Placing a moist kiss on the top of her hand, he wondered why this slip of a girl had seized his interest so quickly. She possessed none of the . . . attributes he usually sought in his female companions. As he stood there, he smiled and winked. "Miss Anthony, I believe this will be a most entertaining journey. I look forward to seeing you again soon."

Fortune felt the color rise in her cheeks. There was something so exciting, so...different, about the way he kissed her hand, as if he were promising that something special would happen. And he had yet to release his grip. The top of her hand burned as if he'd singed it with his lips. Never having experienced any sensation so odd before, she jerked her hand away, gingerly caressing it with the other.

"I— Well, I'm not sure that—" she stammered, wondering what she should do. She did like this man. She liked the way he made her feel. Smiling, she lifted her chin and said, "Mr. Gregory, I believe that I shall look forward to seeing you again, as well."

Anxious to leave his company before she lost her nerve completely, Fortune strode toward the companionway, hoping that Beaumont Gregory wouldn't follow her. "Well, this is a new beginning. Maybe Fortune Rosalynd Anthony should be a new woman," she said aloud to herself, and then glanced around to see if anyone had overheard. Apparently she was alone in the narrow hallway.

Pausing outside her parents' cabin, she tried to rein in her runaway emotions. It would never do for Letha Anthony to suspect that her daughter had breached the bounds of acceptable behavior. Letha's lectures could go on for hours at times. After making sure that her dress hung straight and that her face displayed no hint of the peculiar sensations that pulsed beneath her skin, Fortune opened the door.

From the moment she saw her parents, she knew something was wrong. Her mother lay in bed, moaning and fanning herself. Giles Anthony sat nearby, murmuring endearments to his sick wife.

In an instant, Fortune realized that this trip wouldn't be as pleasant as she'd thought. Nursing her mother could be an exasperating experience. "Oh, dear, Mother, are you ill?"

Letha's eyes fluttered open momentarily before falling shut again. She appeared to be too weak to talk.

"Your mother's never been happy at sea." Giles patted his wife's hand solicitously. "There, there. You'll be getting better any time now."

"I'm sorry you're not feeling well, Mother. Is there anything I can do?" Fortune started to close the door behind her, but she heard a sound and turned around. "Oh, hello, Mrs. Allen, Mr. Allen. How nice to see you."

Jemima Allen smiled at Fortune. "How very nice to see you again, Fortune. Were you and your parents about ready to go to the dining room?"

Fortune glanced back at her mother. "No, ma'am. My mother's not feeling very well, and—"

"Oh, dear, is she experiencing seasickness?" Concern was evident on Mrs. Allen's pretty face.

"Yes, ma'am, I think so." Fortune looked back at Mrs. Allen. The woman wasn't much older, if at all, than Fortune. She was attractive, but a little plump. She looked like a contented cat. Fortune smiled at the idea and then said, "I'm sure she'll be all right soon."

"Tsk, tsk," Jemima said, shaking her head. "I hope so. I've heard of cases lingering on and on."

Fortune tried not to frown. If her mother heard the comment, then the likelihood of a quick recovery would be remote. Letha Anthony was extremely susceptible to suggestion.

Giles looked past Fortune and saw the Allens standing in the companionway. "Good evening, Mrs. Allen, Selwin." He glanced at his wife, clearly recognizing that she wouldn't feel like going to the dining room for supper. "Would you mind if Fortune accompanied you to supper? I'm afraid that Letha is too ill to eat."

"Of course Fortune may go to supper with us." Jemima Allen turned to Giles with a radiant smile. "Don't you worry about a thing. In fact, I'll sit with Letha while you all go."

Fortune felt a tug of guilt. She should stay with her mother and let her father go to supper. "Father, I can stay with Mother while you—"

"No, no, daughter, go on. Ask to have something sent to me here." Giles stood and walked to Fortune's side. He

smiled down at her and put his arm about her shoulders.
"Enjoy yourself, my dear. We'll be fine."

"Now, Giles, I insist," Jemima said, pushing past Fortune and into the cabin. "I haven't had a chance to chat
with Letha in a long time. Nola Bell and I will do just fine.
You go on to supper with Fortune and Selwin."

Nola Bell poked her head out of the other room. "Miz
Allen, you take yo'sef on to supper, too. I's been looking
after Miz Letha since she was a squallin' baby. I ain't about
to let nothin' happen to her now."

"Well, Nola Bell, I'm sure you're right," Giles said,
shrugging his shoulders. "Shall we go, ladies? Selwin?"

The arrangements were made, and Fortune went to supper with her father and the Allens. During supper, Fortune listened eagerly as Selwin Allen spoke of the grand and
glorious West, of California. His job was to recruit set-
tlers, and he'd come to Charleston for that reason. The
Anthony family and three other families from the Charleston area were now on their way to claim land. Several other
passengers on the packet were employees of the packet line,
going ahead to set up offices; others were soldiers or government employees going to take posts in the new territory.

"I tell you, the land is so fertile and the climate so fair
that it puts Charleston to shame." Selwin Allen slapped his
knee and shook his head. "I never would have believed it.
Everything's new and challenging, too."

Giles glanced at his daughter. He noticed the signs of
excitement bubbling up in her. He didn't know why, but
lately, Fortune had come to dislike Charleston as much as
he did. "And the government is going to give me eighty
acres free and clear? It's more than a man could ask for."
Giles mused, picturing the vast expanse of land that eighty
acres represented to someone who had nothing, an unloved second son. He just couldn't get the free land out of
his mind.

"Eighty acres for you, and another eighty for Mrs. Anthony." Selwin fished in his pocket, retrieved his watch and
gazed at it for a moment. He shook his head sadly and

stood. "Although I have very much enjoyed your company, I really must be going. A bit of work to do."

Fortune thought back to when Mr. Allen had first approached her father. She had seen that her father's first inclination was to say yes immediately, but he had looked at his wife and daughter, wondering how the change would affect them. "It's quite a plateful to contemplate on short notice," he'd said, and Fortune had seen her hopes dwindling.

Selwin had stood, nodded to the ladies and followed Giles from the room. "This is a wonderful opportunity. It won't come your way again. You can get in early, while the choice land is still available. I know your situation here is . . . well, less than satisfactory. What with Roger returning and all."

"I appreciate your kindness." Giles had walked with his friend to the door. "Thank you for stopping by. I'll speak with you again tomorrow or the next day."

Excitement had truly welled up in Fortune then. Her father hadn't said no. There was still a chance. She could hardly sit still. More than anything else, Fortune wanted to leave Charleston. Life here had become intolerable for her.

She had always loved the city and the surrounding area, the lush outer islands, the gentle surf, the vast plantations. Charleston displayed an innate grace, a charm, that she found exciting. There were theaters, musicals, races, balls, and parties of every description. The people were gracious and happy, eager to share their passion for living with all guests who visited the city.

All of her excitement about Charleston had dissipated. Now she wanted to leave, never to return. No matter how hard she tried, she could no longer walk down Meeting Street with the same joy she'd once experienced. Standing on the promenade at The Battery no longer gave her that familiar sense of wonder. All the beauty and grace of the city seemed to have been swept away by high tides, or buried by the muck that had lain beneath the surface, unseen by most of the planters and their families.

For several days, she had held her breath, silently praying that her father would agree to go to California. A new beginning. To Fortune, California represented everything that was new and wonderful in the world. It represented independence, growth, opportunity, a chance to live again instead of merely existing.

"I hate Charleston," Fortune had said, flopping down on her grandfather's brocade sofa. "I want to go."

"Now, Fortune, darling, that's not nice." Letha Anthony had admonished, looking up from her needlework. "Sit up straight. And take out that last stem. I declare, you'll never learn to embroider if you don't pay attention."

"Yes, ma'am," Fortune had answered, dutifully retrieving the napkin she'd been embroidering. Feeling no remorse for her outburst, she had taken her needle and carefully removed the stitches her mother had criticized.

"Letha, you must know I can't remain here now that Roger has returned. The situation is damnably intolerable." Giles had jumped up and begun pacing. "If only he hadn't come back. Why couldn't he have remained in England, drinking and gambling?"

"But, Giles, to leave all our friends...our family...to go to the ends of the earth..." Letha, once again, had used the only real excuse she could muster. "And what of Fortune? She's practically engaged to that nice Dennis Forrest. He's the catch of the city—the state, even."

Fortune had given her mother a withering glare and instantly regretted it. Letha Anthony couldn't know why Fortune disliked Dennis so much. And Fortune, painfully aware of her mother's frailty, had never told her. She had never told anyone. The whole incident made her feel dirty, humiliated.

"Mother, this is such a wonderful opportunity!" Fortune had cried, trying to reinforce her father's pleas. "Mr. Allen said that, in addition to our hundred and sixty acres, we could eventually buy more, much more. Think of all the exciting people we'll meet, and the new places we'll see."

"Fortune, dear, there are plenty of very nice people here in Charleston. You don't have to travel to the wilderness to meet interesting people." Letha had frowned and put down the napkin she was embroidering. "Don't slouch, dear. You *have* an opportunity, a marvelous opportunity to marry Mr. Forrest. I can't think for the life of me why you'd turn him down. After all, his parents are quite wealthy and well-respected."

Fortune had swallowed hard. She didn't like lying to her mother, so she had said, "I simply can't abide the man, Mother."

That was true enough. His attack had left her feeling unclean for months. Marrying him was out of the question. Marrying *anyone* was out of the question. She craved independence. She could never get that if she was married. Besides, her parents' marriage wasn't as splendid as her father always pretended. Fortune suspected that her mother didn't love her father, though she didn't know why. He positively doted on her.

"My darling, many marriages begin with less than a loving relationship. Learning to love a man is quite—"

"For the love of all the angels, Letha, I've grown tired of this argument! Let's discuss the opportunity before us. We must come to a decision about California." Giles had lit a cigar and taken a long puff, studying his daughter. His scowl had softened. "Do you really want to leave Charleston that badly, Fortune? I mean, your mother is quite correct in her assessment of marriage, and your marriage would be no different."

"I want more than anything to leave Charleston." Fortune hadn't known how to express her true feelings without causing more problems.

Living with her grandfather, almost as a poor relation, was something she couldn't stand any longer.

Fortune did hate Charleston, especially during the last few months. Life had become almost unbearable to her. Living with her grandfather who saw only the good in his wastrel elder son and only the bad in his younger son, Fortune's father, was trying enough, but her uncle Roger had returned—ostensibly to assume his place as head of the family. All of Giles's hard work throughout the years, keeping the plantation solvent and caring for all his invalid father's concerns, meant nothing. The prodigal had returned.

Now that Uncle Roger had returned to take his place as the head of the family, matters were even worse. His simpering young wife was the crowning blow. The girl was younger than Fortune, and automatically assumed that everyone in the household was there to serve her and her husband. Fortune couldn't stand to see her father so ill-used. "I hate Charleston," she had reaffirmed.

And then there was the Simpsons' party. It would live in Fortune's memory forever as the most humiliating time of her life. Her attitude had changed that night, and no matter how hard she tried to forget, she couldn't. And she had to see Dennis Forrest almost every day. To make matters worse, he acted as if nothing had happened—unless he could arrange to be alone with her. His actions were too abominable even to think about.

Now he'd asked for her hand in marriage. Neither of Fortune's parents could understand why she so vehemently rejected the proposal of one of Charleston's wealthiest young men. And she simply couldn't tell them.

Giles had looked at his wife. He and Fortune had discussed Letha's frailty, and how the trip would affect her. They had concluded that if they took the route across the Isthmus of Panama, she would fare much better. The other routes were much longer and more harrowing.

Fortune's thoughts sped forward to this morning, when they had left her grandfather's plantation, Pleasant Point, forever. Roger Anthony and his new wife were still abed when the carriage pulled away. Fortune hadn't looked back. She felt as if the shackles of slavery had been lifted from her. She caught Nola Bell's eye and then smiled at Boaz. They, too, had been set free. The two slaves had belonged to Giles for a long time, but today they were free. As a gift for their service throughout the years, Giles had arranged for their freedom. Hoping to go to a place where blacks could not be bought and sold as slaves, Boaz and Nola Bell had asked to come along.

Fortune had been delighted. She'd grown up tagging after Nola Bell and Boaz. Now she counted them as friends.

The sound of conversation intruded on her reminiscences, and Fortune looked up in time to see Selwin Allen leave the dining room. His wife remained. She and another woman were discussing a mutual friend. Fortune glanced at the small party assembled at the supper table. Captain Houser had introduced everyone, but most of the conversation so far had come from Selwin Allen. Fortune hadn't had an opportunity to talk to anyone else.

As Selwin departed, another man joined the group remaining in the dining room. One look at his broad shoulders and the square set of his jaw and Fortune knew who he was. Beaumont Gregory. He was soon followed by a man she recognized as having boarded the ship with Mr. Gregory.

Color sprang to her cheeks as Mr. Gregory gazed steadily at her for a few seconds before seating himself directly across from her. *Stop it,* she scolded herself. *He's just a man, an ordinary man.* But Beaumont Gregory was no ordinary man, and no matter how hard Fortune tried to convince herself that he was, she couldn't. Willing herself not to look at him any longer, she glanced at the girl next to her.

Seated to Fortune's left was a young woman named Amelia Sloan. She was pretty enough, but her coloring was almost garish. Her hair was black, nearly blue-black, and her eyes were dark green. Beneath a slightly patrician nose, her mouth was a vivid red, even though Fortune was sure the girl hadn't painted her lips. Fortune decided that, with clothing in the right colors, Amelia might be fine. Dressed as she was, however, in the palest of pinks, she looked like a painted doll. Trying not to appear obvious, Fortune peeked at Mr. Gregory to see if he was still watching her. Though he was talking to his friend, he was still staring at her.

Fortune looked at the two men. Apart from Selwin Allen, they were the youngest men she'd seen on board. Mr. Gregory looked to be in his late twenties or early thirties, and the other man could be about the same age. Both had dark hair, but Mr. Gregory's was a little lighter, a dark brown where the other man's was black. But the difference was in the eyes. The other man's were a sort of washed-out blue, so light that it was almost impossible to tell their color. Beaumont Gregory's were green, as dark as the Atlantic glittering in the sun.

Fortune averted her eyes. Jemima Allen smiled at Fortune when she caught her eye. Fortune returned her smile and then glanced at Beau. He was watching her closely.

She needed to get her mind off the man once and for all. She couldn't wilt beneath his gaze. Since Amelia was nearer Fortune's age then anyone else on the ship, she decided to make friends with the girl. Fortune forced a cheerful smile. "Hello, my name's Fortune Anthony. I'm happy to have someone close to my age on board."

The girl smiled. "Me, too. I'm Amelia Sloan. This is my mother."

"Hello, Mrs. Sloan. I'm Fortune Anthony." Turning to look at the older woman, Fortune smiled as charmingly as possible. "I'm very pleased to meet you."

"Hazel Sloan, of the Georgetown Sloans." Mrs. Sloan gazed at Fortune for a moment. "Pleased to make your acquaintance, I'm sure."

Glancing back at Amelia, Fortune tried to appear cheerful. "Would you like to walk the deck early in the morning?" Fortune asked, hoping to have some company for her daybreak stroll. Back at home—no, Pleasant Point wasn't home anymore—she had walked several miles a day. The exercise had made her feel robust and had given her time to think. Through her eyelashes, she could see that Mr. Gregory had turned to answer a question Captain Houser asked. Flooded with relief, she smiled gaily at Amelia.

"Uh, how early?" Amelia asked, fluttering her dark lashes. "I don't get up too early."

"Oh," Fortune mumbled, a bit disappointed. "I usually walk very early, but we can still spend some time together when you get up."

"Oh, yes. That would be nice." Amelia turned to her mother. "Would that be all right, Mummy?"

Mrs. Sloan looked at Fortune and then at Amelia again. "Well, I suppose it would be." She directed her gaze to Fortune for a moment. "Where is your mother, dear? Would I, perhaps, know of your family?"

"She's not feeling well, Mrs. Sloan. Our servant is sitting with her while Father and I have supper." Fortune could tell almost immediately that Mrs. Sloan was one of those society types who instantly categorized people. Fortune refused to satisfy the woman's curiosity by telling her more than was absolutely necessary. "I don't think we have relatives in Georgetown."

Fortune didn't like the way the conversation was going. Apparently Amelia had no mind of her own. She would be a dutiful daughter, and someday an obedient wife, but as a friend for Fortune, the girl was dreadfully dull. *Too bad that Mrs. Allen is married,* Fortune thought. *I'll wager that she's much more interesting than Amelia.*

Without putting forth any effort at all, Fortune engaged Amelia in polite conversation that wouldn't upset Mrs. Sloan. Having a great deal of experience in handling haughty mothers over the years, Fortune knew exactly what to say and what not to say. She smiled at Mrs. Sloan. "Mrs. Sloan, would it be all right for Amelia to join me tomorrow afternoon in our parlor? It's very small, but she and I could get to know each other while we embroider."

Mrs. Sloan beamed at Fortune. "Well, I think that's a fine way to spend the afternoon, but why not come to our parlor? I'm sure that with your mother ill, the noise of you two girls would be most disturbing."

"Thank you, ma'am, for your thoughtfulness," Fortune said, biting her tongue to keep from saying something truly sassy. "I'll see if I can get away. My father may want me to keep my mother company."

Beau listened to the conversation. He'd spent years listening to just such drivel in his mother's parlor. Women could be awfully mean sometimes, and, he surmised, this Mrs. Sloan was one of the meanest. Her demeanor might be gentle, her words softly spoken, but Beau knew that her tongue was rapier-quick. He suddenly felt sorry for Fortune. If Mrs. Sloan were angered, Fortune would taste the sting of her words.

He looked again at Fortune. She was even more beautiful than he'd imagined. Here in the soft glow of the lamps, her hair shone like spun gold. Her high cheeks and small nose were aristocratic, but he remembered her musical laugh and her sassy remarks. Fortune might come from a society family, but her spirit had never been tamed.

Watching her pretend to be the perfect companion for the mindless Amelia, he wondered how long that friendship could last. Mrs. Sloan wasn't the sort of woman who would welcome the friendship of a girl who didn't abide by the rules of genteel society. Fortune Anthony might know the game, but, Beau decided, lighting a cigar, she wouldn't be above bluffing her way through a hand if necessary. *Yes, by the ace of spades, he already liked this Fortune.* She was a spirited woman, feisty enough to take his bet. Playing the game with such a woman might be interesting. If, of course, a man had leanings in that direction.

Beaumont Gregory, however, did not.

Chapter Two

While the gentle swells of the Atlantic rocked her, Fortune lay in her bed and thought of Beaumont Gregory. What a handsome man he was! Eyes the color of the emerald Atlantic on a bright summer day... And he seemed to be able to read her mind. His hair reached his collar and tended to curl into dark ringlets that sprang free around his face. Even with her eyes closed, she could see his fingers absently brushing the errant locks aside as he'd listened intently earlier this evening as Captain Houser described the perilous trip around Cape Horn.

And then Beau had turned his eyes to her. Her face flamed once again as she remembered the way he'd looked at her, as if they shared some secret. Well, they did. With a smile, she recalled their wager. What fun! He had continued to stare at her. Two can play at that sort of game, she mused, wondering how he'd like to be the object of such close scrutiny.

She yawned. Her eyelids felt heavy. Across the room, her father snored fitfully, and her mother moaned in her sleep. I guess this will be a difficult journey, she decided, sighing, and then she fell asleep.

Before the sun rose, Fortune was dressed and slipping out of the cabin, trying not to wake her parents. She tiptoed up the stairs to the deck and inhaled the cool, salty air. She loved the ocean, its smell, its rhythms—everything about it. As she took her first few steps toward the railing in the darkness, she decided that if she had been born a man she might have become a sailor.

The sound of the waves slapping at the side of the ship and the brisk snapping of the sails greeted her as she strolled along, testing the damp boards to see if they were slippery. When she found that she could walk without sliding, she increased her pace until she was almost marching.

Fortune was nearly alone on the deck. She knew that the ship would soon be bustling with activity with the coming of daylight. The heat of the day would probably keep most of the other passengers below, however. She tried to think of something interesting to do.

Back at Pleasant Point, she'd always enjoyed her early-morning walks around the vast estate. While walking, she'd imagined that the beautiful plantation would be willed to her father and then to her. She could almost see herself someday, sitting astride her horse and directing the planting or harvesting of cotton. For many years she'd followed her father as he rode through the fields, giving instructions here and there. Fortune could practically have supervised the planting at the age of eight.

She had always hoped that her grandfather would see reason and give the plantation to her father, but he hadn't. He'd held on to the foolish dream that her uncle Roger would return to take his place as the next head of the family. Roger had returned. In the few months she'd observed him, Fortune had seen quite clearly that he'd never make a planter. He knew nothing about it and didn't care.

Quickening her step, she shook her shoulders. She didn't want to start this glorious day thinking bad thoughts. She said a prayer of thanks for her many blessings, and then turned to watch the sunrise. The sky to the east was strewn with a few clouds that were beginning to lighten.

Beau watched Fortune for a few moments. She seemed to be absorbed in the sunrise, which promised to be spectacular. He could hardly see her, but he felt a strong urge to talk to her.

"Beautiful out here this time of day, isn't it?" Beau asked, stepping out of the shadows.

Fortune whirled around and found herself facing Beaumont Gregory. "Good morning, Mr. Gregory," she said in a soft voice. "I didn't expect to see you out this early."

"The man who lies abed while others get ahead of him will soon harvest the inferior crop of his laziness," Beau recited with a chuckle, resting his elbows on the railing. "If I had a coin for each time my father said that, I could buy the California Territory."

Fortune smiled up at him. They were very close. She could feel the heat of his body; it seemed to reach across the space to warm her. "My mother often speaks in platitudes, too." She thought about that for a moment. "Whom do you think has the leisure to sit around and think up all those weighty thoughts?"

"A rich man who has no crop to look after, no merchandise to sell and no wife to bedevil him," Beau quipped. Then he sobered. Why had he added "wife"? True, Beau's mother had often driven his father past the limits of civility, but Beau had tried very hard to forget that part of his life. "My good friend Patrick Meade, who now lies snoring in his bed."

The scent of lilacs seemed once more to surround the space where she stood, and Beau inhaled deeply. How he loved that fragrance. He turned slightly to gaze down at her. His hand touched hers, and a spark raced through him, heating every cell in his body. "A man with nothing else to do," he amended, and quickly moved to break the contact.

Fortune's fingers tingled where he'd touched her. She stared at her hand for a moment, wondering what had happened. Glancing back at him, she smiled slightly to hide her confusion and tried to concentrate on what he'd said. So, he wasn't looking for a wife to take to San Francisco. Maybe he'd find one once he arrived. Fortune knew there were few women out there, but perhaps he could find one. A man could hardly run a homestead without a wife. She chose to ignore his reference to a wife, and said, "I suppose you're right. A man who has a crop to harvest seldom has the time to sit and ponder life's little mysteries."

Beau grinned. She'd taken the remark as he'd intended it, and apparently hadn't dwelt on the word *wife*. He knew few unattached young women who would have ignored the word. "Exactly. But I see that we happen to be among the leisure class this morning, and the sunrise promises to be one of the most brilliant I've ever had the pleasure of witnessing."

Fortune looked across the ocean as the sun peeked above the horizon. The clouds were shaded with pinks and lavenders, and then with scarlets and purples, as the golden sun made its way on its upward course. "It is a beautiful sunrise. This is going to be a shining day."

Beau glanced down at Fortune. Once again, the crimson sunrise tinted her golden hair to a color very similar to that of a strawberry basking in the sun. What a glorious color! The gray shadows stole away, chased by the warm sun, and Beau felt sad. Soon the deck would be bustling with activity, and he would no longer be alone with Fortune. She looked up at him, and he felt the magnetism of her eyes. Fighting the urge to kiss her, he cleared his throat and scanned the deck. "Shall we walk for a while, now that we can see where we're going?"

Fortune nodded and began to walk. For a few seconds, she'd thought he was going to kiss her, but he hadn't. You have an overactive imagination, young lady, she scolded herself. Why would he want to kiss you? He as much as warned you moments ago that he wasn't interested in a wife, and he probably meant any entanglement with a woman.

As they strolled along, the breeze picked up. Fortune loved walking with the wind blowing in her face. The spray that occasionally reached them as they neared the prow was cool. Soon her skin felt tight and her gray morning gown was dotted with dark spots of water. Nola Bell would fuss, but Fortune didn't care. She'd never felt so alive and fresh in her life.

"Where are you from, Mr. Gregory?" she asked, lifting a hand to keep her chignon from tearing away from its pins in the stiff breeze.

"Near New Orleans," he answered, his attention caught by her slender hand. Even the movements of her hands fascinated him. He'd never seen a woman move with such innate grace before—and yet she didn't seem to know how she affected him.

Beau sensed that he was on dangerous ground here. His life brought him into contact with many women—all of them unlike Fortune Anthony. Her sincerity seemed to capture his interest as no other woman ever had.

"I've never been to New Orleans," she admitted, feeling sad that he wouldn't be going as far as San Francisco. "I suppose you're going home, then."

"Home?" Beau considered the word for a few seconds. He hadn't been home in years. His father had left the plantation soon after his wife's death, but then there hadn't been much to leave. There was no money, and the plantation had been foreclosed upon. "No, I'm not going home."

For a moment, Fortune smiled inwardly. Maybe he was going to San Francisco after all. She hesitated to question him further. Perhaps he didn't want her to know where he was going. Thinking about that, she gazed up at him. He was a handsome man...not in the usual sense, but handsome nevertheless. His slightly patrician nose gave him a classical appearance, much like the pictures of Greek statues she'd seen in her father's books.

Fortune wondered why he was apparently so opposed to marrying. Had he been married before? Was he in love with a woman who had scorned him? She could ask him none of these questions, yet they clamored to be voiced. Forcing her thoughts back to the original question, she studied him. Again, she liked what she saw. An honest face, she concluded. "Will you be leaving us in New Orleans?"

He grinned, and a dimple formed in his left cheek. "No, I'm going all the way. San Francisco is my goal."

"I see." Fortune somehow couldn't imagine him as a farmer or a merchant, but she supposed that she might be wrong. What else was there for a man to do in the new territory? The knowledge that he'd be traveling with them all the way comforted her. She instinctively felt that he'd know what to do in an emergency situation.

Although Fortune didn't really expect an emergency, she knew that the person who expects the unexpected is seldom surprised. That seemed to be such an ambiguous statement, but she found it interesting. The Isthmus of Panama was only fifty miles wide, so she doubted that very much could happen in so short a journey. The little group of travelers would wait in Panama City until the *California* picked them up and took them on to San Francisco. "Have you ever been to San Francisco, Mr. Gregory?"

"No, but I look forward to it." Beau gazed out over the water pensively. A new beginning. That was what he was looking for. A place where nobody knew him and nobody knew his family. A place where everyone was equal and he had a chance to make his fortune. "I think that California is going to be bustling with people soon. Crowds will go after the free land, and towns are going to develop overnight. The wise man who's there when that happens will be the man who gets rich."

So, he was interested in getting rich. She wondered if he came from a poor family. He looked like a gentleman, and he had the manners of a planter's son—well, most planters' sons. Maybe he was a second son, like her father, and would inherit nothing from his parents. She could certainly sympathize with that situation. "Do you think that California is as wonderful as Mr. Allen says it is?"

Beau thought about it for a moment. "Well, I think his enthusiasm is partly generated by the salary the government pays him to find people to populate the area. But he could be telling the truth."

"If you really don't believe him, then why are you going?" Fortune asked, and then immediately regretted it. She knew that people went to unpopulated areas for a number of reasons, and some of the reasons were very personal. "I'm sorry. I shouldn't have asked that."

Beau chuckled. He couldn't get over how easily they could talk about things that were, well, out of the ordinary for a young woman to be interested in. "I really don't know. Why are you going?"

Fortune realized that when she'd asked the question, she opened herself up to his questions, too. Well, fair was fair.

"My father..." She stared at her fingers, which were clutching the railing. "My father is a second son, Mr. Gregory. We have little inheritance. California seemed to us to be a land of opportunity."

Beau nodded in agreement. "That's what everybody says. I hope it's true."

She gazed steadily at Beau. "I hope so, too, Mr. Gregory. For all our sakes." From behind her came the noises of the ship coming to life. She didn't want to spend too much time with this stranger. After all, he didn't want a wife, and she didn't want a husband. What she needed was a friend, and it looked as though Amelia might be her only chance on the ship. "Gracious, I know my parents must be looking for me by now. I've been out here so long."

"Have you? It seems that we've been here but a few minutes." Beau glanced around. The ship's crew were beginning to work, calling back and forth to each other as they did. "I suppose I'll see you again at breakfast."

"Perhaps," Fortune said, smiling because he appeared to like her. Why are you acting like this? she asked herself. She thought she must be like one of those little twits who were absolutely moonstruck every time a man looked at them, and she found the image distasteful. "I... Good day, Mr. Gregory."

Beau watched Fortune walk way. Her dress swung gracefully around her. Despite the Atlantic swells, she was as surefooted as any sailor. "Remarkable."

"Uh...was you speakin' to me, mister?" a sailor standing nearby asked.

"No. No, in fact I wasn't." Beau felt a little foolish and rushed after Fortune. He caught up to her as she reached the stairs. "Forgive me, Miss Anthony, for not escorting you to your cabin."

Fortune turned, a little surprised to find Beau standing directly behind her. "There's nothing to forgive, Mr. Gregory. I'm quite capable of walking to my cabin without assistance."

Beau recalled her steady yet graceful gait. "I'm quite sure you are, but it was inexcusable of me nonetheless."

He placed his hand on her elbow, and they walked down the stairs. Fortune's cabin was near the stairway, and she stopped outside the door. "This is as far as I go, Mr. Gregory. Thank you for escorting me."

"I believe, Miss Anthony, that we could perhaps dispense with the stringent formalities and address each other in a more... relaxed manner." He grinned. "As if we were friends, in fact. After all, we're apparently going to be spending a great deal of time together."

Fortune tried very hard not to smile, but her attempt was unsuccessful. "While I might agree with your suggestion in theory, my good Mr. Gregory, I fear that the other ladies aboard, being of tender upbringing, might find our sudden familiarity a trifle disturbing—one of those ladies being my own mother."

"I must say that you've dredged up a dilemma to which I hadn't given sufficient thought. Perhaps we could discuss this in more detail during our evening stroll...." Beau looked down into the bluest eyes he'd ever seen, then at her lips. They were a deep pink, like cherries about to ripen. For a moment he couldn't speak; he wanted to take her in his arms and kiss her, kiss her the way a woman should be kissed. "Say an hour after supper?"

Fortune attempted to look angry. "Why, Mr. Gregory, are you suggesting that I would walk, unchaperoned, with a man—a gentleman I'm hardly acquainted with at all? After dark? I say, Mr. Gregory, I find that..."

Beau saw the smile flirting with the corners of her lips and eyes. How very beautiful she was. He touched his finger to her lips and said, "Shhh. One hour after supper."

Fortune said nothing. She opened the door and went inside. Her father was already out of bed and dressed, but her mother still lay moaning.

Giles looked up from his chair. "Did you have a nice walk, daughter?"

"Yes, Father." Fortune moved toward one of her trunks. She removed a light bonnet and then turned to her father. "Would you like to go to breakfast? I can stay with Mother."

"Nola Bell can stay here. We'll both go." Giles went into the adjoining room. When he returned, he was pulling on his coat. "Let's go, daughter."

They left the room quietly, going out into the corridor, where they met Selwin and Jemima Allen. "Hello, Mr. and Mrs. Allen," Fortune said, smiling. She already liked Jemima a great deal and looked forward to having her for a neighbor when they settled in California.

"Why, good morning, Fortune, Mr. Anthony," Jemima replied, tucking her hand through the crook in Fortune's arm and leaving the men to talk among themselves. "I'm happy to see you up this morning."

Fortune studied the young woman for a moment. "I'm always up early."

"That's a good thing," Jemima said, smiling. "I think that's what gives you such lovely skin."

"Thank you, Mrs. Allen." Fortune tried not to blush. Compliments always embarrassed her.

"Please, call me Jemima," she said, laughing cheerfully. "After all, we're going to be cooped up on this boat like a flock of chickens, aren't we? I'd like to be good friends."

"I'd like that, too," Fortune agreed.

Breakfast passed slowly for Fortune. Beau didn't appear for the entire time she was in the dining room. She and Jemima got along very well, and Fortune was sorry she'd promised to go to Amelia's room to embroider.

The afternoon was interminable, worse than she could ever have imagined. Mrs. Sloan quizzed Fortune for the entire time they were together. Poor Amelia hardly said anything at all. Her stitches were perfect and she worked quickly. Fortune, on the other hand, slaved at her embroidery, though she knew that when she returned to her cabin, she'd have to remove nearly every stitch.

For the remainder of the afternoon, she sat with her mother. She wiped her mother's brow with cool cloths, but there was no change in her condition.

During Fortune's lifetime, she'd nursed her mother back to health on many occasions. She knew the routine well. Though she secretly believed that a great many of her mother's illnesses were imagined, she never voiced her opinions. She suspected her father felt the same way, but he never said anything, either. All the illnesses occurred during times of anxiety. Letha simply didn't adapt well to change.

Fortune placed her hand across her mother's forehead. There was no fever, but with seasickness there seldom was. Jemima had told her that several other passengers were ill, as well, including Mr. Allen. Fortune felt relieved that she could travel by sea without succumbing to the incapacitating illness.

At suppertime, Fortune and her father went to the dining room together. When she went inside, she saw Jemima right away. "Hello, Mrs....Jemima," she said with a warm smile.

"Here, dear." Jemima patted the empty chair beside her. "Sit with me."

Fortune happily seated herself next to Jemima. Amelia and her parents sat across from her. She smiled sweetly at Mrs. Sloan. She didn't care that the woman had taken a dislike to her. Mrs. Sloan simply didn't matter. However, Fortune did take great pleasure from being as cheerful and cordial as she could be, knowing that would irritate Mrs. Sloan, who couldn't bare her claws in front of all these people.

"Fortune," Jemima said, peering at the people around them. After apparently assuring herself that nobody was paying attention to them, she whispered, "Guess what?"

Fortune shook her head. "I can't guess. Tell me."

"I... Well, I think..." She glanced around again and leaned closer to Fortune. "I...I'm with child."

Smiling broadly, Fortune clasped Jemima's hand. "I think that's wonderful. Do you know when... I mean, can you tell when it's going to come?"

Jemima smiled shyly. "I'm not certain, but I think maybe soon after we arrive in California."

"Jemima!" Fortune exclaimed aloud, and everyone's eyes turned to her. She blushed. "Sorry," she said, lowering her head. How could she have been so silly? She peeked up at Jemima. How could Jemima have been so silly? She whispered, "Jemima, don't you know it's dangerous to travel... I mean, what if something happens? We don't have a doctor on board."

"I'll be fine, Fortune. Don't worry." Jemima looked around at their fellow travelers. "I'd appreciate it if you kept this our secret."

"Doesn't Mr. Allen know?" Fortune asked, staring at Jemima's husband, who was lost in conversation with her father.

Jemima gazed at him fondly for a few seconds and then turned back to Fortune. "Heavens, no! He wouldn't have let me come, and I... I simply refused to stay at home this time."

As soon as supper was over, Fortune grabbed Jemima's hand and nearly dragged her out to the deck, offering limp excuses to her father and Mr. Allen. When they reached a fairly secluded spot where Fortune thought they could talk, she stopped.

"Pooh!" she exclaimed, placing her hands on Jemima's shoulders. "How is it possible that he doesn't know? I mean, he must see—" Fortune stopped in midsentence. She was treading on dangerous ground. What went on between a man and his wife was private, and she had no business broaching the subject.

Jemima blushed and then turned to look out over the water. "You're right, of course. But I've taken steps... I mean, I don't let him see me.... What I mean to say is—"

"No need to say anything." Fortune slid her arm across Jemima's shoulders. "I apologize for even suggesting that you should confide in me."

"I need to confide in someone. I mean, Selwin and I haven't... Well, our marriage is..." Jemima's voice dropped to a whisper and was carried away by the wind.

"Jemima, forgive me." Fortune felt awful for having embarrassed her new friend. "Just forget I asked. We can be great friends without you ever having to say anything about—"

"No, Fortune." Wiping a tear with one hand, Jemima patted Fortune's hand with the other. "If we're going to be good friends, you have the right to confront me for making such an irresponsible decision. It's just that while Selwin was in California the last time, I fear that he had...well, that he found a woman friend. I simply couldn't let him go back alone."

"What a...what a horrible thing, Jemima." Fortune embraced her. "Well, whatever comes, we'll face it together."

Jemima fished a handkerchief from her reticule and sniffled quietly. "Thank you, Fortune. I just knew we could be close friends." She looked at Fortune with tears glistening in her green eyes. "I really need a friend."

"Me, too." Fortune hugged Jemima close. "We can stand against the world, you and I."

After a few moments of silence, Jemima sighed. "Thank you for understanding, Fortune. I think I'll retire for the evening now."

"Good night, Jemima," Fortune said, releasing her friend. "You can always count on me."

For several minutes, Fortune stared across the undulating sea. Why would Selwin Allen be so cruel? What had he done that made Jemima know about his...his light skirt in California? Fortune considered confronting him with the truth and then tossing him overboard. He deserved it. Yet she knew that she'd have to treat him as if she knew nothing about his personal affairs. She must hold everything Jemima had told her in the strictest confidence.

"Fortune Anthony can keep a secret," she told herself as she turned to begin her evening walk, hoping to rid herself of some of her anger. She found herself facing Beau. "Oh, hello, Mr. Gregory."

"Good evening, Miss Anthony," he said, bowing from the waist. "What a pleasant surprise."

"Surprise?" she asked, wondering what he could mean.

He glanced around to see if anyone could be listening. "I just said that in case someone thought you were meeting me here intentionally."

"Oh, yes." Fortune shook her head to clear away the cobwebs. "I was thinking of something else. I'm sorry."

Beau turned and looked toward the companionway. "Yes, I overheard a part of your conversation."

"You overheard!" she exclaimed. "Oh, how dreadful! This is simply awful!"

"I can't imagine why," he replied, turning her to face the railing. He stood there beside her for a few seconds. "I can keep a secret, too."

"Didn't your mother ever tell you that eavesdropping isn't nice?" she asked, the slightest trace of a smile creasing the corners of her mouth.

"Many, many times," he admitted ruefully. "She told me over and over about all my shortcomings."

"I didn't mean to pry." Fortune touched his arm, trying to comfort him in some way. She didn't know why, but that admission had clearly made him sad all of a sudden. "This is a terrible night to have a conversation with me. My tongue is wagging so hard that I've stepped on it twice or thrice already."

Beau laughed. "Oh, I'm not so sure. I think Mrs. Allen would have told you everything anyway. She needs someone to talk to, and you're the most intelligent female on board this ship."

Fortune grinned, rarely having been so flattered in her life. "I believe I should say thank you, but I'm not sure. From what I've seen of the women aboard, it wouldn't take much intelligence to win that race."

"How right you are. I think Mrs. Allen is pretty smart, though." He stopped to consider what he'd seen of her. "In fact, she may be smarter than her husband."

Fortune smiled sweetly and batted her eyes, though she doubted he could see her well enough to notice. "From what I know of men, that isn't difficult at all."

Chapter Three

The days settled into a routine. Fortune's mother almost never left her bed. Fortune and Jemima came to be close friends, and they shared much laughter—and a few tears.

"You know, Jemima," Fortune remarked as the packet drew into New Orleans, "I never thought I'd find so dear a friend so quickly."

"Neither did I," Jemima told her.

While they were waiting on the levee for their trunks to be unloaded, Fortune and Jemima watched the limited activity in the harbor. "I thought there would be hundreds of ships docked here," Fortune remarked, looking at the wharfs. "Why, I doubt that there are more than twenty."

"If that," Jemima said. "I suppose this is the wrong season for activity. These ships seem primarily to be carrying produce and the like."

"You're possibly right." Fortune fanned herself and looked up into the blazing glare of the sun. "It's awfully hot."

Wearing a heavy veil to prevent sunburn, Letha Anthony joined the two young women. "Fortune, why don't you have on your bonnet? I declare you're going to be as dark as Nola Bell if you don't mend your ways."

"I forgot, Mother. They're all packed away. In my eagerness to see New Orleans, I forgot to protect my skin."

"You'll regret it, I'm sure." Letha was sagging in the heat, hardly able to stand. "I do hope Giles finds a carriage straight away."

"Shall I go look for him?" Fortune hoped her mother would take her up on the offer. "You know him. He may be all afternoon."

Letha nodded. "Please do. Jemima and I will wait here."

"I'll be right back, Mother."

Letha called after her daughter. "Fortune, don't speak with any strangers. And, stand up straight."

Fortune straightened her shoulders and nodded to her mother. Sometimes Letha Anthony could be a torment to those she cared about, but Fortune found her mother easy to forgive most of the time. She hurried up the gangway to the deck and began to search for her father.

She found him rather quickly and passed along the message from her mother. "She's really peaked, Father. I think she may faint."

"I'll get a carriage for you ladies," Giles told her. "Selwin and I can follow along. I've already sent word to the St. Louis Hotel, so they're expecting us."

"Thank you, Father. I'll tell Mother." Fortune kissed her father on the cheek and headed back to the levee to report to her mother.

At the gangway, she ran into Beaumont Gregory. "Oh, hello, Mr. Gregory."

Beau bent from the waist, took her hand and kissed it. "Good afternoon, Miss Anthony. May I escort you somewhere?"

"No, thank you." Fortune removed her hand from his grasp and cradled it gingerly in the other. She couldn't think what was the matter. It felt warm and tingly where he'd touched it. "My mother is waiting for me."

Following Fortune's gaze, Beau spotted Mrs. Anthony. "I see. Well, perhaps I'll see you while we're in town. I certainly hope so."

"You're very kind, Mr. Gregory." Fortune knew her mother was watching. She didn't know exactly why, but she was sure Letha would disapprove of Beau; she didn't know enough about his background and his family. Fortune smiled and turned to leave.

Beau reached out and caught her arm. Flutters radiated along her arm from his touch. She looked up at him. "Was there something else?"

"Yes, Miss Anthony, there was," he replied, grinning broadly. The dimples appeared again in his cheeks. "I want to advise you against walking the streets alone at night. Since you don't know New Orleans, you might chance to find yourself in a district that poses some danger to innocent young ladies."

Scarlet splotches suffused Fortune's cheeks, and her eyes opened wide. "Th-thank you—for your warning," she stammered, and hurried down the gangway.

When she reached her mother and Jemima, Fortune knew she was in trouble. She could see the look of consternation on Letha's face, even through the veil.

"Fortune!" Letha exclaimed, snatching her daughter's hand. "Who on earth was that forward man? And why did he accost you? Have you been— Has he— I want an explanation right now, young lady!"

Knowing that whatever she answered would be wrong, Fortune settled on the truth, or as near to the truth as she could venture. "Please, Mother, you're causing a scene. He's Mr. Gregory, a gentleman who's traveling with our group to California."

"A planter?" Letha stared at the man, lifting her veil to see better.

Jemima shook her head. "I don't think he's a planter, but I don't know exactly what he does. He never said."

Letha glared at Fortune. "What has he to do with you?"

"Nothing, Mother. I met him on the ship at meals." Fortune hoped her mother wouldn't question her further, at least not here on the dock. She glanced around, hoping to spot someone or something that might divert Letha's attention. "Oh, there's Father with a carriage!"

A carriage was pulling up to the levee, near where they were standing. Giles tucked his wife and daughter inside and gave the driver an address. Jemima rode with them. Soon to be followed by Giles Anthony and Selwin Allen, the ladies headed for the St. Louis Hotel.

For the first time on the journey, Letha Anthony looked alert. "My gracious, what a lovely city," she remarked as they passed by stucco homes with ornate wrought-iron railings and verdant gardens.

Soon the fragrance of spicy food washed over them as they rolled past a restaurant. "Oh, that smells delicious!" Fortune exclaimed, trying to see into the dim interior. "This is so exciting!"

From the carriage, Fortune could see very little. Houses stood within walled gardens that blocked most of them from sight. A few were enclosed by wrought iron and displayed a beautiful style of architecture. "Oh, Mother, isn't that garden beautiful?" Fortune slid to the edge of her seat to see better. "Look, Jem, what a lovely array of flowers."

"It truly is," Jemima agreed, fanning herself. "I must say that it's rather warm here."

Fortune hardly noticed the heat and humidity. Once again excitement surged through her, and she craned her neck out the window of the carriage to get an even better look.

"Fortune Rosalynd Anthony!" Letha exclaimed, jerking on her daughter's arm. "Conduct yourself like a lady, or I'll be forced to punish you. I can't imagine what you're thinking about, acting like some hoyden, hanging out the window like that. What will people think?"

Refusing to allow her mother's chastisement to lessen her enthusiasm, Fortune sat back in her seat and cupped her hands together primly. "I'm sorry, Mother, but I don't see that it matters very much what the people of New Orleans think. We'll be here no longer than ten days, and—"

"Fortune! Have you taken leave of your senses?" Letha laid her head back and closed her eyes. "What have I done, Lord, to deserve such a naughty child?"

Jemima stifled a laugh and winked at Fortune. "Oh, Letha, leave her be. She's just happy to be here, in a new, exciting place."

Letha's head snapped up like a doll on a string. "Jemima Allen, how can you side with her in this matter? You know that women are judged by their conduct, and hers is reprehensible.''

"Letha, she's young," Jemima continued, a distinct twinkle in her eyes. "Nobody here knows her.''

"Just because nobody knows her doesn't excuse improper conduct." Letha glared at Fortune. "If you don't act more ladylike, I'll confine you to our hotel room for the entire visit. I won't abide your antics here."

"Yes, Mother," Fortune said, knowing she must find a way to placate her mother. "I'm sorry if I sounded disrespectful. I meant nothing by it."

"That's better." Letha smiled at Jemima and then peered out the window.

The carriage lumbered down the cobbled street, jostling its occupants as it neared their destination. When they reached the corner of St. Louis and Chartres Streets, the hotel came into full view and the carriage slowed, finally stopping at the entrance.

"Ah, I believe we've arrived...." Jemima remarked as she stared at the tremendous hotel.

"Oh, Mother, look!" Fortune exclaimed, hanging out the window again. "What a beautiful place. Are we staying here?"

Letha glanced at her daughter and grimaced. As Fortune dutifully ducked her head back into the carriage, Letha said, "I'm sure that your father said we were staying at the St. Louis Hotel." Letha leaned forward a little to peer past Fortune. "Oh, my, but it's large, isn't it?"

After the few minutes it took to register at the hotel and secure their baggage, the Anthonys reached their rooms. Fortune hurried inside and went from room to room, marveling at the beds with their luxurious hangings. "How lovely!" she exclaimed.

The Negro man carrying one of their trunks smiled and nodded. "There's mosquito netting 'neath them drapes over the bed."

"Oh." Fortune peered beneath the hunter-green satin. "I see. How convenient."

Fortune had a room of her own. After sharing a cabin with her parents on the ship, she was glad of the privacy.

She wanted time to think about Beau Gregory. He was an enigma. Nothing seemed to fit together. He was going to California. He didn't have a wife and didn't want one. He'd started flirting outrageously with Fortune. He didn't seem to have a business or a trade. She sat by the window and looked out over the harbor. She really wanted to know more about him, but she couldn't figure out how to ask the questions that would give her the information she needed.

Knowing that she probably wouldn't see him until they boarded the ship again, she sighed and sat back in the rocking chair in her room. Over the past few days, she'd come to enjoy her morning and evening strolls with him. Though she'd really wanted to know, she hadn't been able to bring herself to ask where he would be staying while in New Orleans. It simply wasn't ladylike. Most of the time—and particularly now that she'd left Charleston—Fortune didn't care whether she was ladylike or not, but she still couldn't ask a man she'd just met where he was sleeping.

She rose and walked behind the rocking chair. Propping her elbows on its high back, she stared out the window, seeing nothing. Her thoughts were completely on Beaumont Gregory. She could see his clear green eyes as surely as if he were standing before her.

Fortune recalled her wager with Beau and smiled. The harmless bet would come to nothing, but it made her life more interesting.

Nola Bell came in. "What's wrong with you, chil'?"

Fortune spun around so quickly she almost overturned the rocking chair. "Wrong? Nothing? Whatever gave you the idea that something's wrong?"

"I seen you looking like you was in a dream." Nola Bell cocked her head to one side. Her black curly hair was now sprinkled with gray, but her black eyes were as sharp as ever. "Ever since we been on that boat, you been up to something."

"You're imagining things." Fortune walked to the front of the chair and sat again. She couldn't look Nola Bell in the eye and tell a lie. "I'm just the same as always."

"Yeah, and I's about to sprout me a pair of wings and fly to California," Nola Bell said, opening the trunk. "I got my eye on you. You ain't 'bout to do nothing you and ol' Nola Bell be sorry for.''

"Oh, you treat me like a baby." Fortune stood again. She simply couldn't be still this morning. Looking down at the street, she watched people bustling to and fro, calling to each other, laughing, talking. "I think this is a nice place. People seem so friendly."

"Humph! Don't smell good!" Nola Bell snorted and shook out one of Fortune's dresses. "I be a happy woman when we gits where we going and I doesn't have to pack and unpack no more. It a shame and a disgrace for a girl to have this much stuff to pack and unpack, pack and unpack."

Fortune giggled, and she was relieved when Nola Bell smiled at her. "I'll be happy, too, Nola Bell. I think California is going to be the most exciting place in the world. A place where we can all be free and happy."

Nola Bell looked up from the trunk. She gazed at Fortune for a long moment and then rocked back on her heels. "You know, Miss Freedom and Happiness, one don't necessary mean the other. You can be free and sad, too."

Fingering the smoothly worn wood of the rocker, Fortune thought for a moment. "I know you're right, Nola Bell, but deep down inside, I feel that I'm going to be happier where we're going. I can see the difference in Father already. And, Mother—"

"Chil'," Nola Bell said quietly. "Your mama ain't gonna be happy nowhere. She carryin' a deep hurt that ain't ever healed and ain't never gonna."

Astonished, Fortune stared at Nola Bell. "What are you talking about? I never heard Mother say anything like that before."

"No, you ain't, and you ain't never going to." Nola Bell closed the trunk. "I's going to git that good-for-nothin' Boaz to come and take this trunk somewhere."

Fortune leapt to her feet. "Nola Bell, you come back here! You can't just say something like that and leave me—"

But she was talking to a closed door. "Whatever could she mean?" she asked herself aloud.

For the remainder of the afternoon, she kept herself
busy. Letha took to her bed to rest, still feeling the effects
of traveling by ship. Giles, along with Selwin Allen, left the
hotel to discuss the purchase of supplies for their home in
California.

Jemima came by for a chat. "Do you think we could go
for a walk?"

Fortune smiled happily. "Oh, let's do. I want to see everything. I'll tell Nola Bell."

Nola Bell was pressing one of Letha's dresses when Fortune found her. "What you up to, missy?"

"Nothing, Nola Bell," Fortune answered truthfully.
"Jemima . . . Mrs. Allen and I are going for a walk."

Without looking up, Nola Bell shook her head gravely.
"If'n you wants to know what I thinks, I thinks that you
and that Miz Allen is like two rosebuds on a bush. You is
fixin' to blossom." She put the iron back on the brazier and
picked up another. She gazed at Fortune for a long time. "I
jes' don't want you bloomin' at the wrong time and the
wrong place. N'Orleans is the wrong place, and this is the
wrong time."

Fortune stared for a moment. "I don't know what you're
talking about. You sound like you've been drinking heavily from Father's gin decanter."

"Now, don't you be gettin' sassy." Nola Bell shook her
finger at Fortune. "You know I ain't never taken so much
as a thimbleful of that awful-smelling stuff. May the Lawd
strike me down dead if that ain't a fact."

"Oh, I was teasing, Nola Bell. I know you wouldn't do
such a thing." Fortune grinned at her success in stirring a
response from the former slave. "I won't be out long."

"You put on a bonnet or you ain't going nowhere," Nola
Bell called as she returned to her ironing.

Fortune paid no attention to the servant's admonitions.
"Come on, Jemima. I can't wait any longer."

The two women walked down the stairs into the hotel
rotunda, where a slave auction was in progress. As they
hurried out into the street, Fortune marveled that such an
event could take place in a respectable hotel.

Strolling along, they occasionally stepped into a shop to examine the wares. First they rounded the block. They started out on St. Louis Street, then turned right onto Royal, right again onto Toulouse, and finally right onto Chartres. Their walk, thus far, had been fairly short.

"Jem, since we've been all the way around this block, shall we explore the streets two blocks away?" Fortune asked, hoping Jemima would agree.

Jemima looked at the little watch she always wore on a chain around her neck. "Well, I suppose we have time."

"Oh, good, good, good!" Fortune repeated merrily as they hurried along Chartres to Conti.

They sauntered along, crossing Royal, enjoying their walk. They turned right and walked a ways down Bourbon Street, until they met a tall, slender Negro woman who stopped abruptly and stared at Fortune.

Jemima glanced at the woman and then at Fortune. Fortune seemed to see nothing but the woman blocking her path. "Come on, Fortune, we can't dawdle. We'll be late for supper."

Ignoring Jemima, the Negro woman raised her hand and touched Fortune's forehead. "The direction of your life has changed. He with the eyes of the sea will bring you peace. You will not complete your intended journey, but that which you seek will be granted."

Fortune stood stock-still. She couldn't take her eyes off the woman. Instead of black eyes like Nola Bell had, this woman's were almost a clear blue, accentuated by the blue-black color of her shining skin. As the woman spoke, Fortune's attention was caught by the rich hue of blue tissue that cradled the woman's pink tongue. She'd seen Negroes with the same odd coloring back in Charleston. "Yes," Fortune squeaked, hardly aware of her surroundings. "I know."

"Your name will be raised on the voices of other tongues in praise. *Fortune.* Sadness, joy, both are in store, and much strife, but contentment will arise out of grief." The woman moved her hand, brushed it against Fortune's mouth. "Your future lies at Charleston."

Without giving Fortune a chance to reply, to say that she'd left Charleston forever, the Negro woman hurried on. Fortune glanced over her shoulder, shook herself, then looked at Jem. "That woman had me caught in her spell until she mentioned Charleston."

"I was beginning to worry about you," Jem said, hugging Fortune. "You had a strange, distant look in your eyes."

"Did I? I feel so…I don't know, strange, maybe. She has a powerful presence, doesn't she?" Fortune asked, turning around to watch the woman walk away. She was too late. The Negro woman was gone, as if she'd simply disappeared.

Jemima turned slowly around and caught Fortune's arm. "I think we've had enough excitement for one day. Let's go back to the hotel."

Fortune nodded and followed along. The woman's words rang through her mind like the clear tones of a bell, words she was unlikely ever to forget. "Did you understand what she said?"

"I'm not sure. She… Did she call your name, or was she speaking of your fortune?" Jem asked, stopping and glancing back over her shoulder. "This is too eerie, Fortune."

Instead of continuing on, they turned at Toulouse and hurried back toward the hotel. The shops they passed along the way held little interest now.

Fortune looked at a man crossing Royal Street, heading their way. He looked familiar to her, but with all that had happened she couldn't think clearly. Her eyes seemed out of focus.

Beau saw Fortune and smiled. He'd been looking for her as he'd reacquainted himself with the Vieux Carré. He was from New Orleans, but his home lay outside the city proper. He had written a note to a good friend, hoping to visit with him for a few days while waiting for the ship to leave for Panama City.

He grinned at Fortune. "Good afternoon, ladies. May I escort you somewhere? Sometimes the streets are unsafe for two such lovely ladies to be wandering about unescorted."

Jemima returned his smile. "Thank you for your kind offer, but we haven't far to go."

Beau hardly glanced at her. He couldn't keep his attention from Fortune. She looked a bit distracted, as if something dreadful had happened. "Is something wrong?"

"Wrong?" Fortune repeated, gazing steadily at his eyes. "She said 'the eyes of the sea.'"

"Who said that? What are you talking about?" he asked, beginning to worry. "Tell me what happened."

Jemima shook her head. "Nothing, really. A Negro woman stopped us and said a few things to Fortune that have, well . . . left her a bit unnerved."

"What things?" Beau asked, staring at Fortune. She looked as if the life had been drained from her.

"I don't know, exactly. I can't remember." Jemima tried very hard to recall what the woman had said, but her mind was almost blank. She looked at Beau. "I can't even remember what the woman looked like."

"Do you think it was a voodoo woman? Did she touch Fortune?" Beau asked, even more concerned now that he'd heard Jemima's words.

"Yes," Jemima admitted, looking at Fortune. "She touched her forehead and lips."

"I don't really believe in all that hocus-pocus, but many people here do. What do you think?" he asked, glancing about.

"This is very strange indeed." Jemima sighed, a little puzzled. "I don't really know what to think. But she's been getting more withdrawn ever since that woman talked to her."

"Doesn't hurt to be safe," Beau took Fortune's arm and guided her into a small restaurant nearby. As he seated Fortune, he waved to a Negro man at the back of the small establishment. "Henry, is Marie here?"

The man glanced at Fortune and nodded. "I send for her."

"What's wrong?" Jemima asked, now concerned that she'd have to explain all this to Letha.

"I'm not sure. Sometimes it's hard to tell exactly what's going on." Beau touched Fortune's cheek, and she turned to look at him. There was a blank look in her eyes.

An old Negro woman entered through the back door. She took one look at the situation and asked, "What the child have done?"

"We don't know exactly, Marie," Beau admitted. "It may be the heat. It may be the humidity."

Marie frowned and shook her head. "She been magicked. I be back."

Beau watched the woman waddle out the way she'd come in. Then he looked at Jemima and shrugged. "I guess we'll wait."

After a few minutes, Marie returned with a tiny velvet bag drawn shut with silken cord. "You—" she pointed a thick finger at Beau "—go taste filé gumbo."

"Yes, ma'am," Beau said, and rose. He walked back to where Henry was stirring a large kettle of aromatic stew. "Marie sent me to taste this."

Henry grinned and took a spoon from a rack nearby. "Best in t' city."

Beau touched the spoon to his lips and winced. "Hot!" He blew on the mixture for a moment and then tried again. "Excellent," he declared, and asked for three bowls of the concoction.

Marie summoned him back to the table. "Lady fine. Nothing ill meant."

Fortune turned her pale face upward and smiled wanly. "I don't understand what happened. We were walking along, and this woman stopped us. She mumbled a few words...*future, Charleston, sad, happy....* I don't quite remember it all."

Nodding, Marie said, "Eat gumbo. Keep gris-gris next to heart."

Though she hadn't thought she had an appetite, Fortune could have licked the bowl clean. "My, but that was delicious. If I didn't have to eat supper with my parents, I'd have another bowl."

Jem laughed a bit shakily. "Are you all right, Fortune?"

"I feel fine. Everything's just a bit hazy." Fortune sipped from her cup of tea. "Ugh! This isn't the most pleasant-tasting liquid. What is it?"

"Drink all. Will help." Marie stood across from Fortune and folded her arms.

Fortune had the feeling that Marie would hold her down and force her to drink the tea if she didn't do it voluntarily. "Well, perhaps it isn't so bad."

Beau laughed. "I see you recognize the futility of disagreeing with Marie. She's a tough woman."

"You see who tough when bottled spirits light bonfire in head." Marie smiled fondly at Beau. "I know you come crawling back for Marie to help."

"I've quit that carousing, Marie." Beau got up and hugged her. "But, just in case, I'll try to be respectful."

"Good. How long you home this time?" she asked, glancing from Beau to Fortune. Then she grinned. "Charleston."

Beau looked at her, puzzled for a minute. "We met on the trip from Charleston. And I'll be home for about another week. We're leaving for California."

"Too late in year. Snow blanket trails in autumn." Marie frowned suddenly. "Too much snow. Many people stranded."

"We're going by way of Panama City." Beau touched Fortune's shoulder. "Well, Miss Anthony, if you're feeling better, we'll go."

Fortune stood, as did Jemima. "Thank you, Marie. I don't know exactly what you did, but I feel better. My head's much clearer now."

"Black lady mean no harm. Powerful. Not trained." Marie hugged Fortune. "She mean well."

Fortune stared at Marie for a moment. "I think I knew that. I wasn't afraid of her."

Jemima shook her head. "I was. She seemed to have Fortune under some sort of spell."

"No mean bad for Fortune." Marie looked at Jemima for a few seconds and then grinned. "He be healthy, strong. Make much pain at birth, much happiness in life. Wait."

She bustled off into the back room and returned with another little velvet bag. "For birthing. Make easier."

Beau looked away. Uncomfortable because he instinctively felt that Jemima was shy about her condition, he pretended not to hear. After a few seconds, he said, "Well, shall we go?"

Fortune walked back to the hotel between Beau and Jemima,. With each step she felt better. Marie had said the woman was powerful but untrained. Fortune understood that the young Negro woman had meant no harm, but her touch had somehow set things askew. "You know, I've heard some of the slaves talking about voodoo, but it seemed like something impossible. I've heard that the practitioners can do lots of things, charms and spells and such."

"Many of the New Orleans Negroes came over from Haiti and brought the voodoo rites with them." Beau stopped across the street from the hotel. "I doubt very seriously if your parents, Fortune, or your husband, Mrs. Allen, would appreciate my accompanying you inside, so I'll leave you here."

"Thank you, Mr. Gregory," Jemima said, taking Fortune's arm. "I'm sure you're right."

Fortune didn't want to leave him, but she had no choice. "Thank you and good day."

When they entered the hotel, the slave auction was over. The rotunda and its barren platform served as a reminder, but there were no crowds of people waiting to purchase slaves, no people bound in chains, waiting to learn what the future held for them.

Even though she felt better, Fortune was glad that she didn't have to weave her way through a throng. Now that the mass of humanity was gone, she could smell the luscious odors emanating from the hotel's kitchen and bakery.

"You know, I feel as if I could eat again right now," Fortune said, inhaling the spicy fragrances. "I hope Mother and Father will want to eat early."

"Perhaps they will." Jemima stopped outside Fortune's room. "Are you all right? I must admit you gave me a scare."

"Oh, it was nothing, Jem," Fortune protested. "I was just stunned by the woman's audacity. I mean, I'm not used to strangers coming up and putting their hands on me and spouting riddles about my future."

"You're probably right," Jem agreed with a sigh. She held up her gris-gris and smiled conspiratorially. "Still, it's nice to have some form of protection—even if it's all in fun."

Fortune slipped into her room without encountering her parents or Nola Bell. Once inside, she stripped to her chemise and pantalets and climbed into bed. Within a few seconds, she was sound asleep.

Beau strode across the ornate rotunda and mounted the stairs. He went directly to his room and sat down, propping his feet on the low table in front of the sofa. Today had been interesting.

His thoughts turned to Fortune Anthony. She seemed to be a different sort of girl from those he'd known. Her quick sense of humor always amused him, and her spirit intrigued him. Few planters' daughters were as spunky as she. He compared her to the very correct Miss Amelia Sloan. What a contrast between the two. Women like Mrs. Sloan had been after him for years to marry their simpering little girls—at least until they'd learned that the Gregory fortunes were in such a condition that their properties had been foreclosed upon.

Not that he would have expected anything different. Throughout time, women had sought rich husbands for their daughters. Somehow mothers forgot that love and respect between husband and wife were important. They forgot that while they were searching for good wealthy husband material, the young daughters were hoping for love. He chuckled. If Mrs. Anthony had been well, she might have acted as Mrs. Sloan did.

Well, if you had to have one of the two, he thought, you'd be much better off with Fortune.

A knock interrupted his deliberations—just in time. He wasn't looking for a wife of any sort. When he opened the door, Patrick stepped in without waiting to be asked. After a second, Beau laughed and said, "Well, do come in and make yourself comfortable."

"What? Oh, yes. Thank you." Patrick moved to a chair and sat, his legs hanging across the arm of the chair. "Where've you been? I've been looking for you all afternoon."

"I've been reacquainting myself with New Orleans." Beau didn't really want to discuss Fortune with anyone right now, so he didn't mention her. "Stopped by Antoine's for a bowl of filé gumbo."

"I stopped in there, too. He said you'd been there earlier with two young ladies." Patrick raised one eyebrow suggestively. "*Two* young ladies? I'm sure this story is a fascinating one."

"Oh, it's nothing, Patrick." Beau dropped onto the sofa and shook his head. "Antoine just needs something to gossip about. You know him."

"I've known Antoine as long as you have. I've never heard him gossip about anyone," Patrick said in defense of their friend. "Damn good food, no gossip. Said something about some sort of curse."

"Oh, for God's sake, Patrick," Beau said, and jumped up. "It was nothing. Nothing intentional anyway."

Knowing that he couldn't really get out of explaining the situation, Beau related the entire incident as he paced the floor, finishing with "And that's all there was to it."

Patrick looked unimpressed. "I seem to recall your spending a great deal of time taking the early-morning and late-evening air with a certain Miss Anthony while we were on board ship. You expect me to believe—"

Beau turned to glare at Patrick, knitting his brows together in a thunderous expression that stopped his friend in midsentence. "What are you getting at?"

"Nothing. Just making an observation." Patrick grinned at his friend. "I've never known you to be interested in any lady who didn't have a price tag."

"All women have price tags," Beau answered dryly. "Some of them are just more open about it. Did you notice that Sloan twit?"

"How could I miss her?" Patrick asked, rising and striding over to the sideboard that held a silver tray with several cut-glass decanters. "Drink, old man?"

"No, thank you." Beau watched as Patrick poured a glassful of amber liquid. "But help yourself."

Patrick returned to his seat with a grin. "I might just do that. Hate to see brandy go to waste."

"That Sloan girl was very eager to catch my eye. It got to the point that I hated to go to supper on the ship," Beau said, shaking his head in disgust. "If Mrs. Sloan had told me once more what a sweet, obedient girl little Amelia was, I'd have come down with terminal seasickness. And she kept asking me if I knew that she was Hazel Sloan of the Georgetown Sloans."

"I'm glad she wasn't after me." Patrick sipped his drink thoughtfully and then grinned. "Woman must have a vision problem. Else she'd have been after me instead of you, don't you think?"

Beau groaned and rolled his eyes. "I'd be delighted to pass her on to you. When I see her, I'll mention that you're interested."

Patrick shook his head vehemently. "No, thanks. I'm no more looking for a wife than you are. Of course, that Fortune Anthony is another matter. I might consider changing—"

Once again Beau glowered at Patrick without speaking.

"On the other hand, I'm not really interested in marriage, and she's definitely the marrying kind." Patrick put down his glass and gazed at his friend for a moment. "Oh, yes, I forgot what I came for. I discovered, quite by accident, that there's a game tonight that practically begs for our attendance. Lots of big players."

"Reputable place?" Beau asked, his interest piqued.

Patrick lit a cigar and nodded. "Yes. As I understand it, some of the gentlemen are in town for . . . an evening's entertainment."

Beau grinned, recalling his wager with Fortune. He'd have to find a way to tell her of his occupation without making her angry. He glanced at Patrick. "Well, I suppose entertainment doesn't come without cost. We're a couple of entertaining fellows, don't you think?"

"I was hoping you'd see it that way." Patrick stood and walked toward the door. "Shall we say nine o'clock?"

Chapter Four

Throughout supper, Fortune craned her neck, looking for Beau. Since they'd met him coming from the direction of their hotel, she decided that he might actually be staying under the same roof.

Letha watched her daughter for several minutes. "Fortune, what is your problem? You're like a kitten following a bouncing ball. What are you looking for?"

Fortune's gaze immediately returned to her mother's face. "I . . . I was looking to see if Amelia might have come in. I guess . . . I sort of told her that we'd do something together while we're here."

Jemima smiled. She knew who Fortune was searching for. "Why, Fortune, I don't think they're here this evening. I was sort of looking for them myself." She turned to Letha. "I'm just so sorry that you weren't able to get to know Amelia and her mother. Very nice people."

"Well, I'm sure you're right, but Fortune shouldn't gawk as if she'd had no upbringing at all." Letha sipped her milk. "Are you finished with your supper, Fortune?"

"Yes, Mother," Fortune answered, placing her napkin beside her plate. "I can't eat another bite."

Jemima laid down her spoon. "I declare, that bread pudding was the best I ever ate. I'm sure I could have forgone supper and eaten three helpings of that."

"You're right, Jemima," Letha said, smiling graciously. "I don't know when I've eaten so much. That roast pork was delicious."

Fortune listened to the two women discuss the merits of the meal while she continued to scan the vast dining room for Beau. Even if he wasn't staying at the hotel, he might have come there to eat.

Jemima glanced at Fortune and then turned to Letha again. "Are you planning to attend the ball here tomorrow night?"

"Oh, I don't know. I'm sure you have to be invited, and—"

"Oh, no..." Jemima nudged Fortune under the table. "They have a huge ball almost every Friday evening. Anyone can attend."

A ball? Fortune couldn't remember ever having gone to a party where she'd actually had a good time. Here, in a strange city, where she knew no one—almost no one—it might be different. "Oh, Mother, please? May we go?"

Letha considered the matter. Fortune was getting past marriageable age. This might be a good opportunity for her. "Well, I suppose. I'll ask your father to make the necessary arrangements."

Fortune almost leapt up and hugged her mother. Surely Beau would attend. This would be a wonderful opportunity for him to see her at her best. "What shall I wear?"

For the next few minutes, the ladies discussed what they could wear. Even though she had no money for a ball gown, Fortune decided to go out early the next morning, as soon as the shops were open, and look at ready-made gowns. Maybe she could find some way to make one of hers look acceptable. She mentioned her idea. "Will you go with me, Jem? And, you, too, Mother," she added quickly.

Jemima looked worried for a few seconds. "Of course I will. Letha, will you join us?"

Looking relieved, Letha shook her head. "No, I don't think so. The heat is oppressive. I never knew that any place could be worse than Charleston. I declare, it simply saps the life right out of me. All I want to do is lie down and be still."

"But, Mother," Fortune protested, "I know we can't afford a new gown for me, but I'd like to find some new laces or ribbons and..."

"Well, you and Jemima can go without me. Take Nola Bell if you like, although I doubt seriously if she'll want to take to the streets during the hottest part of the day." Letha rose; it was a signal that supper was over. "Come along, Fortune. Your father won't want us down here alone so very late."

The three ladies retired to their rooms. Fortune pirouetted around her room like a ballerina until she collapsed into a chair. Then she opened the armoire to see which of her dresses could possibly be made presentable enough for a grand ball.

Fortune could hardly sleep that night. She paced back and forth, taking first one dress and then another from the armoire. She held each of them in front of her, considering the color and cut critically as she tried to decide what to wear. When she hung the last dress back up, the hotel had taken on a deep silence as had the streets below.

Walking to her window to peer out at the fascinating city, Fortune wondered where Beau was. What did a man do in New Orleans, a man who was unmarried?

She knew she should dress for bed, but she simply couldn't settle down. The prospect of a ball was just too exciting to put out of her mind.

Fortune leaned against the windowsill of her third-story room and looked out. Lights dotted the streets here and there, twinkling as the wind blew past them. The silence was pervasive, as if the whole town had gone to sleep.

New Orleans was a city of seasons, she knew. During the heat of summer, few visitors came this far south. But in wintertime New Orleans swelled with visitors from all parts of the country. Still, it seemed to be *too* quiet....

Beau laid his straight on the table, despite the drunken threats of one of the "gentlemen" Patrick had mentioned. When Beau had first entered the stylish gambling saloon, he'd been met by the portly man who owned the establishment. Right away he'd recognized that the place was decent, an honest man's club.

However, he'd learned quickly enough that some of the guests were less than honest. Two of the "gentlemen,"

Thomas Humphrey and Abe Williams, were visitors to the club, as he and Patrick were. All evening long, Thomas and Abe had swilled down brandy and ale as if they were thirsting to death. At first, Beau hadn't cared. Though he never consumed spirits while he gambled, he didn't begrudge others their pleasure.

And then he had realized that neither man had much skill. Both were boisterous and boastful. After it had become apparent that the two were bad losers, Beau had tried to leave. Abe had threatened to shoot him on the spot if he rose from his seat.

Patrick had shrugged, trying to appear nonchalant. Beau had sat down again. As the evening had progressed, the two braggarts had become more and more intoxicated. For a while Beau thought that they might lose consciousness from the spirits. He was wrong.

The more the men lost, the more surly they became. Though Beau carried a gun in his boot, he didn't want to use it. Gambling was frowned upon, but nonetheless overlooked, in New Orleans—unless something illegal happened, like murder. And Beau had been in enough scrapes with the New Orleans authorities. Even if he was defending himself, Beau didn't want to hurt anyone. He had had to kill before, and, though it had been in self-defense, it still haunted him. He had agonized over it for many months, and he still regretted what had happened.

Not even Abe could goad him into another incident like that. Beau sat there, eyes boring into the man directly across from him.

The man was easily read. Beau knew that Abe had lost again, and he knew the man would likely bluster and argue, but he hoped that was all that would come of it.

"Ye just had to do it, didn't ye, friend?" Abe wobbled to his feet and stood there swaying, his finger pointing accusingly at Beau.

Beau tried to look relaxed, but his nerves were singing with tension. "What's that, friend?"

"Don't think I ain't been a-noticin' all them cards. You've the luck of the Irish, and you ain't even Irish." Abe swayed so far to one side that he almost toppled over, but he caught himself at the last second.

The man's words were so slurred that Beau could hardly understand him. Thomas Humphrey's eyes were opening and closing, as if he were falling asleep. Beau couldn't say anything to Patrick, but he hoped his friend was alert enough to know that something had to be done immediately. Abe was a dangerous man. "Say, friend, I suggest that we quit for the evening. I've an early appointment and—"

"You'll not be a-leavin' this table with all my money." As Abe swayed backwards, his chair toppled over. "I'll not be havin' me money goin' home with a cheatin' bastard such as yerself."

Beau was careful not to make any sudden moves. The man was so intoxicated that he probably couldn't shoot straight, but Beau didn't want to chance it. He had to find a way to outsmart him until he could sober up. "Look, Abe, I haven't cheated you. Nobody has. Now, if you don't mind, I'll—"

"Ah, but I do mind." Abe pulled his coat back, revealing the butt of a gun protruding from the waist of his trousers. "Now, if you'll be steppin' back from the money, I'll just be leavin' with what I came with...and what you came with, too. Ought to teach ye a lesson."

During the evening, Beau had left all the money he'd won on the table. It was the gentlemanly thing to do. The bills were neatly stacked in front of him, as were Patrick's bills. Abe's stack had dwindled until there was nearly nothing left. Beau glanced at Patrick and then at Patrick's stack, hoping that his friend would get the message. Beau stood slowly, and Patrick did the same.

Patrick shook his head sadly. "I'm sorry, Abe, but my friend's a damnably good player, and he's honest."

"And you think I'll be a-trustin' you to give a character reference to this thief?" Abe asked, wavering unsteadily. "Do I look like I come in from the fields this mornin'?"

A crowd had gathered some short distance away. Beau was concerned that one of them might be injured should there be gunfire, but he wasn't about to stand there and let this drunken lout kill him. After a moment, he decided that he had no chance of talking Abe out of this course of action. He considered his options.

Beau reached for his money, as if to slide it across the table to Abe. "If you insist," he said, never taking his eyes off the irrational man.

Patrick did the same. For once, Patrick seemed to understand what Beau was doing. When both men had their hands on their money, Beau brought his knee straight up as hard as he could, toppling the heavy table over, right into Abe's body.

Beau grabbed his money, and Patrick his. Assorted cards and cash, along with glasses and bottles, crashed to the floor. "Come on, Patrick!" he shouted. The two men strode to the door.

The owner of the establishment came toward them shaking his head. "Sorry, gentlemen. They's not regular patrons. Never will be."

Beau handed him a few dollars to compensate for any damage. "Thank you for your hospitality, but I think we'll be leaving."

As soon as they were in the street, Beau said, "I know Abe'll follow us. You go that way, and I'll go the other."

Beau didn't have to look back to know that the running footsteps he heard behind him belonged to Abe. The man was having trouble keeping his balance, but he didn't fall too far behind. "Once I get to the hotel, I'll be safe," Beau muttered, wondering how he'd let Patrick talk him into this.

Beau was a man who liked to maintain control of a situation. This time, unfortunately, that control had been wrested from his hands by a bottle of spirits. He vowed to anticipate such difficulties in the future.

He hurried down Toulouse Street, hoping to lose his attacker. He was in such a rush, looking over his shoulder, that he forgot to turn onto St. Louis Street. Abe didn't know where Beau was staying, so the man wouldn't come back looking for him at the St. Louis Hotel unless he saw Beau go in there. He decided to go around the hotel, perhaps hiding in the shadows of one of the doorways, so he turned up Chartres. Abe wasn't too far behind, but Beau was beginning to feel safer now that he'd almost reached his hotel.

"Yer a lily-livered cheat!" Abe screamed from behind him. "Come on, Thomas! He's gettin' away, blast his soul to the devil!"

The epithets continued to ring out all along the street. Beau wondered if he'd be arrested for disturbing the peace, but didn't waste time thinking about it. He just wanted to get away from the screaming, foulmouthed drunk, who was already intent on murder.

Fortune heard shouts from below. She saw a man, a man who looked a great deal like Beau, slide into a darkened doorway on Chartres Street. He must be in some sort of trouble, she thought. A second man, followed quickly by a third, ran along behind. He was the one who was shouting.

"He got away." The man stopped and glanced around, tottering back and forth, apparently trying to decide what to do. "Bastard got away. We'll find ye yet, ye bloody cheat." Another string of epithets followed as the two men looked here and there.

Now that he was close enough for her to understand what he was saying, she blushed. She had never thought to hear such foul language in a public place. Thinking that she could possibly help—if the man below was indeed Beau— she headed for the door. She tiptoed through the parlor that separated her room from her parents', then hesitated. Soft snores were coming from the room, even though the door was closed. She turned the doorknob as quietly as she could and went out into the hallway. Praying that nobody would see her in the dimly lit corridor, she started toward the stairs.

Beau almost knocked her off her feet as he rounded the corner. "Fortune! What in blazes are you— Never mind." He grabbed her hand and pulled her along with him. Working quickly, he removed his dark blue coat and laid it on a chair in the corridor. Abe might recognize it. Then he sat down and yanked Fortune into his lap, positioned her so that he could see past her. "Shh," he warned. "Don't say a word."

Beau couldn't afford another encounter with the New Orleans police. Nor could Patrick. Beau refused to do something foolish that would end up getting both of them in trouble again, just when they were leaving this part of the country for good. He hoped Fortune would cover him well enough for the two drunks to pass by without noticing him.

Fortune felt the color intensify in her cheeks. She'd never been so intimate with a man before. All sorts of sensations shot through her body as the contact made her realize how very little she knew about men.

"I know he's up here somewheres. That bastard'll be all the sorrier when I gets me hands on him." The curses came from the staircase. "Fool thinks 'e can 'ide from ol' Abe. Where'd the bastard go?"

She looked at Beau, wondering what he'd done to make the man so angry, but she didn't ask. Somehow she knew that, whatever had happened, Beau was innocent. Fortune smiled, and Beau winked.

He pulled her closer into his arms, cradling her, and brought his mouth closer to hers. When their lips met, he felt a surge go through him, as if something within had caught fire and now was burning out of control. He almost forgot about Abe. Concentrating on kissing Fortune wasn't difficult. Beau knew at once that she hadn't been kissed often, but she seemed a quick study.

Fortune held her breath. It hadn't been like this that night at the Simpsons' party. Dennis Forrest had been brutal. He'd grabbed her chin and forced her to accept his clumsy kisses. Beau's kiss was anything but clumsy, and there was no force involved with his caresses.

She shouldn't let him kiss her. Women who were free with their charms were scorned. But Fortune didn't care at the moment. Her whole body seemed to crave his touch.

More yelling came from the staircase. Then: "Quiet, Abe, you jackass. You'll have everyone out of their rooms and madder'n a cock at a cockfight."

The voices quieted, but she could still hear footsteps on the stair. Fortune offered a silent prayer that the men wouldn't recognize Beau. She felt awkward, kissing a man who was almost a stranger and praying at the same time, but she did it.

Realizing that the men would get a better view of Beau as they walked past, she sat a little straighter and slid her arms around his neck. As they got closer, she twisted her head until she completely blocked their line of sight. Fortune couldn't breathe for fear of them noticing Beau.

"Damn folks oughta git a room. Ain't decent," one of the men said.

"Looks like we lost 'im, Abe. Let's be a-goin' and leavin' these two alone. Good luck, friend. She's a fair lass, what I can see of 'er."

Fortune was happy they couldn't see her face, which must have been scarlet. Their words disturbed her, as she wondered if their rowdiness had awakened her parents.

"I'm sure they'll not be welcomin' you botherin' 'em, either. That bloke's like to shoot ye where ye stand for interferin' with 'is lovin'."

"Kiss 'er once for me," Abe said as he walked back toward the stair. "I coulda swore that bloke come in 'ere."

"How would ye know? We's probably been chasin' the wrong bloke. He's a swell from round 'ere, ducked into 'is place when we wasn't lookin'. I swear, the spirits has yer mind fuddled."

The two men continued to argue as they trudged down the stairs. Beau and Fortune sat still, locked in an embrace, for several seconds after the sounds died down.

Fortune looked into Beau's eyes. They were twinkling with the reflection of the light of the candles behind her. Suddenly feeling embarrassed, she tried to stand.

"Wait," he whispered, and kissed her once again, much more gently.

She could hardly breathe. Her lungs still burned from holding her breath. When his mouth moved away from hers, Fortune sat there for a few seconds before standing. "I don't suppose you'd like to tell me . . ."

"Not tonight, my sweet." Beau jumped up. "Now get into your room. They might come back. We'll talk later. Go on."

Reluctantly Fortune slipped back inside the parlor. She thought of waiting to see where Beau went, but then she realized that he wouldn't go anywhere until her door closed. She hurried back to her room on tiptoe.

If Fortune had been excited before, her heart was racing now. Sleep seemed impossible. Once again she whirled around the room, hugging herself. Every part of her body sang with an energy and vivacity that she'd never known before. When she'd first thought that this trip was going to be exciting, she'd been doing little more than hoping. Now her expectations had been realized. This was the most exciting thing that had ever happened to her.

Fortune slept late the next morning. When she got up, her eyes were puffy from lack of sleep, but she dressed as quickly as possible. She could sleep this afternoon after she and Jemima went shopping.

Without waiting for Jemima, Fortune bustled out the door and down the hall to the Allens' suite. Just as she lifted her hand to knock, Jemima opened the door.

"Oh, Fortune, I was just coming to get you." Jemima closed the door behind her. "Are you ready to go? You look a bit tired."

"I'm fine, Jem," she whispered, hardly able to trust her voice. As they passed each door, she fought the urge to knock. Beau might be behind one of those doors. But which one?

When they reached the street, Jemima mentioned a shop where she'd seen some laces and ribbons the day before. The two women hurried along Royal Street until they reached the shop.

Fortune could hardly keep her mind on what she was doing. Her gaze kept drifting to the glass window at the front of the store, just in case Beau happened by. She found a length of lace, a few artificial flowers, some ribbons and a pair of fingerless lace mittens. "Oh, look at this lace fan!" she exclaimed, and then glanced around to see if anyone had noticed her outburst. "These things ought to do nicely," she said, placing her selections on the counter. "Have you found something, Jem?"

"Well, I've almost decided on this Chantilly lace shawl. Do you like it?" Jem asked, draping it across her shoulders and turning for Fortune to see. The beautiful garment hung almost to the floor in a graceful swath of delicate lace.

"It's lovely. The creamy color is perfect with your hair." Fortune found one just like it and draped it across her shoulders. She decided she liked it, too. She picked another for her mother.

"Oh, do you think so? Having auburn hair has been a curse. I simply can't wear some of the really pretty colors."

"If you have a dark green gown, it will be beautiful with that shawl. Perfect for your coloring," Fortune told her. "What do you think of this? I have a fairly simple rose-colored gown. I want to stitch this wide embroidered organdie onto the bodice at the neckline."

"That will be perfect for you. What about the ribbons and flowers?" Jemima asked, looking at the other items Fortune had chosen.

"I'm going to make little bows with the ribbons and sew them with the flowers along the flounce of the dress. Maybe I'll make one for my hair, too." Fortune asked the clerk to send her purchases, along with the bill, to the St. Louis Hotel.

She and Jemima left. When they reached the hotel, Fortune went to her room to prepare her gown for the evening's festivities, and Jemima went along to help.

The afternoon passed quickly while the two women worked. Nola Bell helped by pressing the organdie and the ribbons for them. Letha slept most of the time.

"Do you see this little arrangement?" Fortune asked, holding it forward for Jemima's perusal. "I've sewn the flowers to the bow I made. We'll make several and then see how they look."

Within another hour, the gown was finished. Fortune slipped it on for Jemima to see.

"Gracious, Fortune, that's beautiful." Jemima walked around, looking critically at their additions to make sure all the flowers and bows were correctly placed. "You'll be the prettiest girl there."

Fortune didn't answer. She looked in the mirror and saw herself staring back. The color was good for her. The organdie she'd stitched to the bodice added a great deal to the simple gown. She wondered if Beau would be there to see her. She crossed her fingers and said a little prayer. "I guess I'll do," she said finally.

Jemima left, and Fortune decided to take a nap. "I don't want to get tired tonight," she told Nola Bell. Since the Simpsons' party nearly a year before, when Dennis Forrest had mauled her, Fortune hadn't enjoyed a single social event. But she was really looking forward to this one.

Later, when she walked into the ballroom with her parents, she glanced around quickly.

Jem spotted them and hurried over. "Isn't this lovely, Letha?"

"Yes, it certainly is," Letha answered, staring at the elaborate ball gowns. "It looks as if you and Fortune were right to spruce up your gowns. These ladies are certainly dressed for the occasion."

Fortune didn't see Beau. She tried hard not to act like some heathen who had never been to a ball before. Even though she didn't know these people, she would like to appear sophisticated anyway. She watched the dancers whirling past. "Oh, my, how beautiful and graceful they all are."

Giles tucked his finger in his collar and looked around. "Where's Selwin?"

"He's gone after some punch," Jem answered with a smile.

"I think I'll go, too." Giles nodded to the ladies and walked toward a long table laden with silver bowls.

Fortune really wanted to see Beau. Questions had plagued her all day, even though she'd decided that she might not ask them. The answers might prove embarrassing to them both.

She spotted Mrs. Sloan and Amelia. Smiling, she lifted her new fan in a greeting. Mrs. Sloan caught Amelia by the arm and nearly dragged her over.

"Well, Miss Anthony, how nice to see you again," Mrs. Sloan said, her appraising gaze taking in all three ladies.

"It's lovely to see you again, Mrs. Sloan," Fortune answered, forcing a smile. "Oh, forgive me. Mrs. Sloan, this is my mother, Letha Anthony. Mother, this is Mrs. Sloan, and dear Amelia that I mentioned to you."

Letha smiled brightly. "How very nice to meet you. I understand from my daughter that you were very kind on board ship. She mentioned that she embroidered with you and pretty Amelia one afternoon."

"Why, yes," Mrs. Sloan said. "I'm Hazel Sloan, of the Georgetown Sloans."

Fortune cringed. She knew her mother would be impressed. Jemima caught Fortune's eye and smiled sweetly. Fortune knew that the smile merely masked the fact that Jemima wanted to laugh. Both of them had heard the phrase "of the Georgetown Sloans" more times than they wanted to remember.

"My, but you look lovely this evening, Amelia," Fortune said, feeling sorry for the girl, who had such vital coloring but such a lackluster spirit. "Have you been enjoying your stay in New Orleans?"

"Thank you ever so much, Fortune." Amelia smiled shyly. "I haven't had much of a chance to see New Orleans. Mother says the streets aren't safe for the two of us to be out, and Father can't spare the time to accompany us."

Fortune almost groaned aloud. "I'm so sorry to hear that. This is a beautiful city."

Amelia's eyes widened. "Have you been out?"

"Yes, Jem and I—Jemima and I went out yesterday, and again today." Fortune didn't want to sound as if she was bragging, but she wanted Amelia to know that some women had enough gumption to venture forth from the hotel.

"You know, Mrs. Anthony, the sea trip was rather nice. We met the nicest young men." Hazel Sloan was practically oozing honey, she sounded so sweet. "One young man in particular, a Mr. Gregory. Exceedingly well-mannered and handsome."

"How very nice," Letha replied, hoping that Hazel would find other interests soon. Letha didn't really like the woman, even though she was connected with the Sloans of Georgetown. "I'm so sorry I wasn't more sociable."

Amelia smiled wistfully. "Did you have fun?"

Fortune was sorry she'd said anything. It was clear that she'd unintentionally made Amelia feel bad. "We—"

Beau's voice interrupted the conversation. "Ah, there you are, Miss Anthony. Good evening, Mrs. Allen." He looked at the other ladies. "Mrs. Sloan, Miss Sloan." Finally he glanced at the other woman. "You must be Mrs. Anthony."

Fortune thought her face must be burning with a crimson glow. She felt as if she were on fire. All those disturbing thoughts that had kept her up the night before flooded over her once again, and she peeked up at Beau to see if he showed any remarkable change. She knew that she was much changed.

He seemed not to be. Fortune tried to demonstrate an interest in the conversation, but she couldn't say a word.

Jemima stepped into the breach. "Oh, where are my manners?" she asked, smiling happily. "Mrs. Anthony, I'd like for you to meet Mr. Gregory, who is a passenger on our ship."

Letha looked at him pensively. She recognized him as the man on the boat who'd stopped Fortune. He appeared to be respectable enough. And apparently Hazel Sloan thought he was respectable. "Good evening, Mr. Gregory. How nice to meet you at last."

"Likewise, Mrs. Anthony. I do hope you've recovered from your recent illness." Beau tried very hard to mind his manners. He didn't like playing the gentleman for these ladies, but he felt he owed Fortune an explanation, and this was the only way he'd get to make it.

"Thank you for your concern, Mr. Gregory. I'm doing much better," Letha answered.

She didn't know exactly what to do. Jemima Allen was a perfectly scrupulous young matron, and she'd made the introduction. Still, Letha wasn't satisfied that he was really the gentleman he seemed to be. He had a look about him that made her uncomfortable. A familiar, debonair sort of appearance that touched a memory long hidden.

Beaumont Gregory looked like a gambler to Letha. But the St. Louis Hotel was well respected, as were its occupants. She couldn't cause a scene simply because a man *looked* like a gambler.

"Miss Anthony," Beau said, turning to face Fortune. "May I have this dance?"

Chapter Five

Fortune felt the breath rush out of her. Mrs. Sloan had just intimated that Beau was interested in poor Amelia. What had given the woman that idea? Was he? Had he asked Fortune to dance simply to make Amelia jealous?

No, she decided. Beau wasn't that kind of man. If he was interested in a woman, he'd go directly after her without a ruse of any sort.

Fortune's heart quavered as he took her into his arms and they whirled off to join the group already dancing. She smiled at him shyly, wondering if he, too, felt the same kind of little tremors that chased through her body. She was happy that he'd asked her to dance. She knew that he wasn't looking for a wife, so there seemed an excellent possibility of their becoming friends. After all, he apparently trusted her with his life.

Whatever had happened last night, no matter how awful, the outcome had hinged on her response to him, and she hadn't let him down. She instinctively understood that he needed some sort of barrier between him and the two men, and she'd been it. That she was nearby was of importance, of course, but her willingness to participate in his little charade had boosted her in his eyes, she felt sure.

Still, no matter how hard she'd tried, she couldn't put his kisses out of her mind, even though she knew he hadn't been really kissing *her*. He'd been protecting himself from something. But she didn't care. Her lips had burned for hours, as if they'd been branded by a delicious flame meant only for her. Looking up into his emerald eyes, she wondered if he'd kiss her again. She wondered if the kiss had affected him as it had her. What delightful torment, she thought wryly. Neither of us wants to get married, but we both were caught up in the effect of that splendid kiss.

Beau gazed down at Fortune. Her face was almost angelic, her golden hair framing a beautifully uncomplicated face. There was no hint of deception there. *Honest* was the word he'd use if he was asked to describe her. Fresh and honest. Her skin was sun-kissed, with a soft, rosy glow, and a light scattering of almost invisible freckles graced her upturned nose. Her eyes were dreamy, as if she'd been raised in a garden and knew nothing of the cruelties the world visited upon the unsuspecting.

Neither of them said anything for several moments, and Beau began to wonder if she remembered the kiss at all. She'd been fully clothed, but then again, she might have fallen asleep in her dress and been awakened by the uproar. He'd sensed the passion in her, dormant but alive. Fortune Anthony was an intriguing young woman, and he wanted to know her better.

Finally he shored up his faltering courage and smiled at her. "No questions?" he asked, hoping she'd broach the subject of last night's adventure.

Fortune didn't know what to say. She didn't want him to think that every time he asked her to do something she was going to plague him with questions, but she *was* curious. "I...I think I won't ask any questions. It's not that I'm disinterested. On the contrary, there are many things I want to know. I simply don't know what to ask. I think that... I'm sure you'll tell me what you want me to know."

Beau was so stunned that he faltered and almost sent them tumbling to the floor. "That's an interesting approach."

After a few seconds, Fortune gazed up into his eyes. "Friends trust each other... Beau."

A smile broke across Beau's face. Such a simple thing, and yet it makes me feel so good, he thought, grinning foolishly down at her. "Well, Fortune," he began, but then the dance ended. He glanced around, hoping to spot an alcove where they could be alone. He would have given almost anything to have been in Charleston, where a gentleman could escort a lady into one of those lovely gardens, but alas, none were convenient. In addition, he feared that Mrs. Anthony didn't trust him overmuch, and would likely thwart any attempt of his to leave the ballroom with Fortune.

A gentleman Fortune didn't know came up and asked her to dance. She smiled at Beau. "Perhaps we'll have time to talk later."

For a woman who was a stranger in the city of New Orleans, Fortune thought, she was doing very well. She danced almost every dance. Some of her partners were interesting, some were boring, and she couldn't concentrate on any of them, because she kept wanting to dance again with Beau—even though she knew that her mother would disapprove heartily. As the evening progressed, her mother was beginning to look as if she was wearying of the dance.

Beau caught her as she was leaving the dance floor. "Miss Anthony, I realize that we've already danced this evening and that many are clamoring for an opportunity to partner with you, but would you honor me with another dance?"

"Why, Mr. Gregory," Fortune said coyly, fluttering her fan as she peered over it seductively, "I'm just not sure that doing so would be fair to my throng of admirers."

"Please, Miss Anthony," he begged, catching the humor in her voice. "Don't ask me to debase myself further. I am totally enthralled by your presence and couldn't stand for the evening to end without the benefit of dancing once more with you."

"Well, since you ask so sweetly, I'll relent just this once," Fortune teased, trembling with mirth. She lifted her hands as Beau held out his arms to her. "I just love a waltz, don't you?"

"Methinks thou art teasing," he quipped, and whirled her expertly around the floor. "I also believe," he said, in a more serious tone, "that you're the best dancer here."

"Ah, methinks it is thou who art teasing." Fortune felt flattered nonetheless. She did dance well. Even her dancing master had commented on her unusual abilities. But it was much nicer to hear it from a handsome gentleman, she concluded.

Beau enjoyed dancing with Fortune. She was light on her feet, easy to lead and exquisitely skillful. Not only had she mastered the steps, but she was graceful, as well. He admitted to himself, quite reluctantly, that he loved having his arms around her. Her response to his kisses had sparked a tiny flame that seemed to grow every time he thought of her, and he'd thought of little else since he'd kissed her.

What a perfect evening, Fortune thought, closing her eyes and allowing Beau to guide her past other, less skillful dancers. Occasionally she noticed a couple who almost stopped dancing to watch Beau and her. She liked that. A perfect evening, a dream of an evening, she thought, her mind keeping time with their steps.

"Ah, Miss...Fortune," he began, recalling the warm feeling he'd gotten when she'd called him "Beau." He hoped she felt those warm little tingles when he called her name, as well. "We were about to discuss—"

"That's the bastard now!" The deep masculine bellow brought the music and the dancing to an abrupt halt.

Alarmed by the shout, Fortune glanced around, scanning the crowd. At first she saw nothing out of the ordinary. Then she saw them coming across the dance floor, the dancers parting before them as if the two men were plague-ridden. Judging from their unkempt appearance, the men had done nothing but sit behind a glass of spirits since she saw them last. Their clothing, once fine raiment, was wrinkled and tattered, as if they'd been in a brawl of some sort. They were the same men who'd followed Beau last night.

"I knew ye'd be here, ye cheatin' bastard!" one of them fairly screamed.

Beau, stunned at first, pushed Fortune behind him as the men came closer. Patrick suddenly appeared at his friend's side, as if out of nowhere. Standing rigidly, Beau watched the two men swagger across the dance floor until they were close enough to hear him as he spoke in a normal tone. "I believe you gentlemen are mistaken."

"There be no mistake," Abe said, fishing a gun from beneath his coat. "And there'll be no escapin' this time."

Patrick, his gaze never leaving Abe, stepped forward. "Abe, you're wrong. You know you're wrong. If you'll come with me, I'll—"

Abe glared at Patrick and said, "Ye know 'e's a cheat. I don't know where the man hides 'is cards, but 'e do."

Giles Anthony edged closer to the two men. He didn't know what they were doing, but he knew his daughter was in danger. The second man looked harmless enough—in fact, he seemed chagrined by his friend's behavior, but the man wielding the gun was definitely dangerous.

"Gentlemen . . . Abe, is it?" Giles stepped closer to the men. "May I escort you to the bar for a drink? Perhaps, if you tell your problem to me, I can—"

"Don't be interferin', mister." Abe turned his gun toward Giles. "If you be stupid enough to—"

"Stop!" Fortune screamed, darting out from behind Beau. "Leave my father alone. Have you no sense of decency? You've had your head tucked in a bottle of spirits for so long that you wouldn't recognize the very devil if he were standing before you. Now leave this room at once before I summon the police."

Beau edged closer. He was afraid that if he made any sudden moves Abe would do something really dangerous. The inebriated man might even grab Fortune. Right now, he was stunned by her brashness. Beau was trying to take advantage of that moment, but he had to pace himself carefully.

Abe whirled around to see what woman was courageous enough to try to stop him. He saw the most beautiful woman he'd ever seen. An angel. The collar of her gown looked almost like an angel's wings. Her hair was pure gold, and her deep blue eyes caught his in a determined stare. "Missy, ye don't understand—"

"I understand riffraff when I see it. Now kindly leave this ballroom." Fortune lifted her chin and glared as hard as she could. She was counting on the fact that he was drunk, hoping that while she was speaking and had him distracted, someone could wrest the gun from his hand.

Beau moved closer still, but Abe spotted him and pointed the gun at him again. Beau could see that Fortune was too close to the barrel of the gun to be safe. If Abe fired, she might easily be the one injured. Beau stopped, his heart raging at the enforced inaction, but he couldn't risk endangering Fortune. He prided himself on being in control of every situation, but this was one situation in which nobody seemed to be in control. He was helpless.

"The lady's got the right of it, Abe," Thomas Humphrey said to his companion, locking his hand around Abe's arm. "We ain't got no place 'ere. We'll be beggin' yer pardon, miss. There ain't no reason to call the police. We'll not be botherin' you again. Come on, Abe."

Abe was wavering. He couldn't decide what to do. He knew he had the right man, but he couldn't very well shoot him here in this large group of people. "I'll be apologizin' for offendin' ye, miss."

Thomas, still gripping Abe's arm, led the man back through the crowd. As the two men walked, a murmur rode through the dancers and observers like a ship on a cresting wave. Giles stared, openmouthed, at his daughter, but Beau reacted immediately. He went to her and gripped her shoulders. "Fortune! Why did you do that? Those men are dangerous!"

Fortune looked up at Beau with a triumphant smile. "Men react differently to women most of the time. I could see that no matter what you or my father said, the man wouldn't listen. So I had to act."

"Mr. Gregory is quite right, Fortune," Giles agreed, sliding his arm around her waist. "That man could have shot you."

"Well, he didn't, so why are the two of you making such a fuss?" Fortune glanced from her father to Beau. It was nice that both men were so concerned. Looking past her father's shoulder, she could see her mother making her way through the crowd. Her mother would be more trouble than either Beau or her father.

Patrick reached them and said, "Beau, I told you those men were trouble."

Beau glared at Patrick. "You told me they were trouble? As I recall, you were the one who set up the game."

"Well," Patrick said, "I didn't realize they were ruffians when the club's owner mentioned that one of his members had sent word of some guests who would be there. Since were were guests, as well, I suppose—"

"Never mind the explanation. What's done is done." Beau turned to Giles Anthony. "My gratitude to you, sir, for stepping in." Then he gazed at Fortune. "And you, Miss Anthony, are a very brave but very foolhardy woman. I am eternally in your debt."

"Your gratitude is not necessary, Mr. Gregory," Giles said, with a smile and a handshake.

Letha stood beside her husband, her eyes filled with rage. "Giles! I'm astonished that you would... that you would fraternize with these gamblers. Furthermore, I'm dismayed that such a reputable establishment as the St. Louis Hotel, a place that caters to the finer elements of society, would allow such men to pass through its portals." She turned a venomous gaze on Beau. "Unhand my daughter, sir." Without further comment to either of the men, she glanced at Fortune. "Come with me, Fortune."

"But, Mother—"

"Immediately! Don't annoy me further, Fortune." Letha strode away, confident that her daughter would follow.

"Thank you for a lovely—and exciting—evening, Beau...Mr. Gregory." Wanting to say more, much more, Fortune glanced at her mother and decided that it would be prudent to follow.

Letha Anthony was furious. She flung open the door to their suite and marched in. Without speaking, she began pacing across the ornate carpet while she awaited her daughter's arrival.

When Fortune entered the room and closed the door, Letha slowed her pace in a vain attempt to curb her anger. After a moment, she sat on the edge of the sofa and looked at her daughter.

"Mother, if you're angry with me, please don't be. I simply acted as I thought best. I couldn't stand by and let that man hurt Father."

Letha stared at Fortune as if she could see straight through her. "That is not why I'm angry."

Letha leapt to her feet and started pacing again. After a few moments, she stopped. "That—man is a gambler, Fortune. You don't know what trash those men are. Why, they're worse than . . ."

"It was obvious to me immediately that he was trash, Mother. That's why I used the term 'riffraff' when I addressed him."

Fortune was puzzled by her mother's frame of mind. Letha Anthony wasn't one who got upset easily. She rarely displayed that much emotion.

"I was referring to Mr. Gregory." Letha sat down opposite her daughter and clasped Fortune's hands. "Fortune, my darling, you don't know the dangers. Gamblers aren't like other men. They won't respect you. They don't treat you with kindness and courtesy, like that nice Dennis Forrest. They . . . they're seducers of good girls like you."

It was Fortune's turn to pace. She jerked her hands away from her mother, jumped and started walking. So Beau was a gambler. She smiled when she realized that Beau had won his bet. Well, he'd already kissed her, so they were even. She'd settle that with him later.

For now, she had her irate mother to contend with. She recalled her mother's words. Was it true that gamblers didn't treat women the way Dennis Forrest did? *Well, if that's the case,* Fortune decided, *I'll take a gambler over Dennis any day.* But she couldn't say that to her mother. "Mother, you know I don't like Dennis. He's part of my past, a past I'd rather forget. Besides, I'll never see him again."

"Fortune," Letha began, dismissing her daughter's comments entirely as the frivolity of an inexperienced mind. "You don't know about Dennis. The man worships you. He'd put you on a pedestal and treat you like a princess."

Short of telling the truth about Dennis, Fortune could never convince her mother that he was worse riffraff than the two men who'd interrupted the ball. The truth about Dennis Forrest would have to remain her secret. Fortune could never humiliate herself by telling the truth to anyone. She could never tell anyone, because just thinking about it made her feel dirty, inside and out. She couldn't reveal what had happened to anyone—ever.

Besides, she was protecting her mother's feelings. Dennis had remarked quite often that Fortune, being nothing more than a poor relation, should feel honored that he cared enough to want her.

"Mother, Beau—Mr. Gregory—" At Fortune's use of Beau's given name, Letha's head rose sharply and she leapt to her feet. Fortune had never seen her mother move so quickly. She caught her breath and continued, "Mr. Gregory is a fine man. He—"

"Silence!" Letha exclaimed. "I will not be spoken to as a child by my own daughter."

"Heaven forbid, Mother. I certainly meant no disrespect, but—"

"Fortune, you will refrain from speaking to me of that, that *man*." Letha spat, her chest heaving with indignation.

"Mother, please let me explain about—"

"Hear me well, daughter." Letha's voice was chillingly quiet. "You will not speak his name. The man is trash, nothing more."

"But—"

"Furthermore," Letha continued, her rage unabated, "you will not speak *to* him again. Should you chance upon him, either here or on the ship, you will turn your head and continue on your way. This discussion is closed."

Letha spun and walked out of the room, closing her door firmly behind her. Fortune would have liked it better if her mother had slammed it, but Letha Anthony always acted like a lady.

Fortune sat down to await her father's return. She wanted to talk to him about this evening's events. Though she waited for more than an hour, he didn't come back to the suite. Finally she gave up and went to her own room.

It isn't fair, she thought, dropping into a chair in spite of her springy crinolines. Grimacing with disgust at her mother's refusal even to listen to an explanation, Fortune rose and loosed the tapes holding up her hoops. "Wretched things," she muttered, stepping out of them and leaving them where they lay on the floor.

Fortune strode to the window and stood there looking out. Through the open window she could hear the music drifting in from the orchestra, and she got even angrier. After a little while, she settled down. Her mother couldn't tell her what to do forever. One of these days, Fortune would have to take a stand and confront her mother with the obvious. She was no longer a child whose mind and will were to be discounted without so much as a thought.

When did that transition occur for a young woman and her mother? Would she have to take the initiative? Would Letha finally realize that she was a woman in her own right, and therefore capable of making her own decisions? Fortune doubted it. She didn't know what or why or how or when, but Fortune knew that very soon she and her mother would have to come to some understanding.

For now, Fortune would continue to submit to her mother's rule—in most cases. She would not, could not, spurn Beau, any more than she could fly like a bird. She was not the kind of woman who offered her friendship and then withdrew it for no good reason.

Beau paced the floor. "Patrick, we've got to do something about that fool before he does something else. The man's liable to kill me, or someone else in the attempt."

"What can we do?" Patrick asked gravely. "The man simply won't listen to logic."

After a moment, Beau smiled. "There must be some way to divert his attention from us until we leave."

"I've had my troubles with the police, but I do know one good fellow in the department. Maybe we can convince him of this man's unsavory character," Patrick suggested. "With the added testimony of the owner of the club, we could press charges."

"No, nothing formal. I don't want to do anything radical. I simply want him to leave me alone." Beau stopped walking and turned to his friend. "Let's go see what we can do."

Patrick found his friend from the police department rather quickly. With an occasional word of confirmation from Beau, Patrick explained the situation. "So, as you can see, this man has become a nuisance."

"I'm surprised that we didn't receive a complaint from the hotel. They don't like such men going there." The officer shook his head. "I'll spread the word. Abe Williams, you say? We'll question the club owner about these two men and make a show of following them for a few days. If they feel that we're about to arrest them, then perhaps they'll leave town."

"Sounds reasonable. Thank you," Beau said as he and Patrick left. "Likable man."

"Yes. We met at a brawl one evening. I believe you were out of town." Patrick clapped his friend on the back. "I tell you, it was one hell of a brawl—fairly friendly. Most fun I've had in a long time."

Beau studied his friend carefully for a few seconds. "I think I'm tiring of the brawls—friendly or otherwise."

"You're getting soft in your old age," Patrick quipped.

"I'm no older than you." Beau scowled at Patrick. "As I recall, we both turned thirty in the same month."

The next few days passed so slowly that Fortune thought she would go out of her mind. Her mother refused to allow her any freedom at all. Fortune couldn't leave the hotel suite at any time without her mother, and Letha didn't leave until it was nearly time to board the ship.

Without having once caught sight of Beau again, Fortune rode in silence to the levee, where the Anthony entourage boarded the ship for Panama City. Fortune looked forward to the days on board, and she felt guilty when she realized that she was hoping her mother would be seasick again. If Letha was ill, then Fortune's whereabouts wouldn't be questioned too closely.

As the ship sailed out of New Orleans and down the Mississippi River, churning up muddy ripples, Fortune took a last look at the city that had been like a prison to her for a week. The first few days had been so gay and carefree, so exciting, but then had come her infuriating enforced solitude. Her expectations of New Orleans and all its grandeur had been dashed for Fortune by the closed mind of one woman—her mother.

The trip from New Orleans to Chagres, on the coast of the Isthmus of Panama, would take nine or ten days. Fortune loved the sea. The water of the Atlantic was a sparkling emerald green, but as they sailed south the water had turned into a crystalline blue that glimmered with brilliant highlights. Frequently, as she gazed down into the water, Fortune could see fish swimming and playing beneath the ship. At times, as the prow broke through the swells, she saw schools of small fish that seemed to fly. The darkly iridescent fish would break the surface of the water, skim along it for a few yards and then disappear into the next wave. Occasionally a school of dolphins would play alongside the ship, leaping out of the water and then diving in again. They looked so friendly that many times she wished she could join in their play.

As she might have guessed, her mother took immediately to her bed. She warned Fortune about Beau and then collapsed in a quivering heap upon the bed. Feeling sorry for her mother, Fortune resolved to stay with her more on this leg of the journey, but the fresh air and sea beckoned, and she broke her resolve almost immediately.

She'd glimpsed Beau as he'd boarded with his friend, Patrick Meade, but she hadn't spoken to him. He'd smiled and waved, but continued with his business. Fortune expected to see him later, maybe after supper, when she planned to take her evening stroll on the deck.

As usual, Nola Bell sat with Letha Anthony while her family went to have supper. The small group in the dining room—a number of the passengers had been affected by seasickness—were a cheerful lot. Fortune decided that the gaiety was because this was the beginning of the second leg of their journey.

She could hardly eat her supper after Beau joined the group. After smiling a greeting, she tried to appear interested in the general conversation, but, she felt, with little success. Her gaze was drawn to Beau. She knew that he wanted to talk with her. His smile implored her to be patient with him and told her that all would be made clear. At least, that was what Fortune read in his captivating smile.

Beau was happy to see Fortune. After Letha's public censure, he knew that any chance to talk with Fortune alone while in port was gone. He recognized the feisty mother hen protecting her chick—no matter that the chick was of marriageable age and was now friends with the threatening rooster. He couldn't contain a chuckle as he pictured the situation. Hens and chicks and roosters. His brain must be getting mushy.

Patrick entered the room and grinned at Fortune. He greeted her cordially and sat beside Beau. Mrs. Sloan turned away from both gentlemen, and Beau was delighted. Poor Amelia, he thought, glancing at the girl. She'll never get out from beneath her mother's wing. He studied the two women for a moment and realized that Amelia's husband would never escape that dreaded mother's wing, either.

Was Fortune any different? he wondered. She'd toddled after her mother the other evening at the ball, but he nonetheless sensed an independent spirit within Fortune that was absent in Amelia. A smart man, he decided, might choose Amelia. The young girl would be much more easily dominated than Fortune. In spite of her soft coloring, a glow, almost golden, permeated the air around her, Fortune Anthony would be a force with which a husband would have to contend every day of his life. No docile wife there. A shrew, perhaps, if she was angered.

Well, it mattered little to Beau either way. He didn't intend to be caught in either woman's snare. After his experiences with the fairer sex, Beau had vowed never to marry.

In fact, he might have been better off if he'd chosen another route to California. He could have gone to Missouri and taken the overland trail, but he'd read reports of treacherous high mountain treks, of Indian attacks. However, if he'd gone another way, he wouldn't have met either of these women. Amelia held no attraction for him, of course, but Fortune did. There was something about her that drew him, something indefinable...something intriguing....

When Fortune excused herself, she glanced at Beau to indicate that she wanted him to meet her later. He'd promised her an explanation about the peculiar circumstances that had been the cause of her imprisonment. As she left the dining room, she grinned. What would be her mother's reaction if she knew that Fortune had sat on Beau's lap, allowed him to kiss her and then kissed him back? Apoplexy. Complete and total hysteria, she decided. After all, that was Letha's reaction to a great deal that happened.

Fortune would never be like her fragile, dependent mother. Her life would be filled with fun and adventure. If San Francisco was a small town, with little in the way of social events, then Fortune would generate them. And she would encourage a freer, more relaxed set of rules for society that would reflect the tenor of the exciting new land.

She could hardly wait. But she'd have to.

Beau sat in the dining cabin and listened to the prattle of the ladies for a few minutes. He'd wanted to follow Fortune immediately, but he hadn't wanted the other women to remark on the peculiarity of his sudden departure when he hadn't finished eating.

None of the women beguiled him in the slightest. Only Fortune. And that was because she was different in so many ways. He knew that she had been brought up to live the same helpless, vapid life as the others, but somehow she'd risen above that teaching and become an interesting young woman. A woman who could keep a secret. *There are few of those around,* he thought as he listened to one of the ladies telling Jemima some embarrassing private information about one of her good friends.

If Letha Anthony had known that he'd kissed Fortune in the hallway, he'd have been censured soundly at the ball when he'd asked the young woman to dance. Letha wasn't one of those mothers who would condone improper advances, though he doubted that Fortune would ever relate any such details to her mother. No, Fortune could keep a secret.

When a decent interval had passed, Beau made his excuses to the ladies still present and went up on deck. He

hoped, a little guiltily, that Letha was still suffering from
seasickness. She hadn't been at the supper table, and if she
was feeling the way she had during the crossing from
Charleston to New Orleans, he'd have plenty of time to talk
privately with Fortune and renew their acquaintance.

He realized that Letha had guarded her poor daughter
like a dragon lady after the dance. For some reason, Letha
hadn't seemed as upset that her daughter was in danger as
she was about the fact that he was a gambler. He shook his
head derisively. Women. Who could understand them?

Beau reached the deck and glanced around. He didn't see
Fortune anywhere. Knowing that she liked to stroll along,
peering over the railing of the ship, Beau waited in a darkened area. The sun had almost set, sending long shadows
across the deck, shadows that were perfect for him to hide
in, perfect for him to wait for her. If anyone else came
along, the likelihood of his being seen was remote.

He could hardly wait to talk to Fortune. There was, after all, the matter of the wager to discuss. He knew that she
knew that she'd lost. The knowledge brought a smile to his
lips. Be patient, my boy, he chided himself, peering along
the deck, first in one direction, then in the other.

His decision to stand in the shadows and wait for her was
quickly rewarded. Within a few minutes, Fortune sauntered past him without even noticing him. She stopped, no
more than a few feet away and rested her elbows on the
railing. The moon had risen, giving her hair a soft golden
glow that made him want to reach out and touch it.

Beau could wait no longer. He strode softly toward her,
his footsteps loud enough for her to hear, but not so loud
as to startle her. She turned to face him.

"Oh, hello, Mr. Gregory...Beau." She smiled, her
mouth wide with pleasure. "I'm delighted to see you."

"Not nearly so much as I," he said, joining her at the
railing.

"Isn't it lovely?" She pointed at the moon rising golden
out of the ocean. Storm clouds hovered in the distance, but
seemed to hold back, as if to give the moon its moment of
glory. Within a few minutes, it would change to silver, but
for now the radiance was the color of her favorite ball

gown. A shimmer of gold traced an ever-widening pattern across the gently undulating ocean.

Ignoring the view she was pointing at, Beau looked down at her. "More lovely than I remembered or than I could have hoped."

She glanced up at him puzzled at his remark. He was staring at her, not at the moon. Embarrassed, she turned to the moon again. "This is the most beautiful time of evening, I think. The moon rising, the stars just beginning to wink into view. Did you study astronomy, Mr....Beau?"

He gaped at her. Had she said something about astronomy? What? How could he answer without sounding foolish? "Well," he began, gathering his wits about him, the wager all but forgotten, "I've always loved the evening sky."

"I thought so. I always loved astronomy. My father has an astronomy book." She looked down at her hands for a moment, wishing she could have brought more of her books. Even though they really belonged to her father, she thought of them as her own. She'd managed to bring only a few, and her parents had objected to that because of the weight. Finally they'd agreed to allow her to take a few novels, but she'd tucked in a reading primer for her own children—should she ever have any—a Bible, an arithmetic book, the volume on astronomy and one on geography at the last minute without their knowledge. "I brought it with me."

"You like books, don't you?" Beau loved to read, but he hadn't thought of bringing books with him on this journey. He usually traveled as unencumbered as possible, and this trip was no exception.

"I love them." Fortune gazed up at him, her thoughts captured by the shadows playing across his strong face. "You have a very strong face, Beau. I like that. Do you like to read?"

Beau chuckled. "I have always loved to read. Unfortunately, I didn't remember to bring along any books." He thought about that for a few seconds. "I suppose that men think differently from women. I brought items that I felt I couldn't do without.'' He shook his head in disbelief. "I never thought about books.''

She was bright and inquisitive, and her spirit had yet to be suppressed. He hoped that Letha wouldn't manage to do that. What a shame it would be. Fortune was as fresh as the first morning glories twining along a fence rail.

"Back home, I was always reading.'' Fortune smiled as she remembered immersing herself in the adventures of fictional characters, how it had lightened her days. She wondered whether she should mention the bet, or wait for him to. Did gamblers have a particular set of manners they used? She decided to wait. "Either that or playing chess or walking.''

"You play chess?'' Beau asked, looking at her with renewed interest. He'd come across many who played the game, but he'd encountered few who were good enough to challenge him. Although she was bright, he wondered if Fortune would be a worthy opponent.

Fortune knew what he was thinking. "Yes, I play, and I play well.''

"I'm sure you do.'' Beau knew she'd read his thoughts. "We'll have to play sometime.''

"Perhaps,'' she said noncommittally.

He gazed at her for a few seconds before recalling her statement about bringing books. "Well, I'll know where to go if I need something to read,'' Beau said, leaning against the railing.

"All you have to do is ask,'' she answered and stared out across the water. Now, in the late evening, it was almost black. She sniffed the air. A spicy fragrance drifted around her, flirting with her senses, as she tried very hard not to look at Beau. Every time she saw him, she wanted to throw herself into his arms, to discover why his caresses were so different from the mauling she'd received at Dennis's hands.

Would Beau kiss her again? Had he wondered about that night, too? Had his sleep been tormented by dreams of her, as hers had been by dreams of him?

Beau listened to the rhythmic lapping of the waves against the hull of the boat. The evening breeze was picking up, catching wisps of Fortune's hair and teasing the curly tendrils around her face. He wanted to bury his hands in that mass of hair that was sure to reach past her waist. He imagined himself removing the restraining pins one by one until her hair hung in a glorious swath of curls. When she looked up at him, he felt himself drawn to her. Before he could stop himself—if indeed he could have—he was kissing her.

His arms, seemingly of their own volition, caught her around the waist and drew her closer as her hands edged higher until they were around his neck. Her lips were soft, luscious, when his touched them. Beau relished her response for a moment before gently parting her lips with his tongue. Beginning a tender exploration of her mouth, he felt her waver in his arms, as if she might faint. Beau liked the idea that he could affect a woman that way.

Catching her closer in his arms, he pressed his lips against hers, deepening the kiss and exulting in the feeling of her breasts against his chest. He wanted to lift her off her feet and whisk her to his cabin and make love to her.

But he couldn't. He wouldn't. There was no reason for him to ravish this young woman—other than that he wanted her more than he could recall ever having wanted another woman. That she was innocent he did not doubt. And he wasn't about to take her virginity.

Beaumont Gregory had no use for virgins.

Chapter Six

Beau drew away from Fortune, peering down into her face. The moon had turned to silver, a disc pregnant with promise, rising steadily as clouds gathered closer now. The breeze picked up, steadily billowing the sails. Before long, a storm would batter the ship, but it would be no worse than the one in Beau's mind.

Knowing that if he didn't do something soon, he *would* whisk Fortune away to his cabin and seduce her, Beau released his grip on her. He wouldn't—couldn't—do that. Cool air swirled between them, as if to emphasize his loss, and he almost stepped back to her.

"I...I'm afraid that I need to... Patrick's waiting for me. I told him I'd be no more than a moment," he said, struggling to conceal his true reasons for breaking off the encounter. "Allow me to escort you to your cabin."

"No," Fortune whispered, her words almost whipped from her mouth by the rising wind. "I'm not quite ready to go down. You go...you go on ahead."

Beau wanted to talk to her, but he didn't want to break the mood of the moment with words. He felt bad enough for releasing her without a truthful explanation. He didn't like it, and he sensed that she didn't, either.

Without hesitating further, he kissed her softly on the lips and walked away, the pressure in his groin giving evidence of his true feelings. He knew that this would be another long night, one among many. For ever since he'd met Fortune, she'd tormented his sleep—and at times his waking hours, as well.

* * *

Fortune didn't watch Beau leave. The beautiful September evening had suddenly turned chilly, as if it were closer to the end than to the beginning of the month. She crossed her arms and leaned against the railing. Why did he always affect her like this?

Never one to give kisses lightly, she'd allowed this man more liberties than in all her previous encounters put together. Fortune peered down into the depths. The waters swirled with the wind, and the fish sought safety far below the ship. She glanced up. Clouds shaded the moon like diaphanous curtains of black gauze tattered by the wind. Before long, thicker clouds would completely obliterate the silver moon, pitching the ship into a dark, somber world of watery mayhem.

Rain began to fall in murky sheets. Fortune, gathering her skirts into a bundle, ran toward the companionway. She ducked inside as the rain pelted the deck. She stood there a moment, watching the rain pound into the wood and bounce off again, almost like sleet. Thunder rumbled in the distance, another sign that the storm would be a bad one. Hoping the storm would blow over by morning, she trudged down the corridor to her room.

Her father had already returned from his evening discussions with some of the other men, and he looked her up and down. "Gracious, daughter, you've the appearance of a wet hen."

Fortune considered his words for a moment and then smiled. He always knew what to say to her. "I feel like one, Father. My feathers are wet and sticking to me."

"Go and change into something dry before you catch your death of cold. Your mother would go into fits if she saw you now."

"How is she, Father?" Fortune asked, feeling a little guilty for having forgotten about her mother so quickly after leaving the cabin.

"I'm thinking this storm will make matters all the worse. She's with Nola Bell, moaning and groaning like some dying cow." Giles shook his head sadly. "We knew she was frail when we started on this journey. But there seemed to be no easier way."

"Father, stop fretting. Mother will be all right once we reach land." Fortune strode over to him and patted his shoulder. "What else could we have done?"

"I'm sure we've done the right thing, and she'll thank us for it when we reach the glorious city of San Francisco."

"Tell me about it, Father. Tell me about San Francisco," Fortune said, looking for a place to sit. "What does Mr. Allen say about it?"

"I think if you were to sit down you'd wreck the furniture in that wet garment." Giles chuckled and waved her toward her room. "Go and change. We'll have plenty of time to talk later. We've nine more days aboard this ship."

Fortune realized that her father didn't really want to talk about San Francisco tonight. Something about the way he'd dismissed her warned her to give up—for tonight, anyway. She kissed him on the forehead. "Yes, Father. Good night."

"Good night, daughter."

Inside her room, Fortune turned up the lamp. Her clothes were so wet that she could hardly remove them. Nola Bell would fuss when she saw the rain spots. Tonight, however, Fortune didn't care. She simply wanted to change into dry clothes, crawl between the sheets and think about Beau.

Why had he left her so abruptly? And with such a flimsy excuse? Had she said or done something wrong?

Fortune knew little about kissing, but to her the episode had been pleasant. Well, he'd kissed her on two occasions now, so the experience couldn't have been too bad, or he wouldn't have sought her out the second time.

The sea became rougher, and the ship rocked to and fro until Fortune began to feel a little queasy. Her mother must be terribly sick with this added motion. Despite her squeamish stomach, Fortune finally fell asleep. Beau's image taunted her all night, and she awoke frequently to the howling of the wind and the crashing of the waves.

Knowing that everyone else must be asleep, she tossed and turned, trying to find a position that would release her into a slumber that would seal out the storm's rage. She found no such comfort. All night long, the ship was tossed from wave to wave, much like a ball thrown by children.

Along toward dawn, Fortune finally fell into a fitful sleep again, only to have her dreams filled with Beau's kisses, his embrace. Feeling as if she'd been dragged behind the ship all night, she fell out of bed when her father rapped on the door.

"Fortune, it's time for breakfast," he called without opening the door.

"Coming, Father," she muttered, and wondered if he heard her. "I'll be there in a moment. You go on ahead."

Fumbling, she pulled her nightgown over her head. She bathed in the tepid water that remained in the pitcher and then brushed her hair. She didn't know where Nola Bell was, so she braided her own hair, loosely, and wound it into a bun at the base of her neck. It was plain, but she couldn't do much better without help.

She found a suitable dress and drew it on. The cream-colored poplin dress fitted her well, and it showed her figure to advantage, she thought. Wasting no further time, she hurried out into the corridor and along to the dining room. Even though she could hardly stay awake, she didn't want to miss breakfast. She was hungry.

A smile broke across her face as she hurried down the corridor, and she started to hum. She'd lost the wager, there was no doubt about it. She'd gambled with a gambler and lost. But neither she nor Beau could deny the strange friendship that had developed between them. She knew they were as different as a candle flame and a lightning bolt, but she also knew they were friends—and she liked that.

She found few other passengers in the dining room. Her father was already deep in conversation with Mr. Allen. Beau and Patrick sat talking at the other end of the table. Beau glanced at her when she walked in, but Fortune averted her eyes. She didn't know exactly how to react to him this morning.

Jemima wasn't there, and neither were Mrs. Sloan and Amelia. In fact, there were no other women present. Probably seasick after last night's storm, Fortune decided as she sat down by her father.

Fortune was angry with herself for missing the sunrise. Back home, she always walked early in the morning so that she could see dawn creeping across the land. Here, the sunrise was even more spectacular, and she hated to miss a single moment of it. She ate her breakfast quietly as she listened to the conversation around her.

This morning, the men were talking about gold. Someone had heard rumors about gold being discovered near Sutter's Fort in California. Fortune listened avidly to the conversation. Sutter's Fort was near San Francisco, or so Mr. Allen said.

"I heard tell that there were gold nuggets big as hen's eggs," one man said.

"Hell, I heard they were bigger than hens!" said another.

Fortune didn't know either man. They were new to the ship, having boarded for the first time in New Orleans.

Gold. What did that really mean to her? She knew that her father wasn't the sort of man to go chasing off after gold, not when there was a good plot of land to be had for free. He was much more settled, more mature, than that. But the gleam in her father's eye denied her claim. Would he abandon their plan and go to wherever gold had been discovered?

Would Beau?

Beau listened quietly to the conversation. He'd heard about the California gold strike while he was back in New Orleans. He hadn't given it much thought, except to conclude that if gold had been discovered, then his gambling establishment would be a good place for the men to spend their finds. He had no intention of digging for gold, or however it was they were finding it. He'd wait for it to come to him.

If the reports were true, then before long, California would be overrun with men looking for gold. He decided he would build his saloon quickly and then add a hotel later. All those men were bound to need a place to stay while they spent their money in his saloon.

He glanced at Fortune. Her face was upturned, rapt with attention directed to the speakers. As always, she looked as if she were thirsting for knowledge, soaking up the conversation, storing the words to study them later.

What would she do in a town that was certain to grow quickly? Beau imagined she'd find a husband and settle down. That was what most women wanted. He discovered that he was uncomfortable with that thought. He didn't like the idea of her finding some nice young man and settling down. That idea simply didn't sit well with him.

Maybe she'd open a shop. She was smart enough. He recalled her statement about playing chess. She said she played very well. Beau studied her for a moment. Maybe she played with her father and he let her win. Regardless of who won, Beau was impressed with the fact that she played at all.

He caught himself grinning foolishly and tried to straighten his face. He must look like an idiot, sitting there grinning. Well, it couldn't be helped. He felt good, damnably good, this morning, and he didn't know exactly why. Winning the bet, he reminded himself. That's it. You're happy because you won that bet with Fortune.

He schooled his features into a more acceptable visage when he noticed Patrick looking at him with a strange expression on his face. Beau cleared his throat and tried to appear interested in the conversation. But, when he recalled the wager, he grinned again. Collecting on this one would be interesting. It just might be the most fascinating gamble he'd ever made.

He forced his thought back to the conversation. The men were discussing how the gold strike would affect the land they were to claim.

"By the gods, I won't have a bunch of buffalo-brained prospectors traipsing all over my land," Giles stated flatly. "I won't have it."

"But, Giles, you can't be everywhere at once. Maybe you can work out some sort of deal to split whatever they find on your land," Selwin Allen said with a smile. "That's what I intend to do."

Several men laughed and nodded. Fortune wondered if they thought the prospectors would be honest enough to divide the gold equitably. What was a good split? How much should the prospector take, and how much should he give the landowner?

After a few more minutes of talk, the men left the dining room, and Fortune trailed after them. She knew they wouldn't let her follow them into the cabin where they went each morning to talk, so she turned the other way and went up on deck.

The storm had left the decks washed clean. A brisk wind was blowing, causing the sails to snap and chatter in the lively breeze. The sky was a cornflower blue, and the ocean was the color of an aquamarine, a clear blue-green that glinted with silver. Such a beautiful day, she thought. A perfect day to be sailing the Caribbean Sea. A perfect day to be nearing Chagres, and the next leg of their journey.

Fortune could hardly wait. The conversation about the gold fields had excited her even more than before, though she could hardly believe the rumors. What a wonderful place California must be! Mr. Allen had told them about the fertile land and the mild climate in glowing detail. This was just one more incredible reason to go to San Francisco.

"Beautiful morning, isn't it?" Beau asked, walking up behind Fortune.

"Oh!" Fortune exclaimed, whirling around. She'd been so involved in her thoughts that she hadn't heard him coming. "I thought you were going to listen to more of the gold talk."

"What else is there to say?" He shook his head. "None of those men really know anything, so every word is pure speculation. They heard it from someone else who heard it. Besides, I heard the same stories in New Orleans."

"I suppose you're right," Fortune agreed, feeling a little foolish for getting so excited over a bit of conversation. She wondered why she hadn't heard the rumors, too. "Still, if it's true, it could mean a lot of money."

"And a lot of people," Beau added. "Think how many fools will head west when word gets around. There'll be thousands of them, all looking for one big nugget. It's probably true, though. I understand that an army lieutenant named Loesser had evidence. A cask of gold."

"Even so, it sounds like a fool's errand to me. It's difficult for me to believe such a tale," Fortune said, leaning against the railing. She rubbed the smooth wood beneath her hands and looked down at the water. The sun glinted off the waves, almost blinding her. "It's almost too bright to see this morning. The sky and the water are simply shimmering with silver and blue."

Beau looked around. He loved the morning after a rain. The air smelled cleaner and felt fresher, though the salty tang was still there. "You're right. I do like the fresh air. Would you like to take a turn around the deck?"

Fortune smiled and nodded. "I certainly would. Be careful, though. The rain has left the deck slippery in places."

Tucking her hand in the crook of his arm, Beau strolled along at a pace she could easily match. He had to concentrate on the deck ahead of him to keep from stopping and kissing her. When he'd come looking for her, he hadn't thought that the magnetic attraction would be so potent during the day. But it was.

Some animal magnetism, as he dubbed it, had manifested itself between him and Fortune. He would, somehow, have to learn to deal with it. He couldn't be forever kissing her, stammering some lame excuse and then running away like a schoolboy.

He still hadn't told Fortune why those men had been chasing him. She was bright enough to figure it all out, except for a few minor details—such as the fact of his innocence. He decided that she knew he wasn't guilty of cheating or she wouldn't be so friendly, especially after her mother had practically dragged her out of the ballroom that night. He sensed that Letha Anthony had kept her daughter closeted in their suite for the remainder of their stay. Otherwise he'd have encountered Fortune in the hotel sometime during the week.

Cursing his luck, he shook his head. Why had—what was his name? Abe?—come looking for him again? Beau had concluded that after the effects of all those bottles of spirits wore off, Abe and Thomas would be on their way without causing any more problems. So much for trying to figure out the intentions of other men, particularly drunken ones.

He glanced down at Fortune. When would be the appropriate moment to mention their wager? Not now, not during the day. He wanted to collect his prize when nobody was about. The kind of kiss he expected from her wasn't one he wanted to share with the world.

Fortune looked surreptitiously up at Beau through her lashes. What was he thinking about? He'd been quiet ever since he'd asked her to walk with him.

When was he going to bring up the bet? Fortune suspected that she should be the one, but she couldn't do it now, not when someone might see them. Should she mention it and then set a time when they could meet for her to... pay her debt? She smiled. She liked the idea of owing him a kiss, although technically she didn't owe him anything. He'd already collected.

Her fingers were on fire where his hand rested against them, and the fire was making its way up her arm. Occasionally, as they walked, her hips would touch his and send sensations cascading through her. When she thought she couldn't stand any more, she tried to think of a way of telling him. She was saved the effort. In her musings, she stumbled and nearly fell. Beau caught her and prevented her fall, but he couldn't help himself.

"Damnation!" Beau exclaimed, his feet flying out in front of him. He landed soundly on his buttocks.

"Beau! Are you injured?" she asked, kneeling beside him. She caught his hand in hers, wanting to comfort him in some small way, and she looked up and down his prostrate form. "Shall I summon help?"

Injured? Only his pride. Beau raised himself onto his elbows and laughed. He felt quite foolish. "No, I'm fine. Please don't call anyone."

"Do you think you've broken a bone?" she asked, gazing into his eyes to see if they reflected the pain she thought would accompany a broken limb. She glanced around, looking for someone to send for Nola Bell. She was good in emergencies. "Perhaps you shouldn't move."

"I'm fine. Really I am." Beau stood with as much grace as was possible under the circumstances. He dusted off the seat of his trousers but found them damp rather than dusty. "I should have listened more carefully to your warning," he said—in true gentlemanly fashion, glossing over the fact that the fall had really been her fault.

"Let's stand here by the railing, shall we?" Fortune took his arm and led him to the edge of the deck. She felt awful. She'd caused him to fall because her meandering mind had kept her from concentrating on her footing. She looked at him again, trying to ascertain if he was in any pain at all. "I'm quite concerned that you're injured and not telling me."

"Forget it. I'm fine, and nothing is broken." Beau gazed down at her, laughing. Concern was written in her eyes. For the first time, he noticed that they were the same blue as the morning sky. Her lips were pink, particularly the bottom one, where she'd gnawed it with worry.

Fortune knew that he must be embarrassed. He seemed to be standing without experiencing any pain, so she dropped the subject with a final warning. "Please be careful. This deck is dangerous after a rain."

Beau laughed again. She was so concerned, her face screwed into a visage of worry. "Forget it. I'm just a bit clumsy. Particularly when my feet are flying through the air."

This time, Fortune couldn't help laughing with him. He was so funny at times. "You did look a trifle silly."

He slid his arm around her waist. "I did it intentionally to make you laugh."

"Just as I led you there intentionally so that I'd have something funny to brighten my day," she countered. "Besides," she continued bravely, "I believe you took advantage of me."

"All right. You win. I'm just clumsy." Beau hugged her close, and instantly knew that he'd made a mistake. Touching her caused him to recall her sweet kisses, and he couldn't afford to kiss her out here, in plain view of all the deckhands. He shouldn't even have hugged her. Damnation, he shouldn't even be here talking to her. He refused to be the cause of speculation about her virtue, but what was already done couldn't be retracted. Puzzled by her last remark, he narrowed his eyes and gazed at her. "What do you mean I took advantage of you?"

Fortune shouldn't have said anything, not yet. This was the wrong time. "Well, I... Well, I mean, you knew that..."

"Oh," he said, finally seeing where the conversation was leading. "I see. You're referring to our little wager."

"Yes. You knew that I, well, that I liked you already." Fortune puffed out her chest indignantly and lifted her chin. "You took advantage of me, sir."

Beau knew that if he stood there talking to her much longer he would most certainly take advantage of her. "Uh, Fortune, my dear, perhaps it would be best if we discussed this at another time."

"As you wish," she said, trying to hide her smile. So he, too, wanted the payment of their wager to be made when no one could see them. "Shall we continue, then?"

The dampness on the seat of his trousers bothered him a great deal, and, even though he wanted to remain there on deck with Fortune, he had to change his clothes. He would be mortified if anyone saw him in his present condition. "Fortune, I'm enjoying our conversation, but I feel the need to change my trousers. These are deplorably wet."

"Oh," Fortune said, trying not to laugh. "I apologize. I should have realized at once that you'd want to remove your damp clothing. Please forgive me."

"Nothing to forgive." Beau bowed from the waist, caught her hand and kissed it gently. "Until later, then?"

Fortune nodded. As he backed away, she had to bite her lower lip to keep from laughing. She knew he was embarrassed; still, the picture he presented was funny. She turned back to look at the water until she knew he had disappeared down the companionway.

At supper that evening, a few women were present. Jemima came in, looking pale. She glanced at the food on the table and left without eating. Fortune chased after her. "Jemima!" she called. "Wait."

"Sorry. Can't wait." Jemima disappeared into her room, and the door slammed after her.

Fortune returned to the dining room. She sat down again with her father and smiled at the group around the table. The men hardly paid any attention to her, so involved were they in the talk of gold. Then Beau and Patrick came in together.

Beau looked at the group, noticing Fortune immediately. It amazed him that, whenever he entered a room, his gaze automatically seemed to go to her. He grinned, patted his buttocks and shook his head.

Fortune caught his meaning. His bottom was sore from his fall. She smiled at him in return and tried to look sympathetic, though she wasn't sure she succeeded. He didn't enter into the conversation, but Patrick did. The people at the table had divided themselves into two camps: those who believed the stories of abundant gold for the taking, and those who were skeptical.

Not willing to take a stand, because she didn't really know what or who to believe, Fortune stayed out of the animated discussion. Some reported reading about Lieutenant Loesser and his cask of gold, but others had simply heard of gold being discovered. Many of them speculated that, before long, thousands of men would be headed to California. Fortune agreed with that. Many men would do anything to obtain money without working for it.

Her thought sobered her. Exactly what kind of man *would* be going to San Francisco? She'd have to think about that.

When she could stand no more of the speculation, she excused herself and went up on deck for her evening stroll. She marveled that nobody else ever wanted to walk in the fresh air.

Many of the women complained that the humid air destroyed their hair; others whined about the sea mist damaging their clothes. Fortune cared little for either complaint. She savored the moments alone—or with Beau—gazing out at the horizon. During her walks she would ponder her future, happily anticipating the moment when she'd arrive in California.

That evening, Fortune wasn't alone for very long. Beau joined her. For along time, they stood elbow to elbow and stared out at the last glimmer of light filling the western sky.

Beau had vowed not to follow her on deck. He knew that their relationship could never be; they were too different. She, like most women, would want a husband with whom she could settle down. Beau had no intention of ever settling down. His life of going from gambling town to gambling town would never satisfy a woman, and he was too happy with his way of life to change. Besides, he didn't want a nagging wife who would spend all his money and then complain when none was left. Women weren't to be trusted.

And yet here he was, standing beside her, stealing glances down at her. Could she be trusted? Thus far, she'd proven herself to be different from other women. He'd foolishly risked his feelings before for a woman he thought was different, and he wasn't willing to do it again. No matter who the woman was.

Still, they could be friends. He genuinely liked her. Her smile, her laugh, were easy, and never mean-spirited. Even when he'd fallen this morning, she'd been more concerned with his well-being than with the humor of the situation, though he sensed that one day they'd look back and laugh.

Fortune stared at the moon, concentrating on it as it hung there, naked and proud. She thought of the moon as a woman, a beautiful woman. Last night, she'd been coquettish, clothed in the sensual garb of an approaching storm. Tonight, she was beaming proudly down on the ship, which was little more than a speck in the vast Caribbean Sea. The path she cast, a shimmering trail of silver glitter, rode atop the waves—almost tangible. If ever one could catch a moonbeam, Fortune mused, it would be now.

She was trying very hard to avoid looking up at Beau. Something was simmering between them. Fortune knew that the moonlight would be illuminating his face, highlighting his patrician nose, his high cheekbones. His eyes would be a deep shade, somewhere between emerald green and black in the pale light. Hoping to find him gazing in the other direction, Fortune glanced up.

He was staring at her. She wondered what he was thinking, for he didn't seem to notice that she was looking at him.

Beau felt a tightening in his groin. Fortune was an extraordinary woman, delicate of feature and gentle of disposition. He willed the attraction he felt for her to be purely sexual, but he knew he was lying to himself. There was something else, something he couldn't define—maybe didn't want to define.

"Well," they said simultaneously, and then they both laughed.

"Sorry," Beau said. "Go ahead."

"No, you go ahead." Fortune giggled, feeling like an adolescent. "I've forgotten what I wanted to say."

"Me, too," Beau admitted, chagrined. What a foolish thing to do. The silence had been companionable, not strained. Why had he felt the urge to chatter about nothing? "I do have something to say, however."

"What is it?" she asked, turning slightly to see him better. That was a mistake. Fortune could feel the heat between them, a pulsing sort of heat that sent little tingles along her skin. She couldn't back up without looking a little silly, so she maintained her stance and willed herself to ignore the tremors that were making her so fidgety.

"I wanted to explain about the other night." Beau hardly knew where to begin. He realized he'd never told Fortune that he was a gambler, but it hadn't seemed important. Their relationship was one that was impossible. Nonetheless, he wanted to clear the air.

"You don't have to explain." Fortune closed her eyes briefly and remembered his kisses. How she'd longed for such a moment again, even though she was courting danger. "I'm not going to press you for an explanation."

Beau smiled. That was one of the things he liked about her. One of the things. "I realize that, and I appreciate your restraint. But, nonetheless, I'd like to explain. You see," he began, raking his fingers through his hair. "I'm a gambler."

"I understood that much from the rather seedy gentleman who accosted us in the ballroom." Fortune smiled, remembering how she'd caught the man by surprise.

"Yes, he was a grubby sort of man, wasn't he?"

"Undoubtedly." Fortune met his gaze. Her eyes were locked with his, and she could feel his breath falling softly on her face in warm puffs. She was standing too close, far too close, but she couldn't make herself step back.

Fortune's scent tantalized him, and he groaned.

"Is something wrong?" she asked, placing her hand on his arm. She was afraid he might be suffering from some problem related to his fall.

"There are a lot of things wrong, but this is something you can't help with. Well, you could, actually, but I won't let you." Beau cursed himself inwardly. How could he keep entangling himself with her, when he knew her effect on his body? He did it without thinking, though he had to admit that on some level he knew what he was doing. He had to say this and get it over with. "Fortune, I'm a gambler. An honest gambler. I play the odds and read my opponents. I'm good at judging people, which is an asset for a gambler."

Fortune nodded, glad that he was admitting his trade instead of trying to hide it. She already liked him very much, perhaps too much. She now knew why he couldn't get married. That suited her very well. But they could be good friends, even though theirs wasn't a normal sort of relationship. "I understand how that would be helpful."

"Abe, on the other hand, is not a good gambler. He loses money quickly by betting foolishly." Beau thought back to the game that had caused all the trouble. "He drinks while he gambles. That is a major part of his problem."

"Ah, strong drink and chance. The two don't mix."

"Strong drink and chance are all right, but gambling involves decisions that have nothing to do with chance." He tried to decide how best to explain. "Bluffing is a large part of the game. Sometimes a man has a good hand and doesn't have to bluff. Other times, he thinks he can win with a mediocre hand. That's where the gamble lies."

"I see." Fortune knew exactly what Beau was talking about. She'd seen her father playing cards, had learned the game by hiding behind a screen in the parlor and watching. "Strong drink impairs a man's ability to judge character," she said. "Providing, of course, that he has that ability to begin with."

Beau gazed at her. She was absolutely correct. How astute of her. "True." He studied her for a moment. "You told me you play chess. You haven't by any chance played poker, too, have you?"

Fortune laughed and shook her head. "Never actually played, but I've watched my father and his friends."

"So you know what I mean?" Now he understood how it was that she knew so much. "Well, Abe is a poor loser. Especially after having consumed the better part of three bottles of brandy."

"I see. So he, in his inebriated state, accused you of cheating? And then followed you back to the hotel that night?" Now the story came clear. She'd presumed as much, but it was nice to hear the confirmation that her guess had been accurate.

"Yes." Beau looked down at her. Her lips were upturned, and tiny lines of joy radiated from the corners of her deep-set eyes. "Why were you outside your room that night?"

"I couldn't sleep, so I was standing beside the window. I heard all the commotion and looked down. I saw a man—you—hurrying along the street, with those two men chasing him. I saw you slip into the shadows in a doorway. When I realized who you were, I decided to try to help." Fortune blushed furiously, and was thankful for the dim light. "I guess I never envisioned the kind of help I'd be asked to give."

Beau chuckled, imagining how she must have felt when he'd pulled her into his embrace that night. "Sorry. I shouldn't have."

"Oh, no!" she exclaimed, hoping he didn't misunderstand her. "I didn't mean that I didn't enjoy it. What I meant to say was..." What was she saying? How could she admit such a thing to a man who'd never given her the slightest reason to think that he, too, had enjoyed their kisses.

So, she'd enjoyed it. "I must admit that I rather enjoyed it myself. If I hadn't had those two drunks chasing after me, I might have liked it even more." He considered what he'd said. "Then again, I probably wouldn't have kissed you. And I certainly wouldn't have pulled you down into my lap."

"I suppose not." Fortune smiled, warm all over from his admission that he actually enjoyed kissing her. "Then I suppose that we owe them our thanks."

"You know, Miss Anthony," he began, rather formally, tucking his hands around her tiny waist. "I think you have a very strange sense of humor. Most of the women I've known would have slapped my face for kissing them—whether it saved my life or not."

"Must I reiterate, Mr. Gregory, that I'm not like other women?" Fortune teased, finding their banter amusing. He pulled her closer into his embrace, and she felt a shudder of pleasure race up her spine. "I have, on occasion, used my brain for thinking, as well as for writing invitations to parties and place cards for the supper table."

"I find that rather refreshing, Miss Anthony, and just as remarkable as your kisses," Beau whispered, his lips nearing hers.

He pressed his mouth to hers, savoring the softness and the invitation he always found there. This time, her lips parted without being coaxed, and he plundered the soft inner recesses of her mouth. When he reluctantly drew away, he peered down at her. "Well, almost as remarkable."

Fortune had no time to reply. He kissed her again, more urgently, and wrapped his arms around her as if to imprison her. She was past caring about being imprisoned. Her spirit soared, taking wing on the vast wave of feeling that rose and fell all around her.

This time, it was Fortune who drew away. She gazed at him, shaken by the intensity of their kisses.

Then she stammered an excuse and ran for shelter from her reaction to him.

Chapter Seven

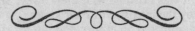

Fortune lay in her bed, staring at the wooden ceiling above her. She was on dangerous ground with Beau. He wanted no part of marriage, had said so more than once. And he was a gambler.

Fortune could hardly have counted the number of times her mother had warned against gamblers. And Letha Anthony was a very strict mother.

As a result of her mother's warnings, however, Fortune had become fascinated with the idea of gamblers, though she'd never really met one until Beau had walked into her life. So far, she didn't see anything really dreadful about him, except that he didn't intend to marry. That wasn't really a problem for her. She didn't want to marry, either. She felt, as Beau must, that marriage was an encumbrance that one could well do without. She'd never achieve the freedom and independence she craved if she succumbed to a husband's dominance.

Smiling foolishly in the darkness, she recalled their wager. He was a shrewd man. Remembering the conversation that had led to the bet, she decided that she'd done everything to taunt him into making the wager, even though she hadn't known the effect her pronouncements would have on him.

She thought of her friendship with Beau. It seemed unlikely that she could be close friends with a man whose kisses made her legs turn to jelly.

He'd kissed her again tonight, which she supposed meant that her debt was paid. Somehow that made her a little sad.

Fortune had liked the idea of owing him a kiss. It had made her days and nights a little more exciting, wondering when he would collect. Ahh, the anticipation is more than the event itself, she thought. Hardly, she told herself. The anticipation of kissing Beau can't even be compared to the actual kissing. There's nothing like that. Nothing at all.

Early the next morning Fortune rose and took her walk. Beau didn't join her, and she missed his company, though she'd decided to avoid being alone with him as much as possible. It seemed that every time they were alone, they ended up kissing and embracing. She enjoyed both immensely. And anything she enjoyed that much must surely be bad for her, she concluded reluctantly as she walked into the dining room for breakfast.

She was early. The room was almost deserted, so she ate quickly and returned to her cabin. Along about noon, Jemima came in and asked her to go to dinner with her.

Fortune noticed that Jemima ate with relish. Apparently her bout with seasickness was past. Being pregnant *and* in rough seas must be terrible, Fortune thought. That was something she'd never have to worry about. There would be no babies for her.

She rather regretted that. Fortune liked children. Having no children would be the one drawback to remaining unmarried. Well, it couldn't be helped. She couldn't have it both ways.

The days passed quickly. Fortune avoided Beau, and he, apparently, avoided her. She considered that regretfully as she watched the mass of land rising on the horizon. Chagres. What a wonderful place it must be. The Caribbean Sea port that would lead her across the Isthmus of Panama to the vast Pacific Ocean, and then to California.

Excitement surged through Fortune. She could hardly stand still. She paced back and forth, hoping for a better vantage point, but found that it was useless.

"We've spotted land," Beau said, coming up behind her.

"Yes," she answered, pointing over the railing. "There. Can you see it?"

"Certainly can." Beau gazed at the horizon for a few moments. "Well, our journey is almost half over."

Fortune nodded. She'd been thinking almost the same thing. "Hasn't it been interesting?"

Beau chuckled, shaking his head. "I suppose it could be termed interesting. I've found certain portions of the trip to be dangerous."

"Yes, perhaps you should stay away from the gambling halls." She grinned at him, displaying perfect white teeth. "My mother says they're gambling hells."

"Well, I'd say she's right in some cases." Beau recalled some of the places he'd played cards. "Some of them are as close to hell as I ever want to come."

He was really talking about his relationship with Fortune, not the incident with Abe. For some reason, Beau felt that whenever he was with her, he lost control. Beau was a man who was always in control—of everything. With her, he simply had no will of his own.

Land loomed larger and larger. Fortune could hardly contain herself. She talked to Beau for a short while and then excused herself. Her parents would, no doubt, be looking for her.

When she reached her room, she checked on the last-minute packing and found that everything had been done to her satisfaction. She'd thrown her clothes into the trunk, only to have them removed and replaced by Nola Bell, who always packed in a way that would prevent at least some wrinkles.

Here in her room, she had but one trunk. Most of their baggage was stored in the ship's hold. Her father had purchased farming equipment, seeds of every description, and the utensils necessary when setting up a new home. There wasn't much room, but he'd packed in as much as he could. Most precious to him were the seeds. The seeds of their future, he'd called them.

Fortune knew she should wait for her parents, but she could no longer contain her curiosity. She returned to the deck, where several of the men had gathered to view the approach to Chagres. By now, the land loomed high above the horizon, and she could see that the cliffs were a verdant green. Though the sea was sunny, above the cliffs were huge dark clouds, hovering ominously, a threatening crown of danger.

The ship sailed smoothly toward the shore. Birds flew overhead, squawking a welcome as the ship's anchor splashed into the water. Native men rowed small boats out to the ship to pick up the passengers and all their baggage.

Fortune waited eagerly. She wished she could be the first one to step onto the new land, but she held back, fascinated by all the activity. When her turn came to be lowered into a boat, she declined. She'd seen some of the men climbing down a rickety ladder, and she opted for that. Drawing the tail of her gown between her legs to control the dip and sway of her crinolines, she descended the ladder. To be dumped like cargo into one of the awaiting boats seemed less than graceful, and it was certainly more demeaning.

When she stepped gingerly into the small boat, she smiled with pride. She was the only woman who had managed to board one of the small boats without the assistance of the men.

Letha apparently didn't share her view. As she was lowered, she shrieked as if she were afraid of falling into the ocean. Once in the wobbly boat, she clung to Fortune's arm.

Beau had watched Fortune. Without faltering, she'd made her way down the unstable ladder and into the boat. He noticed the look of accomplishment on her face and grinned at her. What a woman!

He waited his turn. By the time he approached the ladder, the boat carrying Fortune had gone. He hurried down, hoping that she wouldn't get too far away when they reached Chagres. He wanted to know where they were staying.

No arrangements of any sort had been made in advance. Fortune knew that they'd have to find a hotel when they arrived. From here, all she could see was the waterside village, but she was sure that the town itself would be much more splendid. The houses—huts, really—were made of cane, with thatched roofs. They were built upon poles, and they looked peculiar to Fortune. She assumed that the area was susceptible to flooding.

Perspiring from the immense heat and humidity, she waited until she saw the other ladies trudging across the sand and went to take her mother's hand to help her. Fortune looked up and down the beach. As far as she could see, the high green cliff spread before them. There seemed to be no way around it. She prayed that the city would be in the shade of the cliff, and much cooler than the beach.

Away from the beach, the city would be more normal, she reasoned. She was wrong. There was nothing beyond the beach. Most of the people lived by the sea, not bothering to clear out the jungle that seemed to begin at the edge of the water in places.

One thing she really looked forward to was a bath. A real bath. She would ask for—no, demand—a tub when she arrived at their hotel. After a nice, cool bath, she'd feel much better.

As they walked across the sand toward the little village, Letha kept muttering, "Oh, dear God, what is this place? God save us."

Fortune didn't say anything. She knew that if she acknowledged her mother's muttering, then Letha would launch into a full-scale tirade. Just keep quiet until we get to the hotel, she told herself.

There were no hotels in Chagres.

The people from the ship stood there, gaping at Selwin Allen, who was interpreting for them. Most of the natives spoke no English.

Beau grimaced and moved to the front of the throng of people from America. He asked, in Spanish, where the leader of the village was. There was no real leader. He asked how they could get to Panama City.

The man who answered suggested that they could pay some of the natives who had bongos to pole them up to Cruces. There, they could hire mules and donkeys to take them for the rest of the journey.

Fortune stared in disbelief for a few moments as she listened to Beau's translation. Then she caught sight of Selwin Allen. Had he lied to them? She remembered quite well how he'd spoken of the friendly natives and picturesque villages. But, as she recalled the conversations, she realized he'd never mentioned hotels or other such comforts one might expect on such a trip.

She glanced around. There were several dark-skinned men walking around nearly naked, while there were others who had forsaken clothing altogether. Children played in the muddy paths, squatting naked and staring openly at the people from the ship.

Letha's mouth dropped open in astonishment. "We can't stay here, of course." She turned to her husband, who was glaring at Selwin. "We'll have to go back. It wasn't so bad living with your father."

Hearing her mother's plea, Fortune almost panicked. She prayed that her father wouldn't relent. The idea of returning to Charleston, to Pleasant Point, was abhorrent to her. She simply couldn't face the humiliation of going back to the people she considered her enemies.

Giles shook his head. Even as they spoke, the ship was weighing anchor and hoisting its sails. They had been abandoned.

Fortune knew it couldn't exactly be termed abandonment. After all, the captain had done his job. He'd delivered them to where they'd wanted to go.

Glancing around, she decided that while the men argued over what was to happen, the ladies could sit more comfortably in the shade. She took her mother's arm and led her, protesting all the while, to the edge of the jungle. She spread her daytime shawl on the grass and helped her mother to sit. Several other ladies followed them.

She listened to choruses of "What's to become of us?" "What shall we do?" and "Lord, protect us."

The complaints began to annoy Fortune. Finally she sighed and shook her head. "Ladies," she said, hoping to get their attention, "this isn't so bad. We're all safe. You heard Beau—Mr. Gregory. We can hire some of the villagers to take us to Cruces."

Jemima perked up. "Of course. That's what we'll do. We'll continue our journey."

The other women were more skeptical. Amelia looked positively terrified, as did Mrs. Sloan. Letha was dumb-struck.

Fortune looked overhead. Ominous rumblings were coming from the clouds she'd seen as the ship had sailed in. Within a very few minutes, they'd need shelter. The complaints would start in earnest then.

Glancing around, she saw a dark-skinned woman who was naked to the waist emerge from one of the huts. Fortune jumped to her feet and ran toward her. The woman stopped, as if Fortune frightened her.

"Hello," Fortune said. Then she remembered that nobody here spoke English. *"Buenos días,"* she corrected, and smiled. She knew very little Spanish. How could she convey her meaning to the woman?

As lightning flashed overhead, Fortune pointed toward the sky. "Rain. Need shelter."

As the rain began to fall, she pointed to the sky. Then she held her hands over her head as if to protect it. The woman peered at Fortune as if she were losing her mind. After several attempts to make the woman understand, Fortune showed the woman the women from the ship and then indicated that they needed shelter by pointing at the hut.

The woman began to smile in understanding, then uttered a string of words Fortune could only guess at. She hurried back over to the little group and told them to follow her, then led them to the woman, whom they all followed into the hut. It was primitive, no doubt about it, but it kept off the rain while the men bartered with the natives about the boats.

Their hostess didn't appear to know what to do, but she sat with them, smiling brightly whenever someone spoke. After a few minutes, she offered them a bowl of something that resembled gruel. It was a mealy paste that none of the ladies accepted, save Fortune.

"Muchas gracias," Fortune said, cupping her fingers the way the woman showed her. The gruel was nearly taste-less, but Fortune ate it, smiling and nodding cheerfully.

Soon Beau came to get the women. Rain was coming down in heavy sheets, but there was nowhere in Chagres for them to stay the night, so they had to press on. He handed each of the ladies an umbrella purchased from one of the little stalls where the villagers traded, and they headed out into the storm.

Not all the baggage could be carried. Everyone had to eliminate something before the boats could be loaded. Letha's new set of china—all but six plates and cups—was removed from one trunk, as well as the new silverware. Letha protested loud and long as the delicate dinnerware was placed on the ground. Giles examined his tools, eliminating as few as possible. He wanted everything in two trunks.

Fortune knew she should volunteer to leave behind her books, but she couldn't. While her parents, along with Nola Bell and Boaz, were desperately trying to find room to store their necessities, Fortune remained quiet. She saw Beau standing nearby.

Maybe he could help her. She walked over. "Beau, have you any extra room at all in your trunk?"

When he saw her face, Beau knew exactly what was wrong. "I'll find some room. How much do you need?" Fortune's smile brightened. He went with her to her trunk and looked at the pile of books and then back at his trunk. With a little skill, he could fit most of them in. "We'll manage."

While Letha and Giles sorted through their goods again, Fortune moved her books to Beau's trunk. They rearranged his clothes and other items until the books fit snugly inside the trunk.

"I'll…" she began, her eyes filling with tears. "I'll make it up to you."

"It's nothing. Forget it." He grinned at her and wiped the rain from his forehead. "Besides, I plan to borrow them, anyway."

Fortune thanked him again and then returned to help her parents. After about an hour's work, the Anthonys' trunks were ready to be loaded into the boats.

When she saw the boats, Fortune could hardly believe her eyes. The bongos, as they were called, were no more than hollowed-out tree trunks. Giant logs, perhaps ten to

fifteen feet in diameter, had been dug out to resemble boats.
Rigged above the seating area were small roofs of palm
fronds and long, thick leaves. There were no seats, so everyone had to sit on their baggage.

Three bongos were lined up, ready to be loaded. Fortune and her parents, Nola Bell and Boaz, the Allens, the
Sloans, Patrick and Beau were all assigned to the first boat.
Fortune found herself seated between Jemima and Amelia. The older women sat together, commiserating with each
other over the horrible conditions they were forced to endure.

Fortune stared at the native who was to pole their boat.
Like the other two, he was completely naked and, apparently, quite unashamed. Her mother's eyes widened in
horror, and she turned to Giles and whispered, "The man
is naked! Ask him to cover himself."

Giles shook his head. "I can't. Selwin says they're almost all like this." He pointed to the machete just behind
the native. "I don't think we should bother him."

Beau watched Fortune carefully. At first, he'd noticed
something that seemed like anger. He'd had the distinct
feeling that she thought they'd been fooled by Selwin Allen, but then her face had changed, seemingly as she'd recalled what he'd said. He hadn't necessarily lied to them,
but he had avoided the truth.

As the naked native poled the bongo away from the village, Beau settled back to doze. He'd gotten too little sleep
lately, and the warm, muggy air made him drowsy.

"I'm so mad I could just spit!" Jemima exclaimed in an
ardent whisper to Fortune. "My husband has ... Well, he
never told us about this. He let us think that..." Her voice
trailed off. She could hardly think, she was so uncomfortable.

Fortune fanned herself, wishing she could remove some
of her clothing. Her hoop skirts trapped the heat, causing
her to perspire as if she were in an oven. The rain did little
to cool the afternoon off. Besides the heat, she had to contend with biting insects. She couldn't ever remember being
this uncomfortable.

As they poled up the wide Chagres River, the current became faster. The rain-swollen river had turned into a torrent, and the native poled into a narrow inlet for protection. He tied up the boat and sat down to take a nap.

The other boats followed. Several of the weary travelers complained loudly, but it did no good. The current was too strong for the men to make any progress. As long as it rained, they'd have to stay put.

It seemed to Fortune that it was hours before the rain stopped.

After a while, the current seemed to slow, and the boatman untied the bongo and began to pole forward again. Overhead, trees obliterated the sunlight for long periods of time; it was as if they were passing through a tunnel. Lengthy tendrils of vine hung down from the trees, sometimes reaching the water. The boatmen used machetes to cut through some of the worst places.

Fortune shuddered, hoping that there were no snakes dangling from those vines to fall into the boat. The heat was unrelenting; it even seemed to get steamier as noon approached. Convinced that she'd never be comfortable again, Fortune absently brushed a stray curl from her face. It was so damp with perspiration that the curl stuck to her forehead.

The journey across the isthmus was no more than fifty miles. She silently thanked God for that. Fortune had made herself as comfortable as possible when a blood-curdling screech came from somewhere deep in the jungle.

Amelia screamed and covered her head with her umbrella. Mrs. Sloan and Letha shrieked nearly as loudly.

"What do you suppose that was?" Jemima asked, peering around, clearly expecting to come face-to-face with some wild animal.

Fortune's gaze covered the jungle near the river. "I don't know, and I don't think I want to know."

Every time a howl or screech broke the stillness, the little group all glanced around to see what had made the noise. Fortune felt fairly safe as long as they were in the bongos, but she knew that they'd soon have to make camp. She was somewhat cheered by the colorful birds that flew overhead, sometimes landing in the trees or flying through small holes in the lush green canopy above the river.

They drifted into the sunshine once again, and the heat increased—not to mention the steamy swirls rising from the rainwater that had fallen into the bongo. Fortune felt like the oysters on a New Year's Day banquet table back on Edisto Island—steamed or roasted.

The sun was beating down so hard that they could hardly see for the glare. She wondered how the boatmen could see to pole the bongos forward, but they did. The little group moved steadily up the Chagres River toward Cruces.

When they stopped for the day, everyone was exhausted. The wood in the area was too wet to burn, so they settled for hardtack and beef jerky. Fortune decided that cooking would be out of the question anyway, even if they were able to build a cook fire. The smell of food might entice animals to visit the camp.

Before long, the mosquitoes were awful. Several suggestions were made for eliminating the biting insects, but none seemed feasible. Fortune saw that Letha was miserable. Her mother had always been allergic to the tiny insects, and Fortune didn't like them overmuch herself. After studying the problem for a few moments, she went back to the bongo and opened her trunk. She removed the two Chantilly lace shawls she'd bought in New Orleans and returned to the camp. Silently thanking God that they were so large, she draped one over her mother's head and then sat down and did the same for herself. She didn't really like it, but it was better than being eaten alive. Jemima soon got her shawl, too.

Several other women sent their husbands to retrieve shawls to protect them. One woman, who obviously had no shawl, tore the skirt off a lovely gown and made a tent of it over her head.

Beau spoke briefly with the boatman. He turned to the small group of people, who now numbered a little more than thirty. "We'll need to find a little wood to burn during the night. The mosquitoes will attack in swarms, and—" He looked at the group and decided there was no need to worry the ladies. Those howls all day had given the group plenty to worry about, and he didn't want to add to their concern.

He organized a group of men to search for wood. Beau strode along, watching carefully for jungle creatures. He looked up into the trees and, seeing a length of vine within reach, jerked it hard. He was rewarded for his efforts with a shower of dry twigs. He shouted to the other men as he hurriedly picked up the sticks to keep them from getting too wet.

When the others arrived, he showed them what he'd done. They hurried off to try to find low-hanging vines. After about thirty minutes, there was enough dry wood to burn all night, if they could get a fire started on the damp ground.

Beau and Patrick finally coaxed a small flame to life and hovered close by to make sure it didn't blow out. After it began to eat into a sizable piece of wood that Beau had found beneath some heavily protective shrubs, they relaxed. The rest of the wood would give them some light and protection. Once the fire was burning fitfully, some of the women began to fall asleep, curled up on heavy cloaks they had removed from their trunks.

As the night grew more still, Fortune could hear the muffled whispers of some of their group. After a few minutes, she heard Amelia's whining voice saying, "But I don't want to go any farther. I'm scared."

Fortune was afraid, too. She was afraid of many things. The unknown was frightening enough, but to her, the known was even more so. Returning to Charleston was the one option her parents might decide upon that she would refuse to go along with. She couldn't go back, not now that she'd tasted the splendor and adventure of the outside world.

Fortune sat there, staring at the flames. She was as tired as the rest of the women, but her thoughts were busy. A hundred things crowded into her mind all at once, clamoring to be considered in the quiet evening darkness.

This was adventure—uncomfortable adventure, but what she'd asked for nonetheless. Now she wondered about California. Was it a land of vast jungles and steamy rivers? How could they farm such land? Could the animals be tamed? What sort of house would they have?

Somehow, back in Charleston, she'd envisioned a plantation near San Francisco much like Pleasant Point, with its well-ordered gardens and fields. She remembered the pristine columns reaching from the floor of the piazza through the veranda on the second story, the ornate curved staircase that wound up from the ground floor to the third story, the elaborate ballroom with its gilt-edged mirrors and candelabra. It was a beautiful plantation, to be sure—but one where love did not abide.

Now she wondered what San Francisco would be like. Would she live in a hovel similar to those of Chagres? Had Selwin exaggerated that, too? Would the inhabitants of the city be Indians, Spaniards and Negroes? What would the language be? There were so many questions to be answered that she finally lay down and fell asleep trying to decide which to consider first.

Morning came early to the small encampment. Fortune arose and walked out past the edge of the camp, a ways from everyone else. She wanted to be alone, to take her first walk on the isthmus to have time to think. Knowing that wild animals and poisonous reptiles lived in the jungle, she kept close enough to the others for them to hear her shout.

Creepers hung from nearly every tree. As she brushed past a swordlike plant, she noticed drops of blood well up on her arm. The spikes were sharp and dangerous.

Here and there, the sun dappled the floor of the jungle with light. Where light fell, plants flourished. Fortune discovered a beautiful blooming plant in the jungle. Its delicate pink blossom hung from a tree limb. After a few moments, she realized that the plant had attached itself to a tree, that the blossom was not part of the tree itself, but a parasite.

She reached up to pluck the bloom, but didn't. She knew that it would surely die, and she would rather have the plant live here in this lush green solitude than see it die somewhere along the way, in the boat or on the back of a donkey. Fortune knew that people would soon be waking up, and she decided to return to camp. She didn't want to frighten her mother and father.

When she walked into camp, Beau and Patrick were quietly discussing something across the way. She smiled and waved when Beau shook his head. Fortune knew that he was thinking she shouldn't have gone out alone, but she had been careful. The walk had cheered her in a way that nothing else could—except more kisses from Beau.

Fortune was thinking too much about Beau. She'd vowed to stay away from him, but the bongo didn't allow for much distance. She enjoyed watching him when he didn't know she was doing so. Still, she didn't need to think of him constantly, as she'd done for the past few days.

Breakfast was little better than supper. Everyone had hardtack, jerky and a cup of strong coffee that was full of grounds. She packed up her belongings and trudged along with the others back to the bongo for another day of traveling.

Fortune sat beside Jemima, filled with energy and ready to go. "Everyone seems to have settled down."

"Nothing horrible happened the first day, so I suppose everyone can relax." Jemima tilted her umbrella to keep the sun off her face. "Well, everyone except Amelia."

Fortune gazed at the younger woman. Her face was tear-stained, and her hair hung in tangles about her face. Mrs. Sloan didn't look much better, but she managed a brave smile once in a while.

The Chagres River was dark, and scum floated along with the leaves and limbs broken off by the rain. It seemed, to Fortune, to be a cleansing of the land. The heavy rains came, washing everything clean and bright. Then, in December, came the dry season.

The rain came again right after noon and lasted until the sun was low on the horizon. The palm branches on the roof of the bongo protected them somewhat, and the umbrellas helped, too, but nothing could stop the muggy feeling of being cooked alive. Fortune fanned herself rapidly with her new fan, but it didn't help much. In spite of the elaborately wrapped shawls, the insects occasionally found tender skin to pierce with their stinging bites, and the heat drew perspiration out of her pores in quantities that parched her mouth. The native boatmen showed them how to cut lengths of water vine that quenched their thirst.

After a while, Fortune noticed a blister on her arm where the swordlike plant had scratched her. It must have been poisonous. Alarmed, she glanced at Beau. He was engrossed in conversation with Patrick, but she didn't care. She needed to communicate with their guide.

"Beau," she called, and hardly noticed that every woman within hearing distance turned to face her. She didn't care about that, either—not now. "Look at this."

He rose and walked as quickly as possible across the boat. "What is it?"

"I'm not sure." Fortune peered at the watery blister and then looked up at Beau. "When I went walking this morning, a sharp plant that resembled a sword scratched me. It bled very little, but now I have this blister."

Beau gazed at it critically. Then he motioned to the boatman to look. The two of them chattered for a moment in Spanish before Beau turned back to Fortune. "He says it's a poisonous plant, but that it isn't too dangerous. You'll be all right. But he recommends that you not go wandering off alone again, Miss Anthony."

"Thank you for your help. Both of you. *Muchas gracias, señor,*" she said demurely, pretending to examine a damp spot on the hem of her dress. She was embarrassed. In the future she'd be more careful.

That night, they made camp much as they had the evening before. Fortune's blister hadn't gone away, but it hadn't spread any further.

The boatmen gathered wood, lots of it, and they built a roaring fire about ten or fifteen feet from the travelers. One of the men left alone. Over the fire the other three natives suspended a thick rod. Fortune wondered what they were doing. Could they have found a deer or some other edible animal in the woods?

She watched as the man returned. In his arms he carried a monkey. Fortune was fascinated. She'd seen a monkey but once before, and she thought the animals were cute. She even fancied keeping this one for a pet, if the natives would let her have it.

Within a few seconds, she discovered the terrible truth about their fire. She watched in horror as one of the men took his machete, stabbed the monkey in the chest to kill it and began to skin the dead animal.

Fortune had never been troubled by a weak stomach, but as she watched them, she began to retch. The carcass was then stretched out on the rod above the flame. One of the natives had built a bow to turn the rod, and he nonchalantly pushed the bow back and forth.

She could stand it no longer. Jumping up from her place near the fire, she ran as fast as she could in the opposite direction. Fortune could hear the uproar that her quick departure caused in the encampment, but she didn't care. She had to get away, to get the awful sight out of her mind. But even as she ran, she knew she'd never forget that night or the natives' abhorrent act.

Beau saw Fortune get sick to her stomach, and he knew she'd seen the natives kill the monkey. Then he saw her leap to her feet and dash out of the encampment. He raced after her.

He finally caught up to her and grabbed her from behind. The sudden move spun her around and into his arms, where he felt her body shivering with shock.

Fortune melted into his arms, clinging to him for comfort. Nothing in her wildest nightmares could have prepared her for what she'd seen.

"You're all right," he whispered, stroking her back and holding her as close as he could. "Shh," he soothed. "It's just their way, Fortune—they're not trying to be deliberately cruel."

"Oh, Beau, did you see?" she asked, with a great sob. "This land is so wild and beautiful, so exotic. I wanted to see only the beauty. Now I've seen the utmost of horrors. How can I ever see the beauty again?"

"You will, my darling," he murmured against her hair. "You will in time."

Darling. The word penetrated the revulsion she felt, and she looked up. In spite of the hideous scene she'd just witnessed, a glimmer of light crept back into her mind. Just a glimmer.

Darling.

Chapter Eight

Fortune slept little. As she lay there listening to the night sounds of the jungle, she kept thinking of that poor little monkey. Once he'd been skinned, he looked like a baby.

She knew there were all sorts of cultures in the world; she'd learned that from her reading. Maybe if she had known in advance what to expect, she wouldn't have been so... so stunned. Maybe if the monkey hadn't looked so human.

After all, she ate beef and pork. To these men, such a meal might be repulsive, too. Different cultures, she repeated to herself. I hope that the Californians are more like South Carolinians, she thought.

She turned over, attempting to find a more comfortable spot, but there weren't any tonight. The ground beneath her cloak seemed to be solid rock, and it gouged into her flesh painfully.

Fortune was glad that they were only going to be in this country for a few more days. They would be in Panama City within a week, and a ship would take them from there to San Francisco, where she would begin life anew.

That she didn't actually dislike the jungles of Panama surprised her. The other women seemed to hate it. They would certainly hate it if they'd seen what she had seen. The memory of the natives eating the monkey was still fresh in her mind. Fortune considered the situation. A great part of the problem, for her, was the heat. If she weren't encumbered by voluminous skirts and heavy petticoats, she might

like the place even better than she did. She had to admit
that the country was beautiful.

Everything was more dramatic. The birds were large, and
vibrantly colored. The animals and reptiles were unusual,
though sometimes dangerous. And the plant life...well, the
word that came to her mind was *magnificent*. She thought
back to the fragile blossom she'd nearly picked. During the
day she'd seen hundreds of them, in almost as many shades
of pink and fuchsia and purple.

If she could learn the language, she was sure that she'd
find the natives interesting. The woman back at Chagres
had seemed pleased to have them visit, even briefly. The
nudity of the natives might be a problem. Fortune didn't
know if she'd ever get used to seeing them naked, or nearly
so. She had to admit that it seemed natural for them. It
would never feel natural to her, she concluded.

She tried to imagine some of the other ladies and gentlemen stripping and parading around as if it were nothing out
of the ordinary. The idea was nothing if not humorous.

Fortune was puzzled by her own feelings. While she
should hate a place that was wild and alien, a place where
the people wore no clothes or ate defenseless animals like
that monkey, she couldn't hate it. Now that she'd thought
through the event and tried to understand it, she realized
that she couldn't hold these men responsible for the idio-
syncrasies of their culture, any more than they could her.

Still, the memory was repugnant. From now on, she'd
look the other way if the boatmen started to build a sepa-
rate campfire—or perhaps offer them something else to eat.

As she grew drowsy, Fortune mused that she'd gotten less
sleep on this trip than ever before in her life. If that was
what it meant to live an exciting life, she wasn't sure she
wanted that much exhilaration.

Her eyes came wide open. What was she thinking? She'd
been dreaming of something like this—or similar to it—all
her life. To ask for a challenging life and then be selective
about the components thereof was ridiculous. Either your
life was exciting or it wasn't.

* * *

Beau watched the gentle rise and fall of Fortune's breast in the light of the campfire. Letha lay beside her daughter, guarding her as a mother tiger guarded her cub. He decided that it was a good thing that Letha was so vigilant. Fortune was a beautiful woman. Many men would have enjoyed the chance to take her virginity.

But Beau avoided virgins. He liked willing, experienced women, women who were less interested in a set of antiquated vows than in the emotions and passions that could flourish in a relationship with no entanglements and no restrictions.

One of these days, he might settle down. When he was too old to enjoy himself. Then, maybe, he'd like someone to take care of him. That might be all right.

Fortune would never settle for halfway. She was an all-the-way person if ever he had seen one, committed to everything she did. If Fortune decided to marry, then her marriage would be first-rate. She'd demand—and give—everything to enhance the relationship. In a small way, he envied the man who would one day marry her. That lucky man would be getting the best of the arrangement.

The more he thought about it, the more he thought it was good that he had no serious intentions toward Fortune. She deserved better than him.

Fortune's eyes opened. Filtering through the trees was the first sign of light. With the verdant canopy of leaves overhead, she could hardly tell day from night. She glanced around. Everyone else seemed to be asleep. She peered at her mother. The woman lay there, snoring softly.

Rising as quietly as she could, Fortune looked again at the encampment. She thought she was the only one awake.

Beau seemed to be sleeping soundly across from the dying fire. She tiptoed past him, trying not to make a single noise. The undergrowth was so damp that her footsteps were muffled as she walked.

When she was a safe distance past the encampment, she began to walk more naturally. Fortune wasn't afraid of the jungle, but she was always cautious when she left the camp.

She stayed within sight of the fire and well within hearing distance. Some of the men had tried to stop her walks, but Fortune refused to listen. She felt a compelling urge to investigate the jungle—within reason. So far, they hadn't seen any really dangerous animals. They seemed to be hiding from the travelers, or perhaps they were frightened by the noise.

She hurried to a secluded spot where she could take care of nature's urges and then began to walk for exercise. She loved the mornings.

Used to the cool morning air of Charleston she was surprised to find that the temperature here dropped little by morning. It was also far quieter and more peaceful than Charleston in the morning. Wisps of vapor rose from the moist undergrowth, dancing gracefully on the way through the foliage above. She watched as a vibrantly colored parrot took off, followed soon by several others.

The vivid scarlets, greens and blues of the birds were a stunning sight to behold, and she said a little prayer of thanksgiving for having such a wonderful opportunity. As she walked through the jungle, flocks of beautifully colored blue butterflies fluttered all around. Hundreds of flowers bloomed, a profusion of color that made the jungle seem more alive and inviting. It was like something out of a child's story.

Fortune decided that the others must be getting up, so she hurried back. On a whim, she stopped and picked one of the delicate blossoms and tucked it behind her ear. Maybe it would bring her good luck today.

She almost hated to get back in the bongos. Because of the lack of space, she couldn't move around much. Her legs cramped, and her back hurt long before the end of the day. Many of the others complained because of the heat and insects, but Fortune remained fascinated.

Some of the group became ill that day. She wasn't sure exactly what was wrong with them, but they seemed to feel awful. By afternoon, several people were feverish and could hardly sit up. When they made camp for the night, a few of the sicker ones were wracked with chills, even in the heat.

"Yeller jack," one man said, shaking his head sadly, as they sat around the campfire that night. "I seen it before."

"Do you mean yellow fever?" another asked, eyes wide with apprehension. "I heard that called the yellow jack. But this may be something else entirely. There's no way of telling yet."

Fortune listened with dread. Many times during her life, yellow fever had struck the plantations around Charleston, sometimes killing entire families. Nobody seemed to know exactly what caused it, but because of the epidemics, most of the planters and their families spent the summers in Charleston, away from the heat and swamps.

Mr. Sloan seemed to have contracted the disease. Mrs. Sloan and Amelia were sitting anxiously by his side, patting his face with cool cloths. After a while, Amelia began to cry. Mrs. Sloan glared at her daughter, and the tears abated for a short time. Finally the young girl began sobbing, no longer able to restrain herself. Mrs. Sloan stared for a moment. "Stop it, Amelia. You're upsetting your father."

Amelia paid no attention to her mother. Mrs. Sloan waited a few seconds and then slapped Amelia resoundingly. "I said stop bawling. Things are bad enough."

Turning to one side, Amelia sat there quietly, but her shoulders still quaked with unvoiced sobs. Fortune went over to the younger girl. "Amelia, come with me."

Fortune helped Amelia to her feet, and together they walked the short distance to the edge of the river. The young woman was distraught. For a time they said nothing, but Fortune couldn't stand to see the girl so upset, and finally she said, "Amelia, darling, crying won't help. You've got to be strong. Your father needs you."

"I'm . . . I'm afraid, Fortune," Amelia admitted, sobbing loudly.

"We're all afraid of something, Amelia." Fortune hugged the girl close. "We have to conquer those fears and go on."

Her blue eyes brimming with tears, Amelia looked at Fortune. "You're not afraid of anything. I've seen you ... like that night at the ball, when those horrible men came for Beau ... Mr. Gregory. you weren't a bit afraid.''

"Yes, I was afraid." Fortune thought back to that night. Oh, Lord, she'd been terrified. "I was scared to death, but I couldn't let that man hurt my father."

"But you looked so calm and in control." Amelia, snivelling, blinked back her tears. "You always do."

"If you only knew," Fortune said, wondering how much she could confide in Amelia. "Look, Amelia, your father's ill. We don't know what's wrong with him. He really needs you, and so does your mother."

"She never needed anybody," Amelia countered with a scowl. "Haven't you heard? She's Hazel Sloan, of the Georgetown Sloans. She doesn't need anybody at all."

Fortune chuckled, glad that Amelia saw past her mother's blustering. "Well, even Hazel Sloan of the Georgetown Sloans needs help every now and then."

"Do you really think so?" Amelia asked, her eyes wide-open. "Really?"

"Absolutely." Fortune didn't know how Mrs. Sloan would take this conversation if she heard it, but it was helping Amelia, and that was Fortune's only concern just now. "Now, why are you so upset? We don't know what's wrong with your father. This may simply be some sort of ... something simple. He may feel better tomorrow." Fortune knew that it was important to make Amelia feel better, but giving the girl a false sense of hope didn't sit well with her. "But even if it is yellow fever, we've got to be strong. We've got to do what we can to make him comfortable."

"You're right. I might have known you'd look at it that way." Amelia picked up a twig and twirled it between her fingers. "You never do anything wrong."

Fortune laughed out. "Oh, Amelia, if you only knew. I've spent my life being punished for this or that infraction of the rules. I'm constantly in trouble with my mother."

Amelia giggled. "Are you? Truthfully? Or are you just trying to make me feel better?"

"Both," Fortune said, and then she stood. She helped Amelia to her feet and hugged her. "Let's go back. I'll bet the others are beginning to worry." Fortune started to walk back toward the camp, but then she turned to the young woman. "And, Amelia . . ." she said.

"Yes?"

"I'm always here if you need a friend." Fortune didn't know why she'd said that. She didn't know how much of the whimpering and simpering she could take, but she knew Amelia needed her. Nobody had ever really needed her before, and she rather liked the idea. "That's right. Come to me when you need to talk. We'll be good friends."

Smiling brightly, Amelia led the way back to camp. She strode over to where her mother was sponging off Mr. Sloan's forehead. "Here, Mother, let me do that for a while. I know you must be tired. We'll take turns."

Hazel Sloan stared at her daughter and limply handed her the cloth. Amelia dipped it in the water bowl, wrung it out and then placed it on her father's head.

Fortune smiled and sat down. She felt someone's eyes on her and turned around. Mrs. Sloan was staring at Fortune as if she could see straight through her. It looks as if Hazel Sloan of the Georgetown Sloans is surprised at her daughter's actions, Fortune surmised, leaning back against a thick tree trunk. Good enough. Maybe she'll start acting like a real person.

Fortune had never spent a day like the next. When the group reached Cruces, the next village, several people were really ill. The chances of it being yellow fever were great. Fear of the sick ones had spread quickly among the others. Few people were willing to be close to anyone they even suspected of having the disease.

Well, at least here we can rest and tend to the sick, Fortune thought as the bongos came to a stop at Cruces. She got out and helped some of the others as the trunks were unloaded.

As she and her parents stood there waiting for transportation to the nearest hotel, Selwin Allen and another man marched to the outskirts of the town and talked animatedly with one of the natives. The dark-skinned man kept scowling and shaking his head.

"I wonder what's wrong?" Fortune asked her father. "I don't think Mr. Allen is happy about whatever that man is saying."

Giles shook his head. "I don't know, child. I suppose it's just another stumbling block along the way to our future. It can't be too bad."

Letha fanned her face and frowned. "Well, whatever they're talking about, I'd like them to finish. I need a bath and a nice soft bed."

Fortune nodded. For once she agreed wholeheartedly with her mother. "Me, too."

When Selwin returned to the group, his face was grave. He scanned the little knot of people for a few seconds. "Folks, I don't know what to say. The last time I was here, these people promised to have a place for us to stay. I regret to tell you that no progress has been made toward that end."

A chorus of moans and groans, along with a few epithets, rose from the travelers. Finally, Giles stepped forward. "Selwin, tell us the truth. What do we have to look forward to in Panama City?"

Selwin shook his head. "I don't know. There were no hotels there, but we can stay with some of the residents. I've negotiated to buy mules and donkeys from these people. We'll be in Panama City in three or four days. It shouldn't be long until the ship arrives to take us to San Francisco."

Fortune felt like throwing a stone at Selwin. He'd misled them all the way. The Lord only knew what would happen from here on. She helped her father, Nola Bell and Boaz gather their belongings and pack them on two of the mules Giles had purchased. He bought donkeys for them to ride.

"Damned if I ain't going home," one man said, heading back to the bongos. "People sick and dying, no place to sleep except on the ground. At least I know what I got back home."

Fortune got worried. She hoped her father wouldn't decide to return. Several other members of the group decided that the journey wasn't worth the agony of continuing. They placed their trunks on the bongos and headed back to Chagres to await the next ship.

"Giles, I think we ought to go home, too." Letha placed her hand on her husband's arm. "We simply don't know what's ahead of us. This is far too dangerous."

Please, God, please don't let him give in. Fortune's look implored her father not to go home. She glanced at her mother and saw the agony written there. Fortune felt sorry for her mother, but she couldn't face returning. She'd rather continue alone. She had friends now, good friends. I can always count on Jemima and Beau, she thought with lifted spirits. Even if Father decides to return, I won't go. Fortune's mind was made up. She was going forward, no matter what.

Giles looked at his wife and daughter. He truly felt bad about bringing Letha along on such a harrowing journey. So far, however, none of them were sick. They hadn't been injured. "Letha," he began, trying to gather his thoughts and analyze their situation. "I can't see going home after we've come this far."

"But, Giles, we don't know... I mean, what will happen to us?" Letha saw the futility in arguing with Giles. Their life in Charleston, no matter how hard she'd tried to pretend otherwise, had been miserable. Giles and Fortune truly needed to go on. Letha toyed with the idea of returning to Charleston alone. She could live with an aunt if she had to. No, she couldn't leave her husband and daughter, no matter how bad things got. She'd manage somehow.

Giles enfolded his wife in his arms and patted her back. "Letha, my dear, I don't know what will happen to us, but I do know this. Whatever lies ahead, be it illness, injury or death, it is preferable to returning to Charleston and living with Roger."

Fortune almost let out a whoop of joy. She impulsively hugged her parents, grinning foolishly. "Let's go, then."

Within two hours of their arrival in Cruces, the determined group of about twenty people were headed toward Panama City. A short distance out of Cruces, the trail began to climb, making the way more hazardous.

Selwin, looking over his shoulder, called back to his little band, "This is the old Spanish Trail. Balboa and Cortés used it to bring gold and pearls back to the east coast and ship them to Spain."

Very interesting, Fortune thought as she urged her donkey forward. She peered over the cliff, admiring the breathtaking vistas that were visible from the heights. Frequently the bluffs were steep rock for fifty to seventy feet, broken by ledges that were, at times, dotted with wildflowers and low shrubs. Other cliffs were sheer, falling away for hundreds of feet.

Her bottom was getting a little sore from being jounced around on the animal's bony back, but she said nothing. She was getting what she wanted.

Beau rode along in silence. He'd heard this trail turned rugged, but he hadn't understood just what that really meant. He and Patrick had taken one glance at each other and decided to continue. Neither of them wanted to return to New Orleans or Charleston. Their future lay in California.

He hadn't, however, considered that the trail would lead as high as it did. At times, he could hardly look over the edge. The path led dangerously close to disaster at several points, and Beau could hardly breathe. He couldn't say anything—couldn't speak, in fact—but perspiration broke out on his forehead and it had nothing to do with the heat.

Guiding his donkey as close to the mountain as possible, Beau tried very hard to maintain his dignity. Ever since he'd been trapped on top of a barn when he was a child, he'd hated heights. He simply couldn't get over that fear. Stay calm, he chanted to himself, concentrating on holding on to the donkey.

He chanced a look at a woman and man just ahead of him. They were so sick they could hardly stay on their mounts. Beau didn't think the two of them would make it to Panama City. Mrs. Sloan had surprised him. She and Amelia were taking turns nursing Franklin Sloan, who didn't look too well. Even as hot as it was, Franklin was wrapped in every piece of clothing he could get on, and chills still wracked his body.

Beau felt terrible. These people were in genuine distress, and here he was with his foolish fear. That thought did nothing to make him feel better—or to lessen his irrational fears.

That night they camped on a riverbank. Several of the people around the campfire were dreadfully ill. Fortune could hardly stand to look at them. She felt doubly sorry for Amelia. The poor girl didn't know what to do. Every chance Fortune got, she talked to Amelia and tried to re-affirm their friendship.

Fortune hadn't had much in common with Amelia before this trip, but now that had changed. When this journey was over, they'd spend hours laughing and remembering how awful these few days were. But for now they had to live each horrible moment as it came.

After a few minutes, she could stand no more. The sun was setting, casting long shadows where it reached the earth. She walked down the river a short distance, just out of sight of the group. She was tired of heat and rain and steam and insects and the uncomfortable saddle she had to use. Though she loved the adventure, she had to admit that it did present several problems she hadn't considered before she left Charleston.

She sat down on a rock overlooking the riverbank. Fortune peered over the edge, down into a calm pool of water. She could see several fish, darting and playing in the water near the edge, probably feeding on the bugs that landed on the surface. Just above where she sat, water splattered over the smooth rocks, forming a waterfall no more than ten feet high. Hidden among the verdant greens of the forest and the glimmering pools, the bubbling white water was beautiful.

Beau came and sat down. He leaned back against the rock behind her. "When you sit here, it makes you forget all the problems of the day, doesn't it?"

"Almost," she admitted, turning to look at him. "I just couldn't stand listening to all those sick people anymore and not being able to help. Wouldn't it be better just to die? I mean, if they really have yellow fever? Oh, it's awful."

"Probably. But all of them might not die." Beau shifted to make himself more comfortable and found himself closer to her. Her fragrance, even out here, was stirring. And, though they'd been on a difficult trail all day, she appeared to be cool and calm, as if she'd done nothing more than walk through town. "Some people live."

"I hope so." Fortune sighed and tossed a pebble into the pool. "Let's talk about something else."

"All right. What would you like to talk about?" he asked, gazing into her face. In the dim light, he could hardly see her features.

"Oh, I don't know. But I know I don't want to talk about sickness or death." Fortune couldn't look away. Even in the twilight, his eyes were compelling, almost drawing her toward him.

For a few seconds, neither of them said anything. And then Beau reached out and pulled her toward him. She melted into his arms, resting her head against his broad chest. Warmth spread through him, igniting every part of him with a new glow of sensation.

When he kissed her a moment later, he found that he was starving for the embrace, thirsting for her in a way that could only be satisfied by her kisses. His gentle caress changed into a more urgent need, filled with passion and promise.

Fortune felt that her body must be glimmering in the darkness with an inner light. The deepening kiss set ablaze desires that she'd never known existed, and she found herself hoping that the moment, the kiss, would never end. The effects of his caresses startled her so much that she drew back. Nothing in her life had ever prepared her for such an emotional and physical response to contact.

She stared at him, a wild look in her eyes. Beau wondered if he'd scared her, or if she was just awakening to the passions he'd known were simmering just beneath the cool demeanor most people saw.

After a moment, he was as frightened as she. What was happening between them? Something different, something unfamiliar, something complicated, seemed to be emerging from the friendship that they'd developed, something more, much more.

Eyes full of wonder, Fortune stammered, "I—I think... Oh, I have to go back...."

Beau nodded slowly in agreement. "I think that's the thing to do. For both of us."

The next morning, Fortune lay awake, staring at the canopy of trees over her head. The jungle was waking up for the day, and the sun was dappling the jungle floor with bright splotches of color. Today would be an arduous day of travel, she knew. Another day of heat and rain and steam and insects and all the other terrible things that made the jungle such an ordeal.

Most of the women had taken to wearing whatever lace or delicate shawls they possessed over their heads to keep the insects off. The Chantilly lace ones that Fortune had bought in New Orleans worked wonderfully. She, her mother and Jemima had devised a method of wearing them that protected them beautifully.

They would place the center of the shawl on top of their heads, cross the ends under their armpits, and have one of the others tie them in back. When they were worn thusly, even the most persistent mosquitoes couldn't find a way to get in. The arrangement made seeing more difficult, but they all felt that was a small price to pay for protection against insects.

Riding up the steep and rocky slopes, Fortune once again began to view the journey as an adventure. Her dreams of exotic places, luxuriant, verdant landscapes and dangerous expeditions were all coming true at once. She felt guilty about enjoying herself so much when others were so obviously ill, but she didn't allow that to interfere with her pleasure.

Occasionally she would glance back at Beau. He always seemed to be watching her. Color would rise in her cheeks, but she knew it was less noticeable now, since the sun had tanned her cheeks a little.

Beau studied Fortune as she rode along. Unlike some of the other women, she rode erect in the saddle. Her posture was perfect and showed her nice curves to perfection. As he rode, he felt a tightening in his groin that had become an ever-present nuisance when she was around. Rising in the saddle a little to relieve some of the pressure, he decided he'd have to look at something or someone else. But his gaze always returned to Fortune.

Fortune was exhausted, but she didn't complain. By the end of the day, Mr. Sloan and the other sick people could hardly stay on the donkeys they were riding. Something had to be done. When the group stopped for the evening, the men cut limbs large enough to make litters for the sick. Fortune and some of the other women donated thick woolen cloaks to be stretched between the limbs. They wouldn't be as comfortable as beds, but the sick people wouldn't be in danger of falling off their animals.

They started as early as possible the next morning and finally reached the highest point of their journey. If the climb up the winding mountain trails had been difficult, the way down on the other side was overwhelming. Fortune felt as if she was going to pitch headlong over the head of her donkey.

The litters worked reasonably well, but Fortune found the sound of the poles scraping on the rocks, combined with the retching and moaning of the sick, almost unbearable. She felt sorry for those who were related to the sickest people, for she knew that few of the people with the more advanced cases would live much longer.

Rain began to fall. With the trail as difficult as it already was, rain was something they didn't need. The pace slowed to a virtual crawl, but the travelers were too exhausted to complain.

Mrs. Sloan and Amelia were holding up remarkably well. Mrs. Sloan was apparently a powerful force in the Sloan family. Her directions were distinct, and they were followed to the letter. Amelia had begun to show some strength, as well, and Fortune felt good about that. She thought she might have had something to do with the change.

Letha, on the other hand, seemed to have withdrawn even further. Fortune privately felt that her mother would have been much better off returning to Charleston. Fortune also knew that her father would never have let that happen. He'd have gone, too.

Fortune had little opportunity to be with Beau. The men of the group were always looking for firewood, building some apparatus to conduct the sick more comfortably, or resting from sheer weariness.

The rain fell steadily now. Rivulets of water trickled down the rocky trail, gurgling like a small brook. Fortune saw lizards and frogs beginning to appear here and there, glistening with rain. Once she saw a snake, but she said nothing. If she mentioned it, her mother would be scared to death. Letha was terrified of snakes and was prone to panic every time she saw one.

The riders had little to do. Fortune's donkey followed the one in front of him, and her mother's followed Fortune's. And so it went, all the way from Selwin in front to the last man in the rear. There was nowhere else to go. The trail was no more than nine feet across at its widest point.

When they stopped to rest, Giles said, "Fortune, this afternoon, I'm going to ride in front of you."

"Why, Father?" she asked, rubbing her sore posterior.

"The way is very steep, and I think I should lead." He opened his arms wide and smiled broadly. "Have you ever seen anything so beautiful? If I didn't have land waiting for me in San Francisco, I'd stay right here. I'd find a little piece of land and start my farm here on the isthmus."

"Yes, sir." Fortune was amazed at his words. She let her father and mother pass, happy to hang back, because it meant Beau was lined up just behind her. She liked having her father in a good mood. It made her feel better, too.

In the wider spots, Beau rode alongside her and they relaxed a little, laughing at his jokes and pointing at the splendid scenery. Letha kept glaring back at them, but Fortune didn't care. She deserved a little fun on this trip. She noticed that Beau didn't really look at the panorama before them, but decided he was probably concerned about the others.

Then, somewhere behind them, a mule made a misstep on the rough pathway or slid on the rain-drenched steps. A trunk tumbled off and split open, and all manner of goods spilled onto the trail. "Gracious!" Fortune exclaimed, peering over her shoulder at the mess.

A glittering array of paraphernalia lay scattered in a pattern of brightness on the rocky path. One small cask had broken open, and coins were rolling down the path, faster than the donkeys could carry their passengers. Curses rose from a man toward the rear of the party, and everyone stopped for a few minutes.

Beau cut a length of vine while the man and his wife re-packed what they could find of their belongings. Then, Beau tied the vine around the trunk, securing it as well as was possible. Then the group moved forward again.

They reached a place where rough steps were cut into the stone. Some people, Fortune included, decided to walk their animals. Her bottom was already sore, and the jos-tling it was bound to receive here was more than she could bear right then.

Beau walked along with her. He felt a little better; he trusted his own feet more than the hooves of that damna-ble donkey. Besides, he could get a little closer to Fortune while they walked.

Fortune's parents refused to walk. Giles said, "We paid good money for these donkeys, and we're going to ride them."

Fortune said nothing. She enjoyed walking, even though the terrain was rough. Stones had fallen from the cliffs above, making the trail quite hazardous, so they had to pick their way carefully.

The way down was much steeper than the upward route—and much more dangerous. The group took longer, carefully leading their animals or riding gingerly. Fortune and Beau walked along quietly now, but the silence wasn't uncomfortable for her.

For Beau, it was. He'd taken the outer portion of the track, thus placing himself near the edge of a sheer cliff. When he glanced down, he could see the rocks below, sharp, uneven boulders that almost seemed to beckon to him. As the trail became more narrow, he fell behind Fortune; he was more comfortable walking close to the rising side of the trail.

Fortune thought her parents should dismount and walk. Though walking was more difficult, staying on a donkey's back was even more so. Letha refused flatly, and Giles agreed.

"These donkeys are accustomed to these mountain trails, daughter." Giles held his reins tightly, keeping control over the animal. "Don't worry about us. We'll be fine."

"Please, Father, for just a short way. This trail is too steep to ride," Fortune pleaded.

"No, we're too tired to walk." Giles was adamant.

Steeper and steeper the incline became. Fortune concentrated with all her might on keeping from falling. She judged every step carefully, for there were more and more rocks that had plunged onto the trail from above. Once, her donkey put a hoof down on a stone, which shot out over the edge of the cliff. She could hear it bounding off the boulders below. Before long, she could hardly move slowly enough, the way was so frightening.

"Damn!" Giles shouted as his mount stepped on a stone. The animal stumbled, and its knees buckled beneath it.

Fortune's head jerked up. She saw her father tumble forward over the donkey's head. He rolled perilously close to the edge of the cliff—and then he fell over. His screams, mingled with Fortune's, reverberated through the valley. Then there was a thud when he struck the rocks below headfirst, and his body crumpled and lay still.

Letha shrieked and nearly fell from her mount. Fortune hurried forward, followed closely by Beau. She steadied her mother and nearly ran to the edge of the cliff. *Oh, God, please let him be all right.*

She could see him, about forty or fifty feet below, lying on a large boulder. Blood poured out from several places on his body and head, and he lay with his neck twisted to one side and his left leg curled beneath him at an odd angle.

Beau grabbed Fortune to keep her from scrambling down the slope after her father. Patrick held Letha, preventing

her from going to the edge. By this time, Selwin Allen had
tethered his mount and rushed back to the site of the accident.

Beau looked around at the group. Something had to be
done. Someone had to find out if Giles was still alive.
"Does someone have a rope?"

A murmur went through the little knot of people. Nobody seemed to have one. Finally Fortune looked up at
him. Her voice was choked and strained. "Father...in his
trunk."

Beau and one of the other men found the rope and secured it to a thick-trunked tree. Then Beau glanced around.
Everybody seemed to be waiting for him to descend the
cliff. He wished someone else would volunteer, but nobody did. Every cell in his body screamed as he tried to
prepare himself for what he had to do.

He was about to tie the rope around his waist when Fortune snatched the rope from his hand and said, "I'll go.
He's my father."

"No!" Letha screamed, her voice ringing through the
air. "No, you mustn't."

"I'll do it, Fortune." Beau took the rope from her and
secured it around his waist. He then walked along the edge
of the cliff, mentally chastising himself for attempting the
impossible. There seemed to be no easy way, no moder-
ately easy way. A tall tree rose almost to the level of the
trail. If someone could lower him that far, he could climb
down the tree and make his way on foot from there.

Sliding over the ledge of the cliff was the most difficult
thing Beau had ever done. Perspiration covered his face,
dripping into his eyes, as he was lowered farther and farther down. Finally he caught hold of the top of the tree and
began to climb toward the ledge where Giles lay, unmov-
ing. Working his way down the large tree wasn't easy, but
it was easier than the cliff would have been. His palms were
so wet that his hands could hardly grip the rope.

By the time he reached the lowest limb of the tree, his
rope had about run out. He untied it and gently lowered
himself to the ground. Taking a few seconds to catch his
breath, he gazed up. Above him he could see several peo-

ple looking down from the trail. It looked so far away that he began to wonder if he'd ever have the courage to climb back up.

For now, he had to summon up the courage to traverse the distance to Giles. Beau walked over as close as he could get to the place where the injured man lay. Even from this distance, Beau could discern no movement. The rock that held Giles's body was down a steep slope, about another ten feet.

Beau looked for a way down that wouldn't be too difficult, but there seemed to be none. Inhaling deeply, he started the final part of his descent. He crawled along trying to find secure footing. It seemed to him that the last part of the trip took much longer than the first.

Fortune's gaze was glued on Beau. Shock had set in, numbing her to the sight below, though she realized Beau was in grave danger himself. The slope he was transversing wasn't as steep as the first, but it was dangerous. She realized she'd been holding her breath, and couldn't remember for how long. Her lungs ached, but her heart ached even more.

Her father must surely be dead.

And now Beau was in danger. Being lowered down the cliff wasn't a safe thing to do, but he'd volunteered. Fortune knew he'd done it for her. If he fell . . . if anything happened to him . . . she would never forgive herself.

Her father was dead. She knew it without being told. Beau's risking his life wouldn't change that. There was no way he could have survived that fall. Suddenly, what had been a marvelous adventure had become her worst nightmare.

Nausea welled up in her, and she choked on the bitter taste of bile. She had to be strong, for somewhere behind her, her mother was watching. Silently mourning, even before the pronouncement was made, Fortune turned her concern to her mother.

There was nothing at all she could do for her father.

Nothing at all.

Chapter Nine

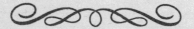

Beau's foot slipped. He slid the last few feet and came to rest beside Giles Anthony. Beau caught his breath for a second as he looked at the prostrate form.

He could tell that Giles's body was broken in many places. Even if he was still alive, they'd never get him back up the cliff alive. Beau caught one of Giles's limp wrists and felt for some sign of a pulse. There was none. He looked for a sign of breathing, even the subtlest sign of a rising and falling chest. There was none.

Giles Anthony was dead.

He wondered how he could turn and signal to those who were waiting. How could he tell them that Giles was dead without breaking Fortune's heart? And how could he tell her that her father was dead without breaking her spirit?

Just beyond where Giles lay there was a grassy place. The grass probably covered solid rock, though. He looked up at the expectant faces above him and shook his head slowly.

In the same instant, he heard a shrill scream. There was only silence from Fortune. He longed to be up there, comforting her, but he had a job to do here.

He went over to the grass and tried to dig a ways with his fingers. The dirt was fairly soft, so he took a stick and plunged it into the earth several times until he had a small hole. So far, he'd hit no rock.

Beau called up to the men on the trail above. "Send down a shovel." This would be Giles Anthony's final resting place.

He waited for a moment and then saw Patrick, shovels strapped across his back, coming over the edge and down the tree, just as Beau had. When he reached Beau's side, the two men began digging.

Fortune held her mother as they sat on a thick log that had fallen beside the trail. Nola Bell paced back and forth, going occasionally to the ledge to peer over. Boaz sat there, tears streaming down his face. Giles Anthony had been good to him. The bond between the two men was strong.

Letha's wailing hadn't ceased since Beau had given the signal that Giles was dead. Fortune could do little except embrace her mother and utter words that sounded meaningless. The world seemed to be crashing in around them, and they had no protection.

Hazel Sloan came over to them. "Mrs. Anthony, I can't tell you how sorry we are." She looked back at the litter where her husband lay. "There are some ways of dying that are better than others. The Lord works in mysterious ways."

"Thank you, Mrs. Sloan," Fortune said, when her mother remained silent. "That's very kind of you. Especially considering your own problems."

"Lord, child, we're all in this together. Who we were doesn't matter anymore, I guess." Hazel sat down with a sigh. A wry smile touched her lips. "It's who we are now that counts."

Fortune looked at the edge of the cliff. She knew that somebody had to go down and say a few words over her father's grave. "Mrs. Sloan, will you sit with my mother for a few minutes?"

"Certainly, child."

Fortune found Jemima and asked her to go to Letha. "I have something to do."

She watched as Jemima went and sat by Letha. The two ladies were busy comforting Letha as Fortune walked away. She found her Bible and put it in her pocket. Then she went to the ledge. "Mr. Allen, lower me down, please."

Selwin gaped at her. "Miss Anthony, you don't realize how dangerous—"

"I realize that I'm going down that cliff with or without your help." Fortune pulled the rope back up and began to tie it around her waist. "If you'd be kind enough to help me, I'd appreciate it."

Several men came forward and helped to lower her to the ground. Fortune dangled in the air like the clapper on a bell for a few moments and then touched the top of the tree.

Beau looked up at that moment. "Good God, Patrick! Look! Fortune, no!" he yelled, cupping his hands around his mouth. "Stop her, Selwin!"

"No, Beau. Let me come." She hurried on down, making her way from limb to limb until she reached the ground. She untied the rope and then followed the same route Beau and Patrick had. She scooted on her behind down the face of the slope that had given Beau so much trouble, clutching at the rocks with her hands when she felt herself slipping.

By the time she reached her father, her fingers were bleeding. Despite the warm sunlight, his body was already growing cold. "Oh, Father," she whispered, touching his face gently. "I'm so sorry. If I'd made you get off that donkey, this wouldn't have happened."

"You couldn't have forced him, Fortune. He was his own man to the end." Beau came up behind her, knelt, and put his arms around her. "This isn't your fault. It was an accident."

"I know, but I encouraged him to come on this trip." Fortune felt tears sting her eyes as her guilt began to flow freely. "He knew that I hated Charleston. He . . ."

"He wanted to leave just as badly as you did." Beau took her arm and helped her to her feet. "Come over here and sit where it's a little softer."

Fortune walked over to the grassy place where Patrick was still digging. She studied the spot for a moment. Her father would have loved it. His final resting place would be on a lovely knoll that overlooked the most beautiful scenery she'd ever seen. "Is the dirt deep enough?"

"Yes, it seems to be," Beau answered. By now, he and Patrick had dug several feet into the soft dirt. "It looks like this place was once a little hollow in the rocks. Over time, dust and dirt blew in and grass and flowers began to grow. The earth is really soft.''

Watching them, Fortune marveled at how easily the shovels bit into the ground. Before long, the hole was deep enough. She stood, walked a few feet away and looked out across the valley while Beau and Patrick moved Giles's body. She spotted a vine that had lovely blooms all along its tendrils. Pulling gently, she unearthed the root and took it back to her father's grave. Beau and Patrick were filling it in.

Tears streamed down her face as she began to read from her Bible. "The Lord is my shepherd; I shall not want . . ." After the psalm, she read the Lord's Prayer.

When the men were finished, she took the vine and pressed its roots into the earth, covering them with a little more dirt. "There. He'd like that."

The three of them went back to the tree, where the rope was still hanging. Beau secured the rope around her waist, and then Patrick yelled to Selwin to begin pulling gently.

As Selwin and the other men took up the slack in the rope, Fortune began to climb. It had been a long time since she'd climbed a tree, but she'd done it many times as a child. When she reached the top of the tree, the men pulled her up and over the edge of the cliff, untied the rope and dropped it again for Beau and Patrick.

"You go on ahead, Patrick," Beau said. "I'll wait."

Beau watched his friend go up the tree and them up the cliff. Fear was already gripping his stomach, twisting and wrenching until the pain was almost unbearable. "You'll be all right," he told himself as the rope fell back to him. "You came down, you can go up."

He practically felt his way from one limb to the next. Perspiration clouded his vision until he could hardly see. His heart raced, pounding with the furious thunder of a thousand drums all beating a different rhythm. After banging his head twice, he wiped the perspiration from his eyes and began to climb again.

Then came the biggest test. Could he release his hold on the tree and swing free for the final distance? "You can do

it,'' he muttered, closing his eyes and opening his hand to
let go of the tree. ''You can do it. You can do it.''

And then he was over the top. He lay there, almost hugging the ground, for a few seconds, his heart still pounding and his chest still heaving. Gradually he got to his knees
and then to his feet.

He walked over to Fortune. Jemima was bandaging her
hands. He sat down and waited until Jemima finished her
task and left. ''Fortune, my dear, I'm so sorry. I wish I
could have done something.''

Fortune looked at him through eyelashes that were separated and spiked by tears. She hugged him impulsively.
''You've done more than enough. How will I ever be able
to repay you?''

''There's nothing to repay.'' Beau stood and smiled down
at her. ''We'll talk later. I think we're going to make camp
just ahead. Nobody really feels like going on, and it's getting too late to see very well, anyway.''

Fortune sat there, feeling numb all over. How she missed
her father already. It wasn't fair. Giles Anthony had
worked, almost as hard as the slaves, his whole life for a
man—his own father—who had never loved or appreci-
ated him. Fortune had loved him. She had adored him. She
remembered days spent in the springtime sun with him,
riding in front of him on his big chestnut stallion as he supervised the planting of the fields.

Her first horse had been chosen for her by her father.
Fortune recalled climbing into her own saddle for the first
time, with her father leading the horse around the lot until
she was comfortable. She remembered the first time she'd
been thrown, how he'd lifted her gently back into the saddle and made her ride again.

Fortune thought of the light in her father's eyes when
he'd seen her in her first ball gown, of his proud words.

''You'll be the belle of the ball, daughter.'' He'd hugged
her, and then scolded her teasingly. ''And I'll not be having you falling in love with some wastrel. The man that
marries my daughter will be a man of the land, a man who
knows the value of the earth under his feet, a man who can

keep my daughter as she's meant to be kept. And he'll adore you from the moment he sees you.''

They'd laughed together. He'd finally relented and said that he wanted Fortune to marry for love. ''If you love the man, then Giles Anthony will be proud to call him son-in-law.''

Fortune and her father had laughed together many times. He had had a zest for life that he had passed on to her, along with his quick wit and sense of humor. He'd passed on his love of the land, his keen ability to judge character, so many things.

Tears stung her eyes as she grieved for the kind man who'd met such an untimely death. But, she asked herself, when is a good time to die? Her father would never have questioned the time of his dying. He had been a religious man who believed that when it was his time to go, he'd go happily.

He'd set out on this journey with high hopes for their future. He'd wanted a new beginning, a place where he wouldn't have to live with the stigma of being a second son, an unloved son.

Fortune loved him with all her heart. If she could have chosen a father, she would have chosen Giles Anthony.

And now he was dead. She'd envisioned many problems they might encounter on this trip, but this hadn't been one of them. Fortune would have to make the decisions now. Her mother couldn't make up her mind about simple issues, such as what gown to wear or what to serve at a supper.

Fortune would have to assume responsibility for both of them. What would they do? How did this affect their claim on the land in California? How would her mother live without her father?

So many questions. So few answers.

Fortune wanted to scream. The atmosphere around the campfire was somber that night. The sound of moaning and groaning was everywhere, as those who were sick were growing ever more ill. Letha had been crying and wailing for hours. Jemima and Nola Bell were trying to comfort her, but their ministrations seemed to have no effect.

Fortune had to get away. She walked a short distance from the campfire and sat down. She didn't want to go too far. The jungle was dangerous at night.

After a few minutes, Amelia came and sat with her. "You don't mind, do you?" she asked tentatively.

"No," Fortune answered, feeling all the fatigue of grief combine with the stretching and straining of unused muscles to make her wearier than she'd ever been. "Please do. I need the company," she lied.

Amelia perked up. "I thought you might. I...I'm really sorry about your father." Amelia glanced away, but Fortune saw her wipe away a tear that had slid down her cheek. "I guess my father won't... I mean, he's awfully sick."

Fortune put her arm around Amelia. "I know. There just seems to be nothing we can do about some things."

"Mummy says he's going to die," Amelia stated flatly, staring straight ahead. "I don't know what we'll do."

A wry smile broke across Fortune's face. "I don't know what we'll do, either. We have a great deal in common."

"Well, I guess I'd better go back. Mummy will be looking for me." Amelia hugged Fortune and rose. "I'll see you later."

Fortune nodded and buried her head in her hands. Poor Amelia. She had to stand by and watch her father die. At least for her the tragedy had come suddenly, without the agony of watching the event drag on for days or weeks.

Death was kinder to some than to others.

"Fortune," Beau said quietly, "may I sit with you for a while?"

"Of course," Fortune answered without thinking. "I'm not very good company, I'm afraid." She smiled. "I even bored poor Amelia so badly that she hardly seated herself before she jumped up to leave."

Beau chuckled and sat beside Fortune. Even in bad times, she still had a sense of humor. "Well, I don't think that's exactly true, but I'm glad she's gone."

"Me, too," Fortune admitted. "I'm trying very hard to be her friend. She really needs one, especially now that her father's dying."

"What about you? Do you need a friend?" Beau asked, stretching his legs out before him and flexing his toes as well as he could in his boots.

Fortune gazed at him. He was so handsome, but his greatest quality was his generosity of spirit. He'd gone down that cliff almost without concern for his own safety. None of the other men had seemed likely to volunteer. He was a friend. A good friend. She smiled thinly. "I have a friend. A good friend."

Beau grinned. "I was hoping you'd say that."

"I don't feel much like talking just now, but I'd appreciate your company." Fortune plucked a tiny lavender flower from the ground and began to twirl it between her fingers.

"Tell me what's concerning you." Beau watched her. She was still very upset. Her mother seemed to have completely lost control. Fortune would have to make all the decisions now, at least for the near future.

"Oh, many things." Fortune didn't know where to begin. She didn't even know if she wanted to voice her concerns. Saying them aloud lent them an air of importance that she didn't want to give them yet.

"What things, Fortune?" he asked, sliding his arm around her shoulders. "I want to know what's bothering you. Friends don't have secrets from each other."

Friends. The word was warm, and filled with kindness. Fortune laid her head on his shoulder, allowing the tears that rimmed her eyes to well up and fall. Could she stand kindness now? From him? Yes. Yes. "Things like, where will we go? Will we still get our land? That sort of thing. Nagging, selfish little things that intrude when I should be comforting my mother."

"Nagging little things have a way of intruding, no matter what's going on." He swatted a large bug that was buzzing around his face. "Like all these insects."

Fortune smiled. "I could lend you a piece of Chantilly to wrap around your head, if you like."

Beau chuckled. There was that sense of humor, even at such a sad time. "I don't think that would really suit me, do you?"

"Well, I'm not sure. I've always thought that a little lace will complement any outfit." She looked him up and down, nodding. "I think maybe a touch at the hem of your trousers, and maybe your sleeves."

"I'll let you know when I need a tailor, thank you just the same." Beau laughed and hugged her close. "We'd better be going back. I'd hate for your mother to think that I'd taken you off to do something horrible."

Fortune's thoughts returned to her mother. "I don't think she'll even notice that I'm gone. She's grieving so deeply that she sees nobody. She may never get over this."

"Were she and your father very close?"

"Oh, I guess so. They never argued, if that's what you mean." Fortune considered the question. It was one she'd asked herself several times. "There always seemed to be something standing between them. My father adored her, but Mother never... I don't even know how to say this. I don't even know exactly what I think." Fortune paused for a few seconds to gather her thoughts. She reflected on her childhood, on the joyous times and the sad times. "Mother never could let go of her feelings. She always kept them bottled up inside."

"She seems rather emotional right now," Beau observed, studying Letha, who continued to weep prodigiously.

"You're right about that." Fortune, too, was watching her mother, who sat some distance away. Letha's eyes were swollen, still pouring out tears, but when she spoke, her words were not of Giles Anthony, but for herself.

"What am I going to do?" she asked, raising her wet eyes heavenward. "What can I do now?"

"She'll get over it," Beau said, twirling a tendril of Fortune's hair around his finger. It felt like the finest silk.

"I don't know," Fortune said, thinking of her mother's heartrending words. "I just don't think she will. She's a hard person to understand. I never have been able to understand her, and I don't think my father ever did. He and

I were much closer. Mother always kept this... this distance between us. I know she loves me, but... I can't explain how I feel.''

Beau sat there for a few minutes more, feeling perfectly miserable. He really cared for Fortune, and it nearly broke his heart to see her in such pain. She put up a strong front, but he knew she was hurting. For the first time in his life, he felt completely helpless.

He wanted to cuddle her, to pull her into his arms and tell her that all of this would go away like a bad dream, but he couldn't lie to her. Beau could do nothing more than sit and listen to her when she wanted to talk, occasionally adding a comment of his own.

"I remember, when I was a little girl," Fortune began with a smile that teased her lips, "Father took me down to see a newborn colt."

"There's nothing prettier than a colt," Beau said, nodding his head. Except maybe Fortune, he added to himself.

"I must have been no more than three or four years old." Fortune sighed with pleasure at the memory. "That colt, we called him Bumbler because he could hardly walk. He sort of jolted along. Anyway, he waddled over to me. We looked each other in the eye and both fell in love."

"You were the same height?"

"Exactly. I think that's why I liked him so much." Fortune gave a little laugh. "He tried to kiss me, well, I thought that was what he was doing. Anyway, he knocked me down. I cried, and it startled him. He fell, too."

Beau laughed at the image her words created. "You scared him as badly as he scared you, I guess."

"I suppose. When he fell, I started to laugh." Fortune's eyes clouded with tears as she remembered how her father had reacted. "My father, the only one left standing, decided to play our game, too. He pretended to fall."

"That was kind of him." Beau chuckled at the thought of Giles pretending to fall for the amusement of his little girl. "Then what?"

"That was a bad thing for him to do," Fortune said, raising her eyebrows mysteriously.

"Why? It sounds sweet to me."

"Well, it was," Fortune admitted, laughing out loud. "Except that he fell into a pile of—"

"Never mind," Beau interrupted, laughing out loud. "I understand."

Beau's laughter was infectious. Fortune remembered how her father had loved to laugh. "You know, Father wouldn't want us to be sad. When I was little, he was always laughing, even when..."

"Even when what?" Beau asked, beginning to get his laughter under control.

"Oh, even when my grandfather was hard on him." Fortune couldn't reveal how badly her grandfather had treated her father. She couldn't betray her father that way. He had always loved his father, whatever that grouchy old man said or did.

"You lived with your grandfather?" Beau asked, beginning to understand why the Anthonys had undertaken this arduous journey.

"Yes. My father ran the plantation for him." Fortune thought of the many wasted years when her father had been a young man, when he could have been building up his own place instead of filling in for his brother.

"What happened? I mean, why did you leave?"

"My uncle returned." Fortune looked at her fingers. They were poking through the bandage Jemima had made. Her palms ached, as did the first joint of several fingers. "He is the older of the two sons."

"I see," Beau said, understanding dawning in his voice. A second son, doing all the work while the elder brother played somewhere else—probably Europe, if he knew the Charlestonians as well as he thought he did. "Why didn't your grandfather buy a second plantation? Many of the planters around Charleston do."

Fortune thought about it. She knew of the custom, but it had never been discussed in front of her. "I can't really answer that, except that my grandfather was saving everything for Uncle Roger."

"Well, I think we'd better rejoin the others." Beau knew that Fortune needed rest, particularly after her ordeal today. "We'll talk again soon, my friend."

My friend. Fortune allowed the words to flow over her like a warm tide. She liked the feeling they gave her. He'd once called her "darling," but "my friend" made her even happier. Many men called women sweet names out of habit, though she didn't think Beau would, but rarely did they call a woman a friend. Fortune really liked that.

When Fortune finally convinced her mother to lie down, Letha did so with a moan. She had, apparently, cried until no more tears would come. Fortune lay there beside her mother, listening to her occasional sniffles, and then to the gentle snore that told her that her mother was asleep at last. Occasionally an animal cried in the distance, and as always, the night was filled with the sound of cicadas.

Fortune rose earlier than usual the next morning. She wanted to go back to the spot where her father was buried. Walking carefully, she made her way back up the trail to the point where he'd fallen off the cliff. It was still too dark to see much, but the stars were beginning to fade.

She sat near the edge so that she could see his grave when the sun rose. While she was waiting, Beau joined her.

"Good morning," he whispered, trying not to frighten her. "You're up rather early."

"I couldn't sleep." Fortune tucked her feet beneath her and pulled her shawl close. The morning air was cooler here than in the valley below. "I wanted to watch the sunrise the way my father will see it every morning forever."

"That's a nice thought," Beau said, sitting next to her. "The ground's a little damp. Did you bring something to sit on?"

"No, the dampness doesn't matter." Fortune glanced at him. The gray predawn light didn't show much, but she could see his profile. She liked the strength she saw in him. His square jaw gave one an impression of power and an intense will. "Thank you, Beau." She leaned over and kissed his cheek.

He slid his arm around her and sat beside her for a few seconds before speaking again. "What was that for?"

"For everything. For being who you are, I guess." Fortune couldn't really have explained her feelings. All she knew was that she'd never felt this way about anybody before.

"Well, in that case, you're very welcome." Beau hugged her close and leaned his cheek against her hair. She hadn't braided it yet, and it felt like satin against his skin. He wished she wouldn't bother with the braids, but he'd never met a woman who would willingly go against the current fashion.

As he considered that idea, he thought that Fortune might just be one who would flout the fashionmongers. She wasn't like any woman he'd ever met.

They sat there, not speaking, until the sun rose. Fortune enjoyed the contact, the companionship of the few moments with Beau, the moments away from the complications and anguish that would return with the sunlight. For now, the sunrise was enough. Subtle blues, purples and mauves at first, and then the brilliant golden globe burst over the horizon into the cloudless sky.

Giles Anthony's final resting place would be the scene of spectacular sunrises forever. Fortune felt a quiet peace settle over her, glad she'd come to witness the first of her father's eternal dawns.

And she was happy that Beau had been with her, too.

Chapter Ten

When Fortune and Beau returned to the campsite, they were greeted by a new onslaught of tears and wailing. Franklin Sloan had died during the night. Hazel Sloan, apparently trying desperately to maintain her dignity, sniffed into a lace handkerchief.

Amelia was sobbing like a brokenhearted child, as was Letha. Fortune was drawn to both, hardly knowing where she could do the most good. Jemima, who was growing heavier with child, went from one to the other, comforting as best she could.

Fortune went first to Letha. She talked quietly with her mother for a few moments. "Mother, Mrs. Sloan was very kind yesterday to leave her husband, who was so very ill, and come over to speak to you. I think you should summon your courage and do the same for her."

Letha looked up at her daughter. "And what makes you think I feel like going to talk to her? My husband died yesterday."

"Yes, Mother, but Mrs. Sloan's loss was more recent. Father wouldn't want us to neglect someone—"

"Leave me alone." Letha turned her back on Fortune. "You never loved your father."

"Mother!" Fortune exclaimed, hurt through to the center of her being by her mother's accusation. "You can't mean what you're saying!"

"Must I repeat myself? Leave me alone with my grief." Letha promptly sat down and lowered her head. Within a few seconds, she was sobbing.

Fortune squatted beside her mother and embraced her. "Mother, don't shut me out. I'm in pain, too." Trying desperately to decide what she could say or do to help her mother, Fortune sighed and willed her own tears not to fall. "I'm going to speak to Mrs. Sloan. I'll try to explain that you're—"

"Don't give that old buffalo any kind words for me. She's a self-righteous ninny, and I—"

"Mother, don't say such things. You're distraught." Fortune signaled for Nola Bell to take over. "Keep her still, and don't do anything to get her excited. She's hysterical."

Fortune reluctantly left her mother and went to speak to Mrs. Sloan and Amelia. She found them talking to Jemima. As she approached, the conversation slowed, leaving her an opening. "Mrs. Sloan, Amelia . . ." She embraced each woman. "I can't tell you how sorry I am. This is . . . such a tragedy. If I can do anything to help either of you over this grief-stricken time, please ask me."

"You're very kind and thoughtful, Fortune," Hazel said, hugging her. "Amelia and I appreciate it."

"My mother is . . . well, she's not herself, and . . ."

"I understand completely," Hazel assured Fortune.

Fortune tried to smile politely. "I know that you and Amelia have many fond memories of Mr. Sloan. In the future, those pleasant memories will comfort you, even as my own memories of my father have begun to comfort me."

"You're an intelligent girl, Fortune, and you're absolutely right." Hazel began to sniff into her handkerchief. "God will provide for us."

"Well, I must return to my mother. Don't forget to call on me if I can do anything for you." Fortune smiled again and walked back across the encampment. She heard Beau and Patrick talking with Selwin about disposing of Mr. Sloan's body.

"I tell you, we've got to burn the body, and everything he touched." Selwin removed his hat and wiped his forehead with his sleeve. "That yellow fever is contagious. It'll have all us puking black if we don't do something now."

Fortune shivered. What a horrible way to die.

* * *

The women waited while the men burned Franklin Sloan's body. Hazel and Amelia stood with Fortune, watching the almost primitive rite. Fortune felt strange, as if some panic had taken hold of the travelers, as if the end were near for all of them. She tried to think of pleasanter things, but the idea still hovered in the recesses of her mind.

When the travelers started down the trail again, everyone but Letha walked. She refused, no matter how hard Fortune pleaded with her. Finally Selwin tied her to the animal to keep her from toppling off.

Fortune walked beside Beau. Her mother no longer noticed anything going on around her, or perhaps she pretended not to. Boaz led Letha's donkey and his own, while Nola Bell walked with her donkey and Giles's, as well as the remaining pack animals.

The way was still very steep, and Fortune watched her mother and her donkey very carefully. She didn't want to lose both her parents in two days.

Around noon, the path flattened out a little, and they were able to ride once again. For a long while, the only sounds that could be heard were the mules' and donkeys' hooves on the stone pathway, and the moans and cries of the sick.

Rain began to fall, not quite as heavily as it had for the past few days, but enough to be a nuisance. Fortune wondered if the rain would eventually cause her hair to grow moldy. Everything else was beginning to.

Several of the people behind her had begun to quarrel. As well as she could make out, they were arguing about who should go in front of whom when the trail narrowed again. Others joined in the discussion, and pretty soon the entire group was involved except for Fortune and her mother and Beau and Patrick. Even Mrs. Sloan shouted at one of the men—just when the woman had shown signs of being human, Fortune thought.

After a while they quieted down, but Fortune noticed that several of them were scowling as if they were still angry. She leaned over toward Beau. "What do you think is wrong?"

"I don't know," he answered truthfully. "I thought we'd all been getting along so well."

"Do you suppose it's the weather? Or maybe everyone's tired." Fortune tried to think of a reason everyone would be easily irritated.

Beau nodded and looked back over his shoulder. A rumble was starting in the back again. "I'd say both. We've been on a difficult trail. We've had two deaths. Either it's scorching or raining or you feel like you're being steamed alive."

Fortune was thrilled when they began to see signs of civilization again. The houses they saw were hardly more than huts, but they signified that the group was coming into Panama City. "Oh, Lord, I'd pay ten dollars for a hot bath."

Beau chuckled and thought, I'd pay a hundred to watch you take it. But what was he thinking? They were friends, nothing more. Friends didn't think of each other in that way.

He was suddenly glad to be reaching Panama City, too. But his reasons were entirely different. They'd been on the trail too long. He needed some feminine companionship that wouldn't have any strings attached.

Having been grouped with so few people, it was natural for him to become attached to them, even particularly attached to some of them. He understood that. He was comfortable with Fortune. He enjoyed her sense of humor. And right now he felt sorry for her because she'd just lost her father. That was all. Nothing more. It was perfectly logical.

The little band rode into the center of town. There were no hotels, as Selwin had finally admitted. But there must be some place for them to go to find rooms for their short stay, Beau reasoned.

He was wrong. Selwin reported that they would all have to find their own lodgings. Beau and Patrick left the group to begin their search.

Fortune watched him go. If her father were here, he would find a place for her and her mother to stay, but she had to assume that responsibility. "Nola Bell, you and

Boaz stay here with Mother and our things. I'll find us a place to stay."

"Lawsy, do hurry. I'll sleep in a barn if'n it don't leak," Nola Bell said, folding her arms across her chest.

Feeling a little abashed at having to go from door to door, Fortune nonetheless did. She dismounted and began to walk. After knocking on more than ten doors and being refused, she felt like screaming. Had these people no pity?

Finally, she encountered a young woman walking along a narrow trail that led out of town. *"Señorita!"* she called, running to catch up with the woman. *"Por favor."* Fortune had almost exhausted her Spanish vocabulary. "I . . . my family and I need lodging."

The woman smiled. "I speak American, some little."

"You do!" Fortune exclaimed, hugging the woman impulsively. "Please, my mother and I need a place to stay for a few days. My father was killed on the way over the mountain from Cruces."

"I have place. Very small."

"Oh, thank the Lord!" Fortune hugged her again. "I'm Fortune."

The young woman looked puzzled. "No charge fortune."

"I . . ." Fortune tried to recall the words of introduction in Spanish, but failed. She pointed to her chest. "Me, Fortune. My name is Fortune."

"Oh, sí. I am called Elena."

"You don't know how delighted I am to meet you." Fortune glanced around. "Where is your house? How much will you charge?"

"We go get mama." Elena headed back toward town. "Bring mama, too."

Fortune didn't know exactly what Elena meant, whether she was referring to her own mother or to Fortune's. All she knew was they were headed back toward Letha, Nola Bell and Boaz.

Fortune and Elena collected the small group waiting at the center of town. Elena rode Giles's donkey, and they made quick work of getting to her house.

When they arrived, Fortune almost cried. It was little more than a hut. The bamboo sides and thatched roof looked almost too insubstantial to remain standing much longer. Elena led them inside. There was a small room that served as a kitchen, dining room and sitting room. Off the sitting area was a tiny bedroom. In the back, off the kitchen, was another tiny room used to store odd furniture, food and other possessions.

Elena indicated the tiny storage room. "This you place. We make beds for you."

It was hardly big enough for one person, much less four. Fortune decided immediately that she and her mother would have to share the room. She'd have to find other accommodations for the servants. "Elena, do you have another building? A barn or something for Nola Bell and Boaz?"

"More rooms?" Elena asked.

"Yes, we need room for them, too." Fortune didn't know how much English Elena understood, and was therefore hampered by the language barrier.

"Come. Come." Elena walked out of the kitchen into the back yard.

There was a small building there, with a little fence around it. Fortune looked at it with trepidation. It looked like a chicken coop, and she hated the idea of putting her servants into that kind of place.

They went inside. In spite of its shabby exterior, the inside was fairly clean.

"No chicken," Elena explained with a shrug. "One day, have chicken."

"Lawsy, when I said I'd sleep in a barn, I didn't know what I was sayin'." Nola Bell shook her head and laughed out loud. "Boaz, git yo'sef to unloadin' all them trunks. We's got our work cut out for us."

Fortune walked back into the house with Elena. The young woman was beautiful, dark and exotic-looking. Her black eyes gleamed with interest and intelligence. She was apparently a native of Panama, probably of Spanish descent. "Elena, how did you learn to speak American?"

"Sisters." Elena smiled broadly, showing tiny, even white teeth. "Holy sisters."

The two young women set about cleaning the storage room while Nola Bell and Boaz unloaded the trunks. As they worked, Fortune discovered that Elena spoke fairly good English. She said a silent prayer of thanks, because with everything else being so difficult, she didn't need the additional problem of a language barrier.

By the end of the day, the little room was cleared of most of Elena's belongings and the Anthonys were moved in. Nola Bell and Fortune made mattresses of fragrant grass that Boaz and Elena had gathered. Letha sat on a mat in the sitting room and continued to cry.

Fortune didn't know what to do for her mother. Words were no help, and neither was any other form of comfort. When the mattresses were made, Letha moved from the sitting room to the tiny bedroom that she and Fortune would occupy and lay down.

Fortune decided to try to make her mother as comfortable as possible. After all, this was only temporary, and in any case it was much better than the trail. She sat down by Letha and put her arms around her. "Mother, please stop crying. This is fine. It's clean and dry and—"

"Fortune Anthony, we were not born to live in such squalor. I refuse to associate with these heathens." Letha glowered at Fortune. "Filth. That's what it is. What will Mrs. Sloan say?"

"Mother, I doubt Mrs. Sloan will say anything. If she's found a place to live, I don't think it can be any better than this one." Fortune was weary, bone-weary, but she knew that she had to remain strong for her mother's sake.

"Whatever you think best, Fortune. I'll leave you to judge. You seem to know everything." Letha lay down with her back to Fortune. "Your father wouldn't have made me stay here if he'd lived. So long ago... He was so handsome...."

Fortune didn't understand what her mother was saying. So long ago? What could she be referring to? Handsome? Her father hadn't been a bad-looking man, but he hadn't had the breathtakingly good looks of someone like Beau. She thought her mother might be dreaming.

Talking to Elena made Fortune feel better. She told her new friend about how her father had died on the trail. "He so wanted to see California. This move was the answer to his every prayer. I'm sorry it ended badly for him. He was a good man."

"Is better he die fast," Elena said. "Death kinder to some."

"Yes, several people have yellow fever. Do you know what that is?" Fortune asked, wondering if it would frighten Elena.

"I know. Is bad. Many die."

"Well, one is already dead. Several others are lingering." Fortune leaned back against the thatched wall of the little hut and felt it give a little. She bent forward to keep from falling through the thatch.

A short while later, Elena fixed a plate of fruit, beans and bread. They ate hungrily, for it was much better than the hardtack and jerky they'd had to eat most of the time on the trail. Letha, however, ate nothing.

Fortune and Elena settled on a price for the room and the chicken house. Fortune noticed that Elena slept on a hammock instead of a mattress, and she asked about it.

"Have only one." Elena smiled cheerfully. "Can buy in village."

Thinking that a hammock would be better than sleeping on a grass mattress on a dirt floor, Fortune agreed. "Tomorrow we'll go into the village. I need to find out when the ship is coming."

Fortune slept well that night. In fact, she slept from almost the moment she lay down until well after dawn. Her last thoughts were of Beau. She fell asleep with his image swimming before her eyes.

The next morning, she crept, shamefaced, into the kitchen, where Elena was grinding corn in a stone basin. "Oh, my, I slept late. I'm usually up very early."

"I up early, too. Much to do." Elena finished making her cornmeal. "Eat. Go to village."

Fortune agreed. She and Elena, along with Nola Bell and Boaz, ate some corn cakes, but Letha refused. Elena had a cow with a calf, so they had fresh milk.

"Nola Bell," Fortune said, thinking about the milk supply. "Do you think you can still churn butter?"

"Humph," Nola Bell snorted. "I been churnin' butter since befo' you was born. How come you think I forgot?"

Fortune grinned and hugged her servant. "I'll see what I can do about getting a churn."

Fortune and Elena went into the village. It was a small village with huts dotting the area. Few buildings were permanent-looking. First, Fortune went to find Selwin Allen to ask about the ship.

"I'm sorry, Miss Anthony," he said. "Nobody seems to know anything about the ship."

"Do you mean there's no ship?" she asked incredulously. What would her mother say? Letha couldn't take much more punishment.

"Well," he said, his forehead wrinkling, "there's one coming. I just don't know when. It was supposed to leave on the sixth of October."

"The sixth of October? That's—why, that's next week!" she exclaimed, wondering what else could happen. If the ship hadn't even left, it could be months before it reached Panama. But Fortune just couldn't worry about that now. There was too much else.

She told him where she was staying and asked him to get in touch with her if he heard anything. Then she and Elena went to the little store. There were no churns. She bought four hammocks, as well as eggs, flour, bacon, corn and other foodstuffs. In this heat, little would keep for very long without spoiling.

She then found a little shop that had a rocking chair and bought it for Letha. Fortune's hopes for a pleasant stay were dwindling as she took note of the size of the town. "Elena, how many people live here?"

Elena looked puzzled that Fortune would ask such a question. "I do not know. Many people. More than one thousand. No more than two thousand."

The population accounted for the small city. Fortune had expected a large port like Charleston or New Orleans. "Can we buy wood?"

"Wood like trees?" Elena asked, frowning.

"Yes. Is there a lumber company?"

"I think no. Why you need wood?"

"Well, I was thinking of unpacking my books if we're going to be here for very long." She thought of Beau. This would be a good reason for looking him up. "I'll have to make a bookshelf."

Elena merely nodded as if she didn't understand the significance of Fortune's remark. "What is need to buy wood? Can cut in jungle for free."

Fortune certainly had the tools to do so. Still packed away in her trunks were many tools suitable for setting up a plantation, or at least getting one started. Her father had planned to start from the ground, leveling trees and building his new home. There were hammers, saws, nails, all the implements necessary for such a venture.

The days passed quickly, and Fortune and Elena became close friends. Occasionally Jemima would walk over to visit, or Fortune would go into the village for information about the ship. They knew the *California* should be steaming toward Panama City, but it hadn't been scheduled to leave New York until the sixth of October or thereabouts. At first she'd thought that another ship would come for them, but she'd discovered that they would have to wait for the *California*. Though she didn't know exactly how long it would take for the packet to go around Cape Horn, on the tip of South America, she prayed that it would arrive soon.

One afternoon, Fortune was in the village to see if there was any information about the steamer and she ran into Beau. "Hello," she said, feeling a little awkward, since she hadn't seen him in a few days.

Beau threw his arms about her and swung her around. He kissed her lightly on the lips and then placed her on the ground in front of him with an apologetic grin. Color ranged into his cheeks in bright splotches. "I—I'm sorry. I hadn't seen you lately, and I suppose I was...just glad to see you."

Smiling happily, Fortune glanced around to see if anyone had noticed them. The natives were the only people around and they didn't care what the *Americanos* did. "Me, too," she said. "I mean, I'm happy to see you."

They talked for a few minutes about adjusting to living in Panama City before Beau asked, "Where are you staying?"

"I'm lodging with Elena Vasquez. Out near the old Spanish fortress wall." Fortune explained how to get to her house. "Come out and see me—us—sometime."

Beau remembered her mother. "How is Mrs. Anthony?"

Fortune hesitated for a few seconds. "Mother doesn't seem to be getting any better."

"I'm sorry to hear that," Beau said, hoping that her mother's problems adjusting weren't affecting Fortune. "Are you still walking every morning and every evening?"

"Oh, yes. I don't know what I'd do if I couldn't get my exercise." Fortune gazed at the fortress wall. The large cannons left by the Spanish were still visible. There were men sitting astride them. "What are those men doing?"

Beau glanced at the wall. "They're looking for a ship. I guess somebody has to tell us when one comes in. There's no real dock here."

"I suppose we'll have to take those awful rowboats out to the steamer and climb up another rickety ladder." Fortune didn't think she'd ever forget the experience over in Chagres. "New Granada. It sounded like such a romantic country when we left Charleston. Panama City sounded like such a metropolitan place. I guess we were all fooled."

Beau chuckled and shook his head. "I guess. But you know, I've really come to like it here. The humidity is awful, but the temperature isn't so bad. It's not a lot worse than New Orleans in the summer."

"But I think it's the same here almost year round." Fortune tried to remember her geography. "I think we're pretty close to the equator."

"You're right."

"Christmas will be coming in a couple of months." Fortune thought back to the wonderful Christmases in Charleston. Her father had always known exactly what she wanted. "I guess we'll be in California by then."

"Maybe." Beau studied the question for a minute. "But I think it's going to take the *California* a long time to go around the Cape. We may be here at Christmas after all."

"It won't seem like Christmas, though," Fortune said, wondering where they could get a fir tree. "It doesn't snow in Charleston, but it's usually pretty cold. Or at least cool."

"Do you miss Charleston?" Beau took her arm and they started to walk.

Fortune thought about her answer for a moment. "No, I don't. Not really. I guess I miss my grandfather, even though he was mean to my father. And he never liked my mother."

"Why not?" Beau asked, hoping she'd tell him more about herself. During the past few days, he'd found himself wondering about her, about her life before he'd met her. He wanted to know what made her different, what made him feel different when he was with her.

"I never really knew. It was like they had an armed truce or something." Fortune shook her head sadly. "I don't think either one of them is a bad person, but they just didn't get along."

"What about your father? Didn't he try to bridge the gap between them?"

"Oh, yes. He was always trying to make them see the good in each other. He'd tell my grandfather about my mother in glowing details." Fortune paused to catch her breath. They were standing by the wall of the fort, at a spot where they could look out over the ocean below. It was a beautiful view. "Then he'd try to explain to my mother why my grandfather was so grouchy all the time. I don't think either one of them listened to anything he said. Not about each other. Not about anything."

"Why didn't you just leave, then?" Beau slid his arm around her shoulders and looked out over her head. "I mean, your father could have gone somewhere else long ago."

"I know. But my father felt he had to stay and take care of Pleasant Point for my grandfather. My uncle Roger was always gone somewhere." Fortune frowned as she remembered all the work her father had done on the plantation, only to have it taken away from him when Roger Anthony returned. "My father was an honorable man."

Beau let the words flow over him. The gentle cadence of her voice, the lyrical quality of her tone, touched a note in him that seemed to respond like a resonant bell. He wanted this woman—and not only as a friend. He wanted to make love to her. Right then.

Fortune stood there. She could hardly talk. Beau's body was pressed close to hers, sending flashes of fire like shooting stars through her body. What was wrong with her? They were friends. From somewhere deep down inside of her, Fortune realized that she wanted them to be more than friends. Her feelings had changed, without her knowing just when. But there was no chance. Beau wasn't interested in a . . . She couldn't even think the word *wife*. Could she?

She stared at Beau for a few moments, wondering what to do. "I . . . I'd better get back. My . . . my mother will be looking for me, and you know how she is."

Breaking free of his hold on her, Fortune almost ran up the pathway toward Elena's house. This relationship was too bizarre for her to comprehend. Could she be falling in love? How would she know if she was? She really knew nothing about love.

In fact, now that she thought about it, she'd never seen what real love could be like between two people. She didn't think her mother had ever loved her father. The thought of a life lived with someone who didn't return one's love brought her little dream world crashing down. Then there was her grandfather's supposed love, a love that was twisted, always centered around money. His kind of love was cold, calculating.

Falling in love?

Never. Fortune would never be dependent on another man. Not for anything. Never again.

Never again.

Chapter Eleven

When Fortune awoke, she lay in her hammock for a few moments. Now that she was accustomed to the feeling of sleeping in the air, she rather liked it.

She glanced at her mother. Letha was staring straight up at the thatched roof. "Mother? What's wrong?"

"Everything's wrong." Letha sniffed, still staring with glazed eyes at the roof. "You shouldn't have to ask."

Fortune sat up and swung her legs over the edge of the hammock. "Come on, Mother. Let's go for our morning walk. I know you'll feel better."

Letha turned slowly and glowered at her daughter. How could she be so unfeeling? Didn't Fortune know that her husband was dead? She was a woman alone now. With nowhere to go. Nobody to care for her. "Go away. I'm not walking again today."

Frowning, Fortune rose and walked over to her mother's hammock. "Mother, you've got to get up. You're going to eat something, and then we're going for a little walk before the sun gets too high. Not far."

"Who are you to tell me what to do?"

"I'm your daughter, and I love you." Fortune decided she was going to have to find a way to force Letha to do the things that were good for her. Her mother had turned into a child in the past few days. Fortune dressed quickly and made her mother get dressed. "Come on. We'll have fun."

Elena fixed a light breakfast, but Letha refused to eat. Fortune knew that her mother would grow steadily weaker if she didn't eat, but forcing food down the woman's throat would be almost impossible. "Come on, Mother. Let's go for a walk. Maybe your appetite will return if you get some exercise. You can't continue like this. You're withering away to nothing."

Letha rose from the little table and headed for her chair. Fortune caught her before she could sit down. "No, Mother. I insist. Just a short walk."

Letha moaned, but she allowed Fortune to lead the way. "I don't know why you persist in forcing me to do these things. Why don't you just let me die?"

Fortune was appalled. She'd never heard her mother sound so depressed. "Come on, Mother. You know you'll feel better. Every day you'll feel a little better. Who knows, you might find Panama City interesting. There's a beautiful view from down at the—"

"Have you been sneaking off to be with that gambler?" Letha asked, stopping to stare at her daughter.

"No, Mother." Fortune couldn't lie to her mother. "I've seen him when I've gone into the village, but I haven't sneaked off to see him. Why don't you like him?"

"Because he's . . . he's trash."

Fortune realized she'd never be able to change Letha's mind, but she had to defend Beau. "Mother, he's been very kind to us. I don't know what we'd have done without him when Father fell."

"What did he do? Nothing. He didn't do anything to save my husband." Letha jerked her arm away from Fortune and began to walk faster.

"Mother, wait!" Fortune called, and hurried to catch up. She tucked her mother's arm into the crook of her own. "That's not nice, Mother. Beau climbed down that cliff at great peril to himself to see if he could do anything for Father."

"You're just like your father. Spiteful and deceitful." Letha broke away again and began to hurry away. She started down a slope that was littered with small stones and vines.

"Mother, stop!" Fortune exclaimed, running after her. "You'll fall!"

"Leave me alone." Letha lifted her skirts and began to run.

Fortune knew, deep inside, that Letha was headed for trouble. But, no matter how fast she ran, Letha seemed to go faster. "Stop!"

"Aiee!" Letha screamed and tried to stop on the loose pebbles. Her feet flew right out from under her, and she started to roll down the hill toward the river.

Her scream echoed in Fortune's head, bringing back the memory of her father's death. "Mother!"

Fortune ran with all her might. Her feet ached, as her thin kid slippers did little to protect the soles of her feet from the stones and pebbles, but she continued to run after her shrieking mother. "Oh, God, no! Please don't do this to me again!"

With scarcely a thought for her own safety, Fortune hurried after her mother. When she got to the place where Letha had fallen, Fortune understood part of the reason. A snake was crawling into a small hole in the ground.

"Help!" Fortune screamed, hoping that someone would hear her. She didn't know whether the snake had bitten her mother or not, but she knew there was a good chance it had. "Boaz! Elena!"

Rushing on, she saw that Letha's body had come to a stop at the edge of the river. One of her legs was twisted badly, and she didn't seem to be moving. Out of the corner of Fortune's eye, just coming into sight, was Beau. Maybe he'd heard her scream. Fortune reached her mother and found her unconscious. Quickly she reached for her mother's hand and found a weak pulse.

By that time, Beau had caught up with them. He knelt beside Letha. "What happened?"

"A snake. Mother saw it and fell. I don't know if it bit her or not." Suddenly Fortune was reliving her father's death, those dreadful moments before she'd known for a certainty that he was dead. *Oh, God, don't let this happen,* she prayed silently as she watched Beau.

Beau began to examine Letha. Her skirts were wound up almost to her waist, and he didn't waste any time being delicate. He saw immediately that her leg was broken. It looked pretty bad. But he saw no snakebite. "I don't think the snake got her. It probably just scared her."

"She's terrified of snakes," Fortune said, thankful that she didn't have to deal with a venomous snake, as well as a bone that was likely broken. "Can you help me get her back to the house before she comes to? That leg is likely to be painful."

Beau lifted the unconscious woman easily. He estimated that Letha Anthony weighed no more than one hundred pounds, and probably less. As he approached the little hut, Letha began to awaken. Her moans of pain indicated that Fortune had been correct.

Elena met them at the door. "Bring her here." She pointed to the pile of grass mattresses that Fortune and Nola Bell had made when they first arrived. "Will be better."

Fortune hurried over, wringing her hands. "How did you know to—"

"I heard you scream. Saw mother fall." Elena helped to lower Letha to the mattresses.

Beau stood and walked out the door. He looked around for something to protect the broken leg. It had to be kept straight, or it wouldn't heal correctly. Soon Elena joined him. They explored the area and found several tree limbs that might be satisfactory.

Elena and Beau returned to the sitting with the limbs. Elena took one look at Letha's leg and shook her head. "Very bad. I go get Damita. She help."

Beau settled into the lone chair in the room to wait. He could hardly ask Fortune to go for a walk when her mother was in such a condition, but after the leg had been tended, maybe they could go outside and talk.

He'd missed her, particularly after she'd hurried off so quickly the other day. Beau wasn't exactly sure what sort of turn their relationship had taken, but he felt sure that they'd passed some significant marker. He'd given up trying to give his feelings a label. The labels he considered made him extremely uncomfortable, so for now he'd simply continue to call what was between them friendship. A special friendship.

Fortune held her mother's hand and whispered soft words of comfort to the distraught woman. After a few minutes, she looked at Beau. "Thank you, Beau. You always seem to be around when I need you."

"I'm glad. We're friends, remember?" He slid forward on the chair and laced his fingers together around his knees. "Would you like to sit here?"

"No, I think I'd better stay here with Mother. But thank you for asking." Fortune felt her mother's eyes on her and looked down.

Letha glared at her daughter with a look almost akin to hatred. "I told you I didn't want to walk." She raised her head a little. "What's he doing here? I won't have a gambler in my house."

"Mother, be nice," Fortune said gently, laying her hand across Letha's forehead to see if she had a fever. "He carried you all the way back from the river."

"That man had his filthy hands on my—on me?" Letha cried, not bothering to mask her disgust. "How dare he?"

Fortune glanced at Beau and was glad to see that he didn't appear to be too angry. She was furious with her mother. "How dare he? Who else would have done it? We're not in Charleston any longer."

She tried not to shout, but her voice rose slightly above its usually gentle tone. Letha had been taking advantage of people ever since she'd arrived in Panama City, and the time for her to stop had come. Fortune put her hands on her hips and lowered her voice. "Please apologize to Beau at once."

"Oh, don't be a stickler for manners, Fortune," Beau said quietly. "Your mother doesn't like me, and I know it. We'll get along just like that."

"Don't be giving orders to my daughter." Letha raised herself up even further. "I'd appreciate it if you'd leave. Since you know I don't like you, I don't see any reason to prolong this conversation, this torment."

"Mother!" Fortune exclaimed. "I've never heard of such bad manners. I'm ashamed of you."

Letha scowled at her. "You're not to talk to me in that tone of voice, young lady. I insist you usher that cheating gambler from my house at once."

Beau chuckled and rose. "Well, Fortune, I—"

Letha interrupted him. "And don't call my daughter by her given name. Have you no respect for her?" She fell back onto the mattress.

Ignoring her, Beau began again. "Well, Fortune, I think that, in view of your mother's obvious dislike, I should leave." He walked over to where Letha lay and looked down. "Mrs. Anthony, I'm sorry to have found you in such a wretched condition. I hope that when I drop by later I'll find you feeling much better."

"You'd better not come back here." Letha tried to rise, but couldn't. "You have the manners of a goat."

"Why, thank you, Mrs. Anthony. I've always admired goats." Beau grinned at Fortune, who rose and followed him to the door.

They walked into the yard. Fortune felt she had to apologize for her mother's behavior. "I'm truly sorry. I can't imagine why she's taken such a dislike to you."

"Oh, I can. Don't you think maybe she had a bad experience with a gambler a few years ago?" Beau asked, rubbing his chin as he leaned against a tree. "Before you were born?"

"I doubt it. The way she feels about gamblers, I'd be surprised if she'd even talk to one." Fortune knew well of her mother's hatred for gamblers. She'd heard the lectures often enough as she was growing up.

"Well, something had to happen to make her hate us so much." Beau caught Fortune's hand and laced their fingers together. He couldn't stand to be this close to her and not touch her in some small way. "We're not such a bad lot, are we? I seem to recall a certain young woman who also professed to dislike the breed, but who appears to have changed her mind."

Fortune couldn't help smiling. Her fingers tightened on his. "Well, it could be that a certain gentleman cheated a little on the wager. Do you think that's possible?"

"What? You wouldn't dare suggest that I, an honorable gambler, would stack the deck in my favor, would you?" Beau asked in mock horror. He clasped her free hand to his heart and lowered his head until his chin touched his chest. "I'm struck with anguish that you'd think such a thing!"

"I think you'd have made a better actor than gambler, sir," Fortune retorted, lifting her chin until her nose was stuck haughtily in the air. She laughed and leaned against Beau for a moment, savoring the awareness that such close contact evoked.

Beau stroked her hair and inhaled her fresh scent. He clung to her for a few seconds and then cupped her chin in his hands. "I'd better go before your mother tries to come out here and chase me off."

"I suppose you're right." Fortune reluctantly drew back and looked into his eyes. They were flashing green in the sunlight. She liked that look. Then she remembered that Beau had been walking toward her house. "Were you coming out here to see me?"

"Oh, yes." Beau took her hand once more. He wished they could go further, but with Fortune's mother injured, he couldn't take the chance. "I came to tell you that we've gotten no news about the ship."

Fortune spun around to look at him. Why would he come to tell her that? He knew that she was coming to town every day to talk with Selwin. "Oh, thank you. In spite of what my mother says, I really do thank you for helping her."

"Don't worry about it. I've had quite a bit of experience with mothers who have reservations about me." Beau stopped. He knew that Fortune needed to be with her mother. "I'll see you later."

Fortune looked up at him as he leaned to drop a kiss on her forehead. She offered a smile and a wave as he strode away. "Goodbye."

"Oh, yes," he called over his shoulder. "I also wanted to remind you that you've lost our wager, *friend.*"

Smiling foolishly, Fortune returned to the house. Letha was almost sitting up. The look on her face suggested that she was about to have some sort of fit.

"Where have you been? What were you doing out there with him? Did he touch you?" She almost threw the questions at Fortune, questions backed by a full load of animosity. "I've told you to stay away from that man. You don't know how... how loathsome gamblers can be."

"Mother, be reasonable. I was only outside for a moment." Fortune had to convince her mother somehow that Beau was a good man. "He's done nothing to you. Whatever happened in your past, Beau had nothing to do with it."

Letha's face turned the shade of a scarlet sunset. Rage filled her eyes. "Why did you say that? Has someone said something to you about— Tell me, why would you say such a thing?"

Fortune blanched in the face of her mother's fury. She'd never seen such a display of emotion from her mother in all her years. "Why, nobody! I just assumed that, since you hate—"

"Assume nothing about me." Letha collapsed onto the mattress. "Where is that fool Elena? I'm in immense pain. Where is Nola Bell? That woman is never around when I need her anymore. Giles should never have freed her. Made her downright uppity."

"Mother, you know that Nola Bell has served us faithfully for many years. It's unfair of you to say such a thing."

"I'll be the judge of what's fair and what's not." Letha moaned and rolled her head from side to side. "Why can't I just die?"

"Mother, you're not badly injured." Fortune sat down on the floor near her mother. "You've broken your leg. It will heal."

"I have return with Damita." Elena burst into the small sitting room with a large black woman. "She take care of mother."

"I'm not your mother," Letha growled, scowling at Elena. "Who is this person?"

"Mother, Elena already said this is Damita." Fortune turned to the woman and smiled. "Welcome. We appreciate your coming to help."

"She no understand good English like me." Elena said a few words to Damita in Spanish. After the answer, she smiled at Fortune. "She happy to help. Knows good medicine."

The old black woman settled onto the floor and examined Letha's leg with the practiced look of a doctor. She passed her hands up and down the leg, which was now swelling and turning ugly shades of black and blue. After a few seconds, she jerked the leg, eliciting a shriek from Letha.

Letha howled in pain for a few seconds and then glared venomously at the black woman who had inflicted the punishment. "Who are you and what are you doing?"

The woman ignored Letha and removed a small crock of vile-smelling potion from her woven bag. She applied a generous amount to the leg and then wound it in wide green leaves. This done, she took one of the shorter tree limbs and placed it on one side of Letha's leg, ignoring her moaning. Then she selected another and put it on the other side.

Taking a wide leather strap, she wound it around the leg and limbs until the crude splints were secure. Then she found a length of fabric and began to wind it around the splinted leg.

Smiling at her handiwork, Damita poked around in her bag for a moment and then withdrew a small clay jar filled with a fine powder. Elena hurried to the kitchen and returned with a cup of water. Damita poured a little of the powder into the cup and stirred briskly.

She made a motion, and Fortune nodded. "Drink it, Mother. Damita wants you to drink it."

Letha wrinkled up her nose. "I refuse to drink anything that looks like that greenish stuff. It smells, and I imagine it will taste just as bad."

Damita lifted Letha's head and began to pour the liquid into her mouth. Letha choked and finally swallowed a few mouthfuls. Fortune bit her lip to keep from laughing. Apparently Damita hadn't understood that Letha was refusing the medicine.

"How dare you pour something like that into my mouth when I've said I won't drink it?" Letha sputtered.

"Mother, she doesn't understand English. She didn't know you'd refused." Fortune turned away and tried to busy herself for a few seconds while she composed herself. She was almost ready to laugh out loud. Finally she brought herself under control and turned to the three other women again.

"Elena, how much do we owe her?" Fortune asked, wondering if Damita would want American money.

Elena spoke with Damita for a few moments and then turned to Fortune. "She say chicken."

"She wants a chicken?" Fortune asked, wondering where she could find one. So far she'd seen none here in Panama City.

"I get for her tomorrow." Elena turned and explained to Damita what would happen. The black woman nodded and grinned.

"Tell her that we appreciate her help," Fortune called as Elena escorted Damita to the door.

Whatever was in the vile-looking green liquid, it put Letha to sleep within a few minutes. Fortune thought her mother looked more at peace than she had in a long time. She hung a mosquito net over her and then returned to her chores.

Days passed, and Letha got no better. Fortune and Beau would walk each evening, sometimes talking, sometimes not. She sensed a restraint in him that hadn't been present before, and neither of them tried to pursue the physical part of their relationship.

Fortune decided that it was for the best. Their kisses seemed to be leading in a direction that she—and Beau—were reluctant to go. Or was she?

She recalled Dennis's clumsy attempts, and was suddenly filled with revulsion again, almost as much as when the incident had occurred. Beau's kisses and caresses were so different from Dennis's mauling. Fortune knew she should be afraid of Beau's embrace, but fear was strangely absent. She decided that it was because his first embraces had been so different, so gentle. There had been no pressure, no demands. With Dennis, Fortune had known that he would have raped her without a second thought if she hadn't escaped. She was amazed by the difference in the two men and their approaches.

She missed Beau's kisses and caresses, though she told herself that she didn't. Fortune didn't know how to tell Beau about her feelings, but she kept him in her mind most of the day, and in her dreams at night.

Beau told himself every day that he wouldn't go to Fortune's house. It was senseless to do so. The relationship had no future. Neither of them was interested in pursuing a physical relationship. Even if he was—and he most certainly wasn't—Fortune wasn't the kind of woman who'd settle for intimacy without commitment.

Guilt plagued him. He knew that Fortune must be wondering why he'd stopped kissing her and embracing her. He considered discussing it with her, but decided that the conversation would embarrass both of them inordinately.

But, by damn, I miss holding her and kissing her. He cursed and tossed a piece of crockery through the window with all the force he could muster.

Patrick's voice came from outside. "Dammit, man, what in blazes is going on?"

Beau leapt to his feet and strode to the door. He hadn't stopped to consider that someone might be coming to visit him. He opened the door with an abashed grin on his face. "Sorry, Patrick. I—I don't know what made me to do that."

Rubbing a large red spot on his forehead, Patrick glowered at Beau. "I was coming up to tell you that a small group of people arrived with the information that the *California* set out for Panama City on the sixth of October as we believed."

"It will take that steamer until after the New Year to get here," Beau said, thinking of Fortune. She was being driven almost mad by her mother's constant crying and complaining. Letha hated living in that bamboo hut, and she was making Fortune miserable.

Beau and Patrick had set up a small gambling hall in the house where they were living. They'd found a family that was willing to leave for the exorbitant price the two men paid for the tiny dwelling. With so few men in town, the gambling establishment wasn't making much money, but at least Beau and Patrick could keep up their game. After all, even gamblers needed practice.

Fortune found herself looking forward more and more to Beau's visits. Her mother was such a crosspatch lately that Fortune often thought of leaving her to her own devices. Such thoughts made her feel guilty. Fortune realized her mother was still in pain, but she was becoming more and more difficult to deal with. Her demands were increasing in frequency and were often unreasonable.

"Fortune!" Letha called from her bed in the sitting room.

Running as fast as she could, Fortune left Elena hanging clean clothes on the line in the yard and hurried to see what Letha wanted. "What is it, Mother?"

"Fortune, get me some cool water." Letha touched her fingers to her mouth as if it were parched from the heat.

"Mother, I just brought you cool water." Fortune crossed the room and looked into the cup. Keeping control of her anger, she said in a normal tone, "You didn't drink what I already brought."

"It's not cool enough," Letha whined.

"Really, Mother, there's no water any cooler in Panama." Fortune took the cup, walked back to the urn and dipped a fresh cup of water. She took it back to the sitting room and placed it in Letha's hand. "Here you are, Mother."

Fortune returned to her chores.

"What this time?" Elena asked, hanging a petticoat on the line.

"More cool water," Fortune answered simply.

She hated to be angry with her mother, but how could she not be? Letha seemed to look for ways to irritate Fortune and the other residents. Nola Bell had quit coming into the house, as had Boaz. Elena tried very hard to be sympathetic, but she often chided Fortune for not taking a firmer position with her mother.

"She needs to be punished." Elena crossed her arms and shook her head. "She no more than a child. You spoil her."

"Elena, she's my mother, and she *is* injured," Fortune explained, knowing that Elena was right in her assessment. "I can't be mean to her."

"She mean to you," Elena concluded, lifting her bamboo basket. "You mother, she child."

After supper, Fortune changed into a fresh dress. She'd given up her petticoats, except for when she went into town. Maybe that's why Beau isn't attracted to me anymore, she mused.

Then she heard him in the sitting room. Letha was scolding him, ordering him to leave, threatening him, but Beau continued to behave like a gentleman.

Fortune brushed her hair quickly, deciding that, since Letha's behavior was even worse than usual tonight, she'd leave her hair down in order to be out of the hut that much quicker. Quite often she'd tried to convince Beau to meet her a short distance from the house, but he always refused.

She admired him for his position, but she hated to listen to Letha berating him every night. She walked into the sitting room. "Good evening, Beau."

Before he could answer, Letha interrupted. "Where are you going? You don't have on a petticoat! Why isn't your hair braided? You look like—a loose woman."

Beau turned to glare at Letha. For once she'd truly made him angry. "Now look, Letha—"

"How dare you call me by my given name?" Her eyes were wide with confusion, and she was scowling with hatred.

"Because you're acting like a child." Beau continued to stare at her, never releasing her from his penetrating gaze. "I insist that you treat Fortune better. You've got her doing work you wouldn't ask of a slave. You continually berate her for her activities. I won't have any more of it, do you hear me?"

"Beau, I don't think Mother—" Fortune stopped. The slight twitching of a muscle in Beau's neck told her how angry he was.

"Now, if you want to continue to be treated cordially by the nice people you live with, I suggest that you start acting accordingly." Beau closed his mouth. He was about to really get into a discussion of her behavior. "Or else we'll move you to the barn with the *other* donkeys. Come, Fortune."

Fortune was astounded. Letha remained silent as Beau and Fortune left the house on their daily walk. For a few minutes, neither of them talked, but she couldn't stand the quiet for very long, not today. "Beau, you were awfully hard on my mother."

Beau looked down at her. He already regretted his outburst; he knew it was likely to make Letha's behavior even worse. She certainly wouldn't ever welcome his visits now, that was for sure. He didn't know what to say to Fortune. How could he have been such a fool? Why had he had to get involved in her problems? She'd never burdened him with her daily difficulties, and she probably thought she was handling them well.

Only an idiot would do what he'd done. They reached the old Spanish seawall and began to walk along it. This was one of the favorite promenades of the villagers.

"This reminds me very much of The Battery in Charleston," Fortune finally said, realizing that he was too angry to discuss her mother. In spite of the fact that she thought he was right, she felt that Letha would now become even more of a problem. "I used to love to go there when I was a little girl."

She stopped and looked down at the bay. The moon was rising, casting a silvery glow to the dark blue waters. The glints on the waves looked almost like stars, and Fortune was fascinated. This was the loveliest view she'd ever seen.

"You know, I'm beginning to love this place." Fortune leaned back against the wall. "The people here are so...so free and independent and friendly. They simply live their lives without bothering each other."

"I suppose you're right." Beau watched her as she stared out to sea. He'd never seen her look more beautiful. The moonlight kissed her hair with almost an iridescent glow. It was like a halo around her lovely face. He had to apologize for his behavior, he knew that, but he hated to broach the subject again. ''Fortune, I'm sorry. I know I shouldn't have said anything. In fact, I try very hard to just smile and take whatever she says without rancor. But tonight, I couldn't stand by and listen to her talk to you that way.''

Fortune looked up at him with a wry smile. ''She's injured. She just lost her husband. She's in a strange, alien country. Many things make her seem self-centered, even more than before. But she's still my mother.''

''I promise I'll apologize to her, as well.'' Beau felt awful. He'd probably made Fortune angry with him, and he was deeply sorry for that, too.

''No, you don't have to apologize to her.'' Fortune continued to gaze into his eyes. Even in the semidarkness, she fell victim to the compelling nature of his beautiful eyes. ''She deserved to be confronted. My main concern is you. Because you're a gambler, she never really liked you. No, that's not quite right. She never gave herself a chance to like you.''

''Fortune . . .'' He hugged her close. ''You're the most fair-minded individual I ever met. You should be a judge.''

''I'd say that's a career that's not open to me.''

''Well, it should be.'' Beau's arm was draped over her shoulder, and it felt so natural there that he was reluctant to move it.

The mood of the moment changed from serious to playful to tender. He did move his arm. He slid it, and then the other, further around her, and drew her close. When she didn't pull away, Beau gazed down into her eyes, questioning, asking if she felt the same raging emotions as he.

He hesitated, vacillating between wanting to kiss her gently and needing to slake his thirst for the passion he hoped—knew—slept deep inside her, waiting to be awakened. He suddenly realized that he wanted to be the man to awaken those passions. The time for questioning had passed.

Beau lowered his head until his lips softly touched hers, getting acquainted again with the sweet taste of her as he gently parted her lips with his tongue. God, he wanted her more than he'd ever wanted another woman.

What was coming over him? He seemingly couldn't get close enough to her. He knew that some sort of milestone had been passed, that their relationship had passed beyond a beautiful friendship and become something more, much more.

Fortune felt her spirit lifted, felt her body take on a lightness that it had never known. Beau's kisses were different tonight, more passionate, more demanding than ever before. She discovered that her own response was without reticence, without artifice. She wanted this new step in the progress of their friendship as much as he—and maybe more.

Fortune felt herself being drawn into passion's web, deeper and deeper. She couldn't stop herself. Her heart pounded like an ancient tribal drum, forcing her blood into wild surges and pulses that intoxicated her like the strongest of spirits. Where would this lead?

Beau knew what was going to happen. He drew away, feeling the heat of passion throb within his loins. If he didn't stop now, there would be no stopping. Guilt almost overpowered him. Fortune was not at fault here; it was he who had drawn them into this impassioned spiral. He had to break free—right now.

Extricating himself from her embrace, Beau rose and walked a short distance away. What was happening to him? How had he allowed himself to go this far with an innocent woman? His body ached from wanting her, but his mind refused to let him take advantage of her.

Trust. What was it she'd said to him once? Friends trusted each other. *Damn trust to hell and back!* What did he care about trust? Nobody had ever trusted him before; why should she trust him now? Why should that guide his conduct?

Why should he even care? When they reached California, she'd move out into the wilderness with her mother and build a neat little farmhouse. She'd marry some man who'd enjoy busting clods of dirt every day for the rest of his life. Why should Beau care if the man got damaged goods? Besides, in the next few weeks, Beau could teach her a lot about making love. He'd practically be doing her future husband a favor.

He turned back to gaze at her. God, but he wanted her. Her lips were pouty, full with the evidence of his recent kisses, and so damnably inviting that he could hardly restrain himself.

What was wrong with him? Gazing at Fortune he suspected what was wrong. He was getting softhearted.

Chapter Twelve

Fortune sat in the rocking chair and stared straight ahead, seeing nothing. What had happened? She couldn't understand.

Had she done something that repulsed him? Had she been inadequate in some way? Plagued with questions, she rocked until long into the night.

Everything had seemed so wonderful, so perfect, and then the cold world had intruded. Beau had risen and walked away from her. She could see that he was debating within himself, but he had said nothing for a long time. Then, as if nothing had happened, he had brought her back home and left abruptly. She continued to rock, wondering how she would ever discover the truth.

In the next few days, Fortune saw little of Beau. The last time they'd walked together, he had muttered some excuse about business to attend to and ended their excursion rather suddenly.

Fortune suspected that he was wrangling internally with some problem. She thought he trusted her enough to talk with her about it, but it seemed he couldn't. He'd withdrawn from her and walked away. After a few minutes of silence, he'd given her the excuse and walked her back home.

Since that evening, he'd avoided her. The void his absence left was painful. Fortune continued to walk each evening, but it wasn't the same. No matter how beautiful the sunsets, she couldn't enjoy them in quite the way she always had. Something strange was happening, but she couldn't put a label on it.

The daily rains came to an end in early December. The occasional rain was light, more of a mist than actual rain, and the humidity dropped to a more tolerable level.

Letha was somewhat changed. Beau's outburst had, in many ways, made dealing with her much easier for Fortune, but it hadn't shaken the older woman out of her doldrums.

Fortune had decided that Letha wasn't mourning so much for her deceased husband as for her lost way of life. The challenge of living in a new, wild country was something she seemingly didn't want to tackle. Indeed, life itself was, apparently, too much of a challenge for her mother.

Living in Panama City had thus far been a wonderful experience for Fortune. She and Elena had become good friends, for the most part overcoming their initial language barrier.

Their different cultural backgrounds were another matter. Elena felt perfectly comfortable wearing no clothing in the house and very little outside. Fortune couldn't overcome her own inhibitions. While she'd shed the weight and confinement of crinolines and hoops, she couldn't bring herself to disrobe in front of others.

To help Fortune adjust to the heat, she and Elena had modified almost all of her dresses. All the sleeves were gone, and the bodices had been cut much lower. The underskirts were removed, as much as possible, and the thin fabric that was left was shortened so that it allowed air to circulate beneath the skirt.

Fortune went into town nearly every day to check on the ship. Each day she returned with no news, but she persisted, knowing that someday the ship would arrive.

The next time she saw Beau standing with some men outside a little store, he seemed startled by her attire. She smiled and nodded as if she were going on past without stopping, but he caught her arm and turned her around to face him. Glancing up, startled, she hesitated.

"Fortune," he said, gazing down into her eyes.

He didn't know if it was a reflection from the sky—or maybe it had something to do with her bright blue dress— but her eyes were more beautiful than he'd ever seen them. In fact, he noticed that *she* was more beautiful than he'd ever seen her. Her skin had turned a slightly sun-kissed color now that she'd abandoned her parasol and bonnet. The swell of her breasts, clearly visible in the way the bodice was cut, also showed a pinkish-tan color.

"Yes?" she finally said, hardly able to speak. She hadn't realized what a powerful presence he had. She had missed him terribly, more so than she wanted to admit even to herself. She tried to smile again, to pass off her hesitation as nothing more than waiting for him to speak. "I've missed you on my walks each evening."

"I—I've been busy. I... Patrick and I have set up a gentleman's parlor and..." Beau's voice trailed into silence, He realized that she understood he was making excuses. Fortune was an intelligent woman. "What have you been doing?"

"The usual. But now I'm getting ready for Christmas." Fortune glanced around the little town. "I never thought we'd be here at Christmas."

"Neither did I," Beau admitted.

Fortune looked up at Beau. If they could find some way to restrain their... passionate urges, they could be friends. She'd given a great deal of thought to that, but unfortunately his touch denied that she'd controlled her feelings. "Beau, I want to build a small house. A real one. With wood."

"Why?" Beau asked, more surprised at what she'd said than at anything he could have imagined her saying.

"Because of Mother. She hates living in Elena's house. The bamboo walls, the dirt floor...the squalor, as Mother calls it." Fortune shook her head sadly. "She's not getting any better. I'm very concerned. I think if she had a more conventional home she'd feel better."

Beau considered Fortune's idea. He decided that she might be right. Women set a big store by such things as a place of their own. And a cabin wouldn't be too hard to build.

Fortune looked longingly at the men standing or sitting around doing nothing. "I have most of the tools and can get the men easily. All I need is somebody to make sure it's built properly."

"I'll see what I can do. I think I can work something out." Beau rubbed his chin thoughtfully. "We could probably build a one- or two-room cabin in a matter of days with the number of men around here. I'll draw some sort of plan today."

"That would be wonderful." Tears glistened in Fortune's eyes. "I think that would make all the difference in the world...to Mother."

"I'll talk to a few people and come by to see you tonight." Realizing that he was still holding her, Beau released her arm. "Don't worry about a thing."

Fortune went on her way, feeling better. She stopped in at the store and bought more tools and plenty of food. If the men were working, they'd be hungry. Then she went home. Elena owned a large parcel of land closer to town that she wasn't using. Fortune planned to buy it from her.

Fortune could hardly wait for Beau's arrival. She was brushing her hair when she heard him coming up the path, and she hurried to the door. She wanted to avoid another confrontation between him and her mother if possible.

As they walked down the path that had grown so familiar to Fortune, she told Beau of the deal she made with Elena. "So you see, Elena will get the house when we leave. The property remains hers."

Beau liked the deal. All afternoon the thought that Fortune might actually be planning to stay in Panama City had been nagging at him. He didn't like the idea of going on to California without her, because, he reasoned, he'd sort of taken her under his wing, to protect and look after her.

He persisted in denying the other, more important reason—that he'd miss her terribly if she remained in Panama.

Fortune and Beau talked animatedly about the plans. Beau showed her a sketch of a house that would consist of three rooms. There would a bedroom each for Fortune and her mother, and a sitting room that would also double as a dining room. A lean-to would be attached out back for cooking.

"This is wonderful," Fortune said, dreaming of the day when she could move into her new home. It wasn't the dream she'd lived with ever since she'd left Charleston, but she realized that with her father's death that vision had changed. "When can we start?"

"We'll start cutting the logs tomorrow." Beau grinned. He was almost as excited about this project as Fortune. Though his nights were occupied at the gaming tables, his days were dreadfully dull. This project would give him something to fill his time.

"Beau," Fortune began when they reached the wall. "I told you this morning that I've missed you. I...I mean, you seem to understand my moods, and I can talk to you and—"

"I know exactly what you mean," Beau said. "I agree." He looked down at her, saw the serious expression on her face. He fought the urge to kiss her, to wrap his arms around her and draw her into the shadows that haunted the nook and crannies along the wall. "But, Fortune, I've got to find a way to... I mean, I'm very attracted to you, and, as you know, I don't intend to marry. What I'm trying to say is—"

"I know exactly what you mean." She laughed. "That's something we'll have to work on."

He slid his arm around her and hugged her close. "I don't enjoy the days when I don't see you. We won't let that happen again."

Arm in arm, they walked back to the hut. As they approached, Beau noticed its primitive, run-down condition. He was happy to be doing something positive about getting Fortune out of there.

Early the next morning, Beau and five other men appeared at the hut. Fortune was up and waiting for them. She opened the trunks and removed the tools her father had so carefully packed and added them to the ones she'd bought.

The men were soon joined by others. Some were curious at first, but they soon linked with the others. Life in Panama City was boring. At dinnertime, Fortune and Elena brought food out to the woods, where the men were working. By that time, there were almost enough logs to begin building.

By nightfall, the logs were being notched and numbered. Beau was exhausted. He'd worked hard all day, but he enjoyed the tingling in his muscles that told him he'd been idle too long. He ate supper with Fortune and then left. He would need a bath before he sat down at the gambling tables tonight.

The next morning, the sound of construction woke Fortune. She quickly climbed out of her hammock and hurried to see what was happening. Some of the men were already there. They were laying the first logs in place.

Beau arrived soon afterward. He introduced Fortune to Eduardo, who professed to know how to hew the logs to make a real floor. While the others were constructing the walls, he and another man would work on cutting the boards for the floor.

Fortune worked hard, too. In addition to her other chores, she cooked for all the men and made sure they had plenty of fresh water. At times, she even pitched in to help with the construction in her own small way.

When evening arrived each day, she was worn out. With so many men helping, the small cabin was constructed within a week. Fortune had little to put in the cabin, but it was hers—for now.

She and Letha moved in. When her mother was situated, Fortune wandered from room to room, marveling at how good it felt to be in her own home, even if it was a crude cabin. The floors were smooth and even. As she walked across the floor, she smiled. She'd almost forgotten what shoes sounded like on a wooden floor.

Now she needed to make some real furniture. She and Boaz started gathering thick limbs that could be used as bedposts. Working as hard as they could, they made two beds. The rope that held the mattresses up was a part of the same rope that had been used to lower Beau down the cliff when her father had been killed.

"Father, I think you'd be proud of me," she said as she sat in the rocking chair. She closed her eyes and rocked, remembering her father in the happy times. He'd always been so kind to her—a good friend, as well as a good father.

Elena and Damita came in to check on Letha. In spite of the time that had passed since her fall, she seemed to be getting worse instead of better. Fortune had thought that the new house would make a difference, but Letha hardly seemed to notice any difference at all.

Damita talked with Elena for a few minutes after they looked at Letha. Elena motioned for Fortune to come outside.

"Damita say your mother want to die," Elena said sadly. "She have no reason to live."

Fortune couldn't speak. Tears welled up in her eyes. The two women had merely confirmed her own fears. There seemed to be nothing she could do to prevent the inevitable. "What about her leg?"

Once again Damita and Elena talked briefly. Elena shrugged. "Leg healed pretty good. May walk funny."

Fortune thanked Damita and went back into the cabin. She sat in the rocker and stared at the walls. What could she do to help her mother?

Christmas was coming.

Fortune could find no fir tree to cut and decorate, so she made her own. Taking the skirt of an old emerald-colored dress, she devised a tree by using a straight branch as the center. She and Elena made ornaments to go on the tree. They popped corn and strung it; they made bows of red ribbon and lace scavenged from another gown; they made an angel of corn husks to go on the top. Fortune stared at it for a moment. It wasn't the most beautiful tree she'd ever seen, and it didn't have the heavenly scent of cedar or pine, but it was green and shiny.

Walking around the handmade Christmas tree, Fortune started to laugh. "I've never seen anything so ridiculous, but it *is* a Christmas tree."

Elena studied it for a moment. "Well, I like it."

They draped a cloth around the bottom to cover the wooden stand. Fortune sighed. "What I wouldn't give for the smell of pine or cedar."

Nola Bell poked her head in the door, looked at the tree and wrinkled her forehead. "I ain't never seed no satin tree, but I can find the smell of cedar."

Before Fortune could reply, Nola Bell disappeared. Within a few minutes, she returned with a few flakes of cedar shavings. "You know we keeps these to make the moths stay away."

Fortune hugged Nola Bell and placed the shavings beneath the tree. Within a short time, the scent of cedar filled the room.

Still considering the tree thoughtfully, Fortune suddenly had an idea. "Come with me, Elena."

The two women went out into the edge of the jungle. Fortune directed Elena's attention to the profusion of colors dotting the scene. "Let's get some of those lovely flowers. Who says we can't put them on the tree?"

They gathered some of the blossoms and hurried back to the cabin. Using pins, they attached the flowers to the tree, then stepped back to judge their handiwork. Both women smiled at the change. The tropical flowers had combined two cultures and made the tree even more special.

Fortune sighed. "If we only had presents."

By Christmas Day, Fortune had made presents for everyone. Beau was coming for supper, and the event was bound to be festive. Letha allowed Beau to help her into the sitting room to join the group. Fortune had invited the Sloans and the Allens, as well as Elena, Beau, Nola Bell and Boaz, to join in the celebration.

Supper was a wonderful meal of roast chicken with cornbread stuffing, fresh corn on the cob, beans and potatoes. Desert consisted of fruit with heavy cream skimmed from the top of the milk they were getting every day.

"I don't know when I've enjoyed a supper this much," Beau said. He glanced from one of his hostesses to the other. "Fortune, Elena, Nola Bell, I don't know who cooked which part of the meal, but you're all to be congratulated."

Nola Bell was beaming from ear to ear. "You know, Mister Beau, I done all this cooking."

"I thought you might have." He hugged her close and handed her a coin. "Merry Christmas."

Mrs. Sloan's eyes glazed over, and she smiled sadly. "This is truly a beautiful gathering. We should be thankful that we've all survived to see this Christmas Day."

They sang Christmas carols, and Fortune lit the candles. For just a moment, she thought of her father. He would have enjoyed this evening. The warm glow of friendship, and, of course, the beautiful Christmas tree, made the evening wonderful. She smiled happily at her friends. "I've gifts for each of you."

Nola Bell opened hers first. Fortune had made a brightly printed skirt for the older woman. "I declare, I ain't never seed anything this bright that didn't fly off into the jungle, but I love it."

Elena grinned. "I can't wait to see my present."

Fortune watched carefully as Elena opened the little package wrapped in green satin. Inside, there was a little ivory-and-lace fan that had been Fortune's.

"Oh," Elena exclaimed, jumping up and hugging Fortune. "I never see anything this beautiful."

Tears came to Fortune's eyes. She'd come to love Elena like a sister during the past few weeks. The fan was the only gift she could give Elena that was truly unique in this part of the world.

Beau had a pretty shawl for each of the ladies, except for Fortune. Elena had made little cakes to pass out to everyone.

Fortune kept her eyes on her mother. Letha was already looking tired, but she held Fortune's gift reverently.

"My dear," Letha said, loosening the ribbon on the package, "I'd almost forgotten it was Christmas. Everything seems so... lifeless, especially me."

When Letha opened the little box, she was speechless. Fortune had asked Eduardo, who had planed their floors, to make a jewelry cask for her mother. He'd carved it with little birds and flowers and lined it with a piece of velvet that Fortune had rescued from one of her deteriorating gowns. "My dear, this is lovely! Wherever did you find it?"

"Eduardo made it," Fortune answered, choking back tears. This was the first thing Letha had taken an interest in since they'd arrived. "Remember him? He laid our floors."

Letha didn't answer. Her fingers played lovingly over the intricately carved little box. Finally, she looked up at Fortune. "I think I need to rest now."

Beau and Fortune helped Letha back to her bed. Fortune was thrilled with her mother's response to the gift. For Fortune, her Christmas celebration was already a success.

Everyone had opened his or her gift except Beau and Fortune. They kept theirs for last.

"You first," Fortune said, hardly able to contain her happiness.

Beau couldn't wait any longer. He opened the package carefully. He removed a little box similar to Letha's. "Why, this is lovely."

"Open it," Fortune urged.

He obeyed and found a white lawn cravat. "Did you make this? I've seen nothing this fine here."

Fortune nodded. "I asked Eduardo to make a box for your cards. But I wanted to do something myself."

Beau was astonished. "This is wonderful. Open yours."

With shaking fingers, Fortune opened her gift from Beau. There was a satin-covered box. She opened it and found a string of perfect pearls. "Oh, Beau, this is marvelous!" She held them to her neck, and he fastened them for her. "I don't know what to say."

After a short time, everyone left except for Beau. "Shall we go for our evening walk, Miss Anthony?"

"Why not?" she asked, linking her arm with his.

They strolled in a leisurely fashion down the path to the wall. The full moon shone down revealing the Gulf of Panama in all its splendor. They said nothing at first, just enjoyed the pleasant evening. Fortune's fingers often strayed to the strand of pearls around her neck. She'd never owned anything this beautiful in her life.

Beau broke the silence. "You know, Fortune, this has been a wonderful evening. I never even thought of celebrating Christmas here."

"Oh, I think men are likely to pass over the holidays more quickly than women." Fortune touched her pearls. "I'm happy you decided to celebrate with us."

"I am, too." Beau started along the wall, making sure he kept his steps short enough for Fortune's feminine gait. "I don't think I've ever spent a happier Christmas."

"I'm sure you're just being kind." Fortune felt the color rise in her cheeks. Even if he was lying, it pleased her to hear it.

"Oh, no." He stopped to look down at her. "I mean every word. Christmases at home were never like this, even when I was a child."

Fortune felt truly sad. She'd always loved the Christmas season. Apparently that feeling wasn't universal. "Why not? What did your parents do?"

Beau regretted having said anything. He shouldn't have mentioned his past. He never talked about it. But with Fortune, it seemed to come more naturally to him. Somehow it didn't hurt quite so much. "My parents were very formal people. My father spent a great deal of time trying to salvage our plantation. My mother was more interested in her society functions than in her children."

"Oh, that's sad." Fortune slid her arm around his shoulders to comfort him. "Didn't you have a Christmas tree or anything?"

"Yes, we did. But our celebrations always involved many people. My mother's friends came from everywhere, so our Christmases were big events that had little to do with human kindness and feeling." Beau had said too much. He didn't want to reveal any more. "Your little celebration tonight made up for all that I've missed."

Fortune smiled, warmed inwardly by his praise. "Mr. Gregory, you're invited to our Christmas suppers from now on. We'll establish a new tradition."

Beau embraced her, his sadness lost at once in her delightful scent and warm touch. Her first kiss was sweet, innocent; she initiated the contact. Beau peered into her eyes when she drew away. What were those eyes, so dark in the late-night shadows, trying to tell him? Her kiss was tentative, almost as if she were afraid of being rejected.

Fortune was surprised by her own actions. She'd never kissed a man, except for her father. Would Beau laugh at her? Would he scoff at her attempts to be...what? What was she trying to be?

Beau needed no further invitation. He lifted her into his arms, allowing the full length of him to enjoy the physical contact, then cradled her against his chest. He walked slowly over to a little copse of palms that grew near the wall and sat down with her in his lap.

Neither of them spoke. For what seemed like an eternity to Fortune, Beau did nothing except hold her close. Her emotions raced from excitement to passion to fear and back again. She didn't know what she expected him to do, or what she wanted him to do. She just knew that something was missing in their relationship.

They'd grown so close, and yet something was missing. Fortune had no experience at all of falling in love. As his lips touched hers, she wondered if perhaps that was the reason for her inability to label her feelings. After a moment more, she didn't care what she should call her feelings.

Beau's fingers slid beneath the bodice of her gown. Fortune gasped but savored the awareness his touch evoked. Her nipples, usually rosy and round, became tight and stiff as he brushed across one and then the other. She could hardly breathe.

"Fortune," he whispered against her hair, inhaling the combination of fragrances—lilac, grasses, sea air. The smells were invigorating, charging him to ever more spiraling emotions. If he didn't stop soon, he wouldn't be able to. The moment was approaching when Fortune's virginity would be in jeopardy. "Fortune, we mustn't."

Her chest was arched against his fingers, her head thrown back in ecstasy as he traced tiny circles around her breasts. "Beau," she murmured, gazing at his head, which was silhouetted in the moonlight. "You can't know how this feels. I've never felt so...so wonderful."

Beau did know—well, approximately—how she felt. He unlaced her bodice further and took one nipple in his mouth. For a few seconds, he paused, waiting for her to slap him or cry. Her moan of pleasure surprised and pleased him. He leaned back to look at her. Both of her breasts were gleaming white in the moonlight, except for the little dark centers, which were puckered from his touch.

He removed his coat and placed it on the grass. Before he could think more of terminating the encounter, she slid her arms around his neck and pulled him down beside her.

As his kisses and caresses thrilled her, reaching deep within her for some sort of animal response, she relinquished her hold on reality and allowed him to guide her. Fortune's blood raced through her veins, surging, singing the sweet song of desire in every part of her, filling her body with wonder and awe. Fortune felt herself drifting into a dreamy world where everything revolved around sensation. She welcomed that world with a driving response that drew them closer together.

Fortune's heart pounded, thundering in her chest as her breathing increased to a rapid rise and fall. Beau's fingers moved her skirts to one side, and his hand slid inside her pantalets.

"Ah," she gasped when he tentatively stroked the light hair at the apex of her legs.

Beau was beyond stopping. His body sought what it had long been promised. Then the pantalets were off, along with his own clothes. Her skirts were bunched about her waist, leaving bare her chest and legs.

Driven now by a desire he'd never known, Beau carefully played across her tender flesh until he knew she was ready for him. That he wanted her could not be denied. Very carefully, he positioned himself above her, continuing to caress her all the while.

Her gyrating body brought the springy hair between her legs into contact with his throbbing organ. Gently, slowly, he lowered himself until he met with resistance. Kissing her and cradling her head with his hands, he pressed forward until the obstruction disintegrated. Her gasp of pain was swallowed by his kiss.

Fortune's body was on fire. Starting with that painful thrust between her legs and rippling outward, the fire spread to every part of her until she felt as if she would be devoured by its magnificent agony.

The fire grew hotter, licking at every cell, gusting with pleasurable flames that demanded the attention of her most intimate emotions. She was no longer in control of her own movements. She met Beau thrust for thrust as his body bored into hers with a new ferocity, as if he had been awaiting this moment. Her passion spiraled higher and higher, as if the flame had been caught in a whirlwind of desire.

And then the fire exploded into a million stars, a million tiny sensations that shot through her on wave after wave of bliss so sweet that she couldn't breathe.

Fortune knew then what love was. Nothing so spectacular could be born of any other emotion.

Chapter Thirteen

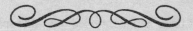

The next morning, Fortune was up before the sun. She danced around her tiny bedroom, humming joyfully as she dressed. Today was her first day of womanhood, true womanhood, and she meant to enjoy every second of it.

She completed her chores in a better frame of mind than she ever had. When she was done, she went into town. She told her mother she was going for news of the ship, but she was really going to see Beau.

When she reached town, she was taken by surprise. There were strangers everywhere. During the past few weeks, she'd gotten acquainted with nearly everyone. Now here were more than fifty people she didn't know, all milling about as if they didn't know what to do. Some of the men whistled at her or called after her, but she didn't look at them. She was too embarrassed.

Suddenly she realized who they were. They were people who were headed to San Francisco. They must have come on the *California*. Fortune hurried around them and went to Beau's quarters. He'd know what was going on.

She knocked on his door. Patrick opened it. "Fortune! What a surprise. Would you like to come in?"

"I . . . Hello, Patrick. Is Beau here?" she asked, hoping he was.

"Yes, he's here," Beau himself called from inside the room. "Come on in."

Fortune stepped over the threshold and into the dim light of the room. She smiled at Patrick and walked into Beau's

arms, though she didn't like the idea of a public display. He
held her tight for a few seconds and then kissed her gently.

"What are you doing down here?" he asked as he led her
to a chair.

"I came to see about the ship." She glanced at Patrick
and didn't sit down. As much as she liked him, she didn't
want to talk to Beau with someone else around. She needed
a confirmation that he still liked her, that he still wanted
her.

Neither of them had mentioned love. She suspected that
he didn't know about it yet. The time would come for that.

"Who are all those people?" she asked finally. "I've
never seen any of them. Did they just come in by ship? Is
the *California* here?"

Beau shook his head. "No. Actually they arrived in
Chagres last week aboard the *Falcon*. They're headed for
the gold fields."

Fortune's eyes widened in disbelief. "Where is the *California?* Where are all those people going to stay?"

"I don't know the answer to either question, Fortune."
Beau glanced at Patrick. "We've heard that some of these
people are less than scrupulous. I want you to stay out of
sight if you can. Elena, too."

"Do you think they're dangerous?" she asked, wondering what would become of the decent citizens of Panama
City.

"I don't know. They stumbled in here this morning, half-
asleep, starving, some of them drunk." Beau grimaced, not
knowing how to tell her the rest. "Fortune, some of those
people, those ladies, are, well . . ."

"Beau! You don't mean that— Gracious!" Fortune exclaimed, hardly believing what she took to be his meaning.
"Where will they—I mean, will they . . . do business here in
Panama City?"

Beau chuckled and hugged her. "I have no idea, Fortune. Let me walk you back home. I don't think you should
try to go through that crowd alone. They're pretty nasty. I
understand that not all of them have through tickets.
They're upset with the steamship company, because there's

not going to be enough room for all of us and them on the *California*. They'll have to wait for another steamer."

Fortune walked along with Beau's arm around her. The crowd hadn't dispersed one bit. She tried not to hear the lewd calls of some of the men, but she did. Beau's arm tightened around her, and his jaw worked with the anger she guessed he was feeling.

Her house wasn't far out of town. In fact, she could still hear the noise of the crowd as they got closer to her door. An idea occurred to her. She needed money badly. Some of them needed passage on the ship. "Beau, all of those people need a place to stay. I can't go anywhere with my mother in the condition she's in. Why don't I sell my tickets and build a boardinghouse?"

"A boardinghouse? Fortune, don't be ridiculous. Those men are . . . well, they're not the sort you'd want to rent a room to." Beau felt that such a venture would be dangerous. And he didn't want to think about leaving Fortune in Panama.

Fortune stopped and looked up at him. "There must be *some* decent people in that mob. That's what I'm going to do."

"Fortune, be reasonable. You won't be able to control this situation." Beau tried to think of an argument that would dissuade her, but he couldn't think of anything that sounded convincing.

Fortune shook her head. "Beau, I need the money. We have to have food and necessities."

Beau knew what it was to have no money. He'd been reared in a home where there was a constant struggle for money; still, his mother had never stopped spending. "Fortune, I have money. I'll give it to you. Whatever you need."

Fortune raised her chin and gazed into his eyes. She'd vowed never to be dependent on a man again, not even a man as kind as this one. "No, Beau. I can't accept charity." She walked a little distance from him and sat on a rock. "Mother won't be well enough to board the ship if it comes anytime soon. She's not really responding to anything. She doesn't eat, and she can't walk."

Beau sat down beside her and enfolded her in his arms. He rested his chin on her head. She was so strong, so brave, so beautiful. "Fortune, don't worry about it. You... If you feel strongly about it, you can pay me back."

She closed her eyes briefly and then smiled at him. "Thank you, Beau, but I can't take your money. I'm going to build a larger house with what little money I have left and the money I get from the sale of the tickets. It won't take long, with all these men in town who have nothing to do."

"Fortune, you can't be thinking of staying!" Beau exclaimed and jumped up. He spun around and faced her. "There's nothing here. Yellow fever runs rampant through here. The malaria is awful. You'll be dead within six months. Sell your father's ticket, but not yours."

She looked up at him. "If it's my time to die, then I'm ready. But don't you see? I can't go now. Mother wouldn't last three days on a ship in her condition."

Beau didn't know what to say. Somehow he had to make Fortune see reason. He had but a few days to do it. "Look, Fortune. The *California* should be here in a few days. When it pulls into the bay, your mother will get better quickly. She hates this place."

"That's true," Fortune conceded. "She really does hate it here. But I don't think she'll be well enough to board a ship." Standing, she grinned at him, hoping to dispel some of his apprehensions. "I've made up my mind. When can we start work?"

Though Beau couldn't see the common sense behind her idea, he acquiesced. There was no dissuading her. They'd build a larger house, one where she could take in boarders. "All right. I'll get the men together again. We'll start tomorrow."

"Thanks, Beau. I don't know what I'd do without you." Fortune melted into his arms. What *would* she do without him?

In a few days' time, the *California* would steam into the bay. Less than a week later, Beau would be gone from her life. The decision she'd made on Christmas night, to make love to him, seemed a little foolish now. Somehow she'd allowed herself to be swayed by her passion, by the power of the moment. It couldn't happen again. She drew away.

"I've got to go. I've so many things to do before the men arrive." Fortune stepped away from him, and a rush of emotions followed. She'd have to get used to that emptiness, and she might as well start now.

As Beau walked back to his lodgings, he cursed himself for not taking more of a role in Fortune's decision. He should have told her he cared for her. That would have stopped this nonsense. If she knew he cared, then she wouldn't be so reticent about borrowing money from him.

Construction began the following morning. Because of the wealth of workers, the work went quickly. More and more men came each day, asking if they could help. The labor was cheap enough, so Fortune always said yes. The house would be done much sooner with more workers. In addition to her chores, Fortune watched over every aspect of the building, offering comments here and there to make the house more what she had in mind.

"Beau," she said one morning as she watched the brown-skinned men hard at work, "why couldn't we make Eduardo a sort of supervisor? He knows more about this than either of us, and he knows most of the men."

Studying the situation for a moment, Beau had to agree. Throughout the construction, Fortune had offered several very helpful suggestions, and this might prove to be the best of all. "You know, I believe you're right."

Eduardo was honored. He took the job with a proud grin. "Eduardo do good work. You be happy."

His children, a boy and a girl, were always along to help him out. That afternoon, Fortune called them in. They seemed so little to be working at a construction site. Both of them were barefoot and nearly naked. She gave them something to eat and sat down to talk to them. As they talked, she had another idea.

When Beau stopped by later, she approached him. "Beau, I have an idea. I want you to send my books out to me."

"What are you going to do with them?" he asked, wondering what she could be up to now.

"Well, there's a reading primer among them. I want to teach Eduardo's children to read." Fortune hoped Beau wouldn't laugh at her. She had so very much to do, but still, her idea seemed like such a good one. The children were very bright, but they'd never have any opportunity to go to school.

"An excellent idea." All children needed to know how to read. But it might keep Fortune away from the construction site and out of town. He was concerned about the way some of the men in town had been looking at her. "I'll do it immediately."

By the tenth of January, Fortune and her mother were able to move into their new home. Instead of logs, the walls were made of stucco. Eduardo had planed the floors and sanded them until they were smooth. The interior walls were of smooth stucco. The entire house seemed cool, much cooler than the log cabin she'd been living in.

Letha smiled as Beau carried her into the house. Fortune knew that it was more like home, but she was afraid Letha would never be at home in Panama, no matter how grand the house. People came from everywhere to see the house. The Sloans and the Allens were among the first.

Soon, people were begging Fortune for rooms. She'd decided that she'd interview them all to make sure they were of sound character before she allowed them to move in. Rent was to be paid in advance.

Before anyone moved in, Fortune needed to restock her pantry. She went happily into town to order her supplies. When she reached the village, she was astounded. The streets were filled with people milling about, some drunk, many angry. As quickly as she could, Fortune made her way to the store. She smiled proudly at the owner. "Carlos, I'd like my usual order, except maybe we should triple it. I'm going to be taking in boarders as soon as I find some who are acceptable."

Carlos shook his head sadly. "I think you have hard time, Miss Fortune. Many people, many bad people."

"Well, there have to be some nice people among all the riffraff," she said, peering out the door.

"What is this riffraff?" Carlos asked, squinting to look into the street.

Fortune laughed and shook her head. "It's a sort of bad person."

"Sí, many riffraffs here now. Come from everywhere." Carlos looked at Fortune for a moment. "You be careful, Miss Fortune. Riffraffs like pretty girl."

Fortune went to a second store, one that had simple tools and household items. There she bought dishes, eating utensils, some large bowls, cooking pots, fabric to make sheets and towels, and several cane chairs. Eduardo was making a dining table for her. She arranged for the items to be sent to her new house and then left.

Hoping to see Beau, she went by his lodgings. She found the place bulging with activity. She stood in the doorway, uncertain about whether or not to go inside. When Beau looked up and saw her, he immediately dropped his cards and came to the door.

"Fortune, what are you doing here?" he asked, ushering her back outside. "For God's sake, you shouldn't be in town."

"Beau, I can't live like a hermit. I do have my business to take care of." Fortune was hurt that he seemed to think she wasn't capable of taking care of herself. "I'll be fine."

"Fortune, you don't know these people. This isn't the elite of society making its way to a new place where they can criticize everyone who isn't like them." Beau tried to think of a way of explaining without hurting her feelings. "These people are gamblers, prostitutes—" he used the word for its shock value "—and even worse. These people are headed for the gold fields. They had nothing to lose by dropping everything and walking onto a boat. No jobs, no money, no families."

His words bored into Fortune with the intended effect. Her face turned pale as he spoke quietly to her, trying to emphasize how horrible this town could become if the crowd got really angry.

"I understand, Beau," she said slowly, thinking of his words. "I'll simply have to find a way of coping with the situation."

"The only way to cope is to avoid a potentially dangerous predicament. Stay at home," Beau pleaded. "I'll make sure you have everything you need."

"Beau, I can't climb into a shell and pretend the bad things in the world don't exist. I simply have to learn to exist right along with them." Fortune considered the situation for a moment. Somewhere in the crowd, a gun went off. Shrieks were followed by another shot. People started to run in the direction of the gunfire. Fortune looked up at Beau and smiled. "That's it. I'll buy a gun."

"Fortune, that's ridiculous." Beau couldn't imagine this delicate flower packing a gun on her hip like some gunfighter. "I won't have you getting killed trying to defend yourself."

"Beau, don't worry. I'll practice until I'm comfortable with the gun. I'm not stupid." She tried to smile reassuringly. "I can learn to hit a target."

"But, Fortune, you don't know what it's like to kill somebody." Beau led her to the shade of a tree, and they sat down. "You can't imagine how that feels, even if you do it in self-defense."

Fortune's eyes widened. Beau had killed someone; she knew it. That was why he'd tried so hard to get away from those men in New Orleans. He hadn't wanted any trouble with the authorities, because there had been another incident. "Beau, I'm strong. I'll do whatever I have to do." She hesitated a moment, knowing that if he wanted to discuss the details of his secret he would. She decided not to press him. "If...if other people are able to kill someone...even in self-defense, and they learn to live with it, then I can. I'm very adaptable."

Beau's arms went around her. Yes, she was strong and stubborn. But she was also innocent, genuinely good inside. He wanted her to stay that way. "Fortune, I don't want you to have to feel that way. It eats you away inside. It deprives you of a part of your humanity."

Almost overcome with sadness at the depth of his feeling, she held him close and kissed him gently. She wanted to chase away all those bad feelings, all those awful memories, and fill that space in his mind with happiness. "Oh, Beau, I'm sorry."

He drew away. "Don't be. I just don't want that to happen to you."

"Don't worry about me. I'll take care of myself." Fortune tried to reassure him, though she doubted she would succeed. "Where can I buy a gun? What sort of gun would you suggest I buy?"

"Fortune, I don't—" Beau stopped in the middle of his sentence. She'd made up her mind, and there would be no changing it. "I'll see to it."

"Thank you, Beau. I knew I could count on you." Fortune leaned against him and smiled. When she was with him, she felt so good all over. The tingles of a simple touch were enough to make her happy. "I want a gun for Elena, too."

Beau shook his head and chuckled. "Well, Miss Gunslinger, I think you ought to go home. I'll get the guns as soon as possible."

"Great. Come for supper." Fortune walked toward home, glad that she'd seen Beau. He always seemed to do the right thing. Humming happily, she suddenly stopped in her tracks. There was a man coming toward her, a familiar-looking man. Dennis Forrest!

She glanced around, but there was no place for her to hide. Lifting her chin defiantly, she strode along with purpose, hoping he wouldn't recognize her.

He called across the way. "Fortune, my darling! Wait!"

Though she wanted to run, she stopped and turned to face him. All the anger she'd felt in Charleston returned. What was he doing here? He must be running from the authorities. There was no other explanation. "Hello, Dennis. What a surprise to see you here."

"I've been out to your house. I must say that it's the nicest place in Panama." Dennis bent and kissed her hand.

Unable to control her response, Fortune jerked her hand away. Taking a moment to restrain herself, she gazed steadily at him. "What were you doing there?"

"Why, I'm just in town. Naturally I would call on old friends," he said, sliding his arm around her waist. "Particularly such lovely friends."

Fortune extricated herself from his embrace and glared at him. "We are not friends, Mr. Forrest. We are acquaintances."

"Well, Letha and I don't see it that way. We had a very pleasant conversation."

"You talked to Mother?" Fortune bristled at his insolence in calling her mother by her first name. "She came out of the bedroom?" Fortune asked.

"Of course she did." Dennis shifted from one foot to the other. "Now that I've seen you, I think I'll just walk you home. I've been invited for supper. I can bring my things then."

"Things? What things?" she asked, praying that her mother hadn't done what Fortune was thinking she had.

"I'm moving in with you. Letha said you were taking boarders." Dennis grinned foolishly and winked. "And I need a place to stay."

Fury raged within Fortune. One of the main reasons she'd wanted to leave Charleston was that she'd kept running into Dennis. Now she'd have to see him every day, whether she liked it or not. She could hardly speak. "I—I can walk myself. I'm sure you have other things to do."

Fortune strode past him, intent on trying to find a way to keep him from moving in. When he followed along, she pushed him back. "Don't bother. I want to be alone."

By the time Fortune reached her home, she had calmed down a little. Letha didn't know what Dennis had done, so there was no reason to be angry with her. *Dennis* knew what he'd done. From the smug look on his face, Fortune realized that he intended to renew what he perceived to be their relationship.

She didn't know what she should do. Since her mother had invited Dennis to board with them, Fortune could hardly retract the offer. She'd simply have to find a way to avoid him.

Elena had moved into the house with Fortune and Letha. Since the house was on Elena's land, Fortune considered her a partner. Elena deserved to be warned about Dennis, particularly with him living there.

Considering the best way to broach the subject, she sat in the little window seat Eduardo had made for her and gazed out into the sunlight. She could see her happiness crumbling about her, her comfortable joy crashing into tiny shards of pain and suffering that would prick her until the day Dennis left Panama.

The one bright spot of her evening would be seeing Beau again. That and the fact that he was bringing out the guns she'd asked for.

Dennis arrived soon after Fortune did. She took him to the bedroom farthest from her own.

He looked at her with a peculiar expression on his face. "Where is your room?"

Fortune bit her lip to keep from cursing him. "Down the hall," she answered curtly, and left the room.

When she went downstairs, she found Beau in the sitting room. "Oh, I didn't know you were here."

"I just got here." He indicated two parcels on the table. "I found the guns you wanted."

"Oh, let me get Elena." Fortune hurried out to the kitchen and brought Elena back to the sitting room. "Look, Elena! Guns!"

"You bought a gun for me?" Elena asked, looking at the two packages. "What I do with a gun?"

Fortune tore off the paper wrappings and removed a gun. The dark metal shone in the sunlight streaming through the window, and Fortune caressed the cold barrel with shaking fingers. "Is it loaded?"

Beau shook his head. "I wanted to show you everything."

He took a twig and lit it from the candle burning on the table. When the flame died, he took the paper wrapping and drew a circle, marking its center with a smaller black orb. "Let's go outside."

He picked up the guns and escorted the two women outside. They walked a distance away from the house and Beau motioned for them to stop. He continued on a ways and set up the paper against a tree.

When he returned to Fortune and Elena, they sat down and listened as he told them about the guns. "Now, here's how you load the revolver. It's a Colt."

Beau demonstrated and then handed a gun to each woman. "Please be very careful."

Fortune took her gun and examined it closely. She loaded it as he'd demonstrated. "What's a Colt?" she asked, rubbing the polished metal respectfully.

"It's named for Samuel Colt. The man who invented it," Beau explained. "Now, put the bullets in the little holes."

Fortune and Elena did as he said, and he nodded his approval. "Give me your revolver, Fortune."

She handed it to him, and he showed them how to pull the hammer back. "You have to do this first to make the gun fire."

He held the revolver straight ahead and squinted as he looked down the barrel. "Keep your arm stiff. Then squeeze the trigger like so."

The deafening boom resounded through the area, and Elena screamed. "Sorry, Mister Beau. I did not expect the sound to be so loud."

"Go ahead. Point at the paper and shoot."

Elena fired first. Dirt and pebbles a foot away from the target flew into the air. "I miss."

"It takes practice," Beau said. "You didn't do too bad."

Fortune held up her gun. She tried to imitate Beau, gazing down the barrel and lining it up with the target. She slowly squeezed the trigger, though it was harder than she'd thought it would be. The gun fired, jolting her hand as the explosion occurred. Her shot struck the edge of the paper, and she grinned triumphantly.

"What in the name of sin is going on out here?" Dennis Forrest had run out of the house and down the path to where they were standing.

Fortune glanced over her shoulder. She was glad that Dennis would know she had a gun and could use it. "Hello,

Mr. Forrest. Mr. Gregory is showing us how to shoot a gun."

Dennis glared at Beau. "I'm sure that if either of these ladies needs protection I shall be up to the challenge."

Beau looked Dennis up and down and then turned his gaze to Fortune. Her face was strained, as if she were holding something awful inside. "Well, Mr. Forrest, that's comforting, I'm sure, but what if you're not around when these ladies need protecting?"

"I shall make it my purpose to protect them." Dennis glanced at Fortune. "Fortune, my dear, give the *gentleman* the gun and return to the house. Letha is concerned about you."

"I am busy learning to shoot this weapon, Mr. Forrest, so that if anyone—any man—attacks me, I can defend myself." She pointed to the target. "If you'll notice, I hit the paper on my first shot. I presume that would give an attacker something to think about."

"Fortune, you don't have to do this. I'm here now." Dennis looked at Beau for a moment. "Sir, I appreciate your kind offer to teach my fiancée to shoot, but that won't be necessary. I'm here to take care of her now."

Beau gazed at Fortune. Her face was as red as if she'd been scalded. "Well, Mr. Forrest, since Fortune asked me to teach her to shoot, I presume she thought she'd have a need of that particular skill. So, if you don't mind, we'd like to continue our lesson."

Beau slid his arms around Fortune and gripped her hands as if to help her aim. "Now, look straight down the barrel and—"

"Sir!" Dennis exclaimed, pulling on Beau's arm. "I must strenuously object to your familiar handling of my fiancée."

Knowing that something was amiss here, Beau turned to look at Dennis Forrest. He didn't seem the sort of man Fortune would be attracted to. Beau knew that this man meant nothing to Fortune, except perhaps as a vexation. "Mr. Forrest, Fortune and I have been close friends for some time now, and she's failed to mention your name at all. She's neglected to mention that she was engaged to anyone. I assume that whatever your former connection was with Fortune, it has ceased to have any meaning whatsoever.''

"There was never any connection." Fortune glowered at Dennis. She'd suspected that he'd react this way when he met Beau. "Mr. Forrest, if you're to rent a room in my home, I would appreciate it if you would stay out of my business."

Dennis's face flamed. He scowled at Fortune and then at Beau. "I presume you're the infamous Mr. Gregory that Letha told me about."

"I am Beaumont Gregory," Beau answered simply. He found the man singularly unpleasant, and wondered how Letha could be taken in by him, as she must have been.

"Then, sir, you must know that Letha doesn't want you near her daughter." Dennis smiled, as if he had somehow triumphed over Beau.

"Mr. Forrest, it matters little to me—"

"Mr. Forrest." Fortune brushed Beau aside. "I am a woman who knows her own mind. From this time forth, do not present yourself as my fiancé. My mother's opinion will not influence my decision in this regard. Now, leave us to our work."

Dennis looked from one to the other, shrugged and returned to the house. Fortune fumed with anger and humiliation. He was even worse than she had remembered.

Beau glanced at Elena, who shook her head. Though he wondered about the relationship between Fortune and Dennis, Beau said nothing. If Fortune wanted to confide in him, she would. For now, the less said the better. He could understand her reluctance to talk about the oaf. Whatever had occurred between the two of them couldn't have been pleasant. Obviously this man had just arrived today, or Beau would have heard about him before now.

Beau decided that he'd have to take more careful note of the people to whom Fortune rented rooms. There could be problems with any of them. He concentrated on helping her to learn to shoot. She might have need of the skill sooner than he had previously thought.

Conversation lulled at the supper table. Fortune could see that Beau disliked Dennis almost as much as she did. Letha came to the table to eat for the first time since Christmas. Though Fortune watched her mother carefully, she could detect no signs of excessive tiring. Having Dennis around had cheered Letha up considerably.

Beau ate quietly, listening to the conversation between Letha and Dennis. It was clear that she liked the man a great deal.

Tension sizzled around Fortune. Dennis was furious that Beau had stayed to supper, and Beau's dislike and mistrust of Dennis was readily apparent. Her own discomfort was enough to make her lose her appetite.

When the meal was over, Beau and Fortune drifted toward the door, as they usually did. The sun was going down, and they always walked then, because it was cooler.

Dennis jumped up. "Where are you going?"

Fortune turned to him and placed her hands on her hips. "If you must know, we're going for our usual evening stroll. I'm sure you're not interested in a long, brisk walk."

She spun around and walked out the door. "Honestly," she muttered as she and Beau strolled down the path.

"May I infer that you're not altogether happy that Mr. Forrest has taken up residence in your house?" he asked, linking his arm with hers.

"You may." Fortune didn't know how to tell him about Dennis, but she felt that he deserved an explanation of some sort. "I've known him since I was a child. He... Back in Charleston, he wanted to marry me. I refused."

"Sounds like an intelligent decision to me." Beau was glad that Fortune was confiding in him, even though he felt she hadn't related the entire story. Maybe she would before their walk ended.

"Believe me, it was." Fortune couldn't tell him about the attack at the Simpsons' party. Even with her present relationship with Beau, as intimate as it was, she couldn't reveal the details of that night.

They walked on a little way in silence. Beau kept looking over his shoulder. Finally Fortune leaned closer and whispered, "Are we being followed?"

"We'd better not be," Beau answered. The thought of that little worm following them was more than Beau could stomach.

His answer made Fortune glad. They were very near the area she privately termed "their place." Upon reaching the spot where they'd made love, both of them instinctively stopped. The shadows of the palms sheltered them from the view of others who might pass by, and the secluded place had become almost magnetic to them.

The thick grasses cushioned her resting place as Fortune sat down. She wanted to be alone tonight, but that meant having Beau with her. His company didn't put any pressures on her. Fortune knew what he was like, what he wanted out of life. She knew that they were of like mind on many issues. Being with him relieved many of the tensions that had plagued her since she'd been in Panama. She hoped that her companionship did the same for him.

Beau pulled her into his arms and held her close. For a while, they didn't speak, didn't move. Just being with Fortune made Beau feel good all over.

Her head was nestled in the hollow of his neck as they lay back and looked up at the stars through the palm fronds that formed their bower. Words weren't necessary. The giving and taking of comfort was enough.

The power of their lovemaking on that first occasion had stayed with him, almost frightening him with its intensity. He had never in his life experienced anything like that evening. The prospect of a similar encounter enticed him, and yet he was charged with a peculiar sense of reverence for their relationship. The change was profound yet undefinable.

After a few minutes, Beau kissed her. Like a man dying of thirst, he drank from the sweet nectar of her giving spirit. Cradling her in his arms, he tried to memorize every nuance of her lovely face, every facet of her beautiful essence.

And then he heard the sound. Pebbles being crunched beneath someone's feet. He knew that it had to be Forrest. He touched his finger to Fortune's lips, though he realized that she'd heard, too. He lay there, comfortable in the knowledge that nobody would see them, especially Forrest. He hadn't the sense to look into the shadows.

Beau waited until the footsteps went past. He and Fortune spent the time in silence, her arm around his chest, her head on his shoulder.

Fortune looked up. The new moon was on the rise, but it gave so little light that Dennis wouldn't ever find them. She rested her head against Beau's strong chest and smiled. What fun!

Wouldn't Dennis be surprised to discover that what she'd so vehemently denied him, what she'd fought to keep him from taking, she'd given freely to Beau? The thought made her pensive. The two men were so vastly different. Both were supposedly gentlemen, though neither of them truly were. Both used good manners in public, but there was still a difference. With Beau, lovemaking was a mutual pleasure; with Dennis, it was for his own selfish gratification.

There were many other differences between the two men. She believed Beau had, for the most part, been honest with her. He'd told her he never planned to marry. She could live with his decision. Dennis was never honest. Dennis fully intended to marry her, and the thought of spending the rest of her life with him was too repulsive even to consider.

After a few minutes, the footsteps went past their little grotto again. From a distance down the path came Dennis's voice calling them. Fortune felt like a child, hiding from the neighborhood bully.

But this game wasn't childish. The passionate game she and Beau were playing was anything but childish. And it was the most exciting thing she'd ever done. Her life was changed, fresh and new.

She was in love with Beaumont Gregory.

Chapter Fourteen

Falling in love. Fortune jubilantly arose from her bed, knowing that her life would be better. Her days were wonderful. She had her wonderful children, who were learning to read and write; she had the best friend she'd ever had in Elena; she had her own business and depended on nobody else; and she was in love.

What else could happen to give her more pleasure? Nothing that she could think of her. Her evening strolls with Beau were very important to her. Whether they made love or not made little difference. It was the simple joy of being together that had changed her life.

The only problems were Letha and Dennis. He was altogether a vexation. Letha was different. Fortune loved her mother and wanted her to get better. Letha seemed better since Dennis had arrived, but she still wouldn't walk, even though her leg was healed; her appetite hadn't returned, and she remained weak.

The idea of leaving when the *California* arrived was growing less and less feasible. Fortune had resigned herself to that fact. She now enjoyed her life in Panama. She had friends: Carlos at the store where she bought her food and staples; Eduardo, who did all her major construction and furniture making; the children she was teaching; Elena, who'd become like a sister. Fortune loved Panama and her new home. Leaving would bring her as much displeasure as the prospect of staying once had.

Fortune's life was almost complete. Even though she'd always denied that she wanted to get married, now her thoughts were turning to that institution. With Beau, the idea held some appeal. She was certain that he hadn't changed his mind, but if their relationship continued to progress as it had in the last few weeks, he just might.

Whatever he did, she was glad they'd made love. She was happy she'd fallen in love. Even if he left on the *California*, Fortune wouldn't be crestfallen. Being in love, the kind of love she had for Beau, was worth the heartache that might follow.

Dennis's presence bothered her. Once he discovered that she didn't intend to allow him any more liberties here than she had in Charleston, he didn't loiter in the house during the day. Finally, when he realized that she and Beau weren't going to alter their evening routine, he stopped eating supper with them.

He'd found other friends. Fortune didn't know who they were, but she was happy to be rid of Dennis as much as possible. Listening to Letha proclaim the man's goodness almost made her ill. If Dennis was as good as Letha claimed he was, then he'd be canonized—before he died.

One evening when they were walking, Beau brought up the subject of Dennis. "Did you know he's gambling like there's no tomorrow? I don't know how much he's lost, but I know he's losing badly."

Beau's comment disturbed Fortune. "What will happen if he runs out of money?"

"All the gamblers in town will cut him off." Beau looked at her speculatively. "And I guess his landlady will throw him out."

"Beau!" She stopped and stared at him. "He wouldn't lose everything he has, would he? Not even Dennis would be that foolish."

"At the rate he's losing now, I'd say there's a good chance that he's already close, unless he brought a lot more money than the other people who've been swarming into town lately."

"Heavens. I don't know what I'd do." Fortune frowned, thinking of her mother. "My mother wouldn't like it if I threw him out. She'd say that wasn't a ladylike thing to do to a gentleman such as he."

"Well, gentlemen such as he cause a lot of grief in the world," Beau said as they settled in their little bower.

"I hear from my mother all the time about what a fine gentleman he is and what a scoundrel you are." She kissed Beau on the cheek and wriggled down into his embrace. "I'll take the scoundrel any day."

"You'd better," Beau teased, holding her back to look at her. With the small amount of light that filtered through the palms, he wasn't able to see her very well, but he pretended to be studying her.

"What are you looking at?" she finally asked, when he'd been staring at her for some time.

"A truly beautiful woman," he answered, holding her close once again. Beau was sorry he'd brought up Dennis, but he thought Fortune needed to know. "A lovely lass."

"You can't see me," she retorted. "But I'll take the compliment."

Their conversation gradually was silenced by their kisses. Fortune relaxed with him, feeling the peace she'd craved all day long. Her life seemed to be almost complete.

She was almost free, and she was certainly independent. She didn't allow anyone to tell her what to do with her life, even though many people tried. Her decisions were hers alone. She'd continue to be independent for as long as she lived.

Fortune was a woman who was responsible for her own actions, and she liked it that way.

Beau's gambling salon was thriving. He and Patrick were working almost all night and a good part of the day at the salon. They now had lodgings near the gambling hall and had converted all the rooms there to public rooms.

Patrick had suggested that they hire a bartender and start serving beverages, and Beau had reluctantly agreed. He never mixed drinking and gambling, but he didn't really object if others did.

Dennis was a frequent visitor there. Beau didn't like having him around, but he lost a great deal of money at the tables and drank quite a bit. Beau treated him like everyone else. The money others lost added to Beau and Patrick's coffers, so they could hardly turn someone out unless he became rowdy.

Beau was concerned about Fortune. He didn't like the idea of Dennis living in the boardinghouse. He'd met the others: a minister, a young couple, a government employee being sent to establish a California office. She still had one room left. Fortune had given the cabin she'd lived in to Nola Bell and Boaz. Both of them worked for Fortune, helping around the boardinghouse.

There had been several break-ins at the saloon. Apparently some of the more unsavory elements in town thought they could find money there. Beau and Patrick tried to be at the establishment as much as possible, but they still couldn't prevent all the robberies.

Crime was growing worse in town. He continually cautioned Fortune against coming into the village any more than she absolutely had to. She had become a crack shot with that revolver of hers, and he made sure everyone knew that she carried one in her new leather boots, but some of the men were becoming more and more brave.

The number of Americans in Panama had risen to about six thousand, with more coming in every day. Beau found them sleeping in the streets many mornings as he walked home just before sunrise. It worried him. With so many people, and so little money and food, trouble was bound to happen.

He thought about the *California*. What would happen when the ship steamed in? Beau knew that the ship couldn't carry more than two hundred people or so. Where were all these six thousand men and women going to go?

Some people were returning to Chagres to await a boat to take them back home. When he found out about those people, Beau always tried to buy their tickets. He figured with all these people in town wanting to go to California, the man who had the most tickets would be in a position to earn a great deal of money. It was a risk, but Beau was a gambler. He thrived on taking risks.

Fortune was furious. Dennis couldn't pay his rent. She knew that her boardinghouse charged far less than many places in town. In fact, some people had doubled and tripled the rent they were charging boarders.

If Dennis were an honest man, someone simply down on his luck, she wouldn't be so angry. But she knew he'd gambled away every cent. Either that or he'd frequented the fancy parlors established by the town's newly arrived ladies of the evening. Fortune suspected he'd done both.

She went into her mother's room. "Mother, I'm going to ask Dennis to leave."

Letha sat up and stared at her daughter. "Whatever for?"

"He can't pay his rent." Fortune knew, had known from the beginning, that her mother would object.

"Oh, Fortune, we can't throw him into the streets simply because he has no money. Why..." She struggled to find just the right words. "Why, he's quality. A good man. Much better than that gambler you seem so fond of."

"Mother, we're not talking about Beau," Fortune reminded her. "The fact is that Dennis has gambled away every cent of his money, except the part he spent at the fancy house."

"Fortune!" Letha exclaimed. "Never say such a thing! A lady doesn't even *notice* such places! And I'm sure Dennis didn't lose his money gambling. It must have been stolen."

"Mother, we're talking about Dennis. He did gamble away his money. He has to move." Fortune tried to think of an argument that would convince her mother. "We need the money."

"Now, Fortune, I'm sure that Dennis is just a little short right now. He'll make it up soon."

"Where will he get the money, Mother?" Fortune asked incredulously, sitting on the side of her mother's bed. "He has no job, no way of earning money."

"Fortune, it isn't decent. We can't ask a person of quality to leave over something as trifling as money. It simply isn't done. I refuse to let you do it."

"We have to face reality, Mother. We're living on the money we make from this place. We have no other money. It's all gone." Fortune, growing exasperated, rose and paced back and forth across her mother's room. "All we have left are our tickets to California. And I may have to sell them soon."

Letha blanched. Fortune couldn't tell if her mother was upset about the possibility of remaining in Panama City or the fact that they had no money.

"We haven't come to that yet." Letha looked out the window. "I'm not going to California."

"What?" Fortune was astonished at her mother's statement. This was the first time the subject had been mentioned. "What do you mean? You want to stay here?"

"Heavens, no. I'm going home." Letha smiled sweetly. "Unless, of course, you marry Dennis. I'm sure we could get along nicely in California together."

"Mother, I'm not marrying him, and that's final. Don't bring the subject up again." Fortune strode to the door. "I'm asking Dennis to leave today."

She went to find Boaz. They looked at the land around the house, selected a good-sized plot and started to clear it for a kitchen garden. Fortune could use some of her father's seeds. The physical exercise, she reasoned, would help her to rid herself of some of the frustrations she'd faced lately, primarily because of two men—for vastly different reasons.

Fortune waited in the parlor for Dennis. She'd made up her mind. He could either pay like everyone else or get out. As of today, he'd lived there a whole week without paying. Now he said he had no money.

When he came down the stairs, Fortune was sitting on the sofa Eduardo had made. "Dennis, I want to talk to you."

"What a pleasant surprise. You're usually not around when I leave."

"Well, I'm going to be here when you leave today." Fortune crossed her arms and counted to ten. She didn't want to lose her temper. "I want you to pack your bags and go."

"What are you talking about?" Dennis stopped and stared at her. "You can't be serious. We're friends."

"We are not friends and I'm serious." Fortune stood her ground. She knew she couldn't waver one bit or he'd take advantage of her.

"I'll speak to Letha about this. She won't have it." Dennis turned and headed back to the stairs. "She's a decent woman."

"Mother has no say in the matter," Fortune said, her voice calm and even. "This boardinghouse is mine and Elena's. Go and pack your things now."

Dennis retraced his steps, ending up standing in front of Fortune. "You don't really mean that. We're too close to being married for you to throw me out. This is a petty squabble. You'll get over it."

"Dennis Forrest, we are not getting married." Fortune enunciated each word very clearly. She couldn't remember how many times she'd told him, but he refused to listen to her. *Why, oh why, won't he leave me alone? Doesn't he know how revolting he is to me?*

"You may not think so, Fortune, my dear." His voice was deadly quiet, as if he had some devious plan bubbling in his mind. "But we're going to be married very soon."

"Leave, Dennis," Fortune said simply, and began to get up. She was beginning to worry. Somewhere in the back of her mind lurked the little girl who hadn't been introduced to womanhood, the same girl that Dennis had nearly raped nearly two years before. What was he planning now?

Dennis pushed her back on the leather sofa and started to kiss her. "Give in, Fortune. You'll never regret it."

"I already regret it," she spat, striking at him as hard as she could. She fought, hitting him in the head and shoulders, but her blows had no effect. Somewhere inside her, panic began to rise, but she refused to give in to it. For a long time, she'd cried herself to sleep at night because of his loathsome behavior. No matter how strong the memories were, no matter how clear the recollections, she would have to remain courageous. She wouldn't let him do that to her again.

"Get off me!" she shouted, with a voice of authority that welled from deep within her. "Now!"

* * *

Beau took a few minutes away from the cigar smoke and tension of the gambling hall and walked out to Fortune's a little early. He had a strange urge to be with her today, even more than most days.

As he neared the house, he heard her shout and began to run. He didn't know what was happening, but he'd never heard her raise her voice, no matter how severe the problem. He reached the front door and hesitated. He didn't want to intrude on a family matter.

He listened at the door.

"Get up, Dennis," Fortune said, fighting to keep her voice calm. Every inch of her rebelled at his pawing attempts to seduce her.

"You stupid bitch. I've given you chance after chance to marry me." Dennis remained atop her, glaring down into her eyes. "You don't have sense enough to recognize the value of intimacy before marriage. We'll call it getting acquainted." He tried to kiss her again.

"Now, Dennis." Fortune slid her gun out of her boot and pressed it into his stomach. "Get off me now."

Shock registered on Dennis's face, and he slowly began to rise.

Beau didn't hesitate any longer. He burst through the door to find Dennis pinning Fortune to the sofa. Her dress was pulled up above her waist, and her hair was disheveled.

"You miserable bastard!" he shouted, lunging at Dennis.

"No, Beau!" Fortune yelled. "Stop!"

Beau stopped. What was happening? Why wouldn't she let him defend her?

Ever so slowly, Dennis lifted himself off Fortune and stood by the sofa, between her and Beau. He never looked at Beau. "You'll regret this, Fortune. You had a second chance to marry me, and you've lost it. You'll regret it."

He turned and looked at Beau. "You're responsible for this. You've turned my fiancée against me."

Fortune composed herself, using one hand to pull down her skirts. "He had nothing to do with this, Dennis. I rejected your clumsy advances in Charleston, and I reject them now. Get out of here. I'll have Nola Bell pack your things.''

Dennis opened his mouth as if to say something but apparently thought better of it. He backed away from Fortune, glared once more at Beau and hurried out the door.

Beau was about to ask Fortune how she'd stopped the assault but then he saw. Her revolver was in her hand. Beau burst out laughing. ''I swear, Fortune, I never thought you'd have to use that gun in your own home.''

''If he hadn't stopped, I'd have divided him in half with a bullet,'' she said, sliding the gun back down into her boot. ''Great boots, huh?''

''Great. Great.'' Beau sat down with her and put his arms around her. ''Fortune, are you all right?''

''I'm fine. Really.'' Fortune lay her head on his shoulder and rested it there for a moment, taking pleasure from the contact. ''This isn't the first time he's done this.''

''Then why is your mother so set on your marrying the bastard?'' Beau asked, ready to go upstairs and reprimand Letha for being so callous.

''She doesn't know.'' Fortune closed her eyes. She'd come close, this time, to losing. Dennis wouldn't have stopped if she hadn't drawn the gun. ''Thanks for the gun.''

Beau pulled back a ways and studied her. ''I'm going to get you a holster. So all these wild men in town can see that you're carrying a gun.''

''That's an excellent idea.''

They discussed the problem of Dennis. Beau felt that he should move into the vacant room so that Dennis would have no reason to think he could come back.

''But, Beau, I now have two vacant rooms.'' Fortune snuggled closer. She was happy that Beau would be living here, though she knew she'd have trouble with her mother. Letha disliked Beau even more now that Dennis had arrived in Panama to poison her mind. Still, Letha didn't own the boardinghouse. Fortune reached up and kissed Beau gently on the cheek. ''But you can move into one of them.''

The arrangements were made. Beau left to pack his bags. He didn't like living so far away from the gambling hall, but he disliked Fortune living here without his protection even more. Some things were simply more important than others.

Fortune smiled at her visitor. Sister Mary Margaret, who was going to be in Panama permanently, had no place to stay. Her church was full of people who were waiting for the *California*. As soon as people started leaving, she'd be able to live at the church.

"I heard that you operate the only reputable boarding-house in Panama City." Sister Mary Margaret smiled and looked around. "You have a very pleasant home."

"Thank you." Fortune kept staring at her. She looked very familiar, but Fortune knew she'd never met the woman. She didn't know any nuns. "I think we can arrange for your belongings to be brought up from town."

"Oh, bless you." Sister Mary Margaret sat erect on the sofa. "I'm very tired. The way from Chagres is very difficult."

"How well I know, Sister," Fortune agreed. "I came by that route, too. I've been here little more than three months myself."

"You came alone? Whatever could have made you do such a dangerous thing?"

"I didn't come alone. My mother is upstairs resting." Fortune knew that wasn't exactly true, but Sister Mary Margaret didn't have to know all the Anthony family's secrets. Letha hadn't forgiven Fortune for evicting Dennis. "My mother fell not long after we arrived. She's unable to walk very well."

"I'm so sorry."

"My father died on the way over the mountain," Fortune explained, still trying to figure out where she'd met the nun or where she'd seen her. Maybe they'd passed on the street in New Orleans. "We were going to California."

"To look for gold?" Sister Mary Margaret asked.

"No," Fortune answered. "We were going to claim some land. Now I'm afraid I'll be staying here." Fortune smiled. She didn't regret her decision. "I really like it. Besides, I think I'm needed. I'm useful for something. I'm teaching several village children to read and write.''

"A worthy occupation," the sister commented. "Well, I think—"

A loud whistling interrupted her. The tune was merry, but a little off-key.

Beau was early for supper. He was surprised to find Fortune sitting in the parlor with a nun. When the sister turned around, he was astonished. He could hardly believe his eyes.

"Hello, Beaumont," she said in a soft voice.

Fortune looked from one to the other. They obviously knew each other, so the introduction she'd been about to make was unnecessary. "Hello, Beau," she said, wonder in her voice. "I gather you know Sister Mary Margaret."

"We're well acquainted," he said, and kissed Fortune's forehead.

When he turned and did likewise to Sister Mary Margaret, Fortune's mouth gaped open. She'd never before seen a man kiss a nun. She had presumed it must be against the rules or something.

Sister Mary Margaret smiled and shook her head. "Now, Beau, don't tease Miss Anthony."

"Oh, please call me Fortune."

"I'm sorry, Fortune," Beau said, his lips turning into a smile. "Sister Mary Margaret and I have known each other since childhood."

"Since birth, in fact," Sister Mary Margaret prompted, with a loving look at Beau. "We're twins."

Fortune looked from one to the other. How could she not have known? The resemblance was striking. "I'm . . . I'm stunned."

Beau laughed. "We don't usually tell people. My sister is a saint, and I'm a sinner, so we hide our relationship. When people see us talking, they just think she's trying to convert me from my terrible ways."

"Oh, that's silly. You know it's not true, Fortune," Sister Mary Margaret said, smiling with pride at her brother. "He may be a sinner, but I still love him."

"What are you doing here?" Beau asked, dropping onto the sofa beside her.

"I am going to be here permanently," she explained. "What are you doing here?"

"Well, I'm on my way to California to seek my fortune." He glanced at Fortune, and was pleased to see that she'd caught his play on using her name. As he thought about it, he realized that both interpretations were true. Fortune was a part of his life now, though he hadn't decided just what part that would be.

Sister Mary Margaret glanced from her brother to Fortune and smiled. "I see. God bless you both."

"Oh, Sister, we're not..." Fortune began, feeling the color spring into her cheeks.

Beau, too, tried to tell his sister that she had misunderstood.

"I'm sorry. I shouldn't have jumped to conclusions." Sister Mary Margaret bowed her head to keep them from seeing her smile. She saw the love in them both. She realized that they'd be good for each other. "I do hope you'll both forgive me."

"You're home early this evening." Fortune tried to cover her embarrassment by changing the subject. She hoped that everyone in town hadn't been thinking the same thing.

"Oh, yes. I completely forgot." Beau grinned enthusiastically. "I'm the bearer of grand news. The *California* pulled into the Gulf of Panama today."

Chapter Fifteen

Beau and Patrick were very successful with their saloon and gambling hall, but the break-ins and thefts were becoming more frequent and more destructive. Beau simply couldn't be there all day and all night.

Living at Fortune's boardinghouse had plenty of advantages. The most important one was being able to protect her from Dennis and other crazed gold-seekers. The other benefits were becoming addictive. He thoroughly enjoyed eating his meals there with the small group of his fellow lodgers. The food was the best in Panama City. Having a clean room in a quiet place had made his life much more pleasant. He was getting much more rest.

Though he continually told himself that those were the reasons he liked staying there, he had another reason: He simply enjoyed being with Fortune. He could no longer deny his attraction to her. He thought of her day and night. He even found himself distracted when playing cards—and that was something that no woman had ever before done to him. His feelings were changing. He almost believed he was falling in love.

Fortune needs me, he told himself sternly, as if to refute his thoughts.

Looking out his window, he could barely see the village. Panama City was an intriguing place, alive with activity and growth. His gambling establishment was very successful, more successful than he could have ever dreamed.

But his dilemma refused to go away. He needed to be at his business to curb some of the robberies. *Damnation,* he cursed inwardly, and his silent words echoed in his mind. He couldn't abandon Fortune; nor could he forsake his business. The quandary remained.

Fortune's little reading and writing class now had four students. Carlos's daughter and Elena's niece had joined the group, much to Fortune's delight. As she and the children studied the lessons, she came to realize that she was a born teacher.

When the lessons were done for the day, each child hugged her shyly and scampered out into the yard to play. They'd be back promptly at ten o'clock the next day, as they had been for several weeks. Fortune put the books away with a sigh of satisfaction. Such lively and inquisitive children made her wish for a child of her own.

She considered her relationship with Beau. Their evening walks were very special to her—and to him, she was sure. Though she would never have believed it possible, their lovemaking had grown even more exciting. Would a baby result from those cherished moments?

What if she did get pregnant? What would happen to her and her baby? Here in Panama, society's rules were much less strict than back home in Charleston. Babies were born out of wedlock all the time without any stigma at all. Could she endure such a pregnancy?

She could. Fortune decided that, should such a thing occur, she'd consider it a blessing. She'd treasure the child with the same devotion that she applied to everything else in her life—and especially to Beau.

Her hands went instinctively to her stomach. Did a child rest inside her now? She wouldn't know for sure for a few more days, but she didn't think so. Fortune thought she would know, would realize the moment the seed had been planted. For now, she must be content with her students.

Fortune decided to go to see Jemima. Since they'd been in Panama, Jemima had visited her only rarely, and Fortune had hardly had time to plan an outing.

When Fortune arrived at Jemima's, she heard a shriek. Running as quickly as she could, she burst through the door and into the empty parlor. "Jemima!" she called, going from room to room. "Where are you?"

"Here," Jemima shouted from the bedroom.

Fortune found her lying on the bed and clutching her distended belly. "Oh, my! Is it time?"

"Yes," Jemima said quietly, closing her eyes and biting her lower lip. "I didn't want to bother Selwin. He's so— Aiee!" Jemima huffed and puffed, her face contorted into a mask of anguish.

"I'll be right back." Fortune raced out the door and over to Carlos's store. "Carlos!" she shouted, looking desperately for him. "Where are you?"

Carlos poked his head up from behind the counter. "Here, *señorita*. What is wrong?"

"I need Damita. Can you send someone for her?" Fortune didn't know where the woman lived, but she was sure he did. "Send her to the place where the Allens are staying. Do you know it?"

He nodded curtly, and Fortune rushed back to Jemima's side. "I've sent for Damita. She helped my mother when she broke her leg."

Without knowing just why, Fortune put the kettle of water on to boil. "Jemima, do you have clothes ready for the baby?"

Jemima nodded, sweat pouring from her face. "I'll be fine. How nice of you to—" Her face contorted once again. "How nice of you to drop by."

Before long, Damita arrived. She took one look at Jemima and shook her head. She muttered in Spanish and motioned for Jemima to spread her legs. Fortune tried to help, but she didn't know what to do. Elena came in soon after Damita and began to translate. Soon, the group of women were working as a team.

Fortune's gaze kept going to Jemima's face. The anguish the woman was suffering was obvious. Fortune didn't know if having a baby was worth all the pain. *And where is the father when all this is happening?* she wondered. *Probably in a saloon.*

And then the baby came. Fortune took the babe from Elena and held it close. The tiny, wriggling creature was dark red and still covered with afterbirth. "It's a boy, Jemima."

Jemima smiled, and then her face wrinkled with pain again. Fortune took the baby to the other room and sat down to bathe him. She'd never held so small a child. When she'd carefully wiped him with a warm, wet cloth, he looked very much different. His eyes were as blue as midnight, and his hair, as it dried, was turning into a puff of auburn like his mother's. Fortune knew that Jemima would want to hold him as soon as possible, so she took him back into the bedroom and handed him to his mother.

The experience touched Fortune. When she was sure that both mother and babe were fine, she returned to the boardinghouse, her mind filled with thoughts of her own child. Fortune wanted a baby, too. Even the threat of a painful delivery couldn't dissuade her now. Fortune wanted Beau's child.

Later that afternoon, Fortune and Boaz raked the garden smooth and started to plow neat rows for seeds. Beau came out of the house and watched from the piazza for a moment. Fortune was trying to plow behind one of the mules her father had bought in Cruces.

Beau tried not to laugh. She was using every ounce of strength she had, but it wasn't enough. He could see Boaz trying to reason with her, but she kept shaking her head.

What Beau knew about farming could be summed up in two words: *very little*. He could recall the slaves on the family plantation planting the fields every spring, but he'd never done it himself. It was clear that Fortune knew what to do, but lacked the physical strength to do it.

Beau removed his coat and shoes and went out into the field. He caught up with Fortune and placed his hand on her arm. Without asking permission, he took the reins from her mouth and copied her style. Firmly gripping both handles of the plow, he put the reins in his own mouth and urged the mule on.

When he had finished the plot, he looked back. His furrows weren't as straight as Fortune's, but they were done.

She and Boaz were following along behind, dropping seeds into the ground.

She glanced up at him. "Thank you. It would have taken me all day to finish that."

"Why didn't you let Boaz do it?" Beau asked, grabbing a few seeds and copying her once again.

"He's not a field hand," Fortune answered simply. "He doesn't know anything about plowing. I couldn't ask him to do that."

"Fortune..." Beau laughed and wrapped his arms around her. "You aren't a field hand, either."

"I know, but it's more or less my garden. Our garden, I guess." Fortune leaned back against him and looked over the rows. She wondered if Beau would be here long enough to see the fruits of his labor, but she instantly put those distressing thoughts out of her mind. She couldn't dwell on them. She just couldn't.

Dennis Forrest was still causing trouble for Fortune. He visited Letha frequently while Fortune was out. After every visit, Letha would rant and rave at Fortune for hours about the sinfulness of Beau's business, about how gamblers were destroying the morals of all the people in Panama.

Fortune could almost see Dennis planting the words in Letha's mouth. It was as if he'd started out planting little seeds of doubt and suspicion, and now, every time he came by, he nurtured and watered and fertilized those seeds until they grew into strong, healthy plants of rancor and hate.

There seemed to be no way of combating his venom. Letha believed every word he said to her.

"Fortune, dear..." Letha called as Fortune came up the stairs after finishing with her students.

Fortune went into her mother's room, knowing that another tirade was coming. "Yes, Mother?"

"Did you know about the shooting last night?" Letha asked, smiling maliciously.

"Yes, Mother. Everyone knows about it." Fortune couldn't deny the shooting had happened.

"Well," Letha said, apparently relishing her story. "I heard that it took place right outside that Mr. Gregory's den of iniquity. That man is a danger to all of us who are law-abiding citizens.''

''Mother, Beau didn't have anything to do with the shooting. He was here.'' Fortune had answered the accusation too many times. ''Did it ever occur to you that perhaps Dennis might have something to do with all this crime?''

''Fortune Rosalynd Anthony!'' Letha clasped her hands to her throat as if Fortune had uttered a blasphemy. ''You know that Dennis is not that kind of man. He's a gentleman of quality.''

''Excuse me, Mother,'' Fortune said, stepping toward the door. ''I think I hear Elena calling me.''

''Fortune, you come back here!'' Letha screamed as Fortune hurried down the stairs. ''I want that man out of my house!''

Fortune left Letha shrieking and went into town. She needed to talk with Beau about the possibility of selling her ticket for the *California*. Her decision had been made. Letha's ticket wouldn't be sold without her permission, but Fortune intended to sell hers if she could find a buyer.

She met Beau coming out of his gambling hall. ''Hello. I was coming to see you.''

''Is something wrong?'' he asked, concerned that there might have been an accident at the boardinghouse.

''Oh, no,'' Fortune answered quickly. ''Nothing like that. I wanted to talk about the possibility of selling my ticket for the *California*. My mother's will probably have to be sold, too, but I want to talk to her first.''

''I see,'' Beau glanced down the street at the growing crowd in front of the shipping company's offices. ''I was going to the offices of the steamer line. I don't think you should go.''

''Why not?'' she asked, her interest piqued. He'd never made such a suggestion before. ''What's going on over there?''

Beau hesitated to tell her. The situation, according to Patrick, was getting worse. The situation, in fact, might well turn into a brawl. He decided to evade the true issue.

"They're going to talk about schedules, that sort of thing. Nothing of real interest."

"Oh." Fortune was disappointed. "I guess I'll go with you anyway. I don't really have anything to do in town, and Mother's in a frightful mood today."

"Fortune, I'm sure that this meeting isn't going to—" He stopped talking. Lying to Fortune made him feel terrible. She deserved to know the truth. "Look, they're going to talk about who can board and who can't. There are likely to be a few discontented men. I think you'd be safer here or at home."

Fortune realized he was trying to protect her, but she needed to be at that meeting. She had an interest in the decision that would be made. "Beau, I deserve to hear what's said."

Beau groaned inwardly. He had known she'd take this stance. She wasn't considering the danger; all that mattered to her was her investment. "I can take care of your interests. I really think there will be a fight. It's simply not safe for you. This crowd quickly degenerates into a mob. They practically attacked Captain Forbes when he came ashore."

"Nonetheless, I'm going." Fortune turned toward the offices and started to walk, then whirled around to look at Beau. "Look, Beau, I appreciate your concern, but I truly think I need to be there."

Shrugging in defeat, Beau caught her arm, and they walked down the street together. Before that fateful August day when he'd met Fortune aboard the ship, he'd been a man who was always in control of his life. Now, he felt that—with Fortune's help—he was so far out of control that it had ceased to be amusing.

Some of his problems weren't her fault, he had to admit, but many were of her making. He had the feeling that they were walking into yet another example of a predicament generated by this spunky woman who was so determined to be independent.

Fortune looked up at Beau. She'd given up the idea of their being no more than friends. In the past few weeks, their relationship had taken on a strange aspect that she couldn't define. She could no longer deny that she loved him. She thought he loved her, but he hadn't said the words. Glancing up at him through a thick fringe of golden lashes, she wondered if he ever would.

They arrived at the offices of the steamship company and joined the throng of people, mostly men, standing there awaiting the employee who would speak to them. Fortune saw Mrs. Sloan and Amelia. She waved and smiled.

Selwin was among the group. When he saw Fortune he came over. "Hello, Miss Anthony."

"Good morning, Mr. Allen. How is your wife?"

Beaming, Selwin bobbed his head foolishly. "She's fine. Fine. And the baby is well."

"Is someone with her?" Fortune asked, feeling a little guilty for not having visited her friend more often.

"Most of the time. Our landlady is there."

Fortune had been so busy with the boardinghouse and her reading students that she hadn't visited anyone lately. She silently vowed to do better. "I'll try to stop and see her before I go home this morning."

"I'm sure she'd appreciate your visit."

Selwin might have said more, but just then a man came out of the offices and stood on a box. Fortune craned her neck to see. The man seemed to be somewhat in awe of the large crowd.

He scanned the throng, as if to judge its character, and cleared his throat. A loud whisper moved through the group like a wave cresting on the shore. Finally he raised his hands in the air calling for silence. "Ladies and gentlemen, please listen carefully." He hesitated. The noise lessened but didn't end completely.

"Silence," he shouted, and waited once again. "I am Captain Forbes of the *California*." A cheer rose from the crowd, and people began to talk again. He waited until the noise died down before continuing. "I have never seen such a phenomenon. I left New York on the sixth of October and headed for Panama. I expected to pick up no more than thirty or so passengers, although the *California* was built to carry one hundred persons."

This time the sound that came from the crowd resembled a roar. Fortune gazed up at Beau. His eyes were scanning the crowd nervously, as if to ascertain when the group would turn into a mob. He smiled, as if to say he'd take care of her. Fortune smiled proudly and pointed to her boot.

"Silence!" Captain Forbes shouted. "We steamed to Peru, where we took on food and water. There were people asking for passage to San Francisco. Since I knew of but twenty or so passengers here in Panama City, I agreed to give them berths."

This time there was no doubt about the roar. Fortune had never seen a mob in action, but she suspected that if the tenor of this speech didn't change quickly, she'd be a witness to violence today.

Captain Forbes held up his hands, and someone fired a gun into the air, silencing everyone. "Now, the steamship company has a contract with the United States government to carry mail and United States citizens. The Peruvians will have to disembark. But we will have to devise a plan for the loading of American passengers. There are far more of you than we can carry in a single trip. I will notify you of our decisions as they are made."

Fortune felt a tug on her arm, and she looked up at Beau. She nodded, and they threaded their way out of the crowd.

"I believe that group of American citizens was about to become a group of savages." Beau took her arm, and they hurried down the street. He wanted to be as far away as possible in the event that poor Captain Forbes said something to ignite the fuel of desperation that lurked in those men.

As they headed for the boardinghouse, Fortune's mind was working. "How do you think they'll work this, Beau? I mean, there are so many people wanting to leave Panama City."

"I don't know, Fortune, but I'm glad I don't have to make a decision and face that group of angry gold-seekers." Beau kept glancing back to make sure they were safe. When they reached the boardinghouse, he told Fortune, "I think you need to be ready for anything. Keep your eyes open for trouble. I'll be back when I can."

Fortune kissed him quickly and bade him goodbye. She knew that he wanted to hurry back to town to arrange for protection for his gambling hall. She knew the boarding-house might well be in just as much danger, so she went looking for Elena. She found her friend cooking dinner.

"Elena..." Fortune began, sinking into a chair. Elena was removing dried corn from the cob. "We may have a problem."

"What problem?" Elena asked, dropping a cleaned cob into the basket at her feet and taking another from the table.

"Captain Forbes from the *California* gave a speech about what the company was going to do with all these people."

"What are they going to do?" Elena cleaned another ear of corn and stared at Fortune. "There are so many Americans."

"He doesn't know yet." Fortune remembered the rumblings within the crowd. "But it's obvious that the ship can't carry everyone at once. Some people are going to be left behind. I suspect that, to be fair, he'll have to establish some order, possibly on the basis of ticket issue dates or the like."

"Fortune." Elena dropped her hands into her lap and sat back. "Are you going to California?"

That was a question Fortune didn't want to answer. More and more, she felt that she belonged here in Panama. She'd even told Beau that she planned to stay. But that had been before she'd discovered she was in love with him. Had her plans changed because of her emotional involvement with Beau?

She looked at Elena. Fortune had never had such a good friend. Within a few hours, her small pupils would arrive for their reading lesson. Her mother lay upstairs; though her leg was completely healed, she refused to arise from her bed, as if she'd been stricken by some debilitating disease.

"I honestly don't know, Elena." Fortune leaned back in her chair and closed her eyes. There were so many considerations to take into account. Even though she had always wanted to be independent, she almost wished that this responsibility had never been given to her. "There are so many things... so many people to think about."

"You want my advice?" Elena cocked her head to one side and continued without waiting for Fortune to answer. "I say leave the place. Panama stink and getting worse every day. People have no money, no education, nothing but dirt and rain and poverty. You go. Life be much better in California. You find nice husband to take care of you."

Fortune opened her mouth to comment, but closed it abruptly. Elena's remarks, spoken in her usual candor, had resolved most of Fortune's uncertainties. For the first time in her life, Fortune could make a difference. Her skills were needed as a teacher for the young, to help them rise above the lack of education, the dirt and rain and poverty that oppressed the people of Panama.

The last part of Elena's statement, along with Beau's actions, reaffirmed within Fortune the need for independence. Over the past weeks, she'd been seduced into thinking that marriage might be a viable option for her. In his concern for her, Beau had assumed that his judgment was better than hers. Maybe it was, but Fortune wanted the chance to exercise her own judgment. If she made a mistake, so be it, but she wanted the opportunity to make her own decisions, right or wrong.

Aside from that, Fortune now had to face the dilemma of her feelings for Beau. She'd grown to love him. She no longer doubted that. Her emerging passions and emotions were due to his expert tutelage, but the results were because of Fortune's inner being, her true spirit. Whatever passion he had discovered had always been there, waiting to be found, much like the gold in California. The love he'd awakened had been there, as well, suppressed because of a childhood in which affections had been strained most of the time.

She looked at Elena with a confident smile. "I'm staying here, where I'm needed."

"Americans. I will never understand them." Elena shook her head wistfully and them smiled. "But I'm very glad you going to stay."

"Me, too," Fortune said quietly. Her thoughts were on Beau. She'd known from the beginning that their relationship could never develop into anything permanent. He wasn't the sort of man to settle down; he'd told her that the first day they'd talked. Over the past few months, she'd tried time after time to warn herself, emphasizing their friendship instead of her growing love. Now she had to face the problem squarely.

Fortune had fallen in love with a man who would never love her in return. She knew that she wasn't carrying his child, and that saddened her. She might have had a baby to remind her of him when he was gone. But maybe this way was better. If the child caused Fortune to think of Beau constantly, she'd never get over him. Was it possible that she'd come to resent the child? She didn't think so, but she supposed it could happen.

Resigning herself to the idea that Beau might leave within a few days wasn't easy. Their walks of an evening had become the highlight of her day. Sometimes they discussed weighty issues; other times, they talked about trifles; occasionally they remained quiet. His companionship meant a great deal to her. She would miss him tremendously.

Beau and Patrick discussed the problem of the growing mob. Alcohol would fuel the flames of hostility, so they decided to limit the sale of spirits to the gambling hall's patrons. The other saloon owners might not agree, but Beau decided to try to work something out with them. He went from place to place, telling them of his and Patrick's plan.

Some agreed, some did not. He had more difficulty when he visited the fancy houses. Many of the madams were unwilling to cut into their profits by not selling beverages, no matter what Beau said.

Beau was sure that if Captain Forbes didn't make a decision soon, riots would occur. He was equally sure that as soon as Captain Forbes announced his decision, riots would occur. There would be no simple answers to such a monumental problem.

Beau walked through the streets of Panama City toward his gambling hall. With each passing day, the stench of human waste had grown, until he almost had to hold his breath in certain areas of town. The Americans who couldn't find lodgings were forced to sleep in the streets. Many were ill, and some were dying. The sight nearly made Beau retch as he threaded his way among them.

These people needed help quickly. Beau noticed a man who'd spent a number of evenings playing cards in the gambling hall. Waving, Beau called, "Henry, will I see you this evening?"

"No," Henry said, coming over to speak to Beau. "We're pulling out tomorrow, headed back home. The little lady can't take this place anymore. She says no decent woman ought to have to live here."

Beau agreed. This town was getting worse every day, as more and more Americans came across the mountains and swarmed into the little town. He clasped the man's hand. "Have you enough money to make it home?"

The sad look in Henry's eyes answered Beau's question. He removed a few bills from his pocket and tucked them into the man's hand. "God go with you. Be safe."

The expression on Henry's face changed perceptibly. He grinned and shook Beau's hand. "You're a good man, Mr. Gregory. Too good for the likes of this town."

"Well, don't tell anyone. Bad for my reputation as a tyrant," Beau joked and moved on. He didn't want everyone to think he was free with his money, but he'd won enough off Henry to make the uncharacteristic generosity palatable. In fact, it made him feel good.

Letha waited until she heard Fortune leave the house for her evening walk with Beau. When Letha was sure they were gone, she went downstairs. Dennis would arrive soon.

Dennis was her only friend. Fortune, though Letha believed her daughter still loved her, had abandoned her for that wicked gambler.

Within minutes of Fortune's departure, Dennis arrived. He took Letha's hand and led her to the sofa. "Letha, my dear, our moment of triumph will be soon."

"I look forward to that time." Letha seated herself and waited for the news she was sure he'd brought. He always told her about the horrible things happening in town and how dangerous the city had become. "Righteousness will triumph."

"How right you are. Won't that be a wonderful day?" Dennis gazed at Letha, joy written all over his face. "Your daughter will be swept from the iniquitous hands of that gambler and returned to your bosom to await her marriage to me."

"Oh, Dennis, none of this would have happened if we hadn't left Charleston. My poor Giles would still be alive." Letha closed her eyes sadly. Though she hadn't loved him, she truly did miss Giles.

"You're right, Letha...Mother... May I call you 'Mother'?" he asked, taking her hand and tucking it in his. "I've always admired your courage. It wasn't your fault that everything went wrong. You tried hard to keep them from making this mistake, I know you did."

"Oh, I did, Dennis, I did!" Letha exclaimed, smiling at his understanding of her situation. Nobody had ever understood her the way Dennis did.

"I'll bet they just ignored your objections," Dennis added, shaking his head as if he were deeply concerned about the way people had treated Letha. "They never realized what a wonderful woman you really are. I'd be proud to call you 'Mother'—or 'wife,' if I were a little older."

Letha blushed at his effusive praise. How Fortune could fail to see this man's merit, Letha didn't know. He was by far the most charming man she'd ever met. "You're so kind. Thank you for your sweet compliment. I'd be honored if you'd call me 'mother.'"

He hugged her quickly and then sighed. "I only wish Fortune could see me as I truly am. That man Gregory undermines me at every turn. I have tried very hard to convince her of my true love, but she's smitten with him."

"I'm afraid you're right." Letha didn't know what else to say. This nice young man had confessed his love for Fortune many times, but her daughter refused to listen to him. Letha thought Fortune didn't deserve such loyalty. "I wish I could do something."

"Oh, Letha... Mother... you've done so much already." Dennis bowed his head and assumed a pained expression. "I can't bear the thoughts of my true love in that... that fornicator's arms." He burst from the sofa and began to pace. "To think that he might have— Oh, it's too horrendous to consider."

"Dennis, calm down." Letha's face burned from her reaction to his sudden eruption. She tried to appease him. "I'm sure that Fortune isn't... I mean, that she hasn't... It's too unthinkable. She can't have allowed that man to take such liberties."

Dennis sat down and took Letha's hand again. He bit his tongue until a single tear fell from his eye. "God knows I love her. I'll kill him if he harms her."

"I'm sure that won't be necessary." Letha patted his hand comfortingly. Seeing that he was distraught, she slipped her arms around him, as a mother would her small child. "Please don't distress yourself so. Fortune won't do anything foolish. I'm sure of it."

"But what about when you get to California?" Dennis asked, with a weary sigh. "You'll be there months before I can get there."

"What do you mean?" Letha asked. She didn't think Fortune really wanted to go on to California now, but she couldn't be sure. Maybe Dennis had heard something she hadn't.

"Your tickets are through tickets, aren't they?" he asked, touching his knuckle to the corner of his eye and sniffling as if he were about to break down. "I have no ticket. I'll be left behind to be tortured by my thoughts. By the time I arrive, he could have... I mean, they might... It's too awful to ponder."

"I'd give you Giles's ticket, but I think Fortune sold it." Letha crossed her arms and leaned back thoughtfully. "But if she hasn't, I'll get it for you. That should solve everything."

"Almost," he admitted, knowing he had her firmly on his side now. Before, she had wavered, seemingly a little defensive about Fortune's actions. His playacting tonight had convinced her. "But what of that gambler?"

"What of him?" Letha asked. She thought the matter was closed until she could find out about the ticket.

"Something must be done about him, or he'll continue to hold her under his influence." Dennis jumped up and began to pace again, pretending to contemplate the situation. He wanted to force Letha to make the suggestion that would seal Beaumont Gregory's fate.

"But what can we do?" Letha asked, puzzled by his continued deliberations.

"We've got to find a way to keep them apart until she regains her senses." Dennis whirled around to face Letha. "But how?"

Letha's eyes opened wider, and she smiled. "We must discover a way to keep him from going to California."

Chapter Sixteen

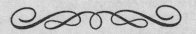

Fortune slumped in her rocking chair, the day's chores completed. Her boardinghouse was full and, even though she was grateful for her booming business, there was a great deal of work for one woman to manage.

Nola Bell wasn't much help anymore. She'd started taking in laundry, and now she had a full-time business going. Boaz had become nearly indispensable to Beau and Patrick, spending a good part of the day tending bar and running errands. Fortune was grateful that the two of them were happily earning their own way and their own place in society.

Nola Bell came to Fortune and sat on the sofa. "I come to tell you that we think we want to stay here. We happy and we got work."

Fortune smiled at her longtime servant and friend. "I'm glad. I've decided to stay here, too."

The smile on Nola Bell's face brightened. "Me and Boaz sure will be glad to have home folks here."

"Me, too." Fortune felt comforted by the feeling of having old friends to keep while adding new friends. It seemed she'd never been so blessed with such good friends. She knew she'd need them all, too. Beau would be leaving soon. She had to keep reminding herself of that.

During the past few days, she'd reconciled herself to the fact that he would soon be leaving. She'd carefully reined in her feelings, trying desperately not to attempt to change his mind or coerce him into staying. Holding her tongue wasn't easy. She knew he was still committed to going and thought he hoped she'd go too.

She couldn't understand that. He didn't want to marry, but he didn't want to break up their relationship, or so she surmised. Would he change his mind and stay?

No, Fortune, she admonished herself. *You can't even think like that. If you do, you'll be completely useless when he leaves.*

Fortune set the table for supper. This was her favorite meal, because Beau was always there. The conversation was usually light, sometimes humorous, but generally entertaining.

Sister Mary Margaret didn't always attend meals, but tonight she was present at the table. Sister Mary Margaret was regaling Fortune with tales of Beau's escapades as a little boy.

"And then there was the time when we climbed on top of the barn. Father always kept haystacks nearby." Sister Mary Margaret laughed quietly, shaking her head as she recalled the picture.

Fortune laughed with her, but noticed that Beau's face turned a little red. Was he blushing? No, it seemed to be something else. Fortune calmed down a little, hoping that Sister Mary Margaret would see the change in his demeanor. Maybe this story was too embarrassing.

"Oh, my, Fortune," Sister Mary Margaret said, laughing harder. "I wish you had been there. I jumped off the barn into the haystack. What fun. Beau refused." Then Sister Mary Margaret glanced at her twin. "Why didn't you jump?"

Beau shrugged and looked briefly at Fortune before turning his attention back to his sister. "I think we've had quite enough of the 'embarrass Beau with childhood stories' class of entertainment for one evening."

Fortune's eyes were on Beau. She suddenly knew the reason he hadn't jumped. He was afraid of heights. The image of his face as he'd edged himself over the cliff in the mountains swam before her. The expression on his face had been one of stark fear. At the time, she'd passed it off as concern for her father, but now she knew the truth.

She reached out and placed her hand over his. How could she have been so preoccupied with her own feelings that she hadn't realized how terrified he was? What courage he'd demonstrated!

Beau smiled at Fortune. She knew his secret. It would remain just that. A secret. His sister still didn't know, and she never would. Fortune knew. That made him feel good inside. Someone special shared his fear with him; he no longer bore the burden alone. Somehow, he realized, he'd never be free of the fear, but now he felt better about it. She wouldn't mention it unless he did.

Fortune heard a noise coming from the stairs. Her mother was making her way very slowly down from her bedroom for the first time in days. Fortune jumped to her feet, toppling her chair over, and hurried to help her mother. "Mother! How nice to have you join us!"

Letha looked at the small group. "Where is everyone else?"

Beau righted Fortune's chair and pulled out another for Letha. "Good evening, Mrs. Anthony. I believe almost everyone is down at the docks, awaiting information about the departure of the *California*."

Glaring at him for a moment, Letha seated herself. "Why? Is it ready to leave? Why weren't we notified? We hold tickets."

"Mother," Fortune said, sitting back in her chair, "nobody knows anything yet. Captain Forbes hadn't given any information."

"There must be some reason. You're keeping something from me. You're both lying to me." Letha noticed that there was a nun at the table, and her tone changed. "Good evening, Sister. We haven't met, but I'm Letha Anthony. I can't tell you how pleased we are to have a gentlewoman such as yourself with us. My daughter has lost her mind, having this ruffian join as at the table."

Sister Mary Margaret glanced at Fortune and then at Beau, trying to bite back her laugh. "Oh, I agree, Mrs.

Anthony. The very idea of having to sit at supper with such . . . well, I'm sure I don't know the correct word."

"It's an insult to all decency." Letha placed her napkin in her lap. "Fortune, the satin stitching on this napkin is very irregular. I want you to take it out tomorrow and replace it with nice even stitches."

Sister Mary Margaret bowed her head. Beau turned to look out the window. Fortune bit her lip to keep from laughing. "Yes, Mother, I'll try to do better. Allow me to introduce you to Sister Mary Margaret."

"See that you do." Letha helped herself to some chicken and dumplings. "Sister Mary Margaret, where are you from?"

"I grew up north of New Orleans," Sister Mary Margaret said simply.

"Oh, how very nice." Letha smiled happily. Here was someone whose presence wouldn't offend Dennis. She could hardly wait for him to arrive. "When did your parents settle there?"

"They moved there from Savannah in 1808."

"Savannah! How wonderful! We may even know some of the same people." Letha was delighted. Here was a woman she could talk with about the good life back home. "Sister, if I may be so bold as to ask, why did you become a nun?"

"My father lost his plantation." Sister Mary Margaret chose her words very carefully. "He and my mother moved into her brother's house. My brother and I couldn't stand her constant complaining and whining about the lack of money, when she'd been the cause of my father's bankruptcy."

"Gracious!" Letha exclaimed, sorry now that she'd asked. If she didn't have that information, she wouldn't have to feel so sorry for the nun. "Well, what happened to your brother?"

Beau was sipping his milk and almost choked. Sister Mary Margaret tried to keep from laughing. "Mrs. Anthony, he's sitting at your side. Beau is my brother."

Letha blanched as she tried to recall what she'd said about him. Well, she decided, whatever had been said couldn't be taken back. She tried to smile pleasantly. "What a coincidence."

The things she'd planned to say to Beau couldn't be said in the presence of his sister, so she had nothing to say for the moment.

Fortune hid her smile behind her hand and dropped her napkin. She bent over to pick it up, attempting to keep from laughing. Sister Mary Margaret had put Letha in her place, and without saying anything untoward.

Supper was a quiet meal after that. Fortune and Beau rose from the table, cleaned it off and excused themselves for their evening walk. When they were a short distance form the house, Fortune looked up at Beau. The smile that teased the corners of his mouth was contagious. Before long, both of them were laughing out loud.

"Laughter is good for you, Fortune," Beau said, catching her hand in his. "It keeps you young and pretty."

"I'm going to be quite interested to see how that looks on you," she teased, smiling coquettishly up at him.

"What do you mean?" he asked with a puzzled expression on his face.

"I'd like to see how you'd look if you were young and pretty." Fortune grinned and fluttered her eyelashes at him. "Try that to see how it works."

Beau stopped and glared down at her as if he were angry. "You're a little fresh this evening aren't you?"

"Why, suh," she began, using her best Southern drawl, "ah don't know what y'all are talkin' 'bout. Ah'm just a simple lil' ol' country girl."

"Uh-huh, a country girl." Beau lifted her off her feet and held her high over his head. He had to look up into her face to see the twinkle in her beautiful eyes. "A country girl? Let me show you how a country boy treats a country girl."

He cradled her in his arms and scooted into their little bower. Placing her on her back, he leaned over her and kissed her with a vengeance.

"Oh, suh, you quite take my breath away."

"That's what I intend to do. You're a little bit of a vixen this evening, I believe." Beau lay beside her and cradled her in his arms.

He stroked her face, still awed by the silkiness of her skin, even though it had been tanned slightly by the tropical sun. Her fragrance, mingled with that of the grass and the sea air, sent his mind reeling. He was consumed with wanting her.

Beau kissed her, taking his sustenance from her. Before long, he'd have to go down to the casino for the evening. For now, he wanted to think of nothing but Fortune. She was a witch, a witch who'd cast a spell over him, but he hadn't resisted. He was a willing captive.

Dennis came to visit Letha. He embraced her when he entered the boardinghouse. "Heavens, but you must be doing much better to have come downstairs."

"I came down," Letha explained, "because I thought that Fortune was here alone with that gambler."

"And was she?"

"No. Sister Mary Margaret was with them."

Dennis glanced around the parlor, hoping he wouldn't see the nun. "Where is she now?"

"Gone to her room to pray, I suppose." Letha sat in her rocking chair and closed her eyes. "You'll never guess who she really is."

"Who?" Dennis liked to be kept up-to-date on people in Panama. He'd made quite a few friends lately who could help him achieve his goals.

"She's his sister. That gambler's sister." Letha crossed her arms and pursed her lips. "Now, can you beat that for irony? A sister and a sinner."

"Well, just because she's a sister doesn't mean she's all that religious." Dennis dropped onto the sofa and grinned at Letha. "Women go into convents for many different reasons, not all of them relating to religion."

"I'm appalled. That's all I can say." Letha shook her head sadly. "What is the world coming to?"

"I don't know." Dennis licked his lips thoughtfully. He needed to implement the second part of his plan. Letha's chattering about this nun was preventing him from goading her into doing the things he wanted. "I do know we have to stop that gambler."

"What can we do?" Letha's interest was piqued by the mention of Beau. "Tell me, please, what can we do with that scoundrel before he ruins my daughter?"

"I'm not sure, yet. I'm still working on a plan." Dennis edged forward and tried to look as if he had a new idea. "I could move back into the house. That way, I could watch him and make sure he does nothing...questionable."

"That's a marvelous idea." Letha considered his plan. It was sound. All she had to do was a find a way to make Fortune let him move back into the house. "I'll see what I can do to help. Perhaps, if you came to visit her, she'd begin to see the difference between you and that gambler."

"I have a good idea." Dennis leapt to his feet and began pacing excitedly. "I'll move back here. We'll get rid of the other guests, and I'll find some nice ladies to move in. That way, Beau won't have a chance."

"Excellent idea. Oh, Dennis, I'm so happy. A houseful of nice ladies." Letha sat back and rocked gently. "It'll be so nice to have someone to embroider with or talk about fashion. Nobody around here knows anything at all. I'm so bored I can hardly keep from screaming."

"I'm quite sure that when these ladies move in the boredom will vanish." Dennis couldn't keep from grinning. Letha was such an easy target. Too bad her daughter wasn't. For Fortune, he'd forego all his plans. "You know, Letha, you're the head of the family now. You should encourage—no, you should order—Fortune to marry me. You know best."

Fortune's breath came in ragged spasms as Beau continued to ply her body with kisses. He'd moved from her lips, down her neck, to her breasts. Now and then a strand of his hair brushed across her stomach, sending shivers through her body.

She laced her fingers through his hair, caressing his head as he teased across her from one breast to the other, keeping the nipples in tight little buds of sensation. One of his hands danced down her stomach, tracing little swirls as he went along, swirls of sensation that took flight within her like a flock of startled butterflies.

Pressing her palms against his chest, she kissed his forehead and then the lobe of his left ear. Her fingers played through the thatch of dark curls on his chest, grazing his taut nipples with pleasure. She knew she excited him.

Fortune moaned and arched against his tender assault. Finally he moved over her, steadying himself for a moment before plunging into the moist recess between her thighs. Her moan became a gasp of pleasure, and she locked her legs around his waist.

Beau rocked back and forth, gleaning every ounce of excitement from her as she urged him on with her feminine mews and moans. He adored her. His body adored her.

Time and time again, he brought her to the precipice of ecstasy, but he refused to send her on that passionate flight of gratification. He slowed their pace, then quickened it until he knew she was eager for release.

"Now, Beau, now," she murmured against his lips as he came close to kiss her again. "Love me now."

"I do, Fortune, I do," he whispered, kissing her deeply.

His tongue explored her mouth hungrily, relishing the sweet taste that he found there. The word *love* richocheted in his mind, and soon his body was keeping pace with the surging of his blood. He could hold back no longer, and he plunged them over that precipice into the rapture that had hovered just out of reach while he'd maintained his rigid control. Wave after wave of pleasure swept through him, like the wake following a ship, powerful and intense.

When at last he lay spent beside her, he didn't want to let her go. Their time together was drawing to an end—unless she changed her mind. How could he ever leave Panama without her?

Fortune was in the best mood she'd been in for some time, and that was saying a lot. She moved around the parlor, sweeping the sand out with a brush broom and humming as she went. She couldn't ever remember feeling this good.

"Fortune," Letha said from the stairway.

"Yes, Mother?" Fortune asked, peering up the stairs.

"I'd like to speak with you."

Fortune stood the broom against the banister and followed Letha to her room. At first, Fortune had been surprised at her mother, thinking she might have dressed for the day, but Letha was still wearing her nightgown. "What is it, Mother?"

Letha said nothing for a few seconds, then slid back into bed. "It's hot here. So very hot. I understand it's much nicer in San Francisco."

Puzzled, Fortune sat on the edge of the bed. "Who told you that?"

Letha hedged for a moment. "Well, it isn't important. Someone did." She fluffed her pillow and lay down. "Fortune, I insist that you consider Dennis's proposal. He worships you. How can you be so muddleheaded?"

"Mother, I won't discuss this with you." Fortune rose and walked toward the door. "I've told you time after time that I won't marry him. It's all a ruse, Mother."

"How can you say that?" Letha sat up and glowered at Fortune. "He's been faithful to you ever since his first proposal, which is a sight more than I can say for you."

"Mother!" Trying to calm herself, Fortune waited for a few seconds before she spoke. "Don't speak of that about which you know nothing. As for me, what I do is no longer... your concern. I'm a woman now, and you must acknowledge that fact if we're to remain friends."

"Fortune, you strike me to the heart. Can't you see that I have your best interests in mind? Dennis is a wealthy young man who loves you. Give up that scoundrel before you get pregnant with his bastard." Letha lay back and turned on her side.

Fortune closed her eyes and tried to think of something to say that would finally convince her mother of the facts. "Mother, I would rather bear ten of Beau's bastards than have one single child conceived in wedlock with Dennis. That man is the scum of the earth, and one of these days you'll find out the truth. I only hope it isn't too late when you do."

Without waiting for a reply, Fortune closed Letha's door and headed downstairs. Before Fortune reached the bottom stair, Letha appeared at the top.

"Fortune!" Letha exclaimed. "I want all of these people out of my house within two days. Dennis and some lady friends are moving in. I've already given him permission."

Turning to gape in astonishment at her mother, Fortune caught her breath. "How dare you do such a thing? This house belongs to me. I shall determine who will live here and who will not. This much you can count on—Dennis Forrest will never live in this house again unless I lie cold in my grave."

Fortune hurried out the door. She could still hear Letha yelling, but she didn't stop. Before she had walked ten paces, she saw Dennis coming from town. She tried to avoid him, but he saw her and caught up with her.

"Hello, Fortune, my dear." He matched his stride with hers. "Where are we going?"

Fortune stopped and glowered at him. "*We* are going nowhere. *I* am leaving you right here."

"Come now, let's forget our differences." Dennis looked at her warily. "Are you still armed?"

"Armed and willing to shoot the...shoot any jackass who touches me without permission." Fortune stared him directly in the eye, never wavering.

Dennis loosened his grip on her arm and took a step away. "You are a tough woman, Fortune. What am I going to do with you?"

"What are you going to do with me?" Fortune repeated, wondering how she could convey her feelings to this man, who persisted in spite of the fact that she'd nearly shot him. "Nothing. Absolutely nothing. Do you understand?"

"I understand more than you think I do." Dennis backed farther away, keeping his eye on Fortune. "Letha has decided that I should move in. I plan to do so the day after tomorrow. Make sure the rooms are vacated. As I told her, I'm bringing some ladies with me."

"You're *not* moving back here. My mother has nothing to do with the decisions that are made about this house." Fury welled within Fortune. "Stay away from me, my mother and my house!"

She spun around and stalked up the pathway.

"Fortune, I wouldn't make hasty decisions if I were you," Dennis called. "There is your health and your mother's to consider."

Fortune stopped, turned slowly and stared at him for a moment. "What does that mean?"

"Oh, just that I think you should be very careful." Dennis grinned maliciously, lifting his eyebrows for emphasis. "There's no way of knowing what will happen, with all the desperate people around here."

"Desperate? Meaning you?" she asked, not taking her eyes from him. She'd known for a long time that she couldn't trust him, but she'd never thought that he would actually threaten her and her mother.

"Who knows? Panama is full of ruffians these days." Dennis walked to where she stood. He traced the line of her jaw with his finger and stared at her. "Anybody could hire one of them to do any sort of awful crime. People need money really bad. They'll do anything for a few dollars."

Fortune controlled her anger. She knew that an outburst would only make him happy. He seemed to thrive on the anger he generated in others. After a few seconds, she turned and walked steadily away without speaking. By the time she reached the house, her hands were shaking. Dennis Forrest was a dangerous man.

Waiting until she was sure he had left, she called Elena. "Elena, stay here in the house until I return. See if you can get Nola Bell and Boaz to come over, too."

"What happening?" Elena asked, studying Fortune's expression.

"It's that Dennis Forrest." Fortune didn't really want to explain, because she was still so angry, but Elena needed to know what to expect. "He's threatened me and my mother."

"But she likes him so much."

"True, but he doesn't care about her. He cares only about himself." Fortune hugged Elena. "I need you to protect Mother until I can get back with help. I'm going to hire a guard."

Fortune hurried down the path. She wanted to run, but she thought Dennis might be lurking about somewhere, watching her. She carried her shopping bag looped over her arm. Maybe that would confuse him.

She decided that she couldn't go to Beau about this, not yet. He had enough problems of his own without adding hers to the pile. Instead, she headed directly to the store in the hope that Carlos might be able to help her. He had lived in Panama all his life, and he would surely know someone who could serve as a guard out at the boardinghouse until Dennis left town or regained his senses.

As she strode on her way, she saw a man she thought she recognized, someone she didn't want to see her. "It can't be," she whispered, and slid into the shadows by the nearest building.

She waited as the man passed, bobbing drunkenly along with a companion. When the two men came closer, Fortune almost gasped aloud. It was *Abe*, the man who'd threatened to kill Beau if he ever saw him again.

Altering her route, she almost ran over to Beau's house and then banged on the door until it opened. Patrick, tucking his shirt into his trousers, flamed with color when he saw Fortune.

"What the—Miss Anthony. Forgive me, I'm not—"

Fortune closed her eyes and pushed past him. "Forget it, Patrick. I have to see Beau now. It's important. Very important."

"One moment. I'll get him. He was tired and lay down to rest for a few minutes." Patrick stumbled out of the room and into Beau's. He shook the sleeping man. "Get up. Fortune's here."

Beau sat bolt upright. "Here?" he asked incredulously, nearly falling out of bed. "What does she want?"

"I don't know, but she said it was important." Patrick slipped back into bed. "Probably wants you to take her shopping or something."

"Patrick, Fortune's not like that. She's—"

Patrick's snores interrupted Beau's retort. It was just as well. Beau pulled on his clothes, combed his hair and hurried into the parlor to see what she wanted at this ungodly hour.

"Fortune, what brings you here so early?" he asked, taking her into his arms.

She let him kiss her and then rested her head on his shoulder. Sometimes she thought that if she could simply lean there and pass all her problems to him, life would be wonderful. But she wasn't ready to relinquish her new-found independence quite yet. "Beau, I was on my way to Carlos's store, and I saw Abe."

"Abe? The drunk from New Orleans?" Beau stared down at her in disbelief. "Are you sure? Lots of men—"

"It was Abe and he was as intoxicated as ever." Fortune locked her hands behind his neck. "I'm afraid for you. Please be careful."

"I will. Don't you worry about me." Beau kissed her again and held her close. "You've got enough problems of your own." He leaned back and looked at her. "Would you like me to accompany you to the store?"

The idea was tempting, but Beau probably hadn't been in bed for long. She couldn't impose on him. "I'd love it, but I think I'd rather let you rest. You need that more than I need a companion this morning."

While she didn't want to go to Beau with her problem, she wouldn't have minded discussing it with him when he was better rested. She kissed him and left, determined to sort out the problem facing her now. However, by the time she entered the store, she hadn't completely pushed Beau's image from her mind. "*Buenos días,* Carlos."

Carlos grinned and greeted her. "What can I do for you this beautiful morning, *señorita?*"

"I have a problem, and I think you can help me." Fortune waited until a customer left the store. She glanced around until she was satisfied that they were alone. With Dennis trying to find ways to stir up trouble, she couldn't trust anyone she didn't already know.

"What wrong?" Carlos asked, peering about as if to see what she was looking for.

"I need a guard. Do you know someone who can shoot a gun and who would be willing to work for me?" Fortune hated to ask such a question. It made her feel as if she weren't capable of protecting her mother, but she knew that Dennis wasn't joking about this. His threat was real.

Carlos scratched his head and then leaned on his elbows on the countertop. "I have my brother-in-law. He...*señorita,* he not very good man like me, but he shoot straight. He loyal."

Fortune thought for a moment. Would she find a *good* man who was willing to work as a hired gun? Probably not, not in Panama. The man she'd have to hire would be on the fringes of society, perhaps with a past that reeked of crime. "How loyal is he?"

"He very loyal. Will do what Señorita Anthony say." Carlos smiled and nodded eagerly. "My sister force him. She mean."

Fortune laughed. "Maybe I should hire her to do the job."

Carlos shook his head thoughtfully. "Too mean. She make brother-in-law do good."

"Does he speak English?" Fortune asked, hoping she could be lucky enough to find someone who was loyal, could do the job and spoke English, as well.

"He no speak as good as me. He just talk pretty good," Carlos said proudly. "I speak extra good, no?"

"You speak extra good," Fortune agreed. "Send him to my house this afternoon if you can. I'd like to talk with him as soon as possible."

"He here." Carlos walked to a door behind the counter and said a few words in Spanish. "He come." After a moment, a man a little less than six feet tall came through the door. Carlos grinned and pointed to the man. "This brother-in-law, Mateo. Mateo, say hello to Señorita Anthony."

"Hello, *señorita.* I shoot people good. I talk good, too." Mateo grinned a toothless grin. "You tell, I do."

Fortune smiled in return. The man was quite eager to assist her, it seemed. Though he was shorter than Beau, Mateo had a thick, muscular build that would probably frighten anyone with any sense. "Mateo, I'm looking for someone to guard my house. My mother, Elena, a nun and

I are frequently there alone. I feel . . . I believe that in these times of high crime, we need a guard.''

"I do," Mateo said, nodding his head vigorously. He turned to his brother-in-law. "Carlos, tell *señorita* I do good for her."

Carlos spouted a few sentences in Spanish that Fortune couldn't follow. His gestures indicated that he was discussing what would happen to Mateo if he didn't do his job well. Fortune tried not to smile. She didn't want either of them to think she didn't take them seriously, or that she was making fun of them. Carlos was turning out to be a good friend.

Fortune explained to the two men about the threat Dennis had made. She hoped they understood that she wanted to be protected from him, not to have him killed.

Carlos said more words in Spanish, and Mateo nodded. After a quick exchange, Carlos leaned forward. "Mateo your man. He take care of you plenty."

"When can he come to work? What should I pay him?" Fortune asked, suddenly realizing that she hadn't given much thought to the situation.

"He come now." Carlos questioned Mateo for a moment and then turned to Fortune. "He work for food and place to stay."

For a few seconds, Fortune thought her plan was about to disintegrate. Then she remembered Elena's shack. Fortune would have to check with Elena, but she was sure everything could be arranged. "All right. We'll go talk to Elena about her hut. Will that be sufficient?"

"Be good. Very good." Carlos grinned as if he considered his part in the settling of the deal a great one. "Mateo wife have baby soon. Need house of own."

"I think we can arrange it." Fortune picked up a few items she needed. She and Mateo left the store with her packages. She made sure her right hand was free in case Dennis started trouble in town.

As they walked toward her house, Fortune and Mateo talked. She learned that he'd been without a job for some time. He and his wife lived with Carlos and his family in a small house behind the store.

"*Señorita,* I do good for you, honest," Mateo assured her, shifting the parcels he was carrying to one hand and taking the rest of them. "Do not worry for nothing no more. Mateo work very hard."

"I'm sure you will, Mateo," Fortune said, wondering exactly how this arrangement was going to work.

She decided that Mateo could sit in front of the house, on the piazza, or inside. The plan might work better if he went from the front to the back occasionally, or walked around the house. Since she and Elena were usually in the kitchen or working in the backyard, there would be little need for Mateo there, except for checking occasionally to see if everything was all right.

Before she reached the house, Dennis caught up with her. He took a glance at Mateo and then turned to Fortune. "Fortune, I've decided that we'll be married right after I move into your house."

Fortune looked at Mateo. "Mateo, this is Dennis Forrest. If he tries to get into my house, shoot him."

"What!" Dennis shrieked, his eyes widening in horror. "What's wrong with you? Have you gone daft?"

"You are what's wrong with me. If it weren't for your constant harassment, I'd be fine. Now, I'd suggest you leave me alone." Fortune leaned over, her hand moving significantly toward her right boot.

"Mateo, or whatever your name is," Dennis began, still glaring at Fortune. "This woman is my bride-to-be. Her mother has made a contract with me. If you interfere in any way, I'll have you thrown in prison."

Fortune realized that Dennis's threat was empty of validity, but she didn't know whether Mateo did or not. She looked up at him. He dropped her packages and folded his arms across his expansive chest. "I work for *señorita*. If she say shoot, I shoot." Mateo turned to Fortune and shrugged. "No have gun yet. You want me break legs instead?"

Dennis squealed as Mateo lunged for him. "Fortune, stop this fool before he hurts me!"

Fortune wanted to laugh out loud. Dennis was acting like a scared child. Mateo was holding Dennis up by the coat and his feet were barely scraping the ground. "Mateo," she said, in a very calm voice, "I believe that Dennis understands and won't give us any further problems."

Mateo slowly lowered Dennis to the ground and released him. "Don't talk bad to *Señorita* Anthony."

Dennis straightened his coat, keeping a wary eye on Mateo. "I tell you, Fortune, before the week is out, you and I will be married. Unless, of course, you'd like to *give* me your boardinghouse. I'd settle for that."

His proposition shocked Fortune. She hadn't expected Dennis to offer any further suggestions regarding the house. "Never."

Stepping out of Mateo's reach, Dennis held himself erect and studied her for a moment. "I hope you know that this fool doesn't scare me. I can get to you, Fortune. Just watch out. I'm tiring of this game. You have until nine o'clock tomorrow morning to agree to my proposal—or else."

Fortune decided that Dennis's sanity was questionable. Even though she realized his defense was mere bravado, she couldn't help wondering if hiring a guard would do her any good. Mateo wouldn't have a problem keeping other ruffians out, but Dennis was intelligent, even if he seldom chose to use his intellect.

When Dennis swaggered away, whistling as if he hadn't a care in the world, Fortune turned to Mateo. "We need to get you a gun right away. We'll ask Beau. You don't know him, but he'll get us another gun."

Fortune and Mateo reached the boardinghouse without further problems. She found Elena and discussed the problem of Mateo with her. "He needs a place for his wife. They're expecting a baby."

Elena readily assented to Fortune's plan. "Can stay in my hut. Very small, but they can stay. I be happy to have him around."

Fortune found a chair and told Mateo to take it to the piazza. They discussed what would be required of him, and he agreed to her terms. As the afternoon progressed, Fortune noted that Mateo sang as he sat on the piazza. For some inexplicable reason, that made her feel better, though he could hardly do so at night, and that was when she needed him most.

When Beau came down the stairs, she introduced him to Mateo and explained her need for another gun. Beau frequently received revolvers as settlement of debts, and he offered to send one over right after he returned to the casino that evening.

"Fortune, I'm really concerned about this man. He makes no sense." He was sitting in the parlor with Fortune, waiting for everyone to come downstairs for supper. "I think he needs to be in an asylum somewhere, where he can't hurt people. I'm afraid he's going to... I mean, I saw how he attacked you the other day."

"I never go anywhere without my gun tucked in my boot. The only time I don't have it within reach is when I sleep." Fortune felt warm inside, knowing that Beau was so concerned for her well-being. "Don't worry."

Supper was especially pleasant. Sister Mary Margaret and the preacher discussed the difference between their religions for almost the entire meal. Fortune didn't have to answer many questions, and she wasn't expected to participate in the vigorous discourse on theology.

She kept looking at Beau. What was he thinking? Occasionally her eye caught his, and he winked or grinned. Maybe he was as glad as she not to have to carry the conversation for a change.

After supper, Beau left immediately for the gambling hall. "I'll get back with the revolver as soon as possible. Let me look at yours for a moment."

He examined it carefully. "I think we need to keep oiling the parts, or we'll have a problem. Several of the guns I've seen lately have been rusted because of the humidity. I'll do it later."

Fortune cleared the table. She was undecided about her walk, since Beau wouldn't be home to escort her. After considering Mateo, she concluded that taking him with her wouldn't be prudent. He couldn't protect her mother and Elena if he wasn't there, so she completed her chores and then pulled a chair out to the piazza.

He sang happily and, after a while, Fortune began to learn the words to his songs. They laughed and sang until the sun was going down.

Then he held out his hand for her to be quiet. "Hear someone coming."

Fortune slid her hand down into her boot and slowly pulled her gun into her lap. She covered it with a fold of her skirt and waited to see who was coming up the trail. When she saw it was Beau, she relaxed. When he came close enough to hear, she called, "You almost got your ears shot off."

"Next time, I'll shout as I come up the path." Beau stepped onto the piazza and held out a revolver very similar to the ones he'd brought for Fortune and Elena.

Before he returned to the casino, he made sure that Mateo knew how to use the gun. Beau questioned the Panamanian as if he were hiring him for his own business, because he was entrusting Fortune's care to this man.

When he was satisfied that Mateo would protect Fortune, Beau kissed her goodbye and left for the gambling hall. He felt that she was safer with Mateo around, and that he wouldn't have to worry so much if he was late getting back to the boardinghouse.

Home. Beau hadn't thought of having a home in a long time. True, Fortune's boardinghouse wasn't really his home, but it had that feeling about it. He couldn't ever remember being so contented with his residence. He enjoyed the nice touches, the home-cooked food, the freshly cleaned room, the nice atmosphere and, most of all, Fortune's companionship.

Home. Why did he think of that word with reference to Fortune? He shook his head as if to clear the cobwebs. The image was still there. *Home.* He rather liked that.

Chapter Seventeen

Fortune finally mounted the stairs and went to bed. As she passed her mother's room, she heard someone talking. A man's voice. Fortune hesitated. Dread nearly consumed her. Dennis had found a way to get into the house.

It was her fault. She'd been out on the piazza with Mateo, talking, singing, passing the time. While she'd been getting to know Mateo, she'd allowed Dennis to sneak into the house.

For a moment, she didn't know what to do. She thought of calling out to Mateo, but she didn't want him to kill Dennis if it wasn't absolutely necessary. She tiptoed back to her mother's door. Feeling guilty about eavesdropping, she pressed her ear to the door to confirm her suspicions. Even though the voices were muffled, she recognized his words.

"I've given her until tomorrow morning." Dennis paced the floor. "Letha, can't you do something? You're her mother."

"I'm doing all I can," Letha whined, lying back on her pillow. She didn't know how he'd gotten into her bedroom, but here he was. She was embarrassed to be lying abed with a man in the room. Reminding herself that he would soon be her son-in-law, she pulled the bedclothes up to her chin. "What else can we do?"

"There are things I can do." Dennis settled into a chair and laced his fingers together. He was thinking of the time when he could lie with Fortune. He'd craved her affections, her body, for so long. Soon she would belong to him.

"Don't you worry. I'll handle this. Fortune thinks she can outsmart me with a native guard. Hah!"

"Dennis, what about the gambler?" Letha asked, gently reminding him of her true interest in his schemes.

"I've got a plan for him, too. He's interfered too many times for my taste." Dennis rose. "Well, I'll bid you good-evening, Mother dear."

Fortune heard him call Letha "Mother" and almost swung the door open. How vile could he get? She heard his footsteps on the floor and scurried to her room. As her door was closing, she heard him on the landing. If she closed the door, the latch would click rather loudly, so she caught it and eased it nearly shut. She hoped he wouldn't notice.

But he did. The door flew open, nearly knocking the breath out of her. Dennis caught her and threw her onto the bed, clapping his hand over her mouth almost before she could scream. The little noise that escaped wasn't loud enough to attract anyone's attention.

Fortune reached for her gun.

"Oh, no, not this time," Dennis said, twisting her arm behind her. He slid his hand into her boot and removed the revolver. "I don't think you'll need this any longer, so I'll be taking it with me."

He laid it on the floor out of her reach. Seeing the door standing open, he kicked with all his might and slammed it shut. "Now, let's see how nice you can be."

Dennis held her arms behind her with one hand and shoved the edge of the sheet into her mouth to keep her screams from being heard. Now that he had a hand free, he removed one boot and then the other, letting them drop to the floor.

Fortune's eyes filled with hatred as he slid his hand inside her dress and caught one of her nipples between his fingers. She could feel his arousal, and she realized that she might yet save herself.

When he relaxed his grip to unbutton his trousers, she steadily moved her hand toward the floor. She prayed that she could reach a boot, if not the gun. One of the boots was standing up. Fortune closed her hand around the soft kid upper of the boot and bludgeoned him with the heel as hard as she could.

When he raised up in dazed fury, she brought her knee straight up, and it caught him squarely on his aroused manhood. He yelped in agony and rolled onto the floor. Fortune dashed for her revolver and leveled it at him. "Get up and get out! If I ever see you near here again, I'll kill you without asking a question." Her tone was as deadly as the gun she held in her hand.

Dennis backed toward the door. His clothes were hanging in disarray, but he didn't pause to rearrange them. He continued edging toward the door. He opened his mouth to say something but the words never came out. The door burst open, pitching him to the floor.

Mateo reached down and lifted Dennis easily by the clothes. "Think you best Mateo, you wrong."

Without asking for permission, Mateo moved steadfastly to the open window and threw Dennis out. Dennis screamed until he hit the ground with a thud. Fortune rushed over and looked out. Dennis scrambled to his feet and started limping away, muttering curses as he went.

"Mateo, this is the second story," Fortune gently chided him. "He could have been killed."

Bowing his head in remorse, Mateo said, "I no count. Don't know numbers. Is bad?"

Fortune laughed and hugged him. "You're a gem, Mateo. Is bad you don't know numbers, but is all right you pitch Dennis through window."

That night, Fortune waited up for Beau. He came home around three in the morning. When she heard him close his door, she hurried along the landing and tapped lightly on his door.

Beau wondered what Mateo could want. Nobody else was awake, so it had to be the Panamanian. Beau swung the door open to prevent the man from knocking harder. It was Fortune, standing there in her nightgown. "Come in," he whispered.

Fortune rushed inside. She felt a little foolish sneaking down the hallway in the middle of the night, but she couldn't wait until morning to talk to Beau. She knew she was in serious trouble.

"Beau..." she began, but she didn't have a chance to finish.

He took her in is arms and held her close. Something was wrong. He could read it in her eyes. He knew that Dennis had been there, had somehow gotten into the house. Filled with rage, he clasped Fortune to him, praying that Dennis hadn't raped her.

"He didn't—? I mean, Dennis... Maybe you'd better tell me what happened, if you can." Beau lifted her and placed her in the middle of the bed. He longed to comfort her, but he didn't know exactly what to do. If she had been raped, she might not want him to touch her. If she had been raped, Dennis Forrest was as good as dead.

"Shh!" She placed her fingers across his mouth and waited while he removed his coat and sat beside her. "Don't get too upset. Dennis was here."

"I know that. I could tell by looking at you." Beau slipped off his shoes, then moved closer to Fortune, still not sure whether she would let him embrace her or not. He slid his arms around her, and she didn't complain. "What happened?"

"He sneaked inside while I was on the piazza talking to Mateo. It's my fault, really. I shouldn't have been distracting Mateo. We were talking and singing. I should simply have hired him and let him do his job. I don't know what's wrong with me. I—"

"Fortune, for God's sake," Beau whispered. "Will you stop yammering and tell me the important facts? I don't *care* if you were singing. I want to know what Dennis did!"

"Oh, sorry. He was talking to my mother. I came upstairs to go to bed and heard them from the hallway." Fortune snuggled closer. This was the first time she'd been in the bed with Beau. She liked it much better than the grass out by the fortress. "I heard him coming, so I darted into my room. He heard me, I guess."

Fortune continued to tell the story, but she could see that Beau was quite anxious about the part when Dennis burst into her room.

"What did he do?" Beau could feel his temper rising. He didn't often lose his temper, but he knew Dennis was in for a real treat come morning.

"He threw me on the bed and then tried to... He held my arms behind my back and took my gun out of my boot." Fortune shook her head in dismay. All the humiliation of Dennis's attacks flooded over her once again. She shuddered with revulsion. "I should have drawn the gun when I heard him coming. I should have killed him."

Beau listened as she continued the story.

"He would have... I mean, if I hadn't smashed him in the head with my boot heel, he'd have..." Fortune couldn't say the word *rape* to Beau. It sounded dirty, nasty, and it made her feel that way.

"Never mind. I understand." Beau held her close, as much to comfort her as to give him time to calm his outrage. He wanted nothing more than to go into town, find that bastard and wring his neck. Beau could almost feel the pleasure he'd glean from closing his fingers around Dennis's neck and choking the life from his worthless body.

"Beau, he wants this place. He's demanding that I force everyone to move." Fortune felt safe and warm in Beau's arms. The vivid memories of Dennis's attack were beginning to fade a little. "He says he knows some ladies who need a place to live. He'll move in with them and we'll all be safe."

"Ladies?" Beau laughed softly. "I know which 'ladies' he's talking about." Cuddling Fortune close, he tried to control his hatred for the man. "Fortune, they're ladies of the evening."

"What!" she exclaimed, almost bolting out of the bed. Beau caught her and pulled her back into the circle of his arms.

For a few minutes, neither Beau nor Fortune said anything. Then Fortune finished the story. Beau chuckled when she told him about how Mateo tossed Dennis out the window. "Remind me to give that man some money above what you pay him," Beau said. "Sounds to me like we both have unsolvable problems."

"What do you mean?" Fortune asked. She'd been so involved in her own difficulties that she hadn't noticed Beau's demeanor. "Tell me what happened."

"We had another robbery. The men came in right after we left last night. Patrick went home for no more than ten minutes to change clothes. When he returned, the place had been ransacked." Beau felt that his problems were minor compared to Fortune's. He hadn't intended to tell her; he'd just blurted it out.

"Sounds like we should combine our resources," Fortune said, resting her head on his shoulder. She closed her eyes, reveling in the feeling of being held by the man she loved, wondering how much longer she would have that luxury.

Beau sat up, almost dumping her off him and looked down at her. "What are you talking about?"

Fortune's eyes opened wide. "Well, I guess I was talking about putting the two businesses together, but that's really impossible."

Beau lay back and drew her into the circle of his arms again. "I guess you're right. But that would solve our problems. We'd *both* be here day and night. I have a guard; you have a guard. That way we'd have protection around the clock and you'd be safe. He wouldn't dare come here with me around."

"Beau!" she exclaimed, then clapped her hand over her mouth. She hoped she hadn't awakened anyone. "That's perfect. That's the solution to our problems. You can bring your gambling hall out here. I'd be rid of Dennis, and you wouldn't be always looking over your shoulder for Abe."

After a moment's consideration, Beau shook his head. "I don't know how we could work it. I mean, the parlor isn't big enough, and—"

"We could build another room! With all these men in Panama looking for ways to earn money, we could complete two rooms in a day or two."

The more Beau thought about the plan, the better he liked it. She was exactly right. He squeezed her tightly. "You're a genius."

Their jubilation turned to passion. Beau's kisses of victory quickly turned into deep, powerful caresses that made him forget his problems. He gently removed her gown, exposing her lovely body to the candlelight. Her skin glowed with a warm ivory color that looked like rich cream. Her hair, fanned out on the pillow, shone with the reflection of the flames.

Beau had to restrain himself to keep from forgetting her slower pace. He'd never been so eager to make love to a woman.

Fortune drew her fingers down his back in lazy circles as she teased his tongue with her own. She wasn't very well schooled in lovemaking, but she'd learned quickly that the things that pleased her pleased him, too. When he rose up above her, she caught his nipple in her mouth and nipped at the tiny bud.

Beau traced a cool trail down her belly with his tongue. "If you don't stop, you witch, I'll leave you behind and seek my own gratification. You're driving me wild."

Fortune slid her legs around him and raised her hips to meet his. "That's the way I want you. Wild as the beasts of the jungle."

Beau moaned. "Torture. You're torturing me."

"And you love it," she answered, drawing his head down so that she could kiss him again.

Though he fought it, Beau was no longer in control of his body. Fortune taunted him, turning him onto his back and then lowering her body over his. As he slid into her warm moistness, he groaned aloud and clasped his arms around her back.

She firmly pulled his hands around to her breasts. "You must do as I say, young man. I'm in charge of this lesson."

"Whatever you say," Beau whispered, reveling in the waves of passion that swept across his body as she rocked gently to and fro. "God, Fortune, you don't know what you're doing to me."

"No," she admitted, leaning forward to kiss his forehead. Her hair fell in a curtain around them, closing the world out of their private haven. "But I'm learning as I go."

Beau tried to help her establish a rhythm that would sustain both of them until her time had come. She moaned as she rocked, feeling him fill her more completely than ever.

When he could take no more of her teasing, he rolled her over and brought them to the rim of the volcano of passion. The lava inside them was mounting, bubbling and boiling as the temperature rose, until it finally shattered into a rapturous explosion of sensation that spiraled through them like the roiling smoke and ash that followed an eruption.

Fortune felt as if she were a feather, settling slowly back to earth after falling from a distant cloud. Her body tingled all over in ripples of gratification, and her eyes refused to stay open. When she awoke, she felt herself being carried. Her eyes opened slowly, and she saw Beau.

He placed her on her bed and covered her up. "Good night, love."

Beau slipped back to his room. He stood there until the sun rose, thinking about what had happened. Making love to Fortune in his bed was quite a different experience from their place near the wall. A bed lent a permanent quality to the event that both delighted and disturbed him. How could he ever leave her now?

Beau slipped out of the house without talking to Fortune. She was, he hoped, sleeping late. She deserved the opportunity. Ever since she'd arrived in Panama, she'd worked harder than any slave his father had ever owned.

He'd wrangled with his emotions all night long. If he remained here much longer, he'd never be able to leave Panama. He wasn't good for Fortune, he'd told himself over and over, finding a myriad of excellent reasons why this had to be true. She needed—no, deserved—a fine, steady man, an upstanding citizen with whom she could live out the rest of her days in peace and happiness. Trouble seemed to follow him. He simply refused to subject her to a lifetime of never knowing what to expect, of never knowing if he was alive or dead.

Before he headed down to the village, he walked out into the kitchen garden, as Fortune called it. Here and there, green shoots were poking through the ground, and he discovered that it made him proud to have been a part of the process. Here and there he found a plant that had been knocked over by the wind or an animal. He bent down and carefully mounded the earth around the tiny seedling.

He noticed that the dirt was as dry as powder. Even though he was in a hurry, Beau found a bucket and filled it with water from the creek. Working back and forth between the garden and the creek, he carefully ladled water onto every plant. He and Boaz would have to find an easier way of watering the plants. During the dry season, water had to be carried to the garden.

The dry air was still and stifling. Even though the rainy season had its own problems, Beau longed for a refreshing afternoon rain. They'd had no rain since before Christmas. After he ladled the last dipperful of water onto the plants, he set the bucket back where he'd gotten it.

"Hellfire and damnation," he cursed, righting another plant. "She's making a farmer out of me. That woman's a witch."

Beau grinned in spite of his accusations. He took a moment to survey the field once more and then walked down to the village. He had a great deal to do today.

When he reached town, he went to Eduardo's house. "Eduardo, I need two rooms built out at Miss Anthony's. Can you gather a few men to help? I want this done immediately. If you can finish it today or tomorrow, I'll double everybody's salary."

Eduardo and Beau talked over the plans for the rooms. Since they were very simple, Eduardo agreed. He left Beau and went to collect a work force.

Within the hour, men were arriving at the boarding-house. Beau purchased additional tools and had them sent out. Then he went to find Patrick.

"Patrick, my friend," Beau said, by way of greeting, "I have a proposition for us that will save us money and grief."

"What could that be?" Patrick asked, pulling on his trousers. "You have the most damnable way of waking a fellow up when he's having the most pleasant of dreams. Couldn't your idea wait until a decent hour?''

"Hardly." Beau threw him a shirt and coat. "You're slower than that mule I was plowing with at Fortune's the other day."

"You? Plowing?" Patrick stopped what he was doing and stared at Beau. "I don't believe it."

"Well, my friend, believe it." Beau laughed and sat down, draping his leg over the arm of the chair. "I wouldn't have believed it if I hadn't been there myself."

Patrick settled into a chair and gazed at Beau for a long time. "You know, that little lady is going to turn you into a real gentleman yet. I never thought I would see a scoundrel like you succumb to the feminine wiles of a society-type woman."

Beau grimaced. Patrick's words were too close to the truth for him to ignore. "I completely agree. I don't know what I'm going to do."

"Get out while you can," Patrick advised him. "You won't see me caught by a woman's guile."

A little uncomfortable with this topic of conversation, Beau decided it was time to discuss their business affairs. "I'm waiting to see about that. In the meantime, I've come to talk about the gambling hall. Fortune and I were talking about security problems. That bastard Forrest somehow got into the house last night and almost raped her."

Patrick leapt to his feet and started scrambling around for his revolver. "Are we off to kill the bastard, then?"

"Not yet." Beau was glad to see that other men were as eager to defend Fortune as he was, although he felt a twinge of jealousy. How many other men were waiting for him to leave so they could move into her life and replace him? As much as Beau disliked the idea of being tied down, he *hated* the idea of Fortune marrying someone else. "Fortune and I struck a bargain. While you sleep the morning away, men are right now working on a new gambling hall for us."

"What?" Patrick spun around and stared in disbelief. "I don't follow this conversation. Maybe after I've had some breakfast."

"Come out to the boardinghouse with me. You'll see."

On the way out to Fortune's Beau explained the plan. Patrick seemed skeptical at first, but he gradually began to see the validity of the plan. "You'll be close by all the time. Fortune's guard and ours will be on duty. By the gods, that's a capital idea! You're a genius."

"True, but I didn't come up with the plan. Fortune did." Beau couldn't take credit for her idea. She was a bright woman, and she deserved to be judged as such.

The noise was louder than Fortune expected. She stood in the doorway, fascinated by the men sitting at the tables. Smoking and drinking, they played hand after hand of cards, never noticing her standing there. Beau glanced at her occasionally, but he didn't make any outward sign that would give her away.

They'd decided to open a door off the parlor so that Beau could lock the doors and windows from the inside, bolt them and then exit into the boardinghouse. None of the patrons could use the boardinghouse door, but it made sense to do it that way.

Fortune closed the door and turned around. Letha was standing behind her. "Mother! What are you doing up?"

Letha ignored her question and pushed past her. Steadying herself against the wall, Letha opened the door slightly. Her eyes widened in horror, and she swung around to face Fortune. "What's going on?"

"Beau and Patrick added some rooms onto the boardinghouse. That way, they're protected and we're protected." Fortune knew that her mother wouldn't like the idea of gamblers being so close, but she felt she had no choice. Dennis had forced her hand.

"What are they doing in my house?" Letha demanded, her voice rising.

Fortune stepped past her mother and closed the door. She took her mother's arm and led her away. "Mother, can't you understand? Dennis is a...a bad man. He's done despicable things. He's threatened us. We need the protection of having people around."

"What I see is that you've succumbed to the charms of a gambler. He's corrupted you. You're...you're just like

your father." Letha turned and went to the stairs. Her steps
were uncertain as she slowly made her way up. "Marry
Dennis. Our problems will be over."

"Marrying Dennis would only create more problems."
Fortune tried to explain without hurting her mother un-
duly. "Mother, the ladies he wants to bring here are not ladies at all. They're..." She hesitated. How could she put
this gently? "Mother, they're fallen women."

"You're lying! Dennis would never do such a thing!"
Letha looked at Fortune, her eyes filled with contempt.
"He told me these ladies were kind and desperately needed
a place to stay. You're just lying to keep me from killing
that gambler."

"Mother!" Fortune exclaimed, rushing over and catching Letha by the arm. "You will do no such thing. I won't
have it. Beau is a fine man. He's been kindness itself
throughout this entire journey. Dennis, on the other hand,
has done nothing but make threats and maul me."

The words were out. Fortune couldn't take them back.
She saw her mother's face blanch and then redden.
"You've mistaken his love, Fortune. He adores you and
would never do anything to harm you. He's seen the way
you act around that scoundrel and is trying to woo you
away from him, nothing more."

"I know the difference between loving and mauling."
Fortune was reluctant to say anything more. If Letha knew
the truth, it would kill her. Fortune had to protect her
mother at all costs. "Mother, I want us to be happy here.
Dennis will be leaving soon. So will Beau. Don't do anything you'll regret."

Beau listened as Captain Forbes made his decision
known. The Americans would be taken from Panama to
San Francisco in the order they'd purchased their tickets.
Those not holding through tickets would have to wait.

The Americans raged. Many of those holding through
tickets were lower-class citizens, ladies of the evening and
gamblers, men who had nothing to hold them in their home
towns. Some were men escaping prosecution for crimes.

Although the steamship *California* had berths for no more than one hundred people, as many as could be accommodated would be taken aboard. A lottery would be held for those who were interested in going. Mayhem reigned among the Americans in Panama. Everyone seemed to want to get to the goldfields first.

Beau sent out word that he had tickets for sale. By the end of the day, the bids on the extra tickets he'd bought from men who'd returned to New Orleans were up to one thousand dollars apiece. Beau sold Giles's ticket for Fortune, and then her own. He made a tidy sum off the tickets that he'd had the foresight to purchase as an investment.

Patrick had also bought extra tickets. He and Beau were delighted with their profits, both on the tickets and on the receipts from the gambling hall at Fortune's, which was doing better than they had ever dreamed possible. Most of the riffraff didn't bother to go all the way out there, so the gamblers who did were more congenial and happier to spend their money.

Letha continued to rage about the gambling hall. Beau didn't care that she shouted epithets at him every time they met, but he did care about her treatment of Fortune.

"Fortune," Beau said as they sat on the piazza one evening before he went into the club. "I think you should build a house for your mother. I think she needs to be where she can't continually harangue you about the gambling hall and the boardinghouse. It's time for her to move on."

"Beau, she's my mother. I can't just put her out." Fortune knew he was right. She'd considered the idea several times herself, but she couldn't bring herself to do it.

"She's getting desperate. I'm afraid of what she'll do," Beau admitted finally.

"You're afraid of her? Of my mother? She hardly weighs ninety pounds." Fortune stared at him incredulously. How could that be?

"I'm not afraid for myself. I'm afraid for you," he explained, getting to his feet. He leaned over and kissed her on the forehead. "I don't want you hurt."

"She won't do anything to hurt me," Fortune answered, looking up into his glittering green eyes. "Don't worry about me."

After he'd gone into the gambling hall, Fortune considered what he'd said. He was right. She simply had to face the facts. Letha would be much happier where she didn't have to see people going into and out of the casino. She needed to go back to Charleston.

Fortune went to her mother's room. She found Letha staring at the wall. "Mother, may I speak with you?"

Letha shrugged, but said nothing.

Taking that as a positive response, Fortune sat on the chair by the bed. "Mother, the Reverend and Mrs. Matthews are going back to Charleston. Why don't you go with them? I could sell your ticket for the *California* and give you some money. I'm really doing well with my boarding-house."

"Would you like to return to Charleston?" Letha asked, a note of hope in her voice.

"No, Mother. I'm staying here." Fortune didn't want to upset her mother, but she had to tell her the truth. "I love Panama."

Letha turned to gaze at her daughter. "So it's come to this?"

Puzzled, Fortune looked at her mother. "What do you mean?"

"You're throwing me out for the gambler?" Letha asked quietly.

"No, of course not." Fortune realized that her mother wasn't thinking clearly, and she hadn't been for some time, but Fortune hadn't wanted to believe it. "Mother, I just want you to be happy again."

"I haven't been happy since I found that I was carrying a child." Letha stared at Fortune. "Your father was no good. He never intended to marry me. Never. He lied. Like all gamblers, he lied."

"Mother, what are you talking about? Father never gambled on anything." Fortune was growing worried. Her mother was making no sense at all now. "You don't have to go. I would love for you to stay here with me. I just want you to be happy.''

''Gamblers always win, Fortune. Remember that.'' Letha turned her back to Fortune and sighed. ''Never fall in love with a gambler.''

Fortune didn't know what to say. She wanted to take her mother by the shoulders and shake her, force her out of this daze that she seemed to be in. ''I'll leave you now. But think about it, Mother. You can go back with the Matthewses if you like. Or I could build you a little house of your own, somewhere away from the casino.''

Letha didn't respond, so Fortune left. Her mother could think about the ideas for a few days and then let Fortune know. Letha seldom made snap decisions, but Fortune realized that this was one time when she might. Letha hated Panama and she hated Beau. That might encourage her to decide right away.

Beau didn't know what to do. The *California* would be steaming out of the Gulf of Panama soon. He had a ticket. He and Patrick discussed the possibility of having two casinos.

''What is it, Beau?'' Patrick asked resting his elbows on the table. ''What's going on?''

''Patrick, I don't want to leave Fortune defenseless. That fool Dennis Forrest will do something drastic. Hell, he almost raped her, for God's sake.'' Beau shuffled the cards and then flipped them, one after another, until the table was covered. ''I don't think it's the first time, either.''

''What are you talking about?''

Beau gazed at Patrick for a moment. ''I think he tried to rape her before she left Charleston. There's something about the way she treated him, even before this last attempt.'' Beau gathered the cards again and began to shuffle. ''I don't want to leave her with that bastard around.''

''So what are you saying?'' Patrick leaned forward and cupped his chin in his hands.

''I think that you should go on to California and get our new place set up. I'll stay here and keep this one going.'' Beau had given a great deal of thought to his proposal, and he hoped Patrick would agree. "That way, we won't have any lapse in earnings."

Patrick considered the proposition. "I see what you're saying." He eyed Beau thoughtfully. "But you will come on to California when I get set up, right?"

"Right." Beau placed the deck of cards on the table. He stacked them neatly and then fanned them out before him. "There are going to be plenty of people here for a while. Why not take advantage of that situation?"

The deal bought Beau some time with Fortune. He prayed that Dennis would win one of the tickets in the lottery, but he didn't. Neither did Fortune or Beau.

On February 1, 1849, the *California* steamed out of the Gulf of Panama with half again as many people as there were berths. Fortune and Beau stood on the dock, waving goodbye to their friends, including Patrick.

Beau realized he'd significantly altered the course of his life.

Chapter Eighteen

Fortune's friends were all gone. She missed Jemima the most. Especially the tiny new baby. Fortune had tried very hard not to visit too often, but she had failed. The baby seemed to draw her.

Now that distraction was gone. Amelia and Hazel Sloan had gone on with the Allens. Of the original group that had crossed the isthmus with Fortune and her mother, only Beau, Nola Bell and Boaz remained.

Over the next few days, Fortune settled into a new routine. She worked in her garden as the sun came up, cleaned the guests' rooms when necessary, helped with the meals, taught the children and thought about Beau. He was constantly in her mind. What would she ever do without him? Even though he hadn't left on the *California,* she knew that he'd leave soon. She decided to live each day as it came and try to leave the worrying for times when it was really necessary.

There were still more than five thousand Americans in Panama. Fortune decided to add to her boardinghouse. The steamship company was trying to establish a regular schedule, but there would be many people in the future funneling through Panama on the way to California.

Fortune and Boaz expanded the garden. Occasionally, Beau would come down to help them. She didn't understand his willingness to do so, but she was glad of it. She had taught him a great deal about farming.

"Why do I need to know how to fertilize a garden?" Beau asked, pulling Fortune into his arms late one night.

They'd walked upstairs to his room, because he needed to change clothes before he went into the gambling hall. "How will that help me win at cards?"

"Oh, I don't know, but my father used to say that a man could learn many things by working in the fields. He believed the earth could teach a man how to live." Fortune smiled up at Beau. She knew that he was teasing her, that he enjoyed his time in the garden as much as she. "Have you learned anything?"

"I've learned that it's torture to watch you bending over and pulling weeds." He kissed her gently and gazed down into her remarkable eyes, feeling that familiar tug on his heart. "You're lovely. Did you know that?"

Fortune glanced at her clothes. "In my farming clothes?"

"In whatever you're wearing." Beau kissed her on the tip of the nose. "I think you must be a witch." He held her for a long moment, reluctant to release her and go to the gambling hall. "So, get on your broom and fly away so I can have some peace of mind. Besides that, I've got to dress for work."

With an air of impertinence, Fortune pointed her fingers at him and said, "I have you under my spell. You will do as I say."

Beau chuckled and then straightened his expression into one of dull compliance. "Yes. Whatever you say mistress."

Fortune tried hard not to laugh. When she could control her voice, she stared into his eyes, and once again found herself caught in the stunning depths of emerald passion. She almost forgot what she'd intended to say. "Every morning you will rise at dawn."

"Yes. Rise at dawn," he repeated in a monotone. "What services would you have me perform when nobody else is around, mistress?"

She snuggled in the warmth of his embrace, still gazing into his eyes. "I would have you weed the garden."

"Yes, mistress," he answered mechanically.

Fortune kissed him and hugged him. Beau turned her very slowly, lifted her and threw her on the bed and fell on top of her. "You're supposed to be in *my* power."

"Well, I was kissed by a beautiful princess, and that broke the spell." Beau kissed her again and again. "If you don't take yourself away very soon, we're going to have a problem. And the solution to that problem might take all night."

"I have nothing on my social calendar that would prevent my becoming involved in a project of lengthy proportions this evening." Fortune gazed up at him. She raked through his dark hair with her fingers and then slid her hands around his neck. "Please, don't rush anything on my account."

"You, young lady, are impertinent." Beau slid off her and stared at her, as if trying to decide what sort of punishment to mete out for her infractions. "Weeding the garden is probably a more fitting punishment, but I feel that a lesson could be taught right here. Perhaps, early in the morning before dawn, you should return to the scene of your crime and yield to the hands of justice."

His hand grazed across her breasts suggestively. Fortune tried to look innocent, batting her eyes at him like a flirtatious virgin. "Oh, sir, if that is what you think I need, I'd be delighted to comply. I really feel that my education in that area has been sorely neglected of late."

"Neglected, eh? We'll remedy that situation." Beau moved closer, touching his mouth to hers, gently at first, and then with more urgency. He parted her lips with his tongue, probing and plundering sensuously until he felt her breath catch. Her fragrance surrounded him, almost willing him to continue his sweet seduction, but he pulled back. "Young miss, be here thirty minutes before dawn. I should have returned from my other, more professional duties by then."

"Oh, sir," she whispered, as if she were in awe of him. "I think you're extremely professional in *everything* you do."

* * *

Fortune lay awake in her bed, staring out the window at the stars. She could see thousands, millions of stars twinkling and watching her protectively. When the moon set, she would rise and go to Beau's room to wait on his return from the casino.

She smiled smugly. Her idea had worked out rather well. Dennis had left her and Letha alone ever since the new gambling club attached to the house had opened. Apparently, with that many people around, Dennis felt he couldn't slip inside or harass her any longer.

The burglaries had ceased, too. With guards posted at all hours, the gambling hall was better protected, and the walk from town must have seemed not worth the effort to the thieves.

Fortune heard a sound and wondered if Beau had come upstairs because he'd forgotten something. She listened for the footsteps to return, but they didn't. She decided that it must have been one of the other guests.

As dawn approached, Fortune slid out of her bed and stole down the hall to Beau's room. She could wait for him there. Opening the door very carefully, she peered inside the dark room and then stepped inside. Something didn't seem exactly right to her. The lamp was out.

Fortune hesitated a few seconds more and then closed the door behind her. She walked over to the lamp, found a match and struck it. After lighting the lamp, she turned and found herself almost in Dennis's arms. Abe and his friend stood on either side of the door.

Before she could scream, Dennis clapped his hand over her mouth. "Get a handkerchief or something to stuff in her mouth."

Fortune bit his hand, but Abe struck her on the side of the head.

Dennis glowered at Abe. "What in damnation are you doing? We don't want her dead."

"Don't matter none to me, chum. I'd like to 'ave a go at 'er before yer friend gets 'ere." Abe looked down at Fortune with lust in his eyes.

Dennis stepped between Abe and Fortune's lifeless body. "Forget it. She's mine."

"Looks to me like she's 'is." Abe removed his hat and scratched his head thoughtfully. "Else she wouldn't come fallin' in that nightgown."

"Don't you worry about her." Dennis lifted Fortune and placed her on the bed. After turning the lamp down low, he motioned for the other two men to hide.

Beau locked the doors of the gambling hall and checked with Mateo, who stood guard outside. Everything seemed quiet. He thought of Fortune upstairs asleep and considered waking her. Their playful banter and kisses before he'd gone downstairs to work had left him filled with desire.

He'd never met a woman who stayed on his mind no matter what he did. As Beau circulated through the second room of the club, extinguishing lamps, he heard a noise. He walked slowly back to the door and peered into the darkness. He could see nothing out of the ordinary, but he knew something was wrong. *Maybe it was Mateo out on the porch,* he thought, and turned to go and see.

As he turned, Abe struck him on the head from behind with a gun. "There ye be, chum." Abe began looking through Beau's pockets. "I'll be takin' back me money from yer game in New Orleans, I will."

"Forget that," Dennis whispered angrily. "Get down to business."

Abe and his friend, Thomas, moved stealthily through the gambling hall, quietly turning the lamps onto their sides and letting the oil run out. Then Dennis struck a match. He glanced down at Beau and sneered. "That's for stealing my fiancée."

"What is the meaning of this?" Letha Anthony slowly looked around the room. She recognized one of the men as the one who'd accosted Beau at the dance in New Orleans. "Dennis, what is going on here?"

"We're burning out the sinners." Dennis shrugged carelessly and tossed the match onto the table with the oil. "The wages of sin."

"Dennis!" Letha exclaimed, staring in disbelief. "You're as bad as Fortune said."

"Probably worse, my dear," Dennis replied, jabbing his elbow into Abe's ribs and laughing. "You'll be delighted to know that, although I've attempted to make love to your stubborn daughter—using a bit of force—I've failed. My quick exile from Charleston was probably one of the smartest things I've ever done."

Fire began to eat away at the table, and Dennis laughed. "That whore didn't deserve to live, anyway. I doubt if the sheriff could have proved I had anything to do with her death."

"You're despicable. Get out now and never return." Letha tried to leave, but found her way barred.

"Now, Letha, my love, you wouldn't want to be hasty. Fortune's sleeping rather soundly. Abe gave her a bit of a tap on the head before we came to visit with the gambler."

"Dennis, if you've harmed my daughter in any way, I'll...I'll—" Letha kicked with her good leg, and it bit into the tender flesh of his arm.

"You bitch!" Dennis struck her across the face, knocking her into the corner. He looked at her for a few seconds. "Looks as if we'll have at least two deaths because of this fire. Let's go."

Before the two other men could slip out a side window, Dennis stabbed them both in the back, left them for dead and ran for the edge of the jungle. Then he hit Mateo on the back of the head, just hard enough to knock him unconscious for a few seconds. When Mateo awoke and noticed the fire, Dennis planned to rush out of the woods and save Fortune's life. She'd be sure to love him then. Everyone would think that the two ruffians, Abe and Thomas, had started the fire. And he would be a hero.

Fortune rubbed the back of her head. What had happened? Her mind seemed a little fuzzy. Something important had occurred, but she couldn't—"Ow!" she exclaimed. Her hand massaged a large sore lump that was the result of having been bashed in the head.

"Dennis!" she shouted, and nearly fell out of bed.

Where was he? What was he doing? Fortune ran from Beau's room and down the stairs. Dennis must be robbing the gambling hall—or worse. *Oh, God, don't let him do anything stupid,* Fortune prayed as she rushed across the parlor.

Smoke was seeping under the door of the club, which was locked from the inside. Panic caught at Fortune's heart, imprisoning her for a long moment as she tried to think. "Mateo!" she called, running to the window. She looked at Mateo's empty chair and groaned. He was slumped on the porch, unconscious.

Fortune raced to the back of the house, opened the door and screamed, "Boaz! Nola Bell! Help!"

All the people inside were in danger. Fortune knew that Beau had to be in the club somewhere, and that he had to be in imminent peril. She'd waken the people upstairs as soon as she could. She screamed, "Sister Mary Margaret! Mother! Fire!"

From the outside, Fortune could see flames in the club, licking at the walls. Everything in Panama was dry because of the lack of rain. It hadn't rained since early December. If she didn't get help soon, the house could burn in a matter of minutes.

Catching her breath, she plunged through the open window of the club. Beau had to be in here somewhere. She prayed that she'd reach him in time. The smoke was thick and black, swirling around the rooms like the menacing evils of hell.

"Beau!" Fortune screamed, stumbling over a chair. She fell onto the floor and found herself lying across something soft. It had to be Beau. "Oh, God, help me," she beseeched, clambering to her feet. She had to find a way to save Beau—if he wasn't already dead.

No, she couldn't believe that. She refused to believe that. She could still feel him too strongly in her heart. Fortune caught both his hands and dragged him toward the door. She fumbled with the tight-fitting wooden bar that secured the door from the inside. Fortune pushed and yanked on the wood until her fingers were bleeding, and it finally came loose in her hands.

She threw it to one side and swung the door open. She dragged Beau out of the burning building and to safety. As she crossed the piazza, she paused to shake Mateo. "Wake up! Fire!"

He moaned and moved slightly. Fortune couldn't take a chance. Because she couldn't drag such a large man, she rolled Mateo off the porch. Maybe that would help wake him up, she thought, and dashed into the house. She could see light in the windows of the house that Nola Bell and Boaz shared. Good. They could start bringing water from the creek.

Fortune sprinted up the stairs and banged on every door, shouting, "Wake up! Fire!"

Sister Mary Margaret appeared in her doorway, dressed in a plain white nightgown. "Did you say 'fire'?"

"Yes. Hurry." Fortune noticed that Elena had stuck her head out the door of her room. "Run! Fire!"

Elena's eyes widened, and she rushed into the corridor. Fortune, Elena and Sister Mary Margaret worked steadily down the row of doorways. When Fortune reached her mother's room, she couldn't find her. "Mother!" Fortune called, wondering what she could do.

She must be in the gambling hall. Fortune prayed that her mother was all right, that she hadn't had anything to do with setting the fire. Fortune rushed past several people who were clogging the hallway and nearly stumbled down the stairs. Sister Mary Margaret was helping them find their way through the smoke that was now filling the house.

Fortune had no choice. She had to go back into the gambling hall.

Gasping for breath, she inhaled deeply and plunged through the open door and into the black smoke. The roof was on fire in one of the rooms. The roar of the blaze was deafening. She tried to search the two rooms as methodically as she could, but the smoke made it almost impossible.

Fortune thought she was lucky. She quickly found a body and tried to lift it. The heavy weight told her that the body belonged to someone else. She couldn't lift it at all. She felt for a pulse. There was none. Right beside it, she discovered another lifeless body.

Her lungs burned and ached as she tried not to inhale the deadly ebony smoke and continued her search. She finally found Letha lying crumpled in a corner. The fire was advancing toward Fortune with sickening speed, but she had to get her mother out.

Letha was fairly light, so Fortune tried to lift her. Her unconscious form was hard to hold, and Fortune ended up dragging her as she had Beau. The backs of her legs were burning in the intense heat. Her gown must have caught fire. The smoke stung her eyes, drawing salty tears that clouded her vision even more. As Fortune neared the door, the roof started to fall in. The burning on the backs of her legs was almost unbearable. She could hardly stagger forward.

Making one last attempt, she threaded her hands under Letha's arms and locked them. When she reached the door, she pitched Letha forward onto the piazza, hoping someone would be there to help.

Fortune jumped off the porch and into the yard. She lay down on the soft grass and rolled until the flames disappeared.

There was a small crowd in the yard now. Mateo came forward and lifted Letha easily. Fortune stumbled behind, finally accepting assistance from Boaz and Sister Mary Margaret.

Fortune saw Dennis standing in the crowd. "You bastard! You murdering bastard!"

Dennis saw Mateo advancing toward him and started to run, but the big Panamanian caught up with him. "No go away until we talk."

Dennis jerked away and ran again. He took the path that Fortune and Beau always used on their evening walks.

Fortune couldn't worry about Dennis. The sun was rising. Mateo would find that criminal and bring him back. She was more concerned about the others. Her mother and Beau were both injured. Fortune found them on a grassy bank at the edge of the yard. Sister Mary Margaret was ministering to them. Elena sat with Letha's hand in her own.

"How are they?" Fortune asked, almost afraid to hear the answer.

Sister Mary Margaret looked up. "Beau's going to be fine. His injury is little more than a lump on the side of his head. I'm afraid your mother is much worse."

Fortune glanced at Beau. He looked as if he were waking up, so she sat down on the grass beside her mother. The backs of her legs ached as she folded them beneath her, but she ignored the pain. Right now, she wanted to see that her mother was all right.

The side of Letha's head was bleeding. Fortune wondered if that injury had occurred when she'd thrown Letha onto the porch, but she couldn't worry about that now. She'd done what she had to do. "Mother, are you awake?"

Letha's eyes fluttered open and then closed again. Fortune slid a hand under her head. Brushing the hair back from her mother's face, Fortune waited to see if there were any other signs of life.

"Fortune..." Letha whispered.

Fortune leaned forward to hear better. "Yes, Mother?"

"I wronged you."

"Mother, don't worry about that." Fortune caressed her mother's face. "Don't try to talk."

Elena gave Letha a sip of water. The older woman almost choked. When she could talk again, Letha continued. "I should have believed in you. Dennis was... He was the scoundrel, not Beau. You were right."

"Shh!" Fortune could hear a timorous quality in her mother's voice. "Conserve your strength. Everything will be fine."

"No, Fortune," Letha said, reaching for her daughter's hand. "I've wronged you for a long time. Your father... he abandoned me. Giles wasn't your father. Giles knew. I... I was so jealous of his love for you. Giles loved you so."

Fortune felt the breath rush out of her. Her legs were on fire, torturing her, but she couldn't rise. She had to comfort her mother. "You don't mean that, Mother."

"No, Fortune. Your father..." Letha's voice trailed off, and for a few seconds she said nothing. "Trevor Russell was your father. A gambler."

So many things were falling into place for Fortune. Her father had been a gambler, which explained all of Letha's malice toward the profession. "Don't worry, Mother. Everything will be all right."

Fortune could hardly sit still. The pain in her legs was excruciating, but she refused to move. Her mother needed her right now. Fortune noticed that Beau was leaning up on one elbow, watching and listening.

"Tell Beau... I'm sorry."

"I'm right here, Letha." Beau reached over and touched Letha's arm. "I understand."

"Forgive..."

"There's nothing to forgive. You were doing what you had to do to protect Fortune." Beau watched the two women carefully. Letha was dying. There was no doubt about that. The pained expression on Fortune's face told him that she realized it, too.

"Take... take Fortune back to Charleston." Letha tried to sit up, but fell back onto Fortune's lap.

Fortune gasped in pain and bit her lower lip to keep from crying out. "Please, Mother, don't talk anymore. Save your strength."

"No, Fortune. I'm going to be with your father. Giles... God rest his kind soul. He will be there, too. I... was never... fair to him. I love you, daughter."

Tears streamed down Fortune's face. "No, Mother. Hold on. Damita will come and—" Letha's head lolled to one side, and Fortune shook her gently. "Mother, don't go. None of this means anything. I need you. I love you."

Letha's eyes fluttered open for a brief moment. "You'll have Beau now. He's... he's a good man. Love him well."

Fortune stood beside her mother's fresh grave. Deep in her heart, she knew that her mother had found peace at last. All those years of living a lie had taken their toll. Her injuries had not truly been fatal, but Letha had had no more will to live.

The house had burned completely. She could rebuild it. There were plenty of men waiting to go to California. Some of them would work for her if she asked, though the pay would have to be small. She'd lost all her money in the fire. As soon as she was feeling better, she'd talk to Eduardo. They would work something out.

Dennis was dead, as well. Mateo had chased him all the way to the old wall. Dennis had climbed it and run along the top, and lost his balance. He fell from the wall and down a ravine. His head struck a rock.

Fortune tried very hard not to hate Dennis. He'd committed many crimes, but she felt he'd lost his mind, that he hadn't been mentally capable of determining right from wrong. Something awful had happened to rob him of his sanity.

All morning, Fortune had lain in her bed, waiting for her mother's funeral. The burns on her legs were bad; in some places the skin had been burnt away completely. Damita had bandaged the wounds and coated them with thick salve that took some of the pain away.

But the real pain was in Fortune's heart. Now, as she looked at the fresh mound of dirt that would serve as her mother's final resting place, Fortune wondered for the first time about her father. A gambler, Letha had said. That explained her irrational hatred of gamblers.

What a burden it must have been to carry such a dark secret for so many years. Her father—Giles Anthony—had known, and he had kept the secret without ever showing any sign that he cared for Fortune any less. Fortune felt tears trailing down her face once more as she thought of the kindhearted man had been her father in every way except that of blood.

And, finally, Fortune thought about her blood father. Had he been as dashing and romantic as Beau? Had Trevor Russell ever loved Letha? Had he made love to Letha and abandoned her without another thought?

Would Beau do the same?

Chapter Nineteen

Fortune rose from her bed. Her burns were healing slowly but they were healing. She and Elena had moved into the small house with Nola Bell and Boaz. Beau had returned to town and reopened the old gambling hall, though he visited almost every day.

Fortune took a sheet and walked slowly to the place where she and Beau used to meet. He was coming to see her. She sat on the sheet to wait.

After a few minutes, Beau arrived. He seemed troubled. "What's wrong?"

He sat down and looped his hands around his knees. "Fortune, it's time for me to go to California."

Fortune felt a knife slide into her heart and turn. "I see," she managed to say, biting her lip to hold back tears. She hadn't cried in a long time, not since her parents had died. Now she was facing the loss of the last precious possession she had—Beau's love.

Though he'd never said the words she was as sure of his love as she was of her own.

"I want you to go with me." Beau gazed at her. He hated knowing that he'd brought pain into her life again, so soon after her mother's death. Fortune wasn't yet physically well herself. "I think you need a change of scenery."

For a moment, Fortune said nothing. She recalled the last few words her mother had spoken. She had told Beau to take Fortune back to Charleston. And she had told Fortune to love Beau well. "Beau, I can't leave. This is my home now."

"Fortune, you've nothing left here. Your home is destroyed. You have no source of income." Beau felt a sense of foreboding well up inside him. Fortune was stubborn, after all. "I can't leave you here."

"Beau, you have no choice." Fortune stared at him, memorizing every feature, reveling anew in the strength of his jaw, the power of his green eyes. "I can't go. I'm committed to help these people. Sister Mary Margaret and I will open our little school and teach these people to read and write."

Leaping to his feet, Beau cursed inwardly. "Fortune, you can't stay. You *cannot* stay. I'd be worried to death about you."

"There's no reason to be concerned. I have friends who'll help me." Fortune tried to smile. "You won't have to...to farm anymore."

"Hellfire and damnation, Fortune!" he exclaimed. "I'm not worried about that godforsaken piece of ground. I'm worried about you."

Fortune rose and picked up her sheet. "Go on to California. I'll be fine. I want to build a plantation outside of town. I want to continue teaching my children. Don't you see? I belong here."

He ignored her reasoning. "My *fortune* lies in California. Yours, too," he said, and then he chuckled at the use of her name. "You could run a hotel, and I could have a gambling hall. We'd be rich."

She leveled an understanding gaze at him and nodded. "I am rich, Beau."

Fortune wrapped her arms around him, savoring for the last time the comfort and warmth of his embrace. When he kissed her, she responded with an assurance born of knowledge. "Now go on. I hope your life is wonderful in California. Stop and think of me occasionally."

It was all she could do to slide her hands down his chest, turn and walk away. The cycles of life were funny, in a wry sort of way, she thought. She'd been conceived by the relationship between a woman in love and a gambler. Now Fortune was breaking her relationship with a gambler who was walking out of her life.

"Fortune," he called after her. "I lo—I care for you. You must know that."

She turned and smiled. He *did* love her. He'd simply have to learn that for himself. "And I care for you. God go with you."

Beau watched her walk away, ever so slowly. He was free. He'd wanted that ever since he'd realized that he cared more for her than he wanted to admit. He was, at long last, getting what he wanted. He was free of encumbrances and was leaving for California immediately. Though he'd attained his goal, he'd never felt so miserable in his life. *Damn her for being a witch,* he thought. He loved her. And that alone was reason enough to leave Panama.

He removed his tickets from his pocket. He'd been sure that Fortune would go with him. Closing his eyes against the compelling sight of her slightly swaying hips, he dropped her ticket on the ground in their little grotto. He was free.

Fortune prayed that Beau wouldn't follow her unless he had decided to stay in Panama. He was probably right. He belonged in a place like California, where everything was more civilized. She tried to convince herself she'd be better off without him anyway, but she failed miserably.

Fortune discussed rebuilding with Eduardo. "I need this done soon, Eduardo. But I have very little money."

"You no worry, *señorita*," he assured her. "We make boardinghouse better."

Within an hour, almost forty men had gathered at the ruins of her boardinghouse. By the end of the day, all the burnt timbers were gone, and the sound of chopping and sawing filled the air.

Fortune and Boaz watched for a while, but then returned to the garden. They watered the vegetable patch by lugging buckets of water from the creek. Fortune passed a stand of trees and stopped. The distance to the creek wasn't too far. She looked at the path she took as she walked with the water bucket. She gazed at the clay banks, where the women of the village often gathered clay to make their pottery. It occurred to Fortune that if the sun-dried clay was spread along the path, it would be possible to run water from the creek to the garden.

"Elena!" she called, dropping her bucket.

Elena came running from the little house. "What is it? Snake?" She glanced around fearfully.

"No, no," Fortune assured her friend. Elena was terrified of snakes. "I have an idea."

She explained her plan for building a clay trench from the creek, and Elena nodded here and there. Fortune concluded, "We could make a little door to close off the trench when the garden was watered enough."

For the next few days, while the men rebuilt the boardinghouse, their wives and children helped Fortune build the pottery trench. Fortune immersed herself in the work with them. When she tried to thank them at the end of the day, they all shook their heads.

"*Señorita,*" Eduardo said, holding his hat in his hand, "they wish to thank you for teaching children. More children will learn."

Fortune was almost overcome by the outpouring of goodwill from her neighbors. Her home was more beautiful than ever. Her garden was watered by a little trench. She felt warm and wonderful inside.

People moved into the boardinghouse. When Fortune had enough money, she sent Elena to buy a pig. "We're going to have a barbecue."

All the workers came with their children, and they danced and celebrated that night. Fortune made sure that there was plenty of roasted corn, beans, tortillas and pork. She couldn't remember ever having felt so good.

She wished Beau could be there to join in the celebration. No wonder he hated Panama. He had never gotten to see these wonderful people when they were happy.

Boaz disappeared. Fortune searched the town over but couldn't find him anywhere. Nola Bell didn't seem too concerned, but Fortune was. He'd never done anything like that in his entire life. Fortune knew a boat had left Panama and wondered if Boaz could have been aboard, but she couldn't imagine him leaving Nola Bell.

Fortune cried herself to sleep that night. She was free and independent, answering to nobody but herself. And she was miserable.

She was going to write to Beau. He'd been gone almost a month, and she missed him terribly. Fortune felt guilty for never telling him that she loved him. If he'd known how much she loved him, he might not have left, she reasoned.

The next morning, she composed a letter. The letter seemed inadequate, but she held it for the next ship leaving Panama. She had to do something to get him back.

A few days later, Nola Bell disappeared. Fortune questioned every person she could find, but nobody had seen the woman. Nola Bell had been like a mother to Fortune all her life. Everybody she loved seemed to be disappearing.

She went to Carlos and asked him to see if he could help her find them. Fortune explained how much they meant to her, and he shook his head sadly. "Many people go away. Maybe they go home."

"No, Carlos." Her voice showed more anger than she wanted it to, but she couldn't help it. The people here were so carefree that a life seemed like nothing to them. She was convinced that they'd been kidnapped or killed. "They disappeared without a trace. They didn't go home or to California. Something is wrong."

Carlos shrugged and sat down. "Who know where they go?"

Sister Mary Margaret offered an opinion. "Maybe they went out into the jungle. Fortune, you can't search all Christendom for these people. Maybe they just went...walking. Give them a few days. They'll turn up."

Fortune jumped up and began to pace. "Sister, I expected more concern from you. You know these people. You know they aren't like that. What is wrong with everyone? Nobody seems to believe me when I tell them that I suspect foul play."

Several days passed, and neither Boaz nor Nola Bell returned. Fortune was convinced they were dead. She went into the edge of the jungle and found a tropical vine like the one she'd planted on her father's grave and placed it on her mother's.

As she mounded the soft dirt around the roots of the plant, she talked to her mother. "Mother, I know that Beau loves me. I've got to go to him. I've got to find a way to tell him that he means more to me than anything or anyone on earth. I . . . I hope you understand."

Fortune got to her feet. She walked slowly back to her beautiful boardinghouse. In a little while, the children would arrive for their lessons. After they left, she'd go and see about arranging for passage to California.

When Fortune arrived at the house, she called for Elena. Elena didn't respond. Fortune went into every room, asking everyone she saw if they'd seen Elena. She searched every place she could think of, but still didn't find her.

It was time for the children to arrive. Fortune's books had been lost in the fire, but she had found paper and had written stories for them to read. She had done the best she could. As she waited for the children, she began to worry. They should have been here thirty minutes ago.

Fortune went to the door and looked out. She could see no one on the trail; nor could she hear the gay, chattering voices she'd grown to love.

Something was terribly wrong. Where could they be? Where were Boaz, Nola Bell and Elena? None of this made sense. It seemed as if the earth had opened and swallowed them up.

She sat in her new rocking chair and rocked nervously, wondering what she should do. There seemed to be no easy answers.

Then she heard a noise outside. *Ah, there they are,* she thought. She'd scold them for being late—and then hug them to her breast. She loved them all.

Fortune ran to the door. Beau was standing there waiting for her. "Beau!"

She opened the door and leapt into his arms. "Oh, Beau, I'm so happy to see you."

He held her close. He knew she'd be furious when she found out what he'd done, but it couldn't be helped. "Come with me."

He distanced himself from her, though all he wanted to do was lose himself in the world of gentleness within her arms. He took her to a rickety wagon and lifted her into the seat.

"Where are we going?" she asked, looking at the array of goods in the bed of the wagon. "What's going on?"

"I'm sorry, Miss Anthony, but you aren't allowed to ask any questions of the driver." Beau jumped in beside her and flicked the reins. The mule plodded along. Beau suspected that if they didn't hurry he'd stop the mule and make love to Fortune in the bed of the wagon. He'd never experienced anything as awful as the few weeks they'd been apart, and he never wanted to again.

The little road led into the jungle. Beau refused to talk to her, and he refused to answer her questions. But for now, just being with him was enough for Fortune. All the questions and answers would come later.

After about a mile, Beau stopped the wagon. "Fortune, before we go any farther, I'd like to apologize for the terrible torture I've put you through. I hope you'll forgive me."

"Beau, what are you—"

"No questions, *señorita*," he said, shaking his head and waving his hand.

Once again he prodded the mule into motion, and the wagon lurched forward through the lush jungle. Fortune never tired of looking at the rain forest. There were no small trees, only thick-trunked giants that soared to a hundred feet above the jungle floor. The sound of monkeys and birds grew louder as they continued their ride.

They soon reached a little clearing where the road hooked sharply back to the left. There was a neatly lettered sign arching over the road that read Charleston Fortune.

"Where are we?" she asked, gaping at the sign. "What's going on?"

Beau stopped the mule and turned to her. He wrapped her in his arms, savoring the delectable fragrance of lilacs that always surrounded her. He'd been such a fool. He knew now that he couldn't ever leave her. "We're home, Fortune. We're home."

Fortune turned to stare at him. What was he talking about? "I . . . I don't understand."

"I've been here for the past few weeks fixing this place up." Beau smiled with pride, recalling all the work he'd done. "I won this place in a game of cards."

Fortune smiled coyly at him. "I seem to recall losing a bet to you. I'm impressed with the way certain wagers turn out."

"You're an impertinent chit. *I* seem to recall that you never paid that debt." Beau kissed her soundly. "Now that that matter has been rectified, I'll continue. We're going to live here forever."

"We are?" Fortune still couldn't believe this was happening. "I've so much to tell you, but I have the feeling that I want to hear what you have to say first."

Beau shook his head and urged the mule on. "Not yet."

Fortune sat on the edge of her seat. As they rode through the gate, the land climbed swiftly. Above the treetops, she could just see the top of a house. Had he built a house for her? She fidgeted with her skirt.

They drew nearer to the house, and she realized that it wasn't new. It was little more than a shack.

Beau stopped the wagon in the yard. Off to one side, she saw a neat garden. The garden was irrigated in much the same way as her own back at the boardinghouse. "Beau! Tell me this instant what's going on!"

He got down and came around the wagon to help her. "All right. You win. This is our home. It's not much, but it's a start."

"I don't understand," Fortune whispered, gazing up into his eyes. "I don't understand any of this."

Elena, Nola Bell and Boaz burst out of the house. Fortune stared in disbelief. "Do you all know that I've been worried sick about you? Why would you run off like that and leave me to . . ." Her voice dwindled into silence. She looked at Beau. "You did this. Why?"

He shrugged. "I couldn't do this alone. I needed help. You wouldn't have wanted to live in this place without having it cleaned up. I hired these good people to help."

Fortune broke free of him and hugged her friends. "I still want answers about this," she said, wagging her finger at them.

Over Elena's shoulder, she saw Sister Mary Margaret emerge from the house. "Good morning, Fortune. How lovely to see you again."

"Don't you good-morning me, Sister," Fortune began, feeling the anger rise. "I came to you and—"

A priest walked out of the house behind Sister Mary Margaret. The nun smiled and said, "Fortune, dear, this is Father Mulrooney."

"Right." Beau stepped up behind Fortune and wound his arms around her. "He's here to perform our marriage ceremony. I sort of figured that this was a wonderful place for two independent thinkers such as ourselves to join forces. I love you, Fortune. I have from the day we met."

Fortune was dumbfounded for a few seconds. She simply couldn't believe what she was hearing. "I...I don't know what to say. I'm speechless."

"Well, it's the first time, I'm sure," Beau said with a laugh. "And probably the last."

Fortune smiled.

"What's that for?" Beau asked, kissing her lightly on the lips.

"Oh, I just remembered what that voodoo woman said. She told me that the man with the eyes of the sea would take me home to Charleston." Fortune felt tears sting her eyes. So much had happened since this adventure began— some bad, some good. "And Mother told you to take me home to Charleston."

"Charleston is our home, Fortune." Beau enfolded her in his arms and held her close. "We belong together. This is going to be a wonderful nation soon. A railroad will be built. People will come from everywhere. We're a part of the beginning."

"That's very fitting, isn't it?" she asked, smiling through tears of joy. "Our beginning and Panama's new beginning will coincide. Let's hope that both flourish."

"They will," Beau promised, kissing her again. "They will. I expect our beginning to flourish into several small

Gregorys very soon. If you don't mind the inconvenience of the ceremony, we'll get that out of the way and then . . . start to flourish.''

* * * * *

HISTORY IN
THE MAKING!

Join Harlequin Historicals as we celebrate our 5th anniversary of exciting historical romance stories! Watch for our 5th anniversary promotion in July. And in addition, to mark this special occasion, we have another year full of great reading.

- A 1993 March Madness promotion with titles by promising newcomers Laurel Ames, Mary McBride, Susan Amarillas and Claire Delacroix.

- The July release of UNTAMED!—a Western Historical short story collection by award-winning authors Heather Graham Pozzessere, Joan Johnston and Patricia Potter.

- In-book series by Maura Seger, Julie Tetel, Margaret Moore and Suzanne Barclay.

- And in November, keep an eye out for next year's *Harlequin Historical Christmas Stories* collection, featuring Marianne Willman, Curtiss Ann Matlock and Victoria Pade.

Watch for details on our Anniversary events wherever Harlequin Historicals are sold.

HARLEQUIN HISTORICALS . . .
A touch of magic!

HH5TH

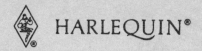 **HARLEQUIN®**

THE TAGGARTS OF TEXAS!

Harlequin's Ruth Jean Dale brings you
THE TAGGARTS OF TEXAS!

Those Taggart men—strong, sexy and hard to resist...

You've met Jesse James Taggart in FIREWORKS!
Harlequin Romance #3205 (July 1992)

And Trey Smith—he's THE RED-BLOODED YANKEE!
Harlequin Temptation #413 (October 1992)

Now meet Daniel Boone Taggart in SHOWDOWN!
Harlequin Romance #3242 (January 1993)

And finally the Taggarts who started it all—in LEGEND!
Harlequin Historical #168 (April 1993)

Read all the Taggart romances!
Meet all the Taggart men!

Available wherever Harlequin Books are sold.

THREE
UNFORGETTABLE
KNIGHTS

First there was Ruarke, born leader and renowned warrior, who faced
an altogether different field of battle when he took a willful wife in
Knight Dreams (Harlequin Historicals #141, a September 1992 release).
Now, brooding widower and heir Gareth must choose between family
duty and the only true love he's ever known in *Knight's Lady* (Harlequin
Historicals #162, a February 1993 release). And coming later in 1993,
Alexander, bold adventurer and breaker of many a maiden's heart,
meets the one woman he can't lay claim to in *Knight's Honor,* the
dramatic conclusion of Suzanne Barclay's Sommerville Brothers trilogy.

If you're in need of a champion, let Harlequin Historicals take you back
to the days when a knight in shining armor wasn't just a fantasy. Sir
Ruarke, Sir Gareth and Sir Alex won't disappoint you!

IN FEBRUARY LOOK
FOR *KNIGHT'S LADY*
AVAILABLE WHEREVER
HARLEQUIN BOOKS ARE SOLD

ROMANCE IS A YEARLONG EVENT!

Celebrate the most romantic day of the year with MY VALENTINE! (February)

CRYSTAL CREEK
When you come for a visit Texas-style, you won't want to leave! (March)

Celebrate the joy, excitement and adjustment that comes with being JUST MARRIED! (April)

Go back in time and discover the West as it was meant to be . . . UNTAMED— Maverick Hearts! (July)

LINGERING SHADOWS
New York Times bestselling author Penny Jordan brings you her latest blockbuster. Don't miss it! (August)

BACK BY POPULAR DEMAND!!!
Calloway Corners, involving stories of four sisters coping with family, business and romance! (September)

FRIENDS, FAMILIES, LOVERS
Join us for these heartwarming love stories that evoke memories of family and friends. (October)

Capture the magic and romance of Christmas past with HARLEQUIN HISTORICAL CHRISTMAS STORIES! (November)

WATCH FOR FURTHER DETAILS IN ALL HARLEQUIN BOOKS!

CALEND